A HOW PRETTY TOWN

(Imaginary toads in a virtually real garden)

BRUCE EVANS

outskirts
press

For Judy, Mark, Audrey, and Matt, by way of explanation.

"The final belief is to believe in a fiction, which you know to be a fiction, there being nothing else. The exquisite truth is to know that it is a fiction and that you believe in it willingly." —Wallace Stevens, *Opus Posthumous: Poems, Plays, Prose*

$$\Delta S \geq 0$$

1

Out of the Cradle Endlessly Rocking

He was an old privileged white man who walked alone through the streets of Edmonds, his mutating hometown on the eastern shore of Puget Sound (now known locally as the Salish Sea), just north of Seattle, from his top-floor condo on the corner of 5th South and SeaMont Lane to a viewpoint bench on the bluff west of Sunset Avenue. Ambling clockwise one day, counter the next, he would go straight like a rook for several blocks before turning perpendicularly, or tack like a knight, two blocks this way, one that, or cut like a bishop diagonally through a park or a parking lot, as mood and memory moved him. He was clinging to the moment, his present suffused with his past. He was constantly rehearsing his back story for the audience of eidolons that haunted him, making his apology, truing or skewing, interlarding interludes, improvising, counterpointing, violating narratives, struggling to wedge his life into the classical constraints of prelude, protasis, epitasis, catastasis, catastrophe, and peripeteia, and leery of denouements of treasured gobs of purgative laughter, or giddy enlightened chortling as ghosts are put to rest, or a tragic transcendence of a sweet prince, or a blooming profusion of yeses. He wanted, impossibly, to cram the universe into one sentence, everything that formed from a ballooning singularity, everything that might rush back into the ultimate black hole, employing a thousand words to make a picture, apprehending or fancying or simply playing, sconcing Easter eggs, stringing clause and phrase after clause and phrase or recursively embedding them within each other, rhapsodic, impressionistic, lush, or angular, oblique, jarring. He was not in the moment, he was incapable of just *being*, but he was where he wanted to be, doing—remembering, reacting, ruing, relishing, reading, writing, recreating, training, playing softball. He had seen enough European castles and cathedrals, enough Venetian canals and Manhattan skyscrapers, enough gold-vermilion leaves in Vermont. He had cycled enough winding paths in Central Park, heard enough reverberating steel drums on Caribbean cruise ships, snorkeled enough coral reefs in tropical waters, seen enough armored alligators from airboats in the Everglades, walked back to shore enough dancing sockeye in Alaska, hiked enough precipitous mountain trails in Switzerland, sniffed enough charming wines in out of the way Sonoma Valley wineries, lazed through enough afternoon baseball games at Wrigley and Fenway. That he had never traveled to South America, Africa, the Middle East, Asia, Australasia, or the Far East did not nag at him. He had no urge to commemorate his 80th birthday by skydiving or riding a camel. In the days that remained to him he wanted to post, on his interactive blog and on Twitter, platforms on which he was followed, he imagined, by a 100 or so vigilants, an inventory of his mind and his town. And to win a gold medal in softball at the Huntsman Senior Games in St. George, Utah.

His clockwise walks he called the Gourmand Way, because on them on his way to the bench he passed two prepossessing waterfront restaurants, Arnie's and Anthony's, patronized by the local gentry. The counterclockwise walks were the Ecclesiastical Way, because on them he passed the original site of the town's Methodist church, which he had attended sporadically as a gradeschooler. The stream of his consciousness was fed by tributaries from literature. He had always been a reader. At four, cradled in his mother's lap, he felt himself becoming part of the browns and pinks of the illustrated *Poky Little Puppy* as she read it to him. As a child, visiting cousins in Seattle, if none of them suggested a game of football or Monopoly or hide-and-seek, he got into their stash of comic books—*Archie, Superman, Captain Marvel Jr.* They called him Professor. In fifth grade, he participated in a summer reading contest for young people at the town's Carnegie Library, tearing through 25 books in 10 weeks. Every few days he dashed up the 15 concrete steps of the stocky brick building with its distinctive Roman-arched doorway and windows (the city hall, courthouse, and jail occupied the ground floor below) and made for the fiction or biography stacks, bypassing the oak drawers of the card catalogue standing free in the center of the stuffy room. He liked the stories of hardscrabble pioneer life by Laura Ingalls Wilder and loved the baseball novels of John R. Tunis, with their clash of competition and their high moral tone, books of versus he would read, often while drinking lemonade, underneath a bough of the cedar tree that shadowed the east side of his house on Maple Street. Roy Tucker, who was the Kid from Tomkinsville, and Old Razzle, Young Razzle, Spike Russell, Highpockets—he remembered them still. One day he sat at a library table and wrote the first two paragraphs of a baseball novel he was going to call *The Kid From Hansville* (a tiny town on the Kitsap peninsula across the Sound from Edmonds) before realizing how incapable he was of completing it. An almost equally keen interest was the Hardy Boys mystery series. After finishing another story demonstrating the insight and ingenuity of Frank and Joe, he would linger on the saggy, faded burgundy upholstery of the couch in his living room, tilt his head back upon a lacy white antimacasser that his mother had crocheted, and try to imagine uncovering a neighborhood crime. He failed at that, too. Once a month he rode his gearless Schwinn bike with the balloon white wall tires to Swanson's Drug Store at Fourth and Main to buy the latest *Sport* magazine and pore over the many feature stories on big-league ballplayers like Robin Roberts and Richie Ashburn, his Philadelphia Phillies heroes. His own play on the town's Little

League baseball team was unremarkable. In high school he read *The Reader's Digest*, to which his parents subscribed and copies of which were always stacked on their plasticized walnut coffee table, and Lincoln Steffens, Upton Sinclair, and John Steinbeck, who were recommended to him by his journalism teacher, Charles Sauvage.

For a long time he had risen from bed early. On April 1, 2019, insistent bladder pressure in the wee hours of the morning caused him to squirm until he gained full consciousness at 2:05, according to the oversize red numerals on his nightstand digital clock. He put on his glasses, tottered to the bathroom, hit a switch and, peering between the black blotches that for him now always accompanied an instantaneous transition from dark to light, pulled from a cupboard beneath the sink a paper towel, a urinary catheter, and a fresh nitrile glove. For the past eight years he had been unable to urinate without assistance. He had vainly waited too long, a urologist, Dr. Rajesh Kumar, informed him when finally he sought consultation about his feeble stream and constant urgency. An ultrasound followed by a cystoscopy revealed a distended bladder and a swollen prostate beyond the help of drugs or surgery. "Your bladder's always half full, and that is killing your kidneys," Dr. Kumar said. "I prefer to think of it as half empty," he replied before being told that his only option was self-catheterization. He placed the paper towel atop the toilet tank, squeezed the pouch at the top of the plastic-wrapped catheter, let the lubricating liquid run while he drew the glove over his right hand, extracted the catheter, emptied the wrapper into the toilet, laid it on the towel, and threaded the thin tube up his urethra until, with a gurgle, it slipped over a threshold and entered the bladder. Instantly a river ran through it, a lemonade waterfall roiling the pool in the bowl. For this relief much thanks, he rejoyced. In 90 seconds he was completely drained. He'd be good not to go for hours now. He slid the catheter out quickly, thrilled by the friction, dropped it on the towel, peeled off the glove, wrapped up all the used pieces, and stuffed the towel into the wastebasket, where it joined a dozen others, the green plastic caps of his med uses protruding at odd angles to suggest the snaky strands of a woman's wild coiffeur, which he regarded stonily. Back in bed, rather than ride out what was sure to be a restless hour before fantasy morphed into dream, he turned on the nightstand lamp, strapped on his Tac head lamp, ricocheting light photon-bombing his thickening, increasingly opaque lenses and his severely macular-degenerated right retina, and picked up his iPad and the composition book where he banked his coinings: neologisms, oronyms, contronyms, aptronyms, oxymorons, onomastics, anagrams, palindromes, puns, double entendres, word searches, cryptics. He waited for words. Where did they come from? He could click on a mental folder but could not command it to open and release its words, let alone release them in either a syntactic or a logical order. But if he waited for them to emerge—sporadically, often, seemingly randomly sometimes—from his buffering unconscious, his mind, itself a fiction, grasping as many as it could as they sought to wiggle free, then consciously buffering and buffing some, rebuffing others, rearranging, rewording, or discarding, he could become a fiction-maker, an orderer, an executor, a self. He waited, scribbled, waited some more, scribbled, revised the scribbles. Then he opened the iPad, logged in to Twitter, and tapped #madamsNxNW: Japanese religion with legs? (6) Love handles? (5,3,4) Ogle one of Shakespeare's howling heroes? (4) A saunter with O'Conner by the Sound? (8) Jewish teacher in tatters novel? (6,2,4) Manifested indifference in Sue's seance? (11) Quality product of a Deist's God? (5) A set of rules for analyzing a former V-P's dance moves? (9). Time, finally, to set notebook and iPad aside, turn out the lights, and ease into sleep, dreaming about the lines.

[*Ooh là là*, Wayne, *plus ça change, plus c'est la meme chose, n'est-ce pas? On dois faire son petit Hemingway et Proust* but allow me to warn you that many readers are going to feel accosted by those Greek terms and annoyed by those cryptics. You are thrusting upon them what at Pendant Publishing my colleague Elaine Benes and I called a "closet" novel. As Jesus enjoined his followers to go into their closets to pray in secret, and as a "closet" drama is one meant to be read not performed, so your stylistic choices (or tics?) bid your readers to take your fiction not to the beach for some breezy page-turning but into their closets—yea, even their water closets!—to labor and linger over, peruse and pause over. At Pendant we commonly advised our fabulists to use the "dramatic method" of storytelling espoused by Percy Lubbock in *The Craft of Fiction*, but clearly we're not going to get anything like a "rattling good yarn" out of you. I foresee *soupçons* of swashbuckling and copulating among a glut of colloquies and a surfeit of set pieces: much self-referential plodding amid the plotting. Don't get me wrong: the "closet" novel, which in my opinion includes *Ulysses*, *Ada*, and *Moby Dick,* is my favorite genre, and I am excited to read these installments of your *recherche.* I loved that little "med uses" Easter egg, and enjoyed some of the others as well, like "books of versus." I relish the opportunity to weigh in at will on the rhetoric of your fiction and the reliability of your narration. It's nice to be back with you! Solveig]

[Wayne, I respond with an exquisite shiver to the Stevens epigraph. It perfectly grasps the rational irrationality of religion. Dave]

[The Stevens is meant to be ironic, right? It's the equation that speaks for you? Or is the equation just another exquisite fiction? Solveig]

He was up—weight 143, pulse in sinus rhythm, steady at a baseline cadence of 70, as dictated by his pacemaker, which had been implanted in 2015 because his resting pulse rate often dropped to 39 after frequent bouts of atrial fibrillation that rendered him breathlessly inactive for hours at a time, and dressed in black skinny jeans, bottoms unrolled, a black sweatshirt, ARIZONA RATTLERS silk-screened in white above the left breast, and black Under Armour compression socks, which gave succor to his neuropathic feet—at 5:05. He pulled his Apple 8 Plus phone from its charging cord, beheld it in appreciation briefly, so thin, so light, so quick, so bright, and tucked it and his wallet into pants pockets. He peeled his Apple watch from its magnetic charger, strapped it on, felt connected: 38 degrees, Partly Cloudy, H—49, L-38. The second false dawn had brimmed, sending its rousing rays through his bedroom skylight, morning becoming electric, but was already conceding the day to clouds pushed in from the west by an on-shore flow of marine air. He had seen tens of thousands of such days, gold, certainly in Edmonds nature's hardest hue to hold, becoming gray. He loved the sun, craved light. For 15 years, after they retired from teaching in their early fifties and until his wife Diane died, they had wintered in Arizona, heatonists, he said, seeking sunsual pleasure, she said, reveling in days that kept their promise from dawn's flaming shook-foil salutation, nature's grandeur, to twilight's spectroscopic ta ta. From age 55 to 70, nearly every day at Desert Edge, a retirement community in Mesa, they played an outdoor sport—tennis, golf, or softball with the Rattlers for him, tennis or golf for her. Nearly every day they carried coffee and breakfast, wine and dinner, to the tiled, lattice-roofed patio of their rented golf course condo and gazed at the facets of the bare Superstition Mountains, embracing the buoyant, dry air as it embraced them. Even after the coming of the basal and squamous cell skin cancers, the Mohs surgeries, and the crinkled skin, they continued to be drawn to the rhapsody of the outdoors, larding themselves with 90 SPF sunscreen and wearing wide-brimmed hats that covered neck and ears. In Edmonds, a how pretty town, as any one would certainly say, it took will, which indeed they had, to find inspiration in the much danker circumambience. Today, he had determined, he would begin the project of rewiring his brain.

He grabbed his iPad and went to the kitchen to pour a 12-ounce glass of water and gag down his daily pills: Sotalol to block atrial impulses to fibrillate, Eliquis to prevent clotting in case a blitzing impulse did blast through, Myrbetriq to caulk his leaky bladder, Levothyroxine to spur his hypoactive thyroid, CitraCal and vitamin D to slow the progression of osteopenia, his crumbling infrastructure, Preservision to reduce infinitesimally the inflammation causing his wet mac d, and fish oil, iron, vitamin C, vitamin B, and vitamin E for general supplementation. Once a week he would take six delayed-release tablets of Methotrexate for the rheumatoid arthritis in his fingers, knees, and ankles. As he swallowed the pills one at a time, pausing after each to make sure none had lodged in his esophagus, which, like the rest of his body parts, had lost much of its elasticity, he also drank in, as always, his sweeping view of the Edmonds Bowl. His wide-windowed condo, 30 feet above street level, the maximum height allowed in the Bowl, looked to the west and the north without obstruction across the town and across the Sound to the forested Olympic peninsula and snowy Olympic mountains, to the Strait of Juan de Fuca, and to Whidbey Island, the bluff bare face of Skagit Head, partially denuded by landslides over millennia, gleaming Doverishly. He could even sit on the toilet and watch the Kingston ferry docking or departing. From anywhere in any room, guest bathroom excepted, he could behold Edmonds, his Edmonds. Though the city limits had expanded southward two miles past the Westgate business center to the Sno-King county line, eastward three miles to the bleak strip malls bordering Highway 99, and northward two miles to a pleasant enough tree-canopied residential area called Seaview, old Edmonds, the true Edmonds, was to be found only in the Bowl. It lay between Pine Street, just an ascending half-block from his condo, on the south; Caspar Street, a mile away, on the north; the beach on the west; and 9th Avenue on the east. Looking beyond the wooded city park and the wetlands to the waterfront of this jewel set on the Salish Sea, he imagined Native Americans roaming the murmuring forest primeval, picking salmonberries, huckleberries, and salal, digging wild carrot roots, or harvesting clams along the shore, then suddenly gazing in wild surmise as Captain George Vancouver and Lieutenant Peter Puget sailed their three-master into the bay and, themselves astonied, espied an ever green and pleasant cove with gently sloping beach and soaring firs, hemlocks, cedars and spruce, some as many as twelve feet in diameter. In his mind a time-lapse film showed the

Olympics upthrusting as tectonic plates collided more than 10 million years ago, glaciers gouging out the Sound as they advanced and then retreated 14,000 years ago, Paul Bunyan and Babe the Blue Ox comically plowing the crevasses deeper, enterprising Seattle logger George Brackett in 1870, while exploring the shoreline in a canoe, taking refuge on the beach during a windstorm and returning two years later to begin logging the hillsides, Brackett in 1884 platting a town, and then his grandfather Bertrand and great-uncle Enos arriving overland from Wisconsin in 1903 to begin sweating on a two-man saw in the logging camps. Edmonds was, had been ever since Brackett's day, a place. Other suburbs between Seattle and Everett were interstices. They had names—Northgate, North City, Shoreline, Mountlake Terrace, Lynnwood, Alderwood, South Everett—but their boundaries were legal, not literal. A driver slipped between their undistinguished and indistinguishable malls and residential areas without knowing when they had left one and entered another. But in Edmonds, sylvan city of hunched shoulders, there was a *there* which suddenly opened up to a driver descending from the trees after traversing its protective eastern hills. Isolated between those hills and additional wooded areas to the south and the north, laved by the Sound, the Sea, it was a singularity sucking in those who came upon it with its reclusive charm and the—help him, will you, Vlad?—cool glory of its whitecapped, snowcapped western marine and mountain horizon. He cherished the name "Edmonds" for its very lack of resonance. It was connotation-free and denotation-irrelevant. The name, he had decided years ago after reading alternative versions of its origin, was probably bestowed by George Brackett in reference to Point Edmund, a promontory on the southwest edge of the Bowl so dubbed by the surveying Charles Wilkes expedition of 1841 and now dominated by luxurious condominiums. Why Edmund? No one knew. Serendipity, he had concluded. The eponymous Edmund's very obscurity deflected preconception and pretentiousness. What was in this name? Nothing. It wasn't in honor of a founder whose history anyone knew, it wasn't in honor of a local tribe, it wasn't a nod to a geographical feature, it wasn't a "Saint" or "San" or "Santa," it wasn't mythopoeic like "Olympia" or "Arcadia," nor was it one of the hundreds of "-burgs," "-boros," "-villes," "-cities," or "-tons" found throughout America. "Edmonds" didn't sound exotic, esoteric, or commonplace. It was the appropriate name for an uncommon place.

[A pretty bland name, I'd say. *Beaulieu-sur-Mer* would be both lovely and à *propos*. But there weren't many French among the early residents, were there? Duval? Guyot? Glen "Frenchy" Rogers, the barber on Main Street? Solveig]

Pills successfully swallowed, he glanced at the Corian countertop dividing the kitchen from the great room and said, "Alexa, give me the question of the day, please," delighting in his power to swirl into life the cerulean and cyan lights of his black pucklike Echo Dot device.

"Good morning, Wayne," said Alexa, whose equanimity and preternatural focus and sincerity he found endearing. "Here is today's question of the day. It is from arts and entertainment and is worth four points. What is the name of the dog on 'The Simpsons?' Is it (a) Snowball (b) Brian (c) Santa's Little Helper or (d) Buddy?"

"Buddy," the old man guessed, having thousands of times surfed past episodes of "The Simpsons" without lingering on a single one, his considerable appetite for verbal play not sufficiently ravenous to overcome his distaste for animation, characters moving grossly against flat backgrounds, their mechanical mouths failing to enunciate their utterances. "30 Rock," "Will and Grace," "Frasier," yes, "Bob's Burgers," "Family Guy," "American Dad," no.

"That's a good guess, but the correct answer is (c) Santa's Little Helper. You have 870 points. Your play streak is at 91 days. Stimulate your brain by playing the 'Question of the Day'. You still have a free game available. To play it, just say 'Alexa, ask 'Question of the Day' to play a game.'"

"No, thank you," the old man said, embarrassed to have failed in front of Alexa and fearful of risking a second defeat. Why couldn't it have been The Thin Man's dog (Asta), Little Orphan Annie's dog (Sandy), Laura Ingalls' dog (Jack), or Sam Fathers' dog (Lion)?

Alexa lost color.

"Lexa?"

She brightened.

"Today is my birthday."

"Happy birthday! Would you like me to sing 'Happy Birthday' to you?

"Yes."

"Okay, let's *do* this. One, two, three: Happy birthday to you, happy birthday to you, happy birthday, happy birthday, happy birthday to you. And many more!"

He smiled.

"Lexa, what's on my calendar for today?"

"What's on your calendar for today? A walk to your bench on Sunset, a workout at HSAC at 11:00, softball practice at 2:00."

He stepped to the hall closet and selected a white polar-fleece jacket and a white New Era ball cap logoed R in black, zipped the jacket to the top, forcing the collar as high as it would go, tucked his iPad between his left arm and his side and, in white New Balance running shoes, descended the three flights of stairs, 30 in all, bumping against the handrail with a hip once on each flight. At the 5th Avenue sidewalk he glanced left—condos running up the hill on both sides of the street as far as his eyes could see; no cars now but swishing streams of them soon to flow into what had become not just a place to catch a ferry to the Olympic peninsula but a destination in itself—and turned right, the Ecclesiastical Way, heading for Starbucks. The quietness of the street, like the qualm before a storm, like the peristaltic convulsing of his bowels before a softball game, excited him. Even when young, though no sharp, sure lad, he knew that morns abed and daylight slumber were not meant for him. Oh, the promise of morning! Every day he cheated sleep and its dreams in eager anticipation of the real phenomena that consciousness would bring and ventured into the world, even if, at 80, that meant only a walk and fresh coffee and online reading of the *New York Times*. What was going on out there? What calamities? What chicaneries? What discoveries? What had Trump tweeted at 3:00 a. m.? And who was getting hits, scoring points, gaining yards? He passed the Gravity Bar, where he occasionally dined on a colorful, meticulously arranged acai bowl, and reached the corner of 5th and Howell—now the site of Hamburger Harry's, a bistro with multiple wide television screens spaced beneath darkly stained exposed beams and rafters that attracted tablefuls of hearty eaters and drinkers who kept one eye on each other and one on ESPN or its cousins and an evolving third on their phones, and before that a garden store—where his paternal grandparents, Bertrand and Mary Adams (the name curtailed from Adamson by a careless or confused clerk when Bertrand's father passed through Ellis Island), had lived, when he first knew them, in the early '40s, in a gray two-story cedar-sided house with a veranda on which he would sit in a cushioned rocker and drink the lemonade his grandmother had squeezed and sugared for him, fascinated by the exotic shades of green or red she produced by adding food coloring to the juice. The house sat on a mostly untended acre lot where he could roam among rampant blackberry vines, nettles, Canadian thistles, and quack grass, or climb the Bing cherry tree or the gravenstein apple tree. Big house on the way to the ferry. Like a wilder farmer boy, at his grandmother's bidding he would enter the wire-mesh chicken coop in the backyard, toss handfuls of grain, step around poop, and extract eggs from nests while the hens clucked and pecked the ground. He would watch with interest as she poured bluing atop the clothes in the washing machine, fed them through the wringer when they were clean, and hung them on the clothesline that ran from the cherry tree to the detached garage at the side of the house. He would stuff himself with the pancakes, waffles, and angel food cakes she made from scratch whenever he stayed overnight with them, her plump arms jiggling as she whipped a wooden spoon through a doughy mixture in a large bowl tucked into her left forearm like a football. She always wore a short-sleeved house-dress, even when weeding the flower beds. At night his grandparents would take turns playing double solitaire with him while they listened to Gabriel Heater, Walter Winchell, Jack Benny, and Burns and Allen on their table model Silvertone radio. Once in a while they would take him to a high school football game or a University of Washington crew race. They were Christian Scientists. They subscribed to the *Monitor* and read something in *Science and Health* and the *Christian Science Quarterly* every day. They attended church Sunday mornings and Wednesday evenings and took weekly shifts supervising the Christian Science Reading Room a few blocks north on 5th. They eschewed tobacco and alcohol and adultery and borrowing and complaining and swearing. His grandmother had gasped in shock the time he tripped coming up the veranda stairs, skinned his knee, and said it hurt like the devil. Yet they practiced a quiet rectitude, never attempting to proselytize him. They were Taft Republicans who voted for Harding, Hoover, Landon, Dewey, Eisenhower, and Nixon and who paid their own way, their innocence the essence of Edmonds, he grew up believing.

The old man and his parents, George and Margaret, had lived in eight Edmonds houses or apartments by the time he had graduated from the University of Washington, obtained his teaching certificate, and struck out on his own, taking a job for an annual salary of $4,200 at the new Edmonds High School at Holmes Corner, 212th and 76th, and renting an apartment in Lynnwood. His mother was always pushing for something better—better neighborhood, better access, better view, more space, less space. After a couple of years in any space, she was ready to apply the modest accrued equity, if any, to something at least different. She had grown up in Greenwood, on the northwest fringe of Seattle, one of nine kids. Although she visited her parents and her sisters occasionally, taking along the old man in their '39 Ford coupe on a Saturday but leaving his uninterested father at home to read the *Digest* or listen to the Huskies on the radio, she cherished the insular beauty of the little town. She yearned to be upwardly mobile, to surpass her lower-class origins, but most of the moves she engineered were horizontal. He had been told that when he was born the family lived in a house on Walnut between 5th and 6th, but the old man's earliest memories were of living with his mother, his father having been drafted into the army in 1942, in a squat house on 6th between Walnut and Alder with a patch of woods to the south and a gravel pit to the west. He often watched in fascination as big dump trucks rumbled in and backed up to the dispensers for a thunderous load of gravel to be dropped into them. He was four, of an age with the girl next door, Claudia, with whom he played occasionally. One day when they were in the woods exploring, both had to go to the bathroom. Rather than return home, the old man unzipped his cords and let fly onto a fern frond. Claudia, amazed, said she couldn't do that. The process seemed simple enough to the old man, so he unbuttoned her jeans for her and reached for her jigger. The jigger was nowhere to be found. Confused, he slipped a finger inside the crotch of her underpants, felt around, and came upon a cleft whose mushy texture he explored with a fingertip. "I can't find it," he said, as confused by her anatomy as Claudia was by his actions. He buttoned her up as she desperately wiggled her hips to keep from going, then she ran home while he went to inform his mother of his befuddlement. His mother, unable to stifle a smile, looked away and said simply, "Girls don't have jiggers."

His father was still in the army when he and his mother moved to a small cedar-sided house—two bedrooms, one bathroom, living room, kitchenette, detached one-car garage—at the end of Maple Street, just above 10th Avenue. Edmonds was an adolescent town and he a six-year-old when he first became conscious of the phenomenon of being there. A day was 24 hours but seemed shorter. It was seldom hot enough for black dogs to suffer, seldom cold enough to run and skid across frozen mud puddles. From the morning that the siren at the fire station roared up the hills in triumph and Nellie McReynolds, the girl who lived across the street, ran out her front door shouting "The Japs have surrendered! The war is over!" while the old man was bouncing a rubber ball against a telephone pole, trying to quicken his reflexes and develop soft hands, his days were, it seemed in retrospect, filled.

After school, weekends, summers, he played whatever sport was in season with the neighborhood boys, the Maple Street All Stars. On the dirt street in front of his house, in the cleared but vacant lot at 10th and Walnut, in Mike ("Monk") Monken's back yard on 9th, in Gary ("Zee") Zylstra's dirt driveway with its 10-foot post and netless basketball hoop on 10th, in the shoulder pads and helmets they requested for birthday presents, in their PF Flyers, with their oddly-bouncing bladdered footballs and basketballs, their Rawlings gloves, their too-heavy Louisville Slugger bats, their taped-over baseballs, their homemade bases—burlap flour sacks filled with straw—they ran drills and scrimmaged and squabbled and fantasized for hours. Sometimes, strapping on holstered cap guns and using hankies for neckerchiefs, inspired by the 12-cent Saturday matinees that they attended at the Princess Theater— handsome Roy Rogers, pretty Dale Evans, golden-toned Trigger their favorites—they would grab imaginary reins and, making clattering hoof sounds by clicking their tongues against the roofs of their mouths, gallop straddle-footedly, left foot leading, through the neighborhood, a posse chasing cattle rustlers, train robbers, bank robbers, or marauding Indians, firing the six-shooters until they caught up with an escapee and either lassoed him and jerked him to the ground or leaped from their saddles and unhorsed him, fists flailing until they knocked him out. Occasionally they would see who was quickest on the trigger. Two would face each other at 10 paces and a third would call "Draw!" Zee always claimed himself the winner of such contests, and always compassionately declared that he had only shot the gun out of his adversary's hand. Or they would play frontiersmen, hooking canteens to their belts and slipping on rucksacks filled with canned heat, potatoes, a jackknife, a screwdriver, wooden matches, a jar of salmon eggs, a cellophane bag of fishing leaders, pre-strung with a small hook and three pieces of buckshot, and head northeast into the then thick woods that now comprise Yost Park, an arboreal expanse stretching from Walnut to Main and featuring an outdoor Olympic-size swimming pool and manicured hiking trails. Using small dead branches found on the ground, they would fight their way through nettles and thistles and blackberry vines and Scotch broom and deer ferns and sword ferns and snake weed and skunk cabbage and Oregon grape, some days pausing to defecate next to a salal bush and wipe with its leaves, weaving among alders and maples and cedars and firs and hemlocks and pines, sampling squishy crimson thimbleberries or crisp vermilion huckleberries on bushes growing out of nurse logs, sliding down ravines mulched by worlds of wanwood leafmeal, crossing gurgling Shell Creek by tip-toeing atop a fallen fir, kicking at mounds of dirt in hopes of finding an Indian skull or an arrowhead, until they came to a small creekside clearing where they could set up camp. They would tie their leaders to the branch they were carrying, hide the hooks with two salmon eggs, and gently toss them again and again into a dark, still pool in the creek, extracting them quickly before they could sink into a snag. Having read *The Adventures of Huckleberry Finn* for an Achievement Award on their way to receiving their Bear ranking in Cub Scouts, they would imagine themselves as Huck and Jim and Tom. When a rare nibble became an actual strike, one of them would lift out of the water with a shout a six-inch jerking Rainbow trout. Immediately he'd conk it with a rock, slit and gut it, cut off its head and tail, and divide it into three pieces while the other two would make a circle of rocks and place three cans of Sterno in a triangle in the center. They would cut the potatoes into chunks in the skillet, light the Sterno, sizzle the potatoes and the trout into a charred crisp that stuck to the ungreased pan, then take turns stabbing the knife into the chunks, which they would pry from the pan and eat off the blade. Summer nights, they'd play catch till dark, which came between nine and ten o'clock, then get into sleeping bags on the old man's lawn, the old man not so much awed as mesmerized by all the stars in a sky unpolluted by carbons or light, mind adrift in a sea of whitecaps, able to discern only the Big Dipper and the north star, slipping without conjecture into sleep, then waking at false dawn to find his hair and bag wet with dew. On chilly, rainy winter days, they played indoors: marbles (pots and chase), Canasta, Tripoli, Monopoly, caroms (on a large board with six netted pockets into which opponents took turns shooting red or green wooden rings with a snap of the middle finger), football, basketball. Football they played in a bedroom on their knees, the goal lines opposite ends of a 12-foot rug. The offensive player would take the ball at one goal line and attempt to smash through his opponents, who in turn were attempting to flatten him on the rug, in four downs. Scoring was rare, bruises were not. For basketball they stripped down to underpants and sleeveless undershirts, makeshift uniforms, and took turns playing one-on-one, dribbling a tennis ball around two chairs, which served as screens, looking for an opening to launch a push shot toward the basket, which was any part of the lintel above the door, or backing in to loft a hook shot. Some winters there might be no snow at all in the temperate Puget Sound climate. When the old man would ask his father "Do you think it'll snow?" the answer was usually "No, it's not cold enough" or, occasionally, bewilderingly, "No, it's too cold." But every couple of years came the vaunted day when dry snow fell like shaken salt and caked inches deep on Maple Street, and the All-Stars, deliriously gathering their rosebuds while they might, wearing jeans and jackets, rubber boots, ski caps, and mittens, ran five or six steps with their sleds held high and belly-flopped onto the glassy, packed surface, sliding smoothly down from 10th to 9th, then careening from one side of the street to the other, madly working the steering bar of their Flexible Flyers, their ruddering lower legs extended to the sky, spewing gobs of laughter as they gained speed on the steep drop from 9th to 7th, until finally losing control and jolting into someone's rockery or fence post, hitting a head, smashing a hand, traumatizing a gut, then shaking it off, wobbling to their feet, grabbing the sled's rope and slip-walking back up the hill in a barrage of boastful or mocking chatter, to do it again and again until, hours later, soaked jeans and aching bodies and the thought of hot mugs of Ovaltine drove them home.

The old man was home, on the couch in pajamas, sick with the mumps and listening with his mother to Oxydol's *Ma Perkins* on their tabletop Philco radio on a May day in 1950, when she told him, his first felt intimation of mortality, that they were going to move. They had stayed in one place for five years essentially because, he later realized, his mother's concern for his feelings balanced her itch for change. The old man went numb, then began to cry. His mother slid over to hug him. They were moving downtown, to a house on 4th between Bell and Edmonds. It had a basement, it would be an upgrade. They'd be closer to the town's stores and activity centers. She was going to get a job at Safeway. The old man sulked and seethed. How could she do this to him? Later he threw away the card that he had made in art class at school and planned to give her on Mother's Day. When she found it in a wastebasket, she brought it to him and said, "Is this what you really think of me?" Aching with remorse, he said, "No, Mom, it isn't. I'm sorry."

Within a couple of months, he was happy about the move. He could be on the beach in five minutes, terrorizing crabs and clams, skipping stones, collecting serpentine pieces of wormholed driftwood. On hot days he would call and ask Sylvia Vose and her brother Vernal, family friends who lived on 4th between Walnut and Dayton, to meet him at the log booms for a swim, after which they would retreat to a niche in the wall of imported granite blocks that buttressed the railroad tracks and warm their icy flesh in the sun. "Awesome," Sylvia would say, referring to all of it—the vast pale blue sky and matching placid sea, the dark evergreens rising from the bank of the peninsula across the way to the tops of the snow-brindled Olympics, and the gleaming sun—looking unsteady to his blinking eye, as if about to uncoagulate and drip messily down the sky—which was slowly restoring them. He and Sylvia could bike to artistic classmate Patty Warfield's two-story house at 3rd and Bell to play 78 records like "On Top of Old Smoky." He could call Sylvia's neighbors, the athletically gifted Johnson twins, Jimmie and Jerry, and Walt Burdett and Dickie Riddle, who lived on 3rd between Main and Dayton, and Dave Williams, who lived on 4th and Bell across the street from the Baptist Church, and invite them to his house to play tackle football on his front lawn, and Zee and Monk were always willing to bike down for a game. He could zip over to the library for a new book and start reading it at Bienz's Confectionary on Main over a Green River phosphate. Evenings he could go to the Princess, where his aunt Mable, his father's sister, was an usher, to take in a double feature plus a cartoon and a selected short subject. After seeing *Young Tom Edison*, he dreamed for days of creating his own telegraph and of transforming the basement, where his mother hung laundry, into a laboratory with some kind of dumb waiter to communicate with the upstairs. He loved it there.

[I loved the blended smell of creosote and train-toilet effluent emanating from the railroad ties! Sylvia]

[Unlike you, Wayne, I did conjecture my way into sleep, looking for the secret, tingling with awe as dark revealed previously hidden light, yearning to put myself in harmony with the order of the cosmos. Gary]

[Halcyon days, indeed! Monk]

Two years later they moved to a house halfway up Walnut, between 5th and 6th, on the opposite side of the street from their first house, because it had a view, his mother said. That was the summer his right leg was in a cast, Dr. Robert Hope's last-resort method of treating the inflammation in his knee, and he got around town on crutches, an outsider looking on while Zee, whose family had recently moved down town to a big white house with a basement on Dayton between 3rd and 4th, and Monk and the Johnsons and Burdett and Riddle were playing Babe Ruth baseball. The previous summer, the bump on the upper part of the shinbone, just below the knee, had swelled achingly. Pain stabbed when he ran or

jumped, and it was too sore to kneel on. In August, Dr. Hope diagnosed Osgood-Schlatter's disease and offered a simple cure: wait,
be patient, play no sports until the pain went away. It was a normal
occurrence in some kids, primarily boys, and he would outgrow it
in a few months. So he sat out the football season, standing on the
sideline to watch Zee and Monk and the Johnsons and his other
freshman buddies practice and then warm the bench at the varsity
games on Fridays. The soreness had not subsided when basketball
season arrived. He sat that one out too. The old man blamed himself for not strictly following the doctor's advice. He could not resist
the temptation to shoot baskets at Zee's backyard hoop or to ride
his bike, pumping with his left leg, tapping with his right foot when
the pedal came round, trying to keep his leg straight, getting off to
push when he came to a hill. There was still no improvement by
March when baseball began. The old man went to practices and
sardonically played a little catch. Finally, when the school year ended in June, his parents took him back to Dr. Hope, who this time put
his leg in a toes-to-hip plaster of Paris walking cast. The old man,
feeling that now he could do no wrong, began swinging his cast all
over town. He walked to the beach and watched his friends swim,
helped them build a leaky raft from scrap lumber that had washed
ashore. He walked to Babe Ruth practice, where he would talk the
coach into letting him take a few swings and attempt to catch fly
balls in the outfield. Within two weeks the foot of his cast was crumbling. His parents borrowed some crutches from a neighbor and,
armpits bruised, again he swung himself all over town. By late July,
the knee no longer ached. In late August, just a day before football
practice was to begin, Dr. Hope, using a hammer and chisel, freed
him. He was stunned to see how much his leg had atrophied in the
two months. And, getting up from the table on which he'd been lying while the doctor worked, shocked to find that he could scarcely
walk. The knee was healed, but he couldn't bend it. He hobbled out
of the doctor's office, and his parents took him home to have a hot
bath. The leg loosened some, enough to walk a bit. In the afternoon

he went outside and jog-walked a couple of laps around the house in a feeble attempt to get himself in shape. Gloom set in. Since second grade he had dreamed of his first day of high school football practice; now he dreaded it. The next day, after putting on pads and uniform, everyone else chattering excitedly, he limped around the track in a warm up lap, Zee and fellow sophomores gliding by him, and winced through jumping jacks and other calisthenics. The old man knew all too well what came next. He tried to disguise his shaking by making little stretching movements. The team circled Coach Howard Howe, 5'8", 140 pounds, who told the biggest sophomore, Dickie Riddle, 6' 2", 200, to come forward. Coach began explaining and pantomiming the fundamentals of tackling: weight low for leverage, short choppy steps for balance, explosive shoulder lead, head to the side, arms wrapping up the would-be ball carrier, legs continually driving. "Wire 'em, wire 'em," Coach growled, whipping his arms forward. "Like this." He told Dickie to run toward him, and, padless and helmetless, met him fiercely, demonstrating all of the fundamentals, and dropped him on his butt. Years later, a struggling teacher and coach himself, the old man realized that this was Coach's version of an Anticipatory Set, focusing interest and establishing his authority. Then came the hat drill in which players took turns going one on one in a rectangular area defined by four helmets, one player trying to imitate what Coach had done as the other tried to run through him. They broke into three groups, each supervised by an assistant coach. The old man placed himself at the back of the line in his group. He heard the thud of pads colliding, the crack of helmets glancing off each other, sounds that used to stir him but now intimidated him. The coach had praise for some like Jimmy Johnson and Zee—"Good job, good job. Attaway!"—admonition for others—"Butt down, butt down! Drive off those legs." Too soon it was the old man's turn to tackle. At the assistant coach's signal, he moved forward hesitantly, off balance, a sharp pain stabbing the wasted flesh at the back of his knee, took a shoulder to the chin and was simply run over, flattened, the back of his head striking the dirt, by the ball carrier. His performance was so bad that the coach, out of charity, made no comment. He stumbled to the end of the other line and became a ball carrier. As he moved forward, again hesitantly, the tackler wired him and carried him backward three yards before dumping him. The drill continued for 10 minutes, all of his friends looking the other way each time the old man's turn came, after which Coach called the team together and demonstrated open-field blocking, emphasizing a scissor kick with the top leg. When they split into groups, the assistant pulled the old man aside.

"Are you all right?" he asked. "These guys are killing you."

"I've got some problems. I just got my right leg out of a cast yesterday."

"Better just watch for the rest of practice," the assistant said.

Humiliated, the old man hovered, trying to will himself part of things. He watched the drills, watched as Coach put the squad into three teams—Zee and Monk and the Johnsons were on second string already— and taught them some of the simpler plays, like Right Buck and Left Buck, of his highly successful single-wing offense. He watched as practice ended with wind sprints. Dejectedly, the old man gimped to the locker room and undressed. The others were bouncing around, jabbering about who looked good out there. Football was back! Senior all-conference tackle big John McDermott, admired by his teammates for his courage and spirit, stripped off his jersey and shoulder pads, gazed at his ample stomach, and sang "All day I faced my barren waist without a drink of water," then shouted "Chief Running Water had three sons—Hot, Cold, and Luke. Bucks were well spent on Springmaid sheets!" In the shower room, hot water roaring, steam rising, happy voices echoing, his friends made a token effort to commiserate with him— "Another day tomorrow, Wayne. You'll get 'em, man." But the next day was worse. His leg was so stiff that he didn't even suit up. After practice on the third day, the old man again standing by and watching, Coach called him into his office and said "Wayne, I'm going to have to cut you. When you finally get your mobility back, you're going to be too far behind. How about being a manager?"

The old man focused all his attention on accepting the offer without showing his devastation. When he told his parents at dinner that he was going to be a manager, his father said nothing, his mother put her head down on her arms at the kitchen table and wept—more for herself than for him, he understood. She had wanted to be like her women friends around town, the mother of a football player. It was Margaret she mourned for.

[Such a shame! More than a year wasted. A simple steroid shot would have had you back in action in a couple of days. Both of my boys had O-S and kept right on playing their sports with the help of cortisone. Maggie and George should have been more aggressive and sought a second opinion. Monk]

A few months later, they moved back to 4th, just south of Main, behind the Beeson Building, to a two-story house, because it was bigger. In his senior year, they moved to a house on Hummingbird Hill, a recently developed area north of Main between 9th and Olympic Avenue, because it was newer. By then he was driving, had a part-time job bagging groceries at Safeway, and was constantly busy with classes, basketball or baseball, movies and dances, so he didn't care as much where he lived, as long as it was near the Bowl. In his freshman year at the U, they moved back down town to an apartment above the *Tribune-Review* building at 5th and Main, because it was just across the street from his mother's work at Safeway. And in his junior year they moved to a new apartment complex on the corner of 3rd and Dayton to escape the Wednesday night pounding of the heavy linotype printing press.

On the north side of Howell, at one time another wild acre of second-growth woods through which he would occasionally wander, sat one of just three strip malls in the Bowl, originally built in the '70s to house an A&P grocery store, its wide asphalt parking lot now fronting Ace Hardware, the Pancake Haus, and the Fun Chinese restaurant. Just past that had been a frozen food storage plant where his parents, who could not afford and had no space for one of those deep-freeze chests that he had seen in a Sears catalogue while searching for pictures of women modeling bras and panties, rented a locker to preserve the wild blackberries they picked, the salmon they caught, and the quarter of beef they bought from a farmer in Alderwood, east of Highway 99, every few months. The space was now occupied by Girardi's Osteria, which teemed with eaters from noon to nine, it and Harry's just two of more than two dozen bistros and cafes offering a, to him, chilly *al fresco* option. He walked on, posturing, reminding himself to contract his gluteus medius, an act which threw his shoulders back and, for the nonce, straightened his curved spine, which was the product of years of defensively hunching, his default mode, hands in front pockets, a bravura attempt at insouciance in the presence of others. To his right, brick condos atop office spaces, which in the aughts had replaced bungalows with lawns and carports or detached garages, crowded each other, their glassed-in sundecks beetling over the avenue. His own, older, condo building was set back from 5th and landscaped in front with boulders, bark mulch, and low-growing junipers.

Walnut Street. When he tasted salty snot trickling onto his upper lip, he set his iPad on the sidewalk and blew his nose. Cold made it run. Heat—from soup or coffee or curries—made it run. Living made it run. Once, years ago, in a post-funeral potluck line, he had seen an old man fail to realize that his snot was falling into a mashed potato-Polish sausage casserole that he was bending over to examine more closely. Now a similar loss of control happened frequently to him. No need for diapers yet, although the odd gas attack sometimes left a faint residue in his underpants, prompting him always to wear black low-rise Jockeys. He used his handkerchief to wipe his eyes as well, swabbing with an index finger. The left, especially, dripped copiously in cold or wind, compounding the blurring of his vision caused by the mac d in his right. Words on printed pages or electronic screens were beginning to anagram themselves into out-of-context dyslexic oddities, reviled relived, reserve reverse, forcing him to shake his head and double-back . Not only did he suffer from the human inability to see the dance of molecules at the quantum level, he struggled to see the macro world clearly as well. The faces of people more than 10 feet away lacked detail, painted roadway lanes were vees instead of straight lines, landscapes were Impressionistically hazy. The monthly shots of Lucentis administered over the past half-year by his ophthalmologist, Dr. Ahmad Jamal, had killed rogue blood vessels and slowed the progress of deterioration but had worked no improvement in vision. Probably he would fail the eye test when required to renew his driver's license in 2020.

He checked his watch, discovered he had four extra minutes. He walked diagonally, a pawn's capturing move, across 5th, a road only at this time of day less traveled, passed Chase Bank, which was located on what had once been the site of Diesel Oil Sales, where Zee's father worked, and went on down to 4th, carefully. He was fond of the town's aging concrete sidewalks, some of them perhaps as old as he. As, 30 years earlier, he had enjoyed stumbling with Diane—"Watch your step," "Mind the gap," they would tell each other affectionately—over the irregular, slick, rounded cobblestones of side vias in Orvieto or Pordenone, their eyes panning the shops and apartments or fixating on menus posted in trattoria windows or on colorful laundry hanging from high bedroom windows, so now he enjoyed the almost anarchic independence of the worn concrete slabs—miniature tectonic plates colliding or drifting apart— that constituted many of the walkways in the core of town. Some were raised from heaving, some depressed from settling, some tilted left, some right, some were separated by one-inch gaps, the worst of which had been filled or patched and painted a cautionary fish-belly white or traffic-cone orange, all of them cracked by gravity and pebbled by water and wind erosion, green spongy moss growing here and there. Each step required an old man's attention, each slab exuded the past.

[The walks are dangerous as hell, but I have to admit I rejoice to see little bits of clam shell in some of those slabs that were made partly of beach sand back in the '40s and '50s. So much more character than the mono-toned, mono-textured white cement or black asphalt replacements that are being planned now. Charlotte]

On the west side of 4th was the Puget Power substation that had been there as long as he could remember, short cedars and one massive blue-green deodar cedar shrouding its guarding fence. There were few NIMBYs in the Bowl when the substation was built. Most residents were just happy to have the power. The heavy, humming transformers that accompanied it they perceived not as ugly but as modern. During its first 100 years, Edmonds was unpretentious and uncomplicated. It took itself and its racial and ethnic uniformity for granted. He could not recall any African-Americans, Latinx, or Asians living in or near the Bowl between his childhood in the '40s, when the population was just over 1,000, and his early adulthood in the '60s, when the population, augmented by annexation, reached the 8,000s. Although Barney McCoy, who lived on Dayton just up from the Masonic Temple and whose nose was flat and skin a shade darker than that of the other Cub Scouts in Pack 360, was said to be part Eskimo, almost everyone in town that the old man knew, he finally realized in college, came from northwestern Europe, the British Isles, or Scandinavia. There were Sorensens, Kjolsos, Engelses, Evanses, Kellys, Currys, Setchfields, Baileys, Tuckers, Sellerses, Goodwins, Husebys, Williamsons, Nelsons, Burdetts, Hawkinsons, Magnusons, Petersons and Pettersons, Lambes, Faircloughs, Swearingens, O'Briens, Clevelands, Millers, Alberys, Deebachs, Duvals, Guyots, Riddles, Coles, Swedbergs, Wagners, Becks, Bienzes, Savages, Kennedys, Kretzlers, Ottos, Astells, Yosts, Dieners, Durbins, Swansons, Hubbards,Tusons, McGibbons, McGinnesses, Andersons, Casparses, and Prestons. There were no "-inis," "-ezes," or "ics," only two "Phillipses," and just one "Karnofski," one "Kuzmoff." Even now, in 2019, the population of the Bowl remained almost 80 percent white, although the City Council had recently recognized the whiteness as an issue and had created a commission to promote diversity of all kinds.

[Yes, everybody looked like us. But, although diversity is welcome, I don't think we have to promote it or apologize for its lack. The Bowl was what it was and will be what it will be. Let it evolve naturally, don't try to force it. Monk]

[What it *was* was an all-white upper-lower, lower-middle class open town. What it *is* is a very white upper- middle class enclave. What far too soon it *will be* without top-down direction is a very white enclave of the 10-percenters, the crazy rich Caucasians. We need greater density, affordable housing for working families and seniors (simpler, cheaper apartments, condos and townhouses; detached accessory dwelling units; an end to single-family zoning; some sort of housing subsidy for people on limited incomes). Charlotte]

[So anyone and everyone is *entitled* to live in the Bowl? Monk]

[It's the upper-middle class that has the sense of entitlement! Charlotte]

[Char, you live in a million-dollar penthouse in the SeaView! Monk]

[And you have a million-dollar view home on 9th! The point is, we have a responsibility to make room for the less fortunate who have been victims of white supremacist heteropatriarchal capitalism. Too many fortunes in America have come from the dispossession of indigenous peoples, the enslavement of African Americans, the production of fossil fuels, or the obvious exploitation of workers. Both of us were overpaid, but at least as a doctor I helped people, and so did you as a lawyer, in spite of the sharkier aspects of your profession. As partial reparation, after I retired, I devoted two years to working for Doctors Without Borders in Congo, and I know you have done *pro bono* work. Charlotte]

Heading north on 4th, the old man passed six consecutive stucco condos wedged tightly, each three levels high with glass-fronted decks, one of which had replaced the '30s-era two-bedroom white bungalow where the Johnsons had lived, before coming to Sylvia's old cedar rambler, stained the same grizzled sepia it had been when built in the early '50s.

He reached Dayton Street and turned right. On the north side of Dayton between 4th and 5th, a parking lot and low brick and cedar buildings housing offices and retail stores had long since replaced the massive, mission-style Hughes Memorial Methodist Church, an ecru stucco structure two stories high, with terra cotta roof tiles, a Roman-arched double-pillared three-door entry, twin Roman-arched belfries, and Roman-arched stained glass windows on all sides. Every Sunday morning a belfry's call to the faithful and rebuke to slackers and non-believers, so many bells floating up and down, was heard from the beach to the hilltop at 10th and Maple. In fourth grade, much to the approval of his mother, the old man answered those calls, attending Sunday school and church, two long hours, with his friends, his Cub Scout buddies, his sandlot cohorts. Some earnestly wore sport coats, ties, and slacks. He wore either dark corduroys or moontans and a white shirt. He was unable, actually did not want, to get something out of the Sunday experiences. He did not under-stand the spiritual. He did not trust the spiritual. As far as he could tell, it wanted to dispossess himself of himself. He often followed and agreed with the moral lessons in the minister's sermons but always shied off, drew protectively inward, when the minister pressed on to the joys of atonement. A few of the hymns could almost inveigle him out of himself. When the congregation rose as one, hymnals open, and roared "Onward Christian s-o-o-o-oldiers, marching as to war," he too responded, more than half-throatedly, to that rousing martial rhythm, ready to fight for the Christian team. "Just a Closer Walk with Thee" produced a tingling in his stomach at "Grant it, Jesus, is my plea-ee-ee-ee," and in "Amazing Grace" his throat constricted and his eyes moistened at "I once was lost but now am found." But even then he sensed that it was tone, an arrangement of notes, not text, working in him, trying to disintegrate him. In July 1951, at the phoned invita-tion of Zee's grandmother Didi, who was a Nazarene, and the voiced-over urging of Zee and Monk, he pedaled his Schwinn up the hill,

standing up to pump and switchbacking half a dozen times to negotiate the 40-degree climb from 8th to 9th on Dayton, and rode in her
'46 Buick to a Billy Graham Crusade for Christ at Memorial Stadium
in Seattle. He was dazzled by Billy's handsomeness—that wavy hair,
that decisive jaw—and his honeyed North Carolina drawl. The way
he would stalk the stage, in command of his audience, the way he
poured out the words, in command of his material. He was glorious.
Finally, as the choir began to hum ever so softly, backgrounding him,
came the moment when Billy called to the unsaved to come forward.
God is speaking to you and calling you to Himself tonight, it is time
to commit yourself to Him, surrender your total person, your intelligence, your will, your body to Jesus Christ the Lord, He must come
first in your heart, it takes a deliberate act of the will, deny yourself,
pick up the Cross and follow Him, you may never have another hour
like this, tomorrow might be too late, accept Christ as your Savior, do
it now, get up and come down right now, be washed clean, avoid the
fires of hell, be with your loved ones for all eternity, your family and
your friends will joyfully wait for you, there are aides waiting on the
field to help you. The dwindling light of the long Seattle summer evening was golden, the sky a darkening azure beginning faintly to twinkle. Dozens of people were rising, converging in the aisles, answering
the call to salvation, descending the stairs to the field below. His pals
were going forward looking back at him, Didi was imploring him to
go forward, he did not want to go forward, he felt no supernal call to
go forward, to be immersed in the evening itself was all he wanted,
to be in the midst of all there was but not ever surrender himself was
what he wanted. He went forward. His friends cheered. Didi cheered.
An usher directed him to a tent. An aide in a corduroy sport coat and
tie greeted him, wrote down his name, congratulated him, patted
him on the back. They sat on folding chairs at a small table.

"Wayne," the aide said, "in order to be saved you must first confess your sins and state your acceptance of the Lord Jesus Christ as
your Savior."

He was dumb to tell the aide how sin wormed within him. He

tried to think of sins he could own up to. He wasn't fully clear on what sin was. Would his grandmother say it was believing that matter was real? He had never killed or stolen. Did swearing and lying count? A minute passed.

"Wayne, just think of something," the aide said, growing impatient.

"Forgive me, Lord, for I know I have sinned," the old man finally mustered, and the aide prayed for him, riffing on the nature of sin and assuring Him that Wayne was penitent.

"And now, Wayne, do you accept Jesus Christ as your Lord and savior?"

"I do."

"Oh, that's wonderful, Wayne," the aide said, grinning. "I am so happy for you. The Lord welcomes you home." The aide presented him with a pocket-size *New Testament*, King James version, and the old man went outside to join his jubilant friends, who all the way home chattered giddily about their conversion experience and their plans to read the *New Testament* every day and to purify their lives. The old man himself was somber. He thought he had probably done the right thing, yet he was haunted by a sense of loss. Nevertheless, the next morning he started in on "Matthew" and, as if it were a library contest, read his way through the *New*. He tackled the mystifying language, giving himself credit for fighting through the many passages he did not understand. The more puzzling, the better. "Let the dead bury the dead." "Sufficient unto the day is the evil thereof." Those lines had stayed with him for the last 68 years. Each chapter was a workout filling him with a sense of achievement but not enlarging his soul. Or did he not even have a soul? Or were feelings soul? His mother was delighted, his father uncommunicative. Although he wasn't quite sure what taking the name of the Lord in vain encompassed, the old man tried to honor the vow he made with his friends to quit swearing and lying. One drizzly day they all retreated from the vacant lot where they were playing workup and went to his bedroom, where they invented baseball lineups using vulgar names for body parts. "Balls" was at shortstop, "Butt" at first, and "Pecker" was on the mound, he recalled. That, he felt confident, was not swearing, although he would never, ever, want his mother to hear him say any words like those. One of the boys told an extended story about the dam man who was in charge of the dam water, all of them feeling that a literal interpretation gave them moral cover. Within a year, however, albeit guilt-gilded, he was saying "God damn it" instead of "gosh darn it," "Jesus Christ" instead of "jeepers creepers," and "hell" instead of "h-e-double-hockey-sticks."

[My family and I also attended. In fact, we went three times during the week-long meeting, so awesome did we find it to be in the presence of Billy and the Holy Spirit. As the son of a Baptist minister I, of course, had already become a Christian but, if I may reference your pedagogical specialty, Wayne, Billy's rousing rhetoric—his glamorous *ethos*, his sin-and-redemption *pathos*, his text-explicating *logos*, waving that open Bible like a conductor a baton—fired my neurons in a way that my dad was unable to do in our little white church with its single steeple at 4th and Bell in quiet, gray Edmonds. Although my views have long since become more complicated, deeper, richer, it's because of Billy that I studied theology and ended up teaching psychology at Big Sur Theological Seminary. Dave]

[We were there, too. Was the whole town? Why didn't we caravan? But that wasn't the Edmonds way, was it? Sylvia]

[I still don't swear! Gary]

He crossed the street and turned left, passing The Red Twig, formerly Brusseau's—a bakery-bistro hangout of his and Diane's, where they could meet friends, get good coffee, and split a croissant, fulfilling a social contract, and before that a dry cleaner's, and before that McKeever's Shell, where he bought gas and had the oil changed in the '49 Ford convertible he owned in high school—and at precisely 5:30 reached the Leyda Building at the corner of 5th and Main, a four-way intersection in the center of which was a modest fountain, its torch-like plume about four feet high, set upon a round brick pedestal, girt by a granite bench, and canopied by an open Tinker Toy-like metal pagoda, that forced cars to go round-about. At one time the building housed Toni's Apparel, owned by Toni Leyda, and Weller's, a men's clothing store that later moved to a new building across Main, just east of Safeway, where as a teen-ager the old man had bought quarter-inch suede belts in pink or purple, polka-dotted short-sleeved shirts with rounded collars worn turned up, and pegged denim pants, a pastel yellow pair of which he was wearing when first touched intimately by a girl. Ten years ago, a Starbucks had commandeered this prime commercial location, placed tables outside, and begun beckoning locals and tourists alike to come and have a cup as the espresso machines kept oozing drop by drop. Brusseau's was gone. All over the country, even in the Bowl now, Americans were in chains.

[So many chains! Not just Starbucks and Best Western but systemic racism and sexism and lookism and ageism and ableism and speciesism—not to mention gross economic inequality. Charlotte]

5:30. Open, then, the door! A crank I am, it occurred to him, amusingly.

"Wayne!" shouted a smiling barista as she turned a key in the lock and bade him enter. "How are you? Grande drip? We're brewing your Ethiopian today."

"Excellent, LaTasha," said the old man. "And a maple scone."

"No high protein feta-spinach-egg wrap? What's the occasion?"

"The first day of the test of my life. Today I start rewiring my brain. I've got six months to take my hitting, throwing, and fielding skills to a championship level."

"Really? You're into neuroplasticity? The text in my psychobiology class says the will can alter brain circuitry by placing new demands on it. You can form new neurons as well as the synapses between them. I mean, you can not only rewire but create new wires!"

"Exactly. Mindful repetition, I've read in several books helpfully recommended to me by Scribd, builds layers on the myelin sheath that insulates your axons. Through practice you can build up the sheath so that signals get transmitted faster and more accurately and produce changes in the brain that enable you to refine your athletic skills. The more reps, the more myelin. Practice makes myelin, and myelin makes perfect—or, in my case, good enough to challenge my peers, I hope."

"I hope so, too. This for that thing in St. George?"

"Right."

Angular-faced girl, cornrowed hair, multiple piercings, rich jewels in an Ethiope's ears and nose. She was lidding the coffee, tonging a scone onto a plate. Another barista, pony-tailed Josh, had stepped behind the counter to help. The old man checked his privilege as he might his image in a mirror, turning to observe the line growing behind him. The half-dozen faces were, comfortingly, he had to admit, white. How guilty should he feel about that? LaTasha seemed unperturbed in the midst of the whiteness, but of course while on duty she enjoyed the systemic protection of corporate power.

[You don't need to feel guilty about that at all—any more than an African American needs to feel guilty about being comfortable in the presence of other African Americans. Don't flaunt your privilege—recognize it, accept it, and, yes, enjoy it—as would a brother among a couple of token whites in a mostly-black pickup basketball game at LA Fitness in Lynnwood. Monk]

[Monk, that's a false equivalence. In view of what happened in Philadelphia last year, it's clear that Starbucks, like most of America, is a white space and that blacks need permission to share it. LaTasha, truly a token, has been given permission to work in Edmonds by the corporation and by the local wypipo because she is willing to use her white voice. Charlotte]

"By the way, Wayne, the other night I referenced you to a friend who went to Edmonds-Maplewood High School as an example of a senior citizen who stays active, and she said she'd seen a picture of you in the Hall of Fame there along with her aunt and your 1984 state championship basketball team. Elizabeth Ann Mann?"

"Elizabeth Ann! Sonnet lover, she claimed when we did a poetry unit in Lit Classics class. Liz Ann, sure. Eighty winters have now besieged my brow, but I do remember her. Played her heart out on the court. A rebound hound. Teammates called her 'The Truck.' Could really use her back bumper to get post position on her defender. Loved that kid. What's she doing now?"

"Not much, I guess. Being a grandmother. Volunteering at the Edmonds Museum. Watching Netflix with her partner. That comes to $5.55, Wayne. Scanning?"

"I am."

He scanned his payment with his phone, sat down with coffee and a scone.

[Ha! Iambic tetrameter—I remember! And thank you for the Elizabethan sonnet! Liz Ann]

He took a window table and faced the fountain, his back to the entrance, the obverse of a gunslinger's tactic, to protect himself against being drawn in by the clusters of retired men who would soon be pushing chairs around for klatching. He rolled his shoulders back, forcing his coccyx to make a right angle with the chair's seat, an L rather than the J that came so naturally now, propped up his iPad, logged in to the free Wi-Fi, and opened the *New York Times*. He scrolled down the Home page, stopping to tap into the many stories whose headlines interested him and occasionally prompted impromptu fashionings of his own, which he typed into the Notes section on his phone. *Public Employees Forced To Exchange Defined-Benefits Pensions For IRAs Now Exceedingly Wroth. Apple To Fund iRaq Reconstruction In Exchange For Naming Rights. Krugman Flogs Deficit Scolds With Keynes.* He liked reading the news online, except for the surfeit of graphics, especially those animatrons that pulsed and darted like an ophthalmologist's field of vision test and those cataracts that descended the screen and required him to tap for their removal. Give him a thousand words and keep your picture. Hard copies, such as those of the *Seattle*

Times delivered to his condo daily, were cumbersome and dim. The iPad held an entire paper in a bright and tidy six-by-eight-inch package. He sipped his coffee, enjoying the hint of cocoa produced by the sweet, unvarnished Ethiopian beans. The scone's maple frosting made lanes of flavor across the papillae on his tongue, reminding him of maple bars past that his mother would bring home from the town's bakery on Saturdays. He had been a fat boy. His mother said he was husky, but he knew he was fat. Some of the kids at school—but not the All Stars—called him "The Fat Man" after the detective on a popular radio show. He was ashamed of the name, but that didn't spoil his appetite. He played many sports, but that didn't keep the flab off. He simply ate too much. Not just one maple bar but two; not just one hamburger deluxe but two. Stacks of thick pancakes saturated with maple syrup, wide wedges of wild blackberry pie à *la mode*, the ice cream melting over the cobalt stain where the berries had bled through the crust, handfuls of chewy chocolate chip cookies. He knew nothing about nutrition. In high school, as his body stretched out, he thinned a bit. By graduation he had reached 5'11" and weighed 180 pounds, parameters he found acceptable for years. He could still get up and down the court in pickup basketball games, still get into a good defensive stance and demonstrate to his players how to drop-step and slide. But in 1977, intrigued by the increasing number of ambitious joggers in skimpy shorts and tee shirts on what were gradually becoming the busy streets of Edmonds—what were they on to? could running actually be something more than a painful means to athletic success or improved health?—he read *The Complete Book of Running* by Jim Fixx, a Mensa member who weighed 240 before converting to a runner's regimen, running away from 60 superfluous pounds and becoming an evangelist for the sport.

[I actually felt a kind of perverse pride in the irony that Fixx died with his Tailwinds on in a race a couple of years later. It was as if he took it upon himself to be the exception that proves the rule that running is healthful. Stu]

["Made lanes of flavor"—I've been wondering how you might incorporate that classic Proustian remembrance. *C'est très agréable*. Solveig]

The old man repented his self-indulgence. He yearned for the physical transcendence of which Fixx spoke: increased self-esteem, the release of pressure and tension, a longer and fuller life spent sailing on a flood tide of endorphins and endocannabinoids, the runner's high. He wanted to be strong, to go long, to attack hills, to join the conspiracy of those with lean and hungry looks. He began to reduce his caloric intake. Ate two, you brute, eh? Not anymore. One would suffice, thank you. It was easy to talk Diane, a P.E. teacher, into joining him. They bought Nike Tailwind shoes. At first they drove from their rambler on Grandview in north Edmonds to the old high school's athletic fields on 6th and jog-walked a few laps, stopping to rest now and then. Within a couple of weeks they were able to finish a mile in nine minutes. Then, afternoons on weekdays if work and weather permitted, mornings on Saturdays and vacation days, they began pounding the pavement, a small circle route at first, maybe a mile, down Bell to 4th, south on 4th to Howell, up Howell to 5th, then back to the field, gradually widening the circle until they were running from 5th and Howell south to Pine, up Pine to 9th, a steep ascent, north to Caspar, west on Caspar to 3rd, south on 3rd to Bell, and back to the field, three miles in all, waving fraternally to other runners whose paths they crossed. That distance sufficed for her, but not for the old man. Eventually he was running another two miles around the track and then loping home while she drove back to shower, do her hair and makeup, and fuss around the house. Four months later he was competing in the 10K races held in nearby towns every summer weekend—in Lynnwood five miles east, in Lake Stevens 25 miles to the northeast, at Green Lake in Seattle, in Redmond, east of Seattle on the other side of Lake Washington. His first took him 50 minutes. So did the second. Surely, he thought, he was capable of better. He talked with Stu Cardinal, the school's cross-country coach—the old man had, in 1969, transferred to the new Maplewood High School built on a hill south of Westgate and had become the girls' basketball coach in 1972 when Title IX came into being—who helped him devise a training plan with a purpose. Twice a week, while Diane jogged a circle route by herself, the old man remained at the track and ran intervals. One day he'd sprint eight 220s, another four 440s. Once a week he'd push himself through extended pain to run a hard mile. The intervals were like vitamins and minerals. He began to get stronger. He became able to break six minutes in the mile. On his two longer runs during the week his pace picked up with no conscious effort on his part. His heart was teaching itself to beat faster for longer. His leg muscles learned to eliminate some of the lactic acid that running produced. He became more lactic-tolerant of that which remained. As the weeks drew on he incurred less and less oxygen debt. He broke 40 minutes in a 10K. After each run he felt justified, purified, washed clean, though not quite all passion spent. Sundays were a special day for each. He would run, Diane would drive to services at the Hilltop Presbyterian Church. Still in shorts, reading the *Seattle Times* in the Morris chair he had inherited from his grandfather, he would rise when she came in the door, smiled a greeting, and went to their bedroom to change. As she dropped earrings and bracelet into the jewelry box on her dresser, he would approach from behind and gently cup both breasts. They would nuzzle as he unbuttoned her blouse, removed it, ran his thumb down her neck chain to her cross of gold, excitement growing for both at this slight sullying, she lubricious, he tumescent, Lucrece awaiting Tarquin, never more chaste than when he did ravish her. She'd turn to offer the fullness behind her white silky bra, he'd free her breasts, unzip her skirt, which fell to the floor as she stepped out of it, and peel off her panties, which she would wantonly dispatch with a flick of an ankle. Lips to lips, lips to brackish lips, tongue to clit until her writhing welcoming groan, her happy moan, lips to tip, then he inside squeezing her legs between his, a slick tight fit, so literally sensational, driving on through delicious throbs of pain until dumbness set in. Or in a chair, she sitting on him, eyes glazed, almost exiting on her way up, sliding slowly, teasingly, down to administer a vaginal squeeze, he shuddering, gasping, fingering her breasts, holding on as long as he could as she rode the carousel to her satisfaction.

[So you "matured," in all senses of the word? Lucky Diane! Solveig]

"Wayne," she once said as they lay seeping after, "except for Jesus, you are the heart of my soul."

"And you are the soul of my heart," the old man said.

They had first met in 1965 at a District mandated in-service class called "Instructional Theory Into Practice" held on four October Saturdays at the new Edmonds High School two miles from the Bowl. He was in his third year of teaching at Edmonds, his alma mater, she in her first at recently opened Meadowdale. He spotted her as he strode past the lectern—trim, bright-eyed, Dorothy Hamill hairdo, a brown flying wedge with bangs down to her eyebrows—and took an empty desk beside her. They shared brown eye rollings as the instructor, an enthusiastic 30-year-old, overviewed this "teacher decision-making model for planning instruction" and started in on "Learning Objectives," the first of seven steps in planning a lesson, featuring task analysis, diagnostic testing, and congruence with Benjamin Bloom's cognitive taxonomy. At the second session, he was there first, same desk. She, seeming to have expected that, said "Hi," and came to sit beside him. She wore a white blouse, blue jeans, black flats, and a powder blue cardigan buttoned only at the top.

"Did you try any of this stuff this week?" she asked.

"Not yet," he said. "Waiting to see how it all fits together."

The second session covered "Anticipatory Set," "State the Lesson Objectives," and "Input." The teacher could, for example, get the students' attention by flicking the lights off and on or writing on the chalkboard a riddle to solve or question to answer while he/she took roll. Having heightened anticipation, the teacher should announce to the students, in infinitive form, what they were supposed to learn in that day's lesson, then proceed with the lesson, identifying and presenting main concepts and skills, explaining clearly by means of such things as examples and diagrams, all the while inviting active student participation.

"I'm Wayne," he said when the session ended, extending his hand.

"I'm Diane," she said, taking it.

"Would you care to get a cup of coffee?"

"I would," she said.

"The Edmonds Bakery?"

"I've never been in there. Sure, why not?"

They agreed that each would drive his/her own car, as he wished he hadn't put it, from the school, situated in a stark neighborhood of strip malls and apartment houses, down steep, tree-lined Main Street, past three-bedroom homes with flowering yards, crimson and white petals of azaleas and rhododendrons not sleeping but bright and alert on a welcome Indian summer day, and into the Bowl, which lay all Danäe to a rare blue sky.

"You know," he said when they were seated with their coffee, both having passed on the pastries that filled the upper tier of a heavy glass case, though he coveted a maple bar, "my mother used to send me on my bike to buy bread here. I always chose white, not wheat. I really liked watching the baker or his wife run it through the slicing machine."

"So you grew up in Edmonds?"

"I did."

"It's such a quaint town. Some day I'd like to buy here. I grew up in Seattle, on Phinney Ridge, near the zoo."

"An area with charm of its own."

"I suppose. We lived on 45th, though. Cars swooshing past all day, going from the U District to Ballard and vice versa. Of course, what I have now isn't any better. I live with a housemate in an apartment on Highway 99."

"And I now live not in Edmonds but two-point-four miles away in an apartment on 196th."

"You've clocked it."

"I have. Give me some time and I'll be living down here again, one way or another."

"So you can go home again?"

Had she read it? His eyes kept going back to the cross on the chain around her neck. Accessorizing? Testifying? Talismaning? But who doesn't knock on wood?

"I'm planning on it. Coffee warm enough?" They had poured it into sturdy mugs from a pot on a two-burner hot plate.

"I actually prefer it a little on the cool side. You get more of the flavor that way. I'm trying to convince myself that there's a hint of cherry in it."

"Really? You mean coffee isn't just coffee?"

"Nothing is just anything. I think you always have to pull back the veil and discover what lies behind or beneath."

"You mean like dark matter?"

"I don't know anything about that. I mean like the spiritual reality behind the material reality. Anyway, when I was a kid, about 12, my dad started taking my mom and my younger sister and I to Napa Valley for our summer vacation. This was long before it became the tourist attraction that it is now. There were only a dozen wineries that welcomed visitors at the time. We'd stay at the El Bonita motel in St. Helena. He loved the whole romance of wine. My sister and I loved the sun and the pool. Mornings we'd spend going to wineries, my sister and I enduring the lectures and the tastings, all the while whining that it was too hot and we wanted to go swimming. We'd hit three places every morning for three days. Linda and I liked Beringer for its cool limestone cave, but the others were drudgery. My mom and dad would ask about Brix and *terroir* and whether the wine had been aged in oak or in stainless steel while they swirled and sniffed and sipped. They'd buy a couple of bottles at each place and finally we would go to the park for a picnic lunch my mom had made—we were thrifty and seldom ate out—and then back to the pool, where we splashed all afternoon, diving, holding our breath while we wrestled underwater, and pretending we were wide receivers by jumping off the side of the pool to catch the sponge rubber football that our dad would throw over the water. So I grew up hearing a lot about wine, and when we were in high school he started pouring us a couple of ounces for dinner. He taught us to always hold the glass by the stem so we wouldn't get greasy fingerprints on the sides and spoil our look at the wine's color, how to suck air in over the wine in our mouths to open up its nuances of flavor—believe me, we did a lot of gagging and coughing as unfamiliar fumes attacked our throats—and to reflect on the wine's structure by considering its acidity and body. So I would say that this coffee—Folger's? Maxwell House?— is thin-bodied, acidic with wild cherry overtones if I'm being generous, just beginning to fall apart because it's been sitting in the pot a wee bit too long, not bitter and flavorless yet but soon to be."

"Who knew? I've always just swilled the stuff for the caffeine, and for something to do, and for a sense of control, and for a connection with my past. My parents perked multiple pots every day, and on those rare occasions when we would make a car trip to the Olympic peninsula or cross the Cascades to Lake Chelan, on those old two-lane roads that ran through as many little towns as possible, they'd stop every couple of hours and get a 10 cent cup of coffee at a greasy spoon. I picked up their habit. I take it you're following in your dad's footsteps? Drinking lots of wine?"

"Not lots, I would say, and I'm not making any trips to Napa Valley, but yes, I have a glass in the evening several times a week. I look for decent but affordable wines in the liquor store."

"We should go out for a glass sometime, and you could teach me."

"We should."

They looked at each other.

"Do you enjoy being a teacher?" she asked.

"Kind of. I like the idea of getting the kids immersed in real literature and trying to make them better readers and writers. Getting them to dig in and read closely. Getting them to communicate their findings in essays filled with textual references. But to tell the truth, I've been foundering." Floundering? He would look them up later. "There's no spark in my classroom."

"The kids are disinterested?"

"Uninterested, yes. Inattentive. I'm only vaguely sure of what to teach and not at all sure of how to do it. I'm hoping that this ITIP program, as mechanical and formulaic as it is, will give me some practical tips on how to structure my classes. Jack Foster, whose Cultural Heritage class I took as a senior and who is now my colleague, thinks it's a farce. He believes that teaching is an art that you either have or you don't. 'You can't teach teaching', he says. That's probably true for him. He inspires just by virtue of who he is. Most of us are not that powerful. We need a framework, a tune, upon which we can improvise, like a jazz musician. Which my father is, by the way."

"Honestly, I kind of feel like you do. I want my girls to be educated physically in the sense that they learn to enjoy their bodies in motion, know how to condition them, and improve their skills and techniques in playing various sports. Right now I just have them line up and count off for teams, then roll the ball out for games. Soccer now, while the weather's good, basketball and volleyball when we have to move indoors, then softball and track in the spring. I love those games myself, but I'm not teaching the girls anything."

"What do you think? Shall we both start experimenting with that anticipatory set stuff and compare notes next week?"

"Let's do. And"—taking out a Papermate and scribbling on a napkin—"here's my phone number in case you need to call me about something."

[Diana, Roman goddess of the hunt. So glad you found an athletic person to settle down with! Solveig]

[I agree with Jack. Gimmicks take the soul out of teaching. Teaching depends as much on who you (the teacher) are as what you do. The acronym ITIP could be said to stand for "I Think I'm Perfect"! Bill]

Thwap! He slapped at a fly that had just parked itself on his table. The coffee sloshed, the fork clinked on his plate. Uh-oh. It wasn't a fly, it was a floater.

LaTasha, bussing the table next to his, giggled. "Did you get him, Wayne?"

He chagrinned. "Nah, false alarm. I've got a bit of a retinal problem."

His watch haptickled him with a reminder: "A moment of deep breathing can clear your mind." But he didn't want to clear his mind; he wanted to submerge himself in its turbidity. As he sipped some now quite cool Ethiopian ambrosia, happily, he was tickled by the suddenly emerged notion that this could be a defining moment, and ultimately Noted, with much buffering and buffing in the process:

Lucifer's Lexicon (*Ambrose-ia for Today's Cynic*)

Trump l'oeil— Post-modern art of governing through tweets that present the elision of reality.

global warming—Modern era of rising earth temperatures, accepted placidly by ordinarily change-fearing conservatives and resisted angrily by ordinarily change-favoring progressives.

micro-aggression—A speech act which, at the macro level, appears innocuous or even complimentary but, at the quantum level, as detected by language string-theorists, produces vibrations derogatory to a socially marginalized group (as when a young female clerk says to an octogenarian of any and all genders, "May I help you, Sweetie?")

post-racial society—An American utopia (in the literal sense of "no place").

bioengineering—Survival of the retrofittest.

---

justice—Revenge dressed up in formal clothing.

multiculturalism—The religious experience of variety.

[All right, let me in on this!

the 99%—The vast majority of Americans, all of whom are convinced that the very rich became so by exploiting them and that it's only fair and just that the wealth of the selfish 1% be distributed by means of taxation to the more virtuous 99%. Monk]

[the 1%—The very richest Americans, all of whom are convinced that they became rich by means of their own talent, effort, and moral virtue and who believe that, although they are of course superior people, everyone could be in the 1% if only they worked at it. Charlotte]

[woke—State of hyperconsciousness in which one is infinitely aware of the infinite number of ways in which another's use of particular words and phrases further oppresses, demeans, and marginalizes an oppressed, demeaned, and marginalized social group and its individual members. Monk]

[tone-deaf—Term applied to the self-whiteous whose use of words like "woke" is an unconscionable culture- appropriation and reveals a woeful lack of awareness. Charlotte]

[stereotype—In regard to a group of people, a generalization that you find offensive.

insight—In regard to a group of people, a generalization that you approve of.

gatekeepers—Editors with whom you agree in regard to their decision to forbid the distribution of a given message in their publication.

censors—Editors with whom you disagree in regard to their decision to forbid the distribution of a given message in their publication.

weaponized language—The rhetorical use of words and phrases to advance causes or present points of view with which you do not agree.

judicial activism—Supreme Court rulings, as in Roe v. Wade or Citizens United, that are based on interpretations of the Constitution with which you do not agree. Gary]

[placebo—A medication or course of treatment that others believe in but you do not.

petty concern—Something that others care about but you do not. Sylvia]

[death—Inevitable ending for all individual animals and plants, the fear of which in humans underlies all religions and philosophies. Dave]

As he listed other candidates for sanityizing by Satanizing—asymmetry, credentialism, implicit bias, systemic oppression, cancel culture—his phone announced, in a chiming arpeggio, a text from Zee.

"happy bday bro! sry 4 l8 ntice but ~xpctd lnch mtg w/ cmpgn mgr @11. c u @ 9 ok?"

The old man, who felt secure only when he had a schedule to follow, checked the time. 6:50. They had originally agreed to meet at 2:00. He had planned to walk to his bench, return home for Greek yogurt (80 calories, 12 grams of protein) and two tablespoons of peanut butter right out of the jar (190 calories, seven grams of protein), then drive to Harbor Square Athletic Club near the waterfront and lift weights before going back to the condo, drinking a smoothie, and resting for an hour. Now that had ganged agley. He skimmed the sports section—the Knicks and Nets had floundered and then foundered and would not make the playoffs, the Yanks and the Mets had opened with wins—squished a last crumb of scone with the back of his fork, dissolved it on his tongue, and edged his way toward the door, nodding to a couple of klatchers.

"LaTasha," he waved, "see you tomorrow. Tell your friend to tell her aunt that I said hello."

"Okay, Wayne, you got it."

Exiting Starbucks, two quick rook lefts put him back on 5th, aiming south. Holding memories at bay, bouncing them back when they tried to insinuate their way into his consciousness, concentrating the way he did when he used to run 10Ks, tucking the iPad between left forearm and ribs, carrying the mail the way "Hurrying" Hugh McElhenny used to for the Huskies in the early '50s, risking a spill on the rugged sidewalk, he beelined in a trot back to the condo, allowing snot and tears to dribble down his face in his hive-bound haste. So much to get done!

He entered the foyer, caught his breath, wiped his nose and eyes with his handkerchief, girded, and began his ascent. When he and Diane first moved in, he had climbed in loud bounds, knees high, lungs full, feet thumping. Nearly forty years later he shuffled up noiselessly, taking an infinitesimal pause on each step, right hand on the railing for balance and propulsion, lungs bellowsing, pacemaker pulsing, heart thumping.

7:00. "Lexa," he struggled to demand between lung spasms as he entered his unit, "play Rachmaninoff."

"Shuffling songs by Sergei Rachmaninoff on Amazon music," she responded, and fulfilled his hopes by selecting "Rhapsody on a Theme of Paganini," whose opening measures soon had him punching the air—"Bom! Bom! Bom!"—twitching his shoulders, and rattle-hop-stepping his feet as he made a smoothie, pouring six ounces of lemonade into the blender and adding, from huge Costco packages, a large scoop of whey protein powder and a cup of frozen strawberries, then a fresh banana and eight ice cubes. As the rhapsody reached the "*dies irae*" refrain, he poured the blended mix into a used Styrofoam cup from the Gravity Bar, popped in a straw, said "Lexa, end music," and sat down at his desktop computer in the south corner of the west wall of the living room. He finished the *New*

York Times and worked his way through *The Huffington Post* and *The Drudge Report*— cringing at the facile liberalism and conservatism, needing always to squirm away from doctrinal certainties, to resist intellectual bullying, but nevertheless curious (and, curiously, obliged) to see what bits of news they had forced into their Procrustean beds; *The USS Mariner*, a sabremetrician's blog about the Seattle baseball team; the *Everett Herald* obituaries (finding today one for the 95-year-old parent of a former student who in 1969 had refused to sign a permission slip allowing his daughter to read *The Catcher in the Rye* in the old man's American literature class); and Facebook, where he seldom posted but daily peeped to keep up with the activities of classmates and teammates and former colleagues and students and players. Already, he was happy to note as he quickly scrolled down, there were a dozen salutations from friends who had been informed of his birthday at the stroke of midnight by an FB algorithm. He would respond to them individually later. He checked his bank and credit card accounts—a Social Security payment deposited at Chase, an automatic monthly Comcast cable and internet charge on Visa—and his mail. The Edmonds Old Settlers' picnic was scheduled for August 11, Classmates.com claimed that his profile was attracting attention, HBO Go had some suggestions for his evening's viewing, Starbucks was pleased to inform him that, as a gold card holder, he was entitled to claim a birthday reward at his convenience, My Fitness Pal had recipes and yoga exercises for him, Scribd had three books to recommend, BookBub had four more, Quora had its usual array of spurious questions and dodgy answers, a softball teammate had forwarded a shaggy dog story, and his high school class steering committee had formally invited him to attend the annual reunion, to be held this year at the Anderson Center Plaza on June 1.

8:15. Done. The hard copy of the *Seattle Times* would have to wait. He would just take a quick peek at his Twitter account. Two responses to last night's tweet: From @eatmyshorts: "WTF?" and from @selectedshortz: "Shinto—embarrassing, not a good pun. Cupid and Eros—too hard, inclusion of conjunction unfair.

Leer—too easy; also, 'howling' an inelegant way to suggest pho-netic correspondence. Flanerie—'by the Sound' better than 'howl-ing' but answer still too easy; not many famous writers named O'Conner. Rabbit at Rest—otherwise good but marred by that mi-grating 't.' Insouciance—a respectable oronym. Rolex—works for me (!) Algorithm—Now that's more like it!" Discerning, judicious, deserved. He rinsed his cup and straw in the kitchen sink, went to his bathroom to fetch a tube of Icy-Hot and apply some to his lum-bar area to warm and relax his degenerative discs, and returned to the living room for stretching exercises, pleased to see tugboat-led cargo ships coming into and going out of the Strait. Commerce! Commoditization! Commodification! Man's smudge, man's smell. Life! Keep it coming!

[Commerce, yes. Commoditization, necessary at times. Commodification, no! Not everything can or should be monetized, Wayne. I really resent the way Edmonds whorishly shakes its booty to attract the tourist gaze. And why on earth would Gary need a campaign manager? Is he running for City Council? Charlotte]

[Yes, Zee is getting ready to announce that he's running for the Council. Guess what—I'm thinking of running too! Monk]

———— ((◦)) ————

The old man was almost always precisely on time for appoint-ments, wanting to keep neither himself nor anyone else waiting. At 9:00 he parked on 7th outside the fence at Civic Field, still faintly dis-oriented by the absence to the south of the 50-foot-high, 80-yards-long covered wooden grandstand that had loomed over the football field since the '30s, the place where, growing up, he had joined throngs to watch football games and 4th of July fireworks displays. Two years ago the aged structure had been demolished by bulldoz-ers and hauled away in trucks in preparation for the development of a modern multi-purpose park now in the planning stages. Zee, always early, had already set up the pitcher's screen on the infield of the softball diamond and was stretching. The old man changed into his rubber-cleated shoes, twice teetering against the bumper of his '15 Santa Fe , threw his bat bag over his shoulder, grabbed a five-gallon bucket filled with softballs, slammed the hatch shut, and squeezed through the entrance to the crude, mangy expanses of poorly-drained clay that had once been the Elysian football and baseball fields of his dreams. To the west, along 6th, were the blocky old two-story wooden Field House, originally a honey-mustard color, now a startling deep barn red trimmed with dark green, the brightest building in town and the current home of the Boys' and Girls' Club, some cracked concrete basketball and tennis courts that dated to the '40s, and a relatively new skateboard facility. In the southwest corner was a *pétanque* court that reminded him of afternoons spent wandering among pickup games in Parisian parks with Diane.

"Happy birthday, Bro," said Zee as they dapped, then shrugged and bro-hugged. "How's it feel to be 80?"

"Feels fine. Feels like 79. I love the smell of analgesic balm in the morning. Smells like possibility! Let's start building up that myelin."

They wore turtlenecks, sweat pants, ball caps, and batting gloves on both hands in the 45-degree weather.

Zee, who, with his high forehead, slitted, half-opened eyes, full head of full-bodied black hair, lightly lined face and unflappable mien, had for decades reminded the old man of Pierce Brosnan, said "Sorry I had to speed this up, Bro. I know you like your schedules. But it's already April, and I'm eager to get started on my campaign for Position 8. Brian has some free time today, and he and I are going to plan for a kickoff session at the Edmonds Center for the Arts next week and work on a statement for the announcement of my candidacy in the *Beacon* and *My Edmonds News* on Thursday."

"So you're really going to do it! Entering the political arena as an octogenarian—I'm proud of you, Bro! I'll doorbell for you, distribute leaflets, answer the phones at campaign headquarters."

"Campaign headquarters would be my house on Olympic View Drive, and I've cut the cord on my landline, so I'll be answering my own cell phone. But I welcome your offer, and I'll put you to work after we get into this thing."

They started, as softball players all over the world do, by playing catch, easy tosses from 30 feet, then moving back to 50. The old man's arm felt good, rested, recovered from last season's rotator cuff inflammation. He was pushing off his back, right, foot well, but his body insisted that he land not on the ball of the left but on the outside of the heel to maintain his balance, shortening his follow-through and limiting his velocity. That could be lived with, however. Entropy guaranteed that the aging base runners he'd be trying to throw out would be a step slower as compensation. In ensuing practices, they'd gradually increase their throwing distance, gaining arm strength, until they reached 90 feet, the maximum for both.

The old man kept glancing around as they threw. "Seventy-three years, Z-man," he said. "Seventy-three years these decrepit grounds have loomed large in our lives. I love the old place, but it's long past time for an upgrade."

"I remember it like it wasn't yesterday," Zee said. "Second-grade class in the Field House because of overcrowding up at the grade school. Mrs. Hill rearranging her seating chart to split you and I up because we talked so much. Playing 'Red Rover Come Over' and 'Farmer in the Dell' with the girls under Mrs. Hill's careful supervision. And all the times we stayed after school with Jimmie and Jerry and Monk and Walt and Dickie and Dave to watch the high school football players practice for a while and then borrow a ball from Coach Howe and get a game going ourselves."

"Right. But two things still stand out the most to me. My agony and Jimmie's ecstasy. That time in Babe Ruth, playing right field, when I chased a deep hit that rolled to the track, picked it up, whirled, hit the football field light pole with my throw, caught the ball when it bounced right back to me, and finally got it to the cut-off man as the batter raced around the bases for an inside-the-park home run, our coach, Jimmie's dad, laughing harder than anybody. And, more to the point for me right now, remember after we graduated we were playing in a summer fastpitch league? They had set up a diamond on the football field with the backstop facing the grandstand? And Jimmie hit a pitcher's drop-ball *over* the grandstand? That's easily 350 feet, and it was still rising when it cleared the roof. And with a wooden bat, not these composite springboards with their high coefficients of restitution that we have today! The rest of us on both teams were happy just to hit one to the grandstand once in a while, and Jimmie rockets it out like Roy Hobbs. Most awesome swing I've ever seen. I want to develop one like that."

"Okay, Hobbs, you ready for turn-and-goes?" Zee said.

"Sure."

They practiced retreating for pop flies without back-pedaling. About 20 feet apart, one would lob a ball over the head of, and slightly to the right or left of, the other. The receiver would pivot sharply and run hard, trying to keep his eyes on the ball, looking it into his glove on the move. These were hard for the old man, especially going to his right when his extended glove hand would sometimes obscure the ball. His declining powers of proprioception made it difficult when moving to interpret the limited stimuli regarding position and equilibrium arising within his body. The dulled nerve endings in his neuropathic feet offered little helpful information. The mac d flattened depth. Often his brain searched desperately to get a Bradleyan sense of where he was while his body in its own wisdom protectively slowed dramatically, giving the brain time to work. Until he reached his 70s, he had been a strong outfielder, able to get a jump on the ball, track it, run unerringly to the spot where it would come down, and snag it if it touched his glove at all. Once, at St. George, in his first tournament there at the age of 60, he had pivoted sharply and sprinted at a 45-degree angle for a ball lined into the gap, collided with the left fielder, who was also running full out, flew backward three feet, his teammate's shoulder bloodying his nose and bending the wire frame of his glasses, and held on to the ball as his head hit the ground. Now he was fearful and unsteady going back, unable to overrule his subconscious, which insisted he take his eyes off the ball and sneak a peek to avoid a collision or a fall even though he had a quarter-acre of open ground between himself and the fence. The old man often worked on his balance at home. Three times a day he would stand next to the couch and, while focusing on the ferry dock, extend his right leg backward and balance on his left for 60 seconds, belaying himself with a hand to the couch if he was unable to control his teetering, then repeat with the right leg. After that warm up he would place one foot on the opposite knee, hands together over his head in praying position. If he went 30 seconds without rebooting, he was lucky. When putting on socks, underpants, pants, or slippers, he would not let himself sit or lean against a wall or a piece of furniture but would stand next to the bed and balance on one leg, falling bedward if necessary. A high school classmate, residing, coincidentally enough, in St. George, he had learned recently on a Facebook feed, had fallen in his bathroom, cracked his head against the counter, and died instantly. A year earlier a softball teammate had fallen while crossing an icy street to get to his mailbox, broken his hip, and never regained mobility. The old man wanted to prevent incidents like those almost as much as he wanted to glide with equilibrium on the ball field.

He and Zee each took a dozen turn-and-goes, getting to and catching more than they didn't get to or dropped, however shaky the process.

Next came ground balls. This was a new drill for the old man. He had been an outfielder for 25 years; this year, his manager had told him, because of his problems with depth perception and balance, he would move to the infield. Having become a defensive embarrassment to himself and to the team, he was relieved to get this news, even though it meant he would incur fresh embarrassments as he struggled to learn the nuances of playing the infield. He and Zee, an infielder since Little League, took turns hitting grounders from home plate to shortstop, going through the bucket of balls, the fielder rolling each ball off to the side. The old man told himself to get the butt down, get the glove down, get the eyes down, stay on the ball all the way. If he could just focus, keep extraneous thoughts at bay. "Down," "down," became his mantra. "Down" he would say as the bat struck the ball, "down" as he looked it into the glove. He managed to stop all of the grounders but juggled a few, even though Zee was hitting them only at medium speed.

"Now, Z-man, the moment I've been waiting for all winter." Both were sweating, turtlenecks sticking to their skins. They drank from water bottles they'd tucked into their bags. "Let's hit."

The old man loved to hit. There was nothing so satisfying to him as a drive that jumped off his bat and streamed into an outfield gap, or one that made an infielder flinch, or a big fly with back spin that carried beyond an outfielder's reach. But he produced very few of any of them. He hit his share of short line drives that fell in front of outfielders, of seeing-eye ground balls, of bloop singles. He averaged .600—a few years ago it had been .750—but there was little explosiveness in his swing. He felt that, although his fielding had declined, he could still improve his hitting. He thought of Jimmie, puffing out his cheeks with the effort, driving his hips, snapping his wrists, and smashing the ball over the grandstand. The Natural. The old man was several fast-twitch fibers short of being Jimmie, but he dreamed of developing a swing like his, a whale of a swing, nasty, brutish and long. Browsing YouTube on his iPad, he had found a dozen videos teaching techniques for hitting softballs with power and watched them over and over through the winter, taking notes, rehearsing slow swings in his living room, inspired by the filmed progress of ordinary hitters becoming power hitters using proper swing mechanics. He had sequenced and memorized the key parts of the swing: grip the bat with the left little finger and ring finger below the bat's knob and wrap the right over the left to increase leverage; get 90 per cent of his weight back on his right leg; tilt the bat toward the pitcher and pull it back until there was tension in the left arm and lat; lift the left leg as if climbing a stair, wind the hips in a slight up-thrust, and aggressively transfer his weight in a big step forward to generate rotational power; lag the bat, then let the left arm lead as the weight transferred; hit the bottom half of the ball, unleashing and snapping the wrists; and follow through completely, releasing the top hand and letting the bat come around to touch his back. Nervously, he got ready. They started with screen ball, Zee on one knee to his side and slightly ahead of him tossing the ball up and the old man driving it into the backstop mesh 15 feet away. On the first swing he lost control of the bat and sailed it into the mesh along with the ball. The grip was so tenuous. He had no control. Were guys really able to hit like that?

"Power shot," Zee said. "You just killed the pitcher. With the bat, that is, not the ball."

"Damn," said the old man. "This is not how I envisioned it."

When the bat flew out of his hands a second time, he decided to slow the swing down. That was better. He could maintain bat control by halving his speed. He was getting the leg drive and the rotation, but falling away somewhat, moving his head and taking his eye off the ball. Balance again. Zee went through the bucket of balls. The old man's timing was off, but he began to put the pieces of the swing together. Practice makes myelin, and myelin makes perfect.

After Zee had taken his turn, swinging the way he had all his life, out on his front foot, little hip rotation, right hand leading left hand but making good contact that produced line drives and hard ground balls—he had such great hand-eye coordination— they went to live BP. Fifty feet away, Zee pitched and ducked behind the screen so as not to get coovered, as the old man took his cuts. Swing and a miss on the first one. The grip, the grip. First things first. As the balls came dropping down from 12 feet at their apex, he decided to forget power and rotational mechanics and focus simply on contacting the ball while maintaining the grip. Not a single ball left the infield but he became a little more comfortable with the grip. When Zee took his turn, he top-hand-lashed ball after ball, not deep but hard. Mid-season form.

"A second bucket?" said the old man.

"I think that's enough for today. You're undertaking a total makeover. Let things settle. We'll be back on Wednesday."

"Okay, you're right. I'm just going to hit for the cycle before we go."

Zee smiled, hoisted the screen over his head, and carried it to his pickup.

Starting at home plate, the old man sprinted to first base, mud splattering the back of his sweat pants, and walked back. Then he hit a double, slowing a bit because of the slick field as he pivoted on his left foot to make the turn at first base, then a triple, trying not to lose pace between second and third, then a home run that left him gasping for breath, unable to speak, his pounding heart having reached its pacemakered limits. But he was confident that he would be fiddle-fit for the opening game of the season.

"Join me next time, Z-man?" he said when finally he could.

"I think you know the answer to that. I'll do what I've done for the past 20 years—play myself into shape."

"See you Wednesday at 2:00," the old man said, "and don't be early."

"Impossible not to be," Zee said. "I have no control over it."

Unaccountably, as he settled into his Santa Fe and fastened his seat belt for the short trip to the Harbor Square Athletic Club, notions that had been flitting through his mind for several days (he had recently re-read Ernest Becker's *The Denial of Death*) coalesced and settled down. He extracted his phone from his sweat pants pocket and thread-tweeted:

#madamsNxNW: Have found the need to develop two new psychological-rhetorical quotients: the Horseshit Quotient, a measure, on a scale of 0 to 100, of the degree to which one deceives oneself; and the Bullshit Quotient, a measure of one's attempt to deceive others. If you tell yourself that fearing death is pointless because death is inevitable (that whistling past the graveyard thing), you register a 90 on the HSQ scale. If you try to persuade others that fearing death is pointless because it's inevitable (that "the coward dies a thousand deaths" thing), you register a 90 on the BSQ scale.

———— ((●)) ————

All of the parking spaces adjacent to the Club and its outdoor tennis courts and its satellite tennis dome and the neighboring commercial facilities and the boardwalk skirting the marsh *cum* bird sanctuary being filled, he circled round to the lot at the Best Western Harbor Square Inn, which fronted on Highway 104. The popular two-story Club, one of the early gentrifiers of the town, built in 1985 and remodeled and expanded several times since, was upscale, spacious, clean, bright, with multiple large windows offering views of the marsh to the south and the Salish Sea to the west. The ground floor featured a juice bar with a granite countertop, a space to lounge on couches and easy chairs, glass-fronted courts and rooms for racquetball , squash, aerobics, yoga, and Zumba, two curtained tennis courts girdled by a rubber running track, a full-length basketball court with glass backboards, a swimming pool, and a women's locker room with sauna, steam room, and hot tub. Upstairs were the men's locker room with its sauna, steam room, and hot tub and two long rooms running east-west, one with cardio and weight machines, the other with benches and racks of free weights and bar bells and multi-purpose stanchions for pull ups, dips, and core work, and an array of ropes, harnesses, stretch bands, medicine balls, balance balls, and kettle balls. He scanned his keyring ID tag at the reception desk and grabbed the towel offered by lanky Pat Dahl, who had begun his career as a Social Studies teacher and boys' basketball coach at Maplewood in the mid-'80s. The morning shifts at the desk and in the locker rooms, picking up towels and replenishing dispensers of soap, shampoo, body lotion, and mouthwash, were often filled by retirees in exchange for Club privileges. "Have a good one, Wayne," Pat said. "You know, I'm thinking of coming out for senior softball this year." "Great," he said, striving to be heard over the whine of a blender mixing a post-workout high-protein smoothie at the juice bar for a tall, trim blonde in her thirties holding a gym bag and wearing a scarlet sweater, white jeans, and scarlet sneakers, her freshly blow-dried hair long and voluminous. "Join my team, the Classics. We could use an infusion of youth." The blonde took her smoothie from Steve the bartender and turned toward the door. "Oh, hi, Wayne." "Hi, Brittany." She was someone he talked with briefly now and then as she bounced from machine to machine (she was a 20-minute dynamo on the elliptical) for an hour, getting her morning cardio work in. She and her husband, Justin, had moved to Edmonds from the Ballard area of Seattle three years ago and opened Harbor Square Micro-Brews. "You just getting started?" "Yeah, I was out practicing softball earlier." "Good for you. Time for me to get over to the shop. As Justin always says, those hopped-up ales aren't going to just craft themselves."

He crossed the slate floor, the tiles a mosaic of tan shades, and climbed the stairs, availing himself of a thick oak hand rail. The locker room floor was a gray wood laminate, the lockers oak, the benches granite. Conscious of the grainy skin on his upper chest, the crepey skin on his upper arms, and the saggy skin on his drooping elephant butt, ever in the grip of body dysmorphic disorder, he chose a reclusive corner locker and changed into black knee-length Nike polyester shorts and a gray Under Armour moisture-wicking tee shirt, put his ball cap back on, tucked his phone into a pocket, and extracted a wireless headset from his gym bag. Entering the machine weight room he spotted fellow Maple Street All-Star Monk, a hard-hitting all-Northwest League linebacker in high school and now a semi-retired hometown lawyer who had given up cigars, lost 40 pounds, and become a Club regular after his heart attack and three-way bypass 10 years ago, and went over to dap.

"Happy birthday, Wayne. You just caught up with me."

"Yeah, thanks, Monk. No work today?"

"Oh, yeah," said Monk, who had a broad bald swath on the top of his head and long gray hair swept back on the sides, an obverse Mohawk, like Larry of the Stooges, "I'm due in court at 1:00. Thought I'd come down here and clear my mind a bit. I have a client who's suing the city. He resents the hell out of the officious Tree Board this town has established because it denied him a permit to cut down a maple tree in his front yard at 7th and Walnut. He's tired of raking leaves every fall, but the Board says that as long as the tree is healthy, it must remain to fulfill its duty to sequester carbon dioxide and keep the Salish Sea from rising up to 5th Avenue. You'd think an enclave of Druids lived here!"

"Good luck with that quixotic quest, Monk! Anyway, I just got done with a little softball practice with the Z-man. He's going to announce his Council candidacy on Thursday. I see him as the Joe Biden of the Bowl, warm, caring, personable, a man of the people concerned about doing the greatest good for the greatest number, only not handsy like Joe."

"Ha. You're right—Zee has always been above reproach. I could live with him on the Council—but I'd rather see me there. I'm going to get the word out next week. If one octo can do it, why not two? Let's strike a blow against ageism. And keep the Council from drowning us in progressive pieties!"

"Hah. Monk, I love it. If Zee is Bidenesque, you're Trumpian, at least in your urge to disrupt, to resist. I already told Zee I'll work for him, but I'm delighted that both of you are going to run."

"Yeah, I think it's going to be fun. Who has the better feel for the zeitgeist of Edmonds—me or Zee? By the way, did you get your evite to the class reunion this morning?"

"Absolutely. And I'll be there. Zee and I have a little presentation to make."

"Not political, I hope. If so, I want equal time!"

"No, not political. Sentimental."

[Zeitgeist, my ass! If Monk is going to run, then I am too. The battle is on for Position 8! This town does not need Mr. Monken's right-wing views. It needs me: AOC. Charlotte]

There were more than 30 other men and women exercising, all of them white. Every few days he would see an Asian or two, but rarely an African American. The seniors were talking and toning, staying within their comfort zones, using light weights and taking long, chatty rest periods, some carrying little towels and diligently using Club-provided spray bottles to sanitize after themselves, a few on the treadmills, watching ESPN on the flat-screen TVs suspended from the ceiling, a few reading books while riding stationary bikes, most of them in shorts and tee shirts, many with a BMI below 25, although one man with a protruding paunch and a woman with a broad backside wore loose-fitting sweat pants and baggy sweat shirts. The young and the middle-aged were variously more aggressive in pounding the treadmills, in attacking the stair-steppers, ellipticals, and rowers, and in pushing and pulling on the weight machines, sweat soaking the brows and hair of some and being wicked away from their torsos by their fuschia or orange or chartreuse tees or tank tops. He occasionally encountered a parent of a former student or player, who generally acknowledged him with a wave and a "Hi," although a few, whose kids he had given a low grade or whose daughters he had not given much playing time, looked the other way. Les Pearson, a retired orthodontist who lived in Woodway Park, his daughter one of many talented writers who had graced the old man's classes and who had for many years been the lead singer for a Seattle grunge band, was there today, slowly riding a bike and musing. After retiring, Les had taken to writing poetry, self-publishing a couple of volumes which were in stock at the Edmonds Bookshop, and often found his brain generating useful images and phrases as he turned the pedals, his subject the quotidian, his style a fusion of the laconic imagism of William Carlos Williams and the manic rhythms of Theodore Roethke, whose attractive wife Beatrice had taught the old man's beginning French class at EHS in 1955. "Hey, Les," he said, "how's the poetry coming?"

"Pretty good, Wayne. I've almost got enough for another book. Been looking back and enjoying some of your old blog entries, too. Those two wine poems, an extended metaphor and a calligram, were a little too form-dependent for me, more artifice than art, but I liked your rather free-wheeling pastiche of Whitman." "Yeah, thanks, Les. I got the idea for the Whitman thing one day when I was cutting across the playfield of the City Park on 3rd, kicking at the grassy leavings of the mowing crew and remembering how I used to play baseball and hunt for Easter eggs there. I'll keep my eyes open for your new book."

Disquieted, as if he had just hit a long but lazy and easily catchable fly and needed to review his swing mechanics, he pulled his phone from his pocket, walked over to an unoccupied chest press machine, sat down, logged into the Club's Wi-Fi, tapped his website icon, and reread.

Wine Tasting

Call it jammy,
plummy, minty,
buttery, toasty,
flinty.

Note peppers,
currants, cedar,
honey, apples,
figs.

Say it's huge
or supple or
its backbone
shows.

Find it glossy,
elegant, profound—

bespeak its utter charm—

but pronounce it
surpassing
only if metaphor
gives way to moan.

The Shape of Sensibility

A slim crystal belly embraces blanc
gold ichor atop a stork stem. Swirl
ed and sniffed, the wine opens herb
aceously. Tongue-rolled sips tingle
surprised oral nooks. Each gent
ly in-drawn breath bursts into
bright wine flames. Exhalation
brings exaltation. Even as it's
swallowed the wine evolves
enzymatically. Such econ
omy: glass emptying,
sipper filling with
sanguinity. As
the moments
pass,
sen
tim
ent
set
tles
to
the bottom of the wine glass.

A Whitman Sampler: Channeling the Good Gray Poet While Coping With Age in the 21st Century

A senior said, What is this grass that I am still on the right side of?
It must be a green sward drawing me forth
An admonishment not to let it grow under my feet
To cherish my roots but not go to seed
To shun the lay-up shot and swing for the pin
A verdant reminder of renewability through medical ingenuity
(Age's ravages, both core and cosmetic, repaired or riposted
Demeter and Persephone perpetuated by Prometheus and Hephaestus)
A hint that there's nothing greener on the other side
A lush carpet for the feet to seize upon daily
Because to die is different from what many suppose, and suckier.

O seniors, fellow seniors,
Finding no sweeter fat than sticks to my own porous bones
I sing the body eclectic
I calibrate myself and sing of myself
And what I've assumed you can assume
For every procedure pertaining to me as good pertains to you—
The freeze-drying of squamous cell growths from head to toe
The Mohs surgeries
The cataract surgery
The injections of Lucentis for wet macular degeneration
The bone marrow biopsies
The infusions of Zometa for smoldering multiple myeloma
The exfoliations
The periodontic gum grafts
The thyroid oblation
The rotator cuff therapy
The ultrasounds

The DEXA scans
The CT scans
The PET scans
The MRIs
The buckets of blood tests
The exponentiation of X rays
The angiogram
The heart pacemaker
The antibiotics for pneumonia
The antibiotics for recurring UTIs
The Sotalol and Eliquis for a-fib
The Methotrexate for rheumatoid arthritis
The Levothyroxine for hypothyroidism
The Myrbetrq for bladder leakage
The cortico steroids for polymyalgia rheumatica
The colonoscopies and endoscopies and cystoscopies
The colon polyps excisions
The testicular cyst excision
The five daily self-catheterizations to countermand the importunity of a puffy prostate
The femoral lipoma ectomy
The sciatic nerve electrical massage

I sing of the craft of
The periodontist
The orthopedist
The dermatologist
The ophthamologist
The endocrinologist
The cardiologist
The rheumatologist
The hematologist
The gastroenterologist
The nephrologist

The urologist —
All those specialists whose Medicaring has preserved my electrical-chemical self
And who stand by to offer me, if needed,
Miracle Ears
eSight glasses
dental implants
carotid scrapings
organ transplants
arterial bypasses or stents
defibrillators
carpal tunnel surgery
vascular stripping
diuretics
dialysis
bone marrow treatment
radiations
metal joints
prosthetic limbs
While I await science's nano-mapping of the human brain and the concomitant promise of wonders to come:
Tissue regeneration
plastic blood
kidney cleansers
high IQ cancer cell killers
gripping hands
artificial hearts
sight-restoring eyes
dementia-defeating pacemakers for the brain
a copious cornuhopia of embedded nano devices and microchips
a Kurzweilian robotic rebooting of a bionic me
At last readying me—Quantified Self and (O!) Qualified Soul—
for an unending ever green passage to India.
Do I contradict myself? Very well, then, I contradict myself

(I am large, I contain multi 'tudes).

[Diane would have appreciated the wine poems. Although she did love to pair adjectives with wines, she was quite holistic in approach to everything. I'm sure the moaning was more important to her than the describing. But she would have disdained Kurzweil and the whole notion of—what can I call it?—*deus ex homo*? This even though she had a pacemaker herself! Linda]

He heard grunting and shouting from the free-weight room— "Come on, you got this!" "One more!" "Give it to me!"—and then a triumphant scream as dropped weights thudded and clanked on the rubber floor. Compelled, self-cajoled, he logged out and entered the room, where he found four men in their tank-top 20s, splendid specimens of their kind, slapping hands, dapping, spotting for each other, urging each other to press on when exhausted muscles sobbed for oxygen in the final reps of their dead lifts, bench presses, and squats. He was awed by their raised traps, rounded rhomboids, epauletted delts, layered tris, busty pecs, ballooning bis, flaring lats, thunderous thighs, globular glutes, and bulbous calves. After all these years, he was still inspired by, never dismissive or cynical of, the narcissistic glamour of others. He and Diane, who was eager to play competitive tennis and to push herself in aerobics classes, had been among the first to join the Club when they moved into their new condo in 1985. Over the years, the old man, who often used to skim *Muscle and Fitness* in the school library, had tried many workout regimens—heavier weights/fewer reps, lighter weights/more reps, more sets/fewer sets, more time between sets/less time between sets, increasing the weight and decreasing the reps set by set/decreasing the weight and increasing the reps set by set, working certain areas one day (bis, lats, back), other areas the next (tris, pecs, shoulders), more days off between workouts, fewer days off between workouts. Whatever he did, the goal was always the same: get bigger, get stronger, get mass, get definition. Keep adding weight or reps or both, don't stagnate. If you can bench 125 pounds today, do 130 next time. If you can do

12 pull ups today, do 13 next time. Keep increasing your max. Don't settle. And always, the result was the same: he got bigger, got stronger, added mass, carved definition, all more than acceptable given his age and ectomorphic frame, until finally he sprained a ligament in a shoulder or an elbow and had to take six weeks off to let the inflammation subside, then revert to benching 10 pounds and doing two pull ups, gradually, over a period of months, getting back to the point where he could, and would, hurt himself again. But for now, he was healthy. Following his latest protocol, every third day working all muscle groups in three sets of descending reps—10,9,8— at the highest weight he could manage that sequence, incrementally increasing the weight only when his tissues begged for more, resting 60 seconds between sets, time spent stretching various leg muscles, multitasking, he'd lifted all winter without injury.

[Wayne, it's healthful to stay fit, and I applaud your effort in that regard. However, your uncritical acceptance of your body dysmorphic disorder is actually a kind of boasting and may also be heard as a dog whistle for fat-shaming. Charlotte]

He tapped his iTunes icon, synced his headset, twisted in the ear buds, and said, "Siri, play 'Stayin' Alive' by the Bee Gees." His pumping-iron playlist was stuffed with songs that had the power to move him—something amphetaminic, surging, soaring, driving, like Benny Goodman's "Let's Dance" or Glen Miller's "In the Mood," something serotonic, bluesy, haunting, like Errol Garner's "Moonglow"—but always he jump-started himself with the feverish pulsation and falsetto orgasmic ululations of the Bee Gees. Oh, those knifing strobe lights and wheeling, shimmering disco balls! Those scintillating gauzy green flashes, light motifs, of a simulated aurora borealis in a boogie wonderland. Those nights at Parker's on Aurora and Pantley's on the Edmonds waterfront and the Landmark Inn in Lynnwood, they the lone married couple, he in his polyester, wing-collared shirt and polyester bell-bottom pants, Diane in her black jump suit with its flared sleeves and flared legs set off by a gold sash belt and open-toed gold heels, ordering the house white, usually Almaden chardonnay ("Thin but clean," Diane judged), waiting for a niche to open in the crush of reveling singles on the dance floor who were presenting, stomping and thrusting and writhing, shaking bootys and breasts in quest of a passion partner for the night, finally seizing an opportunity to demonstrate their repertoire of moves in the Hustle, the 20-somethings grudgingly making room during "Boogie Oogie" or "Hot Stuff" or "MacArthur Park" for their dips and drops and lifts and leans and then nodding or smiling in appreciation as the two returned to their table. Diane had spotted, one spring day in 1978 a couple of months after they had seen *Saturday Night Fever* at the Lynn-Twin Theater in Lynnwood, an ad in the *Edmonds Enterprise*, which had succeeded the *Tribune-Review*, for disco dance lessons at Kennelly Keys, a music store occupying the space on 5th between Dayton and Main that had housed the original Crow Hardware before Crow moved to a new building near the marsh, east of Railroad Avenue. "The idea tickles me," she said. "Let's do it!" The idea excited him as well. To be Tony Manero! To rule the floor! Their instructor, Jeffrey, a slender 25-year-old wearing a dark blue blazer, light blue tee shirt, and bell-bottom blue and white striped jeans, who had, he told them later, sailed through all the advanced classes at the upstairs Fred Astaire studio on 2nd Avenue in downtown Seattle and won competitions in Las Vegas with his partner Lesley, greeted them at the door when they arrived for their first appointment, looked them up and down during handshakes, and led them weavingly through displays of guitars and organs and saxophones and stereos and amps and speakers to stairs that dropped to a roomy but chilly basement with florescent lights and a linoleum floor and a portable record player. "You both look like you're in great shape, so I'm going to teach you the Latin Hustle. Let's start with the basic footwork. It goes tap-step, coaster-step, walk, walk. Tap-step, coaster-step, walk, walk. You both open your bodies slightly on the tap and then close on the step. Guy goes backward on the coaster-step, forward on the walk. Girl goes forward on the coaster-step, backward on the walk. Like this." He demonstrated both parts. "Now you try it. Wayne starts with the left foot, Diane with the right. Tap-step, coaster-step, walk, walk. Don't bounce. Don't try to 'dance.' Dancing is just walking. Stay on balance, heads up and still. Dancing is walking. Tap-step, coaster-step, walk, walk. Wayne, don't hop on the coaster-step, just walk. Diane, that's good. Now walk together. Wayne takes Diane's hand in his left about waist high and puts his right hand just above Diane's left hip, Diane puts her left hand just back of Wayne's shoulder. Practice a few times while I cue some music." When "Disco Inferno" began to throb, a corresponding surge shot through the old man. His boundaries dissolving, his autonomy waning, he just felt like dancing, he was leading Diane through the steps, they were Tony and Stephanie. "Slow down, Wayne," Jeffrey said. "Don't hunch your shoulders. Relax. When you walk-walk, don't mince, land on your heels. Don't try to do too much. Just walk on the beat. Diane, you're fine." After taking a minute to refocus, they repeated the exercise. "Better," Jeffrey said. "Be sure to practice the footwork at home a couple of minutes each day until it becomes second nature. Now let's get into a basic move, the underarm turn. All moves are done on the walk-walk. You go tap step, coaster-step, and then into the move. Like this." He demonstrated with Diane, raising her right arm when they got to the walk-walk, and she knew instinctively not to spin on one foot but to turn by walking in a tight circle. "Okay, Wayne, you take over." They practiced without music, then with music, then went from basic to move to basic to move, developing, the old man thought, a bit of fluidity. "Relax, Wayne. Don't get up on your toes."

After the half-hour lesson, they jaywalked across a quiet 5th to Brusseau's for coffee and oatmeal-raisin cookies the size of salad plates.

"That was fun," Diane said.

"More for you than for me. But I like the challenge. I want to get better. So we need to practice."

Diane shrugged. "I guess. I thought Jeffrey did a pretty good job of teaching, though. No need for an anticipatory set, because we sought him out. We were already primed and motivated. For a diagnostic test he eyeballed us and decided that we could handle—footle?—the Hustle. He could have done more on objectives and overview, so we would know what we were going to do today and what we were going to progress to in future weeks. But his task analysis was good. He really broke down the basics of the dance in logical order and then insisted on repetition while giving us feedback, correction, and praise before moving on to the next phase."

"Praise for you, maybe. Correction for me."

"But you'll get it."

At home, in their two-bedroom rambler on Grandview, every other evening, as Diane sighed quietly, the old man plugged their portable Hi-Fi into the outlet on the patio and they practiced, first the basic footwork, then the underarm turn, then the two together, for ten minutes. In the lessons of succeeding weeks—which both looked forward to, Diane with delight, the old man with determination— Jeffrey would put them through a quick review and then add two new moves. Double underarm turns, multiple rapid spins, reverse turns, reverse spins, underarm turns leading to grip reversals and double arm turns by both, a brief dos-a-dos before facing each other again, underarm turns leading to drops, the old man adjusting his grip as a cue, Diane pivoting, he pushing his arms downward, she lying back almost supine, left knee bent, right leg extended parallel to the floor, underarm turns leading to wrap-ins in which they would walk together in a tight circle, wrap-ins leading to wrap-outs, Diane reverse-pivoting and flaring her right arm, wrap-outs leading to sit-drops, Diane, having been cued by the old man's cross-body lead, sitting abruptly on her left foot, her right leg parallel to the floor, her arms held wide so he could catch her as she sat and flip her back up, wrap-outs leading to leans, Diane spinning back to his side and cocking her right foot on her left knee as they both leaned to their left and held for two counts, wrap-outs leading to dips, Diane executing a spin-and-a-half back to his side, he taking her right hand in his left and stretching her backward across his body as far to his left as he could reach, her torso parallel to the floor, her left arm extending as if having just tossed a frisbee, wrap-outs leading to lifts, Diane leaping from a spin-in to straddle his waist as they reached out their arms and the old man walked in a circle before lifting her down, or Diane quick-spinning in to gain speed, placing her right hand on his right shoulder and vaulting onto his back, he shrugging her up so she was parallel to the floor, gripping her legs with his left hand and her torso with his right and walking clockwise twice before setting her down. When Jeffrey suggested adding solo Travolta-like pointing sequences and independent strutting and hip-thrusting and shadow-boxing and rope-a-doping and fist-winding, like a basketball official making a travelling call, they demurred. They were uncomfortable with posing and preening, with separating dancers and dance. They would call attention not to themselves but to their togetherness in motion. And each week, as the moves multiplied, their home practice sessions grew longer, ultimately becoming an hour every other day. Even Diane, who preferred doing what came naturally, conceded that the volume of material necessitated repetition—first to master the grammar of the moves, morphemes, discrete movements like a tap, a step, a lifting of the arm, blending into larger phrase structures like the basic footwork pattern or an underarm turn, then to integrate them into a strategic rhetoric of motifs, a linking of loose, balanced, and periodic figures by means of theme and variation or point and counterpoint or tonal modulation, enabling them, they hoped, persuasively to please the audience with their idiosyncratically stylized blend of *élan*, emotion, and logic . The rhetoric, in this patriarchal arena of dance, was the old man's responsibility. He was to lead, Diane was to follow. Both liked it that way. Diane had the better grasp of grammar, the better ear, the intuitive feel for phrasal idioms. The old man spoke sometimes with an accent or mangled an inflection. But he found that he actually excelled in improvising choreography, turning moves into meaning, one flowing from another or augmenting another or contrasting with another or parodying another or one-upping another. A life-long pre-planner, he was surprised to find himself delighting in the spontaneous creativity required of him as leader. After the obligatory introductory basic step, he had to choose. The music wouldn't wait, there could be no dithering. He had to establish an essence for their existence on the dance floor. It was adopt and adapt or die. At first, practicing at home or in the basement of Kennelly Keys under Jeffrey's supervision, he tended to stutter, to repeat basic several times while ransacking his mental and muscle memories for material. Or, panicked, he might produce an odd permutation like dog man bites, or—what was he thinking?—abruptly break off into a distracting anacoluthon. But gradually, through repeated trials and errors, he became, in his improvisatory ordering of their bodily movement in space, recursively winging the changes, a creator like his jazz pianist father. He did not know what move he would next make, what angle he would take, as he did not know what thought he would next think, but he knew that something inspired by the beat would present itself and that he could accept or reject its aptness to that context, with a different something instantly replacing a rejected something in a seamless dance of his heart's composing, a different intuitive algorithm each time out on the floor, he and Diane, who instantaneously read his sines, two nearly one in their ad-libbed charade.

He would start with the bis. Imaginary paint cans vibrating at his sides, he strutted to the stanchion in the middle of the room for underhanded pull ups, raising his chin well above the bar he was gripping, ankles crossed to prevent his legs from assisting. Between sets he leaned against the stanchion, planted his heels, and stretched his calves while swinging his buttocks left and right—"UH, UH, UH, UH, stayin' aLIVE!"—and gazing at the female players in pleated tennis skirts and matching visors on the outdoor courts, the reed-choked marsh in the background. He returned to the machine room and frolicked with Gerry Mulligan on a rollicking "Sweet

Georgia Brown" while curling 60 pounds at one machine and pulling down 100 pounds at another, stretching quads and hamstrings in between. He continued to work for an hour, severely stressing all of his major upper body muscles while viscerally responding, stomach jigging, skin prickling, heart accelerating, oxygenated blood flooding tired tissues, to "Imagine there's no heaven," "Nobody gets too much heaven no more," "Goin' to the cabin in the sky," "Now I've heard there was a secret chord that David played and it pleased the Lord," "We are family," "I like New York in June, how about you?""J-j-j-jive talk," "The first time ever I saw your face," "You take your hand in mine," "Chances are," "Warden threw a party" (bopping a few steps between sets), and finished with a bit of core work—rotations on the torso machine, simulating the thrust of the hips in his softball swing, abdominal crunches on a different machine, knee and hip raises on the stanchion, and a set of planks on a soft mat. As he rose to his feet, he put a hand on a wall for balance and looked down through its windowed upper half at the gleaming basketball floor on the ground level. Why not go down and take a few shots? Why not enter the basketball shooting contests at the Huntsman Games, since he was going to be there anyway? With the help of the handrail, he hurried down the back stairs as "And I think it's gonna be a long, long time" kicked in and picked up a loose Wilson Jet basketball, new, its composite skin pebbly and agreeably tacky. For years he had played in pickup games at the Club, first with all-comers, then, in his sixties, only with the over-40 crowd. When, on his 70th birthday, he made a step-through push shot from the free-throw line and then a game-winning pullup jumper for a 3-pointer, high fives and wide grins all around, even from the opponents, he decided that would be the climactic end. He could still shoot, but during those last few years 50- and even 60-year-olds had been knocking him around, zipping by him, or jumping over him as he tried to play defense or rebound. At 60 he had won a gold medal in basketball at St. George with a team from Seattle, but at 80 he didn't trust his balance enough to try again, even against his coevals.

However, at 70 he had also won a gold at St. George in the Hot Shot competition and a silver in the Free Throw/3 Pt. competition. Why couldn't he do it again, be a Rocket Man, against the 80-year-olds? He removed his ear buds, exited iTunes, tucked his phone and headset into his hat, placed the hat next to a side wall, and began to shoot following his old routine, the one he taught his players: first, swishers from two feet, resting the ball on the finger pads of his right hand, launching it with his wrist, imparting backspin off the index and middle fingers, and dropping it into the middle of the cylinder, touching no iron, with an exaggerated Michael Jordan follow through, then from five, eight, and 12 feet, working back to the free throw line where, feet shoulder width apart, knees bent, elbows in, ball in the shooting pocket at chest level, wrist cocked, eyes on the rim, he sought to achieve a smooth continuous motion, as if reaching toward an upper shelf, and place the ball just over the front of the rim, eyes never deviating from the target. At first he was awkward. Not enough leg, too much arm, a lazy wrist, a wandering eye, but soon his muscles began to remember his old high school form, and he made 22 in a set of 25, confident that he could improve on that. The 3-pointers were a different matter. He gradually worked his airballing way back to the 19' 9" arc, pushing hard with his legs and his shoulder, casting off rather than shooting with touch, struggling just to get the range. In a set of 10 heaves, he made two, one an unintended bank. This would be a project. For the Hot Shot contest, a timed one-minute period in which the shooter, rebounding for himself, shot from four different 17-foot spots marked on the floor, each worth three points, and one beyond the arc at the top of the key worth five, he would need to shoot jump shots quickly. That would be a formidable challenge. He hadn't jumped much in the past 10 years. It would take weeks to gain the leg strength and the coordination required. He moved to within five feet of the basket and shot, gathering and going up (about two inches off the floor) while trying to sync his arm motion with his legs. He stopped after just 10, knowing that his calves would for days be too sore to jump if he did any more. But his regimen had begun. From now until October, he would shoot four times weekly. As he let the ball roll away and went to retrieve his phone and headset, balding Alan Barnett, a pulmonologist at Stevens Hospital who in 1999 had tried but failed to prevent the old man's father from dying of pneumonia, and who wore a vintage green and gold Sonics jersey, and bulky Jon Ramsay, a financial planner with an office on 5th, walked onto the floor to warm up for the noon pickup games. "Hey, Wayne!" Alan said. "It's been years since we saw you out here. You gonna join us today?" "I wish," the old man said. "Those days are gone. I've just been shooting around, getting a little exercise." "Well, we miss you, man. You were deadly with those patented 15-foot jumpers." "Yeah, thanks. You guys have fun. I'm heading for the shower." Time to get back home, where he would eat a can of Starkist tuna mixed with a tablespoon of light mayo and a diced dill pickle (260 calories, 48 grams of protein) and a Granny Smith apple (100 calories) while checking email, Twitter, Facebook, and Instagram on his iPad, stuff in his ear plugs, draw his sleeping mask over his eyes, and nap on top of his bed for an hour, grind four scoops of beans from a bag of citrusy Peruvian single-origin purchased at Starbucks and slow-drip a 16-ounce pour-over, settle himself in front of his desktop for two hours to compose for his blog, pour six ounces of frisky Bogle red blend into a burgundy glass and read Carlo Rovelli's *The Order of Time* for an hour or so, eat half of a microwaved PF Chang frozen sweet-and-sour chicken dinner (340 calories, 15 grams of protein), munch a double-chocolate Costco Kirkland power bar (200 calories, 20 grams of protein), then spend the evening in front of his 50-inch Samsung plasma, toggling between the Mariners' opener, a couple of NBA games, reruns of *Seinfeld* and *Modern Family*, and a book of cryptic puzzles.

He went upstairs to the locker room, which was now crowded and noisy with the bantering of middle-aged professionals and businessmen changing for basketball, and nodded and dapped and high-fived his way back to the corner, where he dawdled in his undressing, waiting for the room to clear to avoid exposing his wrinkled rear to the judgment of the male gaze. He checked the fitness app on his watch—10,282 steps, 5.2 miles, 520 calories burned—then turned to Twitter on his phone. Responses already! "@#Edmonds Landing attendant (former student)—These also rate a 90 on your HSQ/BSQ scale: 'Beauty is only skin deep' and 'Age ain't nothin' but a number.'" "@#nophonymaloney—Your belief that you can rewire your brain at 80 also rates a 90 on the HSQ. " "@#howardcosell/tellitlikeitis—Suggest you also add a Chicken Shit Quotient, a measure of one's fear of calling out horseshit and bullshit, as demonstrated in the use of rhetoric (politically correct terms, euphemisms, bromides) to sugarcoat painful truths. If you call someone 'differently abled' instead of 'crippled,' or 'mentally challenged' instead of 'stupid,' you register a 90 on the Chicken Shit quotient."

He winced. Then shrugged.

After a quick shower he entered the hot tub room, flipped the switch for the jets, and immersed himself to the neck for a long soak. It had been an active morning, walking and jogging, hitting and fielding and running, lifting and shooting, a productive morning, laying a foundation, he was pleased, he was so pleasantly tired, the jets massaging his legs and back as he slowly turned this way and that, the roiling surface water splashing his face now and then, its chlorine fumes, hinting of eucalyptus, vaporubbing his nasal passages, its steam matting his hair.

[I lost that case—but fought the good fight against City Hall! Monk]

[City Hall did the right thing. Not only do trees sequester carbon, but a recent study shows that proximity to trees is associated with a broad range of physical and mental health benefits for humans. Charlotte]

[For what it's worth, I've actually never read Roethke, Wayne. Les]

2

Crossing Kingston Ferry

a

Wayne, white man, footsore, relaxing and recovering on the observation deck of the *Puyallup* the day after his long workout, laughing and indicting his tender soles, recalling his lurch of fright at the sudden, explosive, departing whistle blast on his first ferry ride, to Port Ludlow on the old Black Ball Line in 1945, his mother calming him with hugs, seeking perspective as the boat pushed off for Kingston, its wake white but not very turbid, gazed eastward at his town, latitude 47.8 N, longitude 122.36 W, across tiderows of drying black-green seaweed and amber bulbs of kelp spread along the beach, and up asphalt city street escalators—Caspar, Daley, Bell, Main, Dayton, Maple, Alder, Walnut, Pine—to the tree-lined rim of the Bowl, the morning haze lifting, his memory delving, his fictive mind augmenting what had long ago been scanned and saved.

In the late '40s and early '50s the population of Edmonds was less than 2,000. The town seemed to the old man capacious. It was a place for children. Pedestrians, cars, and houses alike had elbow-room. Vacant lots dotted the Bowl, even on Front Street. The Johnson twins could play catch in the middle of 4th for 15 minutes at a time before being interrupted by a car. Sylvia and Patty could run from backyards on one side to backyards on the other, playing hide-and-seek, without looking both ways before crossing. Here and there were two-story Cape Cods or Craftsmen with dormers, but many residences were simple composition-roofed, cedar-sided or -shaked bungalows or ramblers set back from the street and fronted by lawns and flower beds. Most were 1,000-1,500 square feet with one bathroom, two bedrooms, a living room, a kitchen, and a dinette off the kitchen. Having grown up during the deprivations of the Depression and come of age during the rationings of World War II, young marrieds like George and Margaret Adams were cautious with their spending and their reproducing. Linoleum and area rugs covered their floors, formica their countertops. Two children were the norm, one not unusual, three probably an accident. Like the milk in quart glass bottles delivered to the door from an Alderwood Manor dairy by Wes Dawson, Edmonds was uniformly white, with little difference in status signified by the color of collar worn on the job. The huge Gothic manorial estates of tree-dense Woodway Park bounding Edmonds to the south, built by such aristocrats as a Seattle land magnate, the president of Boeing, and the president of Pacific Northwest Bell, were a mile and a world apart from the unpretentious, pre-bourgeois mill town losing its original economic engine and becoming a bedroom community where husband/father drove the family's only car to his job in Seattle while wife/mother kept house and minded the children. Edmonds was quiet, orderly, safe, and clean. Most of its people were loyal, hardworking, thrifty, disciplined, resilient, optimistic, complacent, conformist, insular, unsophisticated. They valued family stability and independence. There were neither many do-gooders nor many rogues or irreverents. Warily, they were beginning to buy things like cars and appliances on the installment plan. Cautiously, they were beginning to embrace consumerism. They were skeptical of big government. They appreciated the G.I. Bill, FHA loans, and Social Security, but were otherwise uneasy about federal assistance. They belonged to booster and service community organizations like the Elks, the Moose, the Lions, the Knights of Columbus, the Masons, the Daughters of the American Revolution, the American Legion, the Rotary Club, Kiwanis. They distrusted crusaders and muckrakers. They were patriotic but not jingoistic. They believed that the future was promising for them and even more so for their offspring. They believed that a circumspect one-wage-earner family could own a modest house and car, put interested kids through a state college, build a cabin on a lake or an island, and save enough for retirement and funerals in their sixties. Many had been taught in the three-story grade school (by Frances Anderson, perhaps, a member of Edmonds High School's first graduating class in 1911, and after college a teacher in the still extant building erected in 1924, now a cultural and recreational center named in her honor, a stucco, many-windowed bastion overlooking the Sound on the hill at 7th between Dayton and Main), or in the striking Art Deco high school edifice at 4th and Daley, the old stories that made them American: America had been discovered by Europeans, settled by brave souls who conquered the wilderness and its inhabitants in quest of religious freedom and economic opportunity, wrenching themselves free from monarchies and autarchies, declaring their independence and enshrining the principles of liberty and democracy in a Constitution written by divinely-inspired Founding Fathers and Framers, advancing civilization westward in covered wagons, pursuing America's Manifest Destiny, fighting a Civil War to end slavery, winning World War I to make the world safe for democracy, benevolently granting women the right to vote, winning World War II to eradicate genocide and fascism, these additional truths—admonished formally in classrooms or in sermons and Sunday school lessons at Hughes Memorial Methodist Church, Holy Rosary Parish, the Edmonds Baptist Church, the Church of the Open Bible, and the First Church of Christ, Scientist, or inferred informally, through observation of daily life—surely self-evident: all citizens are equal and have equal opportunity, every vote makes a difference, racial segregation is in principle deplorable but in practice understandable, Japanese internment camps had been necessary evils, America fights only in self-defense or in defense of freedom, marriage between a man and a woman is the bedrock of society, divorce is almost always wrong, there is men's work and women's work, women need the protection and guidance of men, every girl can grow up to make a house a home, every boy can grow up to be President, every boy can be Thomas Edison or Henry Ford or a Horatio Alger hero, failures in life are owing to lack of character and will power, economic success can be achieved through ambition and self-reliance, small business is the key to a strong economy, socialism and communism are based on a misunderstanding of human nature, personal happiness can be achieved by practicing faith, hope, and charity and observing the Golden Rule.

[Our old U.S. History lessons should have been subtitled "How The West Was Spun"! At long last the old fictions are fading. We're moving from the Old Testament to the New, from Columbus Day to Indigenous Peoples' Day. Charlotte]

[Honor the Indigenous People, yes, but it's wrong to cancel Columbus Day. Columbus is the symbolic representative of the Europeans who came to this land and turned it into a prosperous democracy that—in spite of its flaws—has been and continues to be a beacon of hope to the oppressed throughout the world. Monk]

[There is much to be said for both the old and the new fictions. It's important to see both sides and to maintain civility in the process. Gary]

[Or is a foolish civility the god hobblin' little minds? Charlotte]

The town's business district—from 6th to Sunset, from Walnut to Bell—catered to basic needs and was as simple as the lives of its people. There were three grocery stores on Main in the heart of town: Safeway, The Shopping Cart, and Edmonds Grocery and Market, which also offered delivery service for the barons in Woodway Park. There were six gas stations—Flying A, Union, Chevron, Richfield, and Shell within a block and a half of each other on 5th, and Harry's

Texaco on 3rd at Caspar—plus the Suburban Transportation System bus station at Yost's Auto Company for the increasing number of commuters. There were four taverns—The Sail Inn ("and Stagger Out," the old man and his buddies used to say), the Edmonds, the Up and Up, and Engels'. There were three family restaurants. Brownie's Cafe and Bud's Cafe, both narrow rooms with eating space at a long counter and a half-dozen booths with formica tabletops, served no alcohol and featured ground sirloin, chicken-fried steak, pot roast, and meat loaf. Tuson's Grill boasted a liquor license, had a bar as well as eight leatherette booths with plasticized-wood table tops, and specialized in T-bone, rib-eye, and top sirloin steaks. There was Hoffer's, a malt shop with tabletop juke boxes, The Polar Bear, also a burger and ice cream joint, and Bienz's, a confectionary which sold comic books, soft drinks, ice cream, candy bars, gum, and all manner of penny candy. There were three clothing stores—Weller's for men, Toni's Apparel and Durbin's for women— Kuzmoff's Shoe Repair, Crow Hardware, Reliable Hardware, the Edmonds Lumber Yard, Kurtz and Eckley Welding, Diesel Oil Sales, Sater and Ridenour Heating Oil, Eddy's Electric, Western Auto Supply, the National Bank of Commerce, Hubbard's Realty and Insurance, Swanson's Drug, Edmonds Dry Cleaners, Edmonds Flower Shop, Edmonds Bakery, the 5 And 10 Cent Store, and the *Tribune-Review* newspaper office. There were two barbershops—Bill's and Frenchy's—and one beauty shop—M'Lady's. There was a post office. And there was the Princess Theater, showing each evening Hollywood double features preceded by a Looney Tunes cartoon and a newsreel and on Saturdays matinees for kids featuring cliffhanging serials and cowboy movies starring Roy Rogers or Gene Autry or Hopalong Cassidy.

Other than movies, the town offered its residents little in the way of entertainment. There was an Easter egg hunt for kids at the City Park, the old man occasionally managing to find a gold one, which could be traded in for a 50-cent piece. On the Fourth of July a parade—featuring colorful floral floats with smiling teenage girls in bathing suits throwing Hershey's kisses to spectators, the American

Legion drill team, the high school band playing "The Washington Post March" and "The Stars and Stripes Forever," towering on stilts a bearded Uncle Sam in blue top hat, red cutaway with white stars, and white pants, the town's fire engine, blowing its siren at intervals, the mayor riding in a horse-drawn buckboard, as well as sundry horseback riders, motorcycle riders, Model T drivers, and unicyclists—wound through town and finished at the City Park, where families congregated to picnic on fried chicken and water-melon and play multi-generational softball games, the old man and Zee and Monk always excited to show their stuff against the adults. At dusk they wended their way back to the high school football field for a 30-minute fireworks display that screamed independence and nurtured unity. In August there was the Old Settlers' picnic, again at the City Park, with wheelbarrow races, three-legged races, egg-toss contests, and prizes for the earliest settler present and the oldest and youngest persons present. In September there was the Salmon Fishing Derby, drawing scores of participants and specta-tors who hung around the boathouses to scrutinize the catches, one of which, in 1948, good enough for third place, was a 12-pound hooknose netted by the old man after his father had reeled it to the boat. And in December, at the intersection of 5th and Main, which was barren of fountain and trees, there was the lighting of the Christmas tree set in place by Fire Department volunteers, a 30-foot fir that drew attention away from telephone poles and electric wires, and the arrival of Santa in the city's one fire engine to throw cellophaned candy canes to the old man and 70 or 80 other diving, grasping, wrestling kids. These seasonal events brought a spare but satisfying structure to the year.

There were no art galleries, playhouses, or concert venues. The old man's great-uncle Enos had played trombone in the Edmonds Band in concerts at the Opera House on Dayton early in the centu-ry; his grandfather Bertrand had sung there in the Edmonds Choral Society. Both groups ceased to exist during World War II, and the opera house became the Masonic Temple. The women's Music and

Arts Club held monthly meetings and arranged occasional field trips to exhibits and concerts in Seattle. During the fall and winter, there were Friday night high school football and basketball games, heralded by the pep band's rousing after-school marches through town; in summer there were Sunday afternoon Town Team baseball games against opponents from villages in the Cascade foothills like Monroe, Sultan, or Granite Falls. The consistent success of the football team under Coach Howard Howe (including an undefeated, unscored-upon season in 1949) induced a swelling of civic pride and nearly an idolatry on the part of the old man and Zee and Monk, who attended all of the games and as many practices as possible. But, for the most part, in Deadmonds, as post-war teenagers took to calling it, people entertained themselves by listening to the radio, watching three television channels, working on hobbies, visiting family and friends, fishing, playing cards, going on picnics, attending church, attending club meetings. Paternalist, ethnocentric, sexist, homophobic ("Excuse me, sir, can you tell me where I can find the Edmonds ferry?" "Speaking!") it must surely have been, the old man realized. The outward lives of most seemed to be as temperate as the cool, drizzly climate, but instances of avarice, boorish boosterism, small-mindedness, meanness of spirit, McCarthyism, and suspicion of new ideas would no doubt have been easy for someone less innocent to identify. Alcoholism and infidelity certainly occurred. The old man was aware that Monk's dad Phil, a house painter, bought three fifths of Old Crow every Saturday evening to see him through the Sunday closing of the Washington State Liquor Store. He knew that Patty's mother Pauline had once left her husband for three months to live in Seattle with a Fuller Brush salesman who had knocked at her door. Surely there had been, in the midst of a crowd, even at the hearth of a home, loneliness. He thought of his mother. He thought of his father. There were more than mere traces of Winesburg, Spoon River, Grover's Corners, Gopher Prairie, and Zenith in the Bowl. Year by year some ones married other ones and led, under cement gray skies admitting a certain slant of oppressive light but sometimes backlit to a pearly luminosity and on occasion bursting into blue, unexamined lives, or lives of quiet desperation, or lives of determined stoicism, most, nevertheless, some ones, any ones, no ones, absurdly, off again, on again, singing or dancing in the how pretty town, loving, creating, worshiping, celebrating, Sound, trees, clouds, rain.

[I loved the little town as much as anyone, but let's face it: the females were oppressed and repressed and everyone suffered, themselves included, from the toxic masculinity of the males. Charlotte]

[I admit that I did suffer my share of concussions (fortunately, no reperconcussions, no CTE!) when I played football at Whitman, trying to be a warrior hero. And I feared for my sons when they played football for EHS in the '80s. But the game was so much fun! We all reveled in the culturally approved sadomasochism, inflicting and incurring pain within a system of rules. It felt good to smash somebody. It did not feel good to be smashed in return, but we bore our pain proudly. To live fully, you have to run some risks. And I admit that I'm sometimes guilty of mansplaining. I can be presumptive and aggressive and abrasive. But that's why I succeed in the courtroom. I ask you, when we remove the so-called toxic elements from masculinity, what is left that isn't the same as femininity? Monk]

[Monk, do you even hear yourself? Charlotte]

[I never reveled in it. I did not like either inflicting or incurring pain. I endured it, because that's what guys did to achieve status in their tribes (in my case, the Maple Street All Stars and the males at EHS). In that regard, I was oppressed. Baseball and basketball, now, those I reveled in! Gary]

[So Monk exults "*Vive la différence!*" and Char, no fair lady, demands "Why can't a man be like a woman?" Solveig]

b

"Things never are as bad as they seem, so dream, dream, dream," soothed The Pied Pipers in sweet harmony on the 45 record played in the jukebox at the closing of the Teen Canteen at the darkened Masonic Temple on the second Friday of November 1956 after the football team had beaten Arlington to clinch the Northwest League championship on the frozen dirt of the Edmonds field, temperature, incredibly, in the 20s, a clear night, big bright egg-shell moon in the north, a few stars discernible beyond the moon's glow and the power poles flooding the field with light, as the old man leaned against a wall, arms folded, watching the dancers glide to a stop on the waxed maple floor, Dickie Riddle executing a final dip with his smiling partner, Solveig Lerass. The lights came up. The old man had seen the two dance together several times during the evening. Would Dickie be driving her home? Apparently not. Dickie thanked her and turned away toward Monk and Zee and the Johnson twins who formed an island in a current of kids saying their goodbyes as they flowed toward the exit. Solveig went to get her coat from a wheeled rack at the back of the hall. The old man followed, retrieved his own gray tweed topcoat, slipped it on, turned up the collar.

"Hi, Solveig," he said as she pulled a long woolen navy blue scarf from a pocket of her navy blue coat and wrapped it around her neck.

"Oh, hi, Wayne," she said, moving toward the door.

She was his height, 5'10", with broad shoulders, pale skin, auburn hair swept back to expose her forehead and ears, russet plastic combs constricting it behind her head before it fell lavishly in a broad mane halfway to her waist. Long silvery lashes canopied her ice-blue eyes. The old man had known Solveig since grade school. Mrs. Hill had selected them to serve a month's term as host and hostess, sitting at a table in front and modeling good chewing habits, as their second grade class ate from their tin lunch boxes in the classroom. They sang a duet, "Zip-a-Dee-Doo-Dah," in fourth grade music period. Off and on he had seen her, said hi to her, at Bienz's, the Princess Theater, the beach. She had ridden the truck to pick beans in Redmond the summer they were 12. In eighth grade he had stumbled through one dance with her at a New Year's Eve party at Patty Warfield's. In high school, a blended population of nearly 1,000 students from Edmonds and Esperance and Alderwood Manor grade schools, he spotted her only occasionally in a hallway. They had been in no classes together until this, their senior year, when both were forced into a required course, Family Living, and both elected to take second-year French and Jack Foster's class, Cultural Heritage. She and her parents had come to Edmonds from Ballard shortly after the war, living in a Craftsman with a basement full of pipes and sinks and shower heads at the corner of 6th and Walnut, her father a self-employed plumber whom his parents had once called to replace a rusted, leaking pipe at the back of their toilet in the house on Maple Street, but her family had moved, he had recently heard his mother telling his father, to a new house they had built in Talbot Park, a woodsy development north of Snake Road. He had always found her attractive, doubted she saw him in the same light, and was hesitant to approach her, or any other girls for that matter.

Wrapped in his topcoat, sitting high in the brimming grandstand with Bobby Moore, a lithe, wiry baseball teammate who lived near Chase Lake in the Esperance area, he had been thrilled by the game. Everyone was there: Mayor McGibbon, Police Chief Rassmussen, the Tusons, the Traftons, all the local businessmen and their wives, his parents, the parents and younger brothers and sisters of the players, a cluster of teachers, although not Foster, all drawn toward the light, sucked in by the gravity of the game, both teams undefeated, the staid little town baring its emotions, aching for a win. This was where they had to be. And on the field was where the old man should have been, in the light, the cheerleaders shaking their purple and gold pom-poms for him. Having been cut as a sophomore, he no longer dreamed of playing football, but the phenomena of his waking moments were shot through with epiphenomenal images of himself as a basketball and baseball phenom, making a crossover step and dropping the ball just over the rim and through the net, soaring to grab a one-handed rebound, poking the ball away from a dribbler and dashing down court for a breakaway layup, ripping a fastball into the left-centerfield gap, hook-sliding into second for a double, diving to catch a sinking line drive in right field. He had been so stirred by the playing of the national anthem that as the Tiger pep band hit "and the la-AND of the free-EE" he let drop from his mouth the wild cherry Lifesaver he had been sucking on and ground it with a desert boot into smithereens, no more sugar for him, he would purify his life and become a star. His ears ached with the cold, his face became so numb that he could scarcely articulate speech, but the team, his buddies, exhaling clouds of fog, played through it fearlessly, inspiring the old man at each snap of the ball, helmets clunking, shoulder pads thudding, on defense the shoving of blockers to the ground, the racing to the ball, the fierce gang-tackling, on offense the diving to the frozen earth to make open-field scissor-kick blocks, their bare lower legs getting scratched, scraped, ripped open, the bass drum thumping after big gains, the cheerleaders, pom-pommed hands on hips, high-kicking right-left-right, townspeople yelling, squirming, waving their arms, crying "Go, go, go!" and then, on the last play of the game, Edmonds leading 19-13, ball at their 40, the Arlington back, clever, agile Lee Peterson, whom the old man had played against in basketball as a junior, burst through the line on a quick opener, spurted past the linebackers, Dickie and Monk, and ran full-speed at Zee, the lone safety, Zee staying low and on the balls of his feet, waiting, reading, letting Peterson make his juke and then driving forward with short choppy steps, ramming his shoulder into Peterson's gut, wiring with his arms, and dumping him on his back as the gun sounded, a wave of purple storming off the bench to engulf him and hop-dance with their arms around him, some stotting like antelopes, the old man wobbling to his feet, his legs rigid with cold, cheering and thrusting a fist into the air, so proud of Zee, eyes briefly welling, then grabbing Bobby to give him a hug, purple and gold confetti showering down upon them, vowing to get up 20 minutes early Saturday morning and do pushups and jump rope before working his eight-hour shift as a boxboy at Safeway. Deliriously, the crowd rushed onto the field to congratulate the players and Coach Howe, and the old man and Bobby worked their way to the exit on 6th, then walked the three blocks to the just-opening Canteen, saying "Can't wait till basketball, baby," "Can't wait till baseball, baby," and hung up their coats and descended to the basement to play ping-pong and wait for the football players to show up after they had showered and dressed at the Field House.

When they heard Elvis's "Tutti Fruiti," they went back upstairs to find a throng, at least 20 of them football players in their navy blue letter jackets, chenille block bold-gold "E" sewn on the left breast, Ivy-League shirts, jeans or pastel peggers, and white bucks or desert boots, exuberantly mingling and glowing. Bobby, a bopper, immediately asked Patty to dance, both bending at the knees and waist, 18 inches apart, buttocks projected backwards, arms bent at their sides for balance, up on the balls of their feet, tapping the right toes outward and in, tapping the left toes outward and in, alternating their feet rapidly and decisively, twisting their hips and shoulders, his white bucks and her brown and white saddles tapping in double time. When the song changed to "Heartbreak Hotel," they moved together and clinched and swayed, then bopped again when it became "See You Later, Alligator," and the old man walked around, patting guys on the back, shaking Zee's hand ceremoniously, saying "From Maple Street All-Star to high school all-star! Way to go, Z-man!" When the song became "Standin' on the Corner," he settled sardonically into a place along the wall and watched for a while. As "Moonglow" began, Dickie, 6' 2," 200 pounds, fearsome, fearless tight end and linebacker, smiled knowingly at Solveig and the two waded into the stream and held hands at arm's length, slowly circling clockwise, insinuatingly undulating their pelvises at each step as right-hand notes on a piano carried the lambent melody above the soft, steady beat of bass, guitar, and drums, then coming together as soaring strings superseded the piano, her left hand on his shoulder, his left hand wrapping over and bringing to his chest her right, working it, caressing it, staring into each other's eyes, gliding forward, hesitating in place, gliding backward, an emulation of the most haunting, sensuous dance the old man had ever seen, that of William Holden and Kim Novak in *Picnic*, which had played at the Princess during the summer. When the song changed to "Allegheny Moon," he noticed Zee and Sylvia releasing each other, Zee walking over toward Jerry Johnson, Sylvia, in a long gray pleated skirt and a short-sleeve pink blouse, backing away from the center of the floor, and suddenly he found himself approaching her, saying "Sylvia, want to dance?' "Sure," she said. He led her out on the floor and held up his left hand as if signaling a right turn. She smiled, raised her right arm, clasped his palm in hers, both placing their free hands in the middle of each other's back, maintaining a discreet distance between their bodies. Beguiled by her softness, her lotioned hand, the layer of adipose tissue on her back, he labored in the box step that his mother had taught him, stepping ahead of the beat and onto her feet, saying "Sorry," turning, eddying, unable to go anywhere. "The place looks great," he said. "The streamers, the flowers." Sylvia and Patty helped with decorations for school dances. "Thanks. Great game, tonight, huh? Gary was our hero!" Her dark eyes shone beneath her curled eyelashes. "Yeah, he really was. Can't wait to play those guys in basketball." "Will our basketball team be as good as our football team?" "I hope so, lots of the same guys playing." "Plus you." "Yeah, plus me." As the song ended, Patti Page quavering "For me and for my one and only love," he yearned to dip Sylvia but didn't dare for fear of dropping her. They stopped dead. "Well, thanks, Wayne, that was fun. Maybe we'll have another dance later." And she was off, heading toward Patty and Dickie and Monk. The old man went downstairs, couldn't find a ping pong partner, came back up, leaned against the wall.

Solveig, hands jammed in her coat pockets, navy blue earmuffs adorning her hair, stood outside next to one of the three unfluted Italian columns supporting the flat roof of the concrete porch of the building that had served many civic purposes since its construction in 1909: a basketball court for a girls' team, Frances Anderson its star; a stage for dramatic and musical productions, his grandfather and granduncle Enos playing there occasionally as members of the town's choral society and band; even at one time a small bowling alley; and now a hall for meetings and installations for the Masons, the Rainbows, and DeMolay. Guys in customized Fords, Chevies, Mercs, and Studies were cruising up and down Dayton, racking their pipes on the way up, snapping them on the way down. Kids were descending the stairs, hailing rides or walking briskly toward their cars parked on Dayton or 5th. A long, dark green '56 Lincoln, with wide white walls and a Continental kit, a car that he didn't recognize, swooped to the curb in front of the Temple, and Solveig waved, skipped down to it, and jumped in.

The old man hunched his shoulders against the cold and walked the two blocks to his house on 4th, behind the Beeson Building.

[I loved, loved, loved the Canteen! Our own little excitingly dark, soulful, sonorous world, communal and romantic. Patty]

"Well, I guess if we need a plumber to fix a leak in the future we don't call Kjell Lerass," his mother said to his father Saturday evening at dinner, a pot roast she had put to simmer all day in Lipton's packaged onion soup, his father lifting the lid occasionally and adding water as needed. "While I was checking out June Trafton's groceries today she told me that Kjell and Leona have gone strictly commercial—installation for new businesses, houses, and apartment buildings only. No more being called to replace leaking hot water heaters in the middle of the night for them! They've opened a big demo store full of fixtures on 196th in Lynnwood near Ed's Market. Leona runs the office, Kjell does the contracting, and they've hired three full-time plumbers to do the work. So now they've got that big new house on the water in Talbot Park, a new Lincoln and a new Chrysler, they've joined the Everett Golf and Country Club, and they're going to send Solveig to Whitman next year. Must be nice!"

On Sunday afternoon the old man came downstairs dressed in a gray sweatshirt, gray tee shirt underneath, white gym shorts, and his new Converse, and asked to borrow his parents' '54 cream-of-tomato soup Studebaker Land Cruiser sedan.

"Why?" his mother said.

"Go play basketball with Zee. Get a Green River after at Bienz's."

"It's three blocks to the gym. You can't walk?"

"It's raining."

"It's misting!"

" And I'll be tired afterwards. You're not going anywhere, are you?"

"Coach opening up the gym on a Sunday?" his father said.

"Yeah, sort of."

He parked the Studie at the Field House to avert suspicion from neighbors or faculty members who might happen to be driving by and jogged on the slickening sidewalks through mist to meet Zee, who was waiting, holding his rubber basketball, hair damp from his walk over, outside the west entrance to the gym. Yes, there it was, where they had left it Friday after school, the tip of a piece of white string that they had tied to the crash bar on the inside of the door and fed at floor level through the narrow gap between the door and its latch-post. The old man pinched the string and teased it out six inches, raised it to waist-level, and tugged. The crash bar clicked and released and Zee grabbed the edge of the door and pulled it open. They were in! Laughing, the old man untied the string and threw it into a garbage can while Zee dribbled onto the maple floor and started shooting. The gym was old, dark, unheated, dank. Burlington and Anacortes had intimidating bright new stand-alone gyms with roll-up bleachers, glass backboards, digital clocks and scoreboards, heated tile floors in the locker room, huge shower bays. The Edmonds gym was an integral part of the aging Art Deco building, with access not only from the streets but from the first and third floor hallways. It had wooden backboards, a single scoreboard and an analog clock that turned red in the last minute of a period, cold concrete floors in a dim subterranean locker room, one small shower bay. The thump of Zee's dribbling echoed off the cream-colored concrete walls and the hard, built-in wooden bleachers that loomed within three feet of the sidelines, leaving just enough room for players' benches on one side and a string of bouncing cheerleaders on the other. Zee's damp shoes squeaked and squealed as he cut and pivoted on the maple floor, freshly lacquered for the basketball season. They didn't dare turn on the lights. They had to make do with the gray light coming from a few windows high in the northeast corner.

"I've always loved this place," the old man said as Zee flipped him the ball.

"Me, too."

The old man felt the enormity of tomorrow's first official practice. He had been up early Saturday to do pushups and jump rope. After work, before dinner, in the dark, he had run an Olympiad (uphill on Main to Olympic, north on Olympic to 196th, down 196th to Caspar, down Caspar to 7th, south on 7th past the football field , up the sudden hill between Bell and Main, lungs flaming, then coasting down Main to home). All fall, after school, while Zee and the guys were practicing football, he had been shooting in the upstairs gym of the Field House when it rained or at Zee's outdoor court at the house on Dayton when it didn't. He had to make the team, had to make the starting lineup. His blood surged. He felt quick. He was soaring for rebounds. They fed each other for layups. He felt agile. He was sweeping under the rim for left- and right-handed reverse hooks. They fed each other for outside shots, Zee bending his knees, elbows at his sides, both hands on the ball, thumbs almost touching, launching the ball with backspin, extending, following through, his classic two-hand set, a proven zone-buster, a little short at first, hitting the front of the rim, he hadn't played in a while, then finding the range, like the second-team all-league guard he had been last year, legs, wrists, and eyes coordinating, starting to swish them, the net splashing backward, then the old man shooting his one-handers, right foot forward, weight on the balls of his feet, making more than he missed. Next came jumpers, the old man's favorite shot, the one that felt most natural to him. He would jab fake one way, cut the other, take Zee's pass in a two-foot jump-stop, gather, elevate, hitch slightly at the top of his jump for power as he extended the ball on the pads of the fingers of his right hand, the left just a guide, and release it with arch and backspin. Or catch it, take two hard dribbles, and go up suddenly. This was his shot. If he didn't rush, he was every bit as accurate from 16 feet as Zee. They rested a minute, sweat dripping down their noses even in the cold, soaking into their tee shirts, and drank from the fountain near the entrance to the locker room. They played H-O-R-S-E, they played 21, Zee winning most often. Finally, what they had been building up to, a game of 1-on-1 to 20 by one, winner's outs. Zee beat him, as expected. If the old man didn't come out tight on him, Zee would sink a two-hand set; if he did, Zee, who was quicker, would flash by him for a layup or, if the old man did manage to stay low and slide, cutting him off, Zee would keep his dribble alive, hesitate, juke, get him to raise up, then drive around him or crossover to his left before the old man could recover. For his part, the old man was limited to the jump shot. Zee was quick enough to contest the set shot and also drop step and slide to cut off the drive. The old man lacked facility with the ball. He had trouble keeping his dribble alive. His instinct was to take two hard dribbles and pull up for a jump shot or make a jump stop, head fake, and step around for a push shot. He was fairly good at that. He forced Zee back on his heels a couple of times, he coaxed him to jump prematurely a couple of times, once he even made a reverse pivot and spun by him to bank one in off the board ("That was nice!" Zee said), but usually Zee was able to stay on top of him and make him shoot a forced, pressured shot. Zee won, 20-10. Was he twice as good?

They shook hands.

"Think we're ready, Z-man?"

"I think so."

"I hope so. Big day tomorrow. You need a ride home?'

"Nah. Think I'll jog. Work on my dribbling on the way."

The sky remained gray, but the mist had stopped. The old man walked to the Studie, drove out Puget Sound Drive, and turned down Talbot Road. He drove slowly, his the only car on the new blacktop road, swiveling his head as the road descended past gouged earth, uprooted tree stumps, and an idle bulldozer, eyeing the new houses on their half-acre lots, trying to read the lettering on mailboxes mounted on posts on both sides of the road, not knowing Solveig's address, not knowing what he would do if he found it, just wanting to know that he was on the street where she lived, but in a yard at the bottom of the slope, almost a half-mile into the Park, just before the road began to climb again, his breath quickening in embarrassed guilt and joy, he saw Solveig, in a yellow rain-slicker and black rubber boots, a matching yellow rain hat drooping over her ears but not covering her long mahogany mane, windrowing a heavy littering of umber leaves that had fallen onto the lawn from the two towering maple trees that had been left in place when the house was built. The angular split-level house, with cedar shake roof, vertical clear cedar siding, and a wooden deck all along its perimeter, sat on a low bluff above the Sound and looked directly at Possession Point on Whidbey Island. She lifted her head, she recognized him, he had to stop. He swerved to her side of the road, put the Studie in neutral, rolled down his window.

"Hi, Solveig."

"Wayne! What are you doing out here?" Carrying the bamboo rake, she walked over to the shoulder of the road. He could see the ice-blue of her wide-set eyes.

"Oh, just driving around, killing time. Been playing basketball with Gary and now I'm just waiting for tomorrow and the first team turnout."

"Nervous?"

"Very."

"Oh, I'm sure you'll do well."

"So this is your new place, huh? I heard my parents talking about it the other day. How do you like it?'

"It's a great house. Everything new—I love it. But I don't love the location. I mean I love the view, but we're so far away from downtown Edmonds, and I really miss it. I have to ride the bus to school, I have to have my dad take me to a game or a dance. Before, I could just walk to everything. And I don't really know anybody out here. All my friends live in Edmonds. Patty, Carolyn, Charlotte, Sylvia, Dickie, Dave. I'm trying to talk my dad into buying me a car."

"Yeah, I need a car, too. I'm going to get one right after the first of the year. Been saving my money."

"From your job at Safeway?"

"Yeah. How'd you know?"

"Oh, my mom said she saw you and your mom working in there when she was shopping one day."

"I saw you dancing to 'Moonglow' with Dickie at Canteen. You guys were really good."

"Yeah? Did you see *Picnic* last summer? Somehow Dickie and I just flowed into that dance scene, or it just flowed out of us. It was so much fun. I liked that whole movie. Reminded me of the 4th of July in Edmonds with the parade, the food, the games, all the little kids and the grandparents. And when Millie said 'Go to him, Madge,' my heart just soared. Do you like Kim Novak? She was beautiful, wasn't she?"

"She was. I liked the way she just slightly moved her jaw and lower lip to express emotion. She keeps looking out of the corners of her eyes. She's feeling very deeply but she can't find the words, she's just not a words person, and that hurts her, her lack of language is her Achilles heel, she moves her eyes in panic, she longs to be known, she's more than a pretty face but can't think how to show it."

Solveig smiled and leaned on the rake. "So what do you think of Miss Anderson's Family Living class and *Marriage for Moderns?*"

"Mm, pretty easy, pretty boring. Compatibility, courtship, weddings, responsibilities, money management, home-making, house buying—don't we all learn these mostly by watching our parents? "

"I actually like it. I like the philosophy of partnership, the woman and the man equal but with different responsibilities, they're a paired unity, they grow together. There's useful information about economics, financing and investments, things like that. And of course we haven't gotten to the chapter on sex and reproduction yet!"

"Yeah, saving the best for last, I guess! Anyway, I like Mrs. McAllister's French class better."

"Oh, I do, too. I love her discussions of French culture—their cuisine, their couture, and so on. I think I'm going to major in French in college. I can see myself working as an interpreter or translator in some American embassy somewhere, or maybe writing for a fashion magazine."

"Really! Well, I like writing and reciting the dialogues she has us do, and analyzing the grammar of sentences is just plain fun. But I like Foster's Cultural Heritage class best of all. So many interesting ideas come up in there."

"I really enjoyed *The Great Religions By Which Men Live.* My family is Lutheran, although we only go out to the Trinity Lutheran Church in Lynnwood on Christmas and Easter and Ash Wednesday, but it was fascinating to learn about the eastern religions. Atman and Brahman and *maya*. But throwing the *Bible* in the wastebasket to make a point? I didn't really mind—I got it—but for some people that's going a little too far. Patty was really fuming after class that day, and when I told my dad about it, he said the guy must be a communist."

"You know he was in the Marines in World War II? He's no commie."

"No, I'm sure he isn't. But there might be some people suspicious of him."

"To me he's the most interesting teacher at EHS. He told me the other day that he was the stroke on the Harvard varsity crew when he went back to college after the war ended. I'm going to write a feature on him for the *Wireless*."

The Studie, the old man realized, had been idling at least five minutes. To stay any longer would be unseemly. "Well, guess I'd better get the car back in case my parents need it. Nice to talk to you, Solveig."

"You too, Wayne. See you in class—I mean classes—tomorrow."

He put the car in first and followed Talbot Road to the top of the hill and out of the Park. He looped back to Perrinville, with its one general store, then took Snake Road down to Edmonds, stopping at McKeever's Shell on 5th to get a dollar's worth of gas.

"So what's up, Wayne?" said Donnie Bailey, a classmate who worked there weekends, as he turned the crank on the pump and the numbers reset to zeroes.

"Not much. Just played a little basketball with Zee, then ran into Solveig Lerass and talked to her for a while."

———⟫(⟪●⟫)⟪———

When, in the midst of one of their minutes-long open-mouthed kisses at the beach parking strip in the front seat of his midnight blue '49 Ford convertible with the fender skirts and the dual pipes, on a late gray Sunday afternoon, welcome winter darkness descending early, his left hand, inside her tan car coat but not the soft beige cashmere sweater he had given her for Christmas, alternately squeezing and caressing her substantial resilient breasts, the old man's already open eyes (after their first two dates, he had rejected the claustrophobic solipsism of Hollywood closed-eyes kisses, he wanted to see her fine lashes, her high forehead, the brown redness of her hair, the loosing of the hair from its combs, wanted the car's interior in his periphery, wanted a context) widened as a Great

Northern freight train rumbled by and Solveig lowered her hand to the crotch of his pastel yellow peggers. His hackles horripilating, he stiffened even more. Smiling, Solveig pulled her head back and looked at him. "'Manual manipulation,' the book says. I can't get that out of my mind." She unzipped his pants, slid her hand down and stroked him outside his tartan-plaid boxers. He slid his hand down to the crotch of her black pedal pushers and rubbed with two fingers. She went inside the fly of his boxers and gripped him in her fist, giggling as he leaked a bit into it. He unzipped her and slid the two fingers inside the crotch of her damp white nylon panties and up into her slickness. "No," she said. "Stay outside and just stroke the clitoris." He found something gristly and palpated. She resumed the kiss—it seemed to be important to be kissing while manipulating—and rubbed his hardness faster as they panted into each other's slobbery faces until, with a gasp, keeping his fingers going on her, he released, then moaned as she continued manually to urge more throbbing from him. When he finally subsided, softened and diminished, she extracted her splashed hand from the inside of his soaked boxers and spread her legs wider as he leaned in to his manipulating, their mouths gaping, their tongues tickling each other, their teeth sometimes bumping clumsily, stroking, now tenderly, now aggressively, he had no idea what she preferred, he had no touch, he was almost getting bored, there might be people walking by, and then at last she thrust her pelvis forward and he skated his fingers up and down the little ridge while she murmured and writhed.

They hugged and rested their heads together for a moment. "I think Family Living just became my favorite class," he said.

"And I think *Marriage for Moderns* just became my favorite book," she said. "But, geez, I need to be home by 5:30. Let's get you cleaned up." Opening her pocketbook, which lay to her right on the bench seat, she extracted Kleenex from a packet and swabbed him, both laughing as she elicited a final series of shudders, mopped his boxers, mostly in vain, then slipped a fresh tissue inside her panties and dabbed around. "We're going to have stains," she giggled.

Two weeks later Solveig called to invite him over to study for Foster's Cultural Heritage semester final. "Come about 11:00," she said. "My parents are going to Sunday brunch at the Everett Golf and Country Club, so it'll be quiet."

He parked on the shoulder of the road in front of the walkway adjacent to the concrete driveway that led to a two-car garage. The burled maple trees were bare, their rough bark showing all the way to their tops. The dormant lawn was sallow. She met him at the door wearing a nubby pink bathrobe. Her broad feet, their toenails painted deep red, were bare.

"Hiiiii," she said, tugging his right arm—his left clutched his goldenrod Pee Chee, on the cover of which he had recently written with his black Papermate "Ah foun' mah three-oh ohn Bluebayee Heeoh," and a paperback copy of *Laughing Boy*—and leading him over the bare oak floor toward a chocolate brown velour couch which was angled to provide a view of Whidbey. "What a great house!" he said, tilting his head back in homage to the six skylights that made it astonishingly light inside even on this cloudy day, panning his eyes from north to south, the gleaming avocado refrigerator and stove and the white and avocado mosaic tiles of the countertops and of the kitchen bay window's deep sill, which held terra cotta pots of small green plants, the long birch dining table with eight matching chairs, the long oak console with multiple doors that surely accommodated a 24-inch television set and a turntable and a number of LP record albums, the built-in oak book shelf housing a complete set of *The Encyclopedia Britannica,* the blonde oak rocking chair, the trapezoid-shaped glass coffee table bearing a copy of *Sunset Magazine*, the gleaming black baby grand piano, a hallway that led to bathrooms and bedrooms, a stairway with oak spindle balusters that led to a daylight basement, and then out the western windows—nine panels, each 10 feet high and four feet wide, plus a sliding glass door—to an expansive patio that surrounded a tarp-covered kidney-shaped swimming pool, more lawn, and a concrete stairway with iron railings leading to the beach. "What a great view!"

He set his materials on the coffee table and tossed his top coat over the back of the rocker. They sat. She snuggled up to him and kissed him. "Are you ready for this?" she said, and stood and unbuttoned her robe. Stunned by her audacity, he took her in as if she were a museum exhibit. Three times now they had gotten each other off in the front seat of his car, playing blind man's bluff, but they had not yet seen each other naked. She was so white, that whiter skin of hers than snow, except for the faint blush on her cheeks and forehead and her mauve nipples and her reddish-brown bush. He was hardening. He stood. Her springy breasts filled his cupping hands, her wide belly felt taut. He helped her shrug out of the robe, which she tossed to the end of the couch. He ran his hands over her broad cool ass, he gripped it and squeezed. She lifted his white tee shirt and ran her hands over his chest hair, still patchy, like a newly seeded lawn, and his stomach, softer than hers but less flabby than it used to be now that he had grown to 5' 11". She undid his purple suede belt, unbuttoned his Lee jeans, pulled them down, pulled his white boxers down, he stood revealed, he was on display, he was embarrassed, like the first day of swimming lessons at the Everett YMCA when the instructor told him and Zee and Monk and the rest of the all-male class to undress, shower, and report to the pool naked, he was almost vertical, was he big enough, was he good enough, she dropped to her knees, took him, incredibly, into her mouth, tonguing, tugging, he grabbed her hair in his fists, how sweet was this, and then he shattered into a rag that she had previously pulled from the pocket of her robe. When she was unable to coax any further shuddering from him, she wiped him off, set the rag on the floor, stretched out on the couch with her knees pulled up, and he leaned in to kiss her salty, slimy lips with their surprising whiff of sea brine, his upreaching hands working her breasts, and lap doggedly with his tongue until she was through convulsing and whimpering and he was on the verge of hardening again.

They stood up. "Damn!" she said. "A wet spot." She grabbed the rag, dabbed at herself, scrubbed the wet spot, flipped the cushion over. They hugged and kissed. She invited him into her room to watch her dress. The old man found her thrilling and precious. He nearly swooned at the jut of a haunch, the uplift of a breast, as she reached for a hanger in her closet. "Solveig," he said softly, cautiously, "should I try to get hold of some rubbers?" "Yes," she said.

They were sitting at the dining room table studying, formulating possible essay questions (What esthetic qualities of Navajo life are revealed in the characters' speech and actions? What do the songs, chants, and prayers reveal about Navajo beliefs? What is the role of beauty in the Navajo culture? Does the death of Slim Girl imply a tragic outcome for cross-cultural marriages? Define the term *hozoji*. Compare and contrast the principles of Taoism with the concept of *hozoji*.), Solveig wearing pink pedal pushers and a white blouse, a plate of krumkaka and glasses of lemonade before them, when her parents came home. They looked sternly quizzically at Solveig.

"Hi," Solveig said. "How was brunch? I invited Wayne over so we could study together. Big final in Cultural Heritage this week."

"Brunch was fine," Leona Lerass said. "You should have told us you were going to have company. Hi, Wayne."

"You're right. I'm sorry."

They were going steady. They were in love. In the spacious, knotty-pine paneled basement rec room, on its black shag carpet, Whidbey in his peripheral view, she taught him to dance, again and again recuing "My Prayer" until he could go forward and back, slow-slow-quick-quick, and pivot and hold in place and lead her into an underarm turn and execute a final, graceful dip, and "Rock Around the Clock" until he could double-time tap right-left-right-left and twist his upper body in sync. They went to Canteen on Fridays after home basketball games, mingling and replaying the action with Zee and Jimmie and Jerry and Monk and Bobby and Sylvia and Patty and Charlotte but dancing only with each other, and caravanned, after their final dip on "Dream," to Wilson's Drive-In at 145th and

Aurora to order burgers and shakes and fries from the carhops. On Saturdays they went to movies at the Orpheum, the Paramount, or the Music Box in downtown Seattle. Both felt pity and fury after *Sayonara* ("This would be a good movie for Cultural Heritage," Solveig said), both were inspired by *The Spirit of St. Louis* and *Fear Strikes Out*, the old man vowing to conquer his fear of failing at the plate as well as of being hit by a pitch, both dreamed of participating in dramatic dance scenes after *Silk Stockings* and *The Benny Goodman Story* (both melting, as always, at "Moonglow," their song, both jazzed by Gene Krupa's tom-tomming and kids jitterbugging to "Sing, Sing, Sing" in the aisles of Carnegie Hall), both moved by the tragic heroism of the Colonel and the Commander in *The Bridge Over the River Kwai* ("This would, too"), she admiring Kim Novak's triumph over weasely, conniving Frank Sinatra in *Pal Joey*, he beguiled again by that self-distancing, those twitching lips, the downcast eyes, the pouty drooping lower jaw, he could identify with that. In mid-March, the drive-in theaters opened for the season, the Sno-King on the northern edge of Lynnwood on Highway 99 and the Aurora south of Wilson's. They became regulars on Saturdays, except when she had her period, hooking the speaker to the driver's window but turning the volume off, climbing into the back seat in the dark when the cartoons began, eagerly undressing each other, dropping the clothes in a pile on the floor, he slipping on one of the Trojans that Bobby stole a package of every couple of weeks while stocking shelves at Swanson's Drug store and shared with him, pulling a scratchy wool plaid Pendleton blanket over themselves, cuddling, cocooning, then she stretching out on the seat for him or hoisting herself onto his lap and riding him. They usually missed a few minutes of the first feature but then, his arm around her after reaching forward to turn on the volume, both still naked, lost themselves in the films, both teary at the end of *A Farewell To Arms* (he because of Frederic Henry's loss, she because of nature's injustice to Catherine Barkely), both locked in the cross-cutting tension, seeing the situation from both sides, of *The*

Enemy Below, it seemed so real, both stunned by the eerie com-plexity of *The Three Faces of Eve,* the existence of multiple person-alities a stunning revelation, so un-Edmonds-like, neither of them even knew of anyone who was seeing a psychiatrist, and by the shocking melodrama of *Peyton Place*, could Edmonds in any way be like that, true enough they knew of no important person that had ever come out of EHS and many classes limited themselves to facts or skills but Foster and McAllister presented ideas, math teachers taught inductive and deductive logic, and science teachers espoused the scientific method, kids had sex, certainly, hadn't they just minutes ago, and Sandy Ferlaak had become pregnant in her junior year and been required by district policy to leave school and receive home instruction, but were parents that controlling and pu-ritanical, sex education was part of the curriculum for seniors, guys read *Playboy,* although not in front of their parents, and found it available not at Swanson's in Edmonds but at the new Pay'N'Save in Lynnwood, on weekends a few went to the woods or the beach and drank, certainly alcohol was a serious problem for some, Joe Hatch and Larry Russell had gotten drunk the night after Joe obtained his driver's license and were killed when Joe failed to negotiate a curve going down Maplewood Hill and his '51 Chevy Deluxe coupe with the windshield visor and fender skirts and dual pipes flew into a gulch and hit a tree, the Johnsons' dad spent his evenings at the Edmonds Tavern, Monk's dad hit the liquor store for a fifth of bour-bon every day, and Ken Miller, the Safeway manager, the old man's mother had informed him, had once undergone aversion therapy at Schick Shadel in West Seattle, some of the guys surmised that classmate Dale Lippert, who never showed any interest in sports and who liked to paint scenery for school drama productions, and P.E. teacher Miss Rhonda James, who never wore makeup and who combed back her slick short hair into a DA, were "queer," but ho-mosexuality was seldom a topic of discussion, and incest was never even a consideration, Patty's mother had left home for a while but they hadn't heard any other gossip about extramarital affairs, they were unaware of any evidence of spousal abuse or shady business deals or suicides, some people had more money than others, of course, Woodway Park was a world apart and business men and professionals were moving into north Edmonds and Talbot Park but were there really status differences, cultural differences, except for income wasn't everybody equal, was Edmonds stultifying, repressive, bourgeois or petite bourgeois (was there a difference?), was there anger among the teenagers, desperation to get out, did they want to rise above the town, none of their friends ever seemed to talk that way, or was that because they were too bourgeois Solveig wondered, the old man dreamed of becoming a reporter, starting first with the *Seattle Times* and commuting from Edmonds, and ultimately advancing to the *New York Times*, but thought of the move with a sense of apprehension not relief, Solveig wasn't sure yet what she wanted to be, translator or fashion writer, certain only that she did not want to be in the plumbing business, they would marry, on their honeymoon they would attend the Ashland Shakespearean Festival, in a niche in the granite bulkhead shoring up the bank on the west side of the train tracks, waves swashing ten feet below them, they decided on names for their three children, Samantha, after the luminous Grace Kelly character in *High Society*, for a girl, Oscar for the first boy, Max for the second.

And every Tuesday and Friday through February there were basketball games. He had finally made a varsity, after having been cut from the football team as a sophomore and apprenticing on the jayvee basketball and baseball teams in his sophomore and junior years. In the three-day tryout period he had concentrated to his utmost during the monotonous drills, executing with precision the fundamentals of passing and shooting, miming Coach, pronating his wrists on the chest passes, exaggerating his follow-throughs, taking each part of each drill seriously. He got his butt down, dropstepped and slid. He pivoted with passion. He made 90% of the 25 free throws they shot daily. In scrimmages he fought for loose balls, contested shots, blocked out, passed and cut crisply, ran the plays precisely, even soared over Monk to tip in a rebound ("More lucky than good," he heard Coach say on the sideline to a couple of subs waiting to come in.) He didn't take many shots—and missed most of those few—but he knew he was displaying good form, he was just rattled. There was no question that Coach was going to keep the returning letter-winners—Monk the banger, Zee the scorer, Jimmie the slashing driver, Jerry the jumper—but who was the fifth senior going to be? The old man, who was versatile if nothing else, or Stew Jenkins, a 6'3" stiff whose shots clanked and whom Coach had kept in the program for two years because of his height, or erratic Fred Morton, who would drive successfully to the hoop in a burst of speed one day and throw up blind hook shots another? In the final scrimmage on day three, Stew shot a ball that missed the backboard and hit the end wall. Fred, leading a fast break, threw a no-look pass out of bounds. The old man, leading a fast break, jump-stopped at the free throw line as Stew came at him to defend, faked a shot, and dropped a perfect left-handed bounce pass to a cutting Zee, who laid it in. Coach nodded. Two minutes later, the old man, making one of his signature two-dribble drives, jump-stopped, head-faked, and stepped around Fred to sink a short push shot. Coach smiled. He was in.

But the team and the old man both struggled. Now that he had achieved his lifelong dream of being a starter, he was unable to be a difference-maker. The versatility of his mediocrity was all that he had going for him. In Coach's double post offense, the old man could play either outside or inside with equal lack of effect. As a post man, although undersized, he rebounded well because he fought to find gaps and was relentless in pursuing the ball, and if he set a screen for a guard and a defender ran into him, he could make his free throws. He shot 81% for the season, which turned out to be a school record. But with his back to the basket he was unable to make many post moves—few power drop steps, few running hooks, few turnaround jumpers—so his teammates usually ignored him and looked to find Monk inside instead. As a guard, he passed well and screened well but was limited by his lack of a set shot and by his two-bounce dribble. On defense, he held his own. Inside, he banged, he fought to deny position, he contested shots without fouling, he blocked out. Outside, he got his arm out to deny perimeter passes, if his man did get the ball he gave him a cushion so he could deny dribble penetration, conceding a few more set shots than he should but usually getting away with it. Not that his teammates were much better. Zee, who made first team All-Northwest League, averaged 18 points a game and led the conference in scoring, canning those two-hand sets or keeping his dribble alive long enough to find a little opening for a runner or a baby hook, and Jimmie, so quick, averaged 12 by knifing to the basket for layups, but the other players had little offensive game. The old man averaged four for the season, most of those coming on free throws. His one glory performance happened on a Friday in late December when the undefeated Marysville Tomahawks came to town. The lead changed hands with every basket throughout the game, and the old man, possessed by the possibility of upsetting the league leaders, grabbed six rebounds in the fourth quarter, got fouled setting a screen with 15 seconds to go, swished both free throws on the 1-and-1, fought around his man to steal a pass at the other end, and threw the ball to the ceiling in celebration as his teammates rushed toward him to pound him on the back and Coach shook his fist and said "Attaboy, Wayne!" The win moved Edmonds into third place in the eight-team league, and that was as high as they would go. In January they slowly sank to sixth, out of contention for even the District Tournament, let alone State. Still, he loved it all. The practices, where Coach would put in the game plan against the scout team of second-stringers and they would convince themselves that they could win. The team dinners at players' houses before home games, mothers offering platters of cubed steaks, trays of foil-wrapped baked potatoes, cartons of sour cream and margarine and jars of bacon bits, huge wooden bowls of green salad, bottles of French dressing, and baskets of doughy Parker House rolls from the Edmonds Bakery. The bus rides to away games, 12 varsity players, 12 jayvee players, 10 cheerleaders, two managers, and two coaches crammed together, the girl-ogling, the joking, the razzing, the comradely bonding, the old man letting himself go, almost, briefly, dissolving into the whole, then, the old yellow bus wheezing its way up Highway 99, darkness falling, everyone becoming silent twenty minutes before their destination, feeling the game grow upon them, girding themselves, visualizing, preparing, usually in vain, not to let their teammates down. And the crowds—at home, a gym full of Edmonds fans, with the brassy pep band blaring "Tiger Rag" and "Muskrat Ramble," away, a knot of parents and friends, including Solveig, who filled up the car her parents had bought her for Christmas, an aqua and cream '55 Bel Air hard-top convertible, with Sylvia and Patty and Charlotte and Carolyn. The old man's parents drove to every game, even to Anacortes, two-hours away, and proudly sat among the other parents. His mother always wore something purple or gold—a blouse, a sweater, a skirt, a scarf. They were not yellers, definitely not given to rising to their feet, but applauded all good plays, his no more enthusiastically than anyone else's, and exchanged nods and smiles with their equals.

Baseball was more successful but less enjoyable. The team finished a respectable third, behind Everett and Marysville, and the old man played right field and batted .280, hitting mostly singles to center and left. Only Jimmie at short and Bobby at third had higher averages. Zee, the football and basketball star, was down around .200. But the feeling just wasn't the same. Fewer than a dozen parents and friends attended the afternoon games, most parents, like his mother, having to work, most friends busy with other after-school activities. His father, able to adjust his schedule at Hopper Chevrolet, was the only parent who appeared at every home game. Solveig came to the first two games, then decided that her time would be better spent doing homework. And no one, parent or friend, attended the away games. The spring weather was often miserable, with temperatures in the 40s and 50s, and rain squalls passing through. The Edmonds infield was a clumpy clay strewn with rocks, which Coach required the players to rake into piles and throw to the sidelines before practices or games could begin; the outfield, clipped quack grass, was uneven, with little mounds and depressions that forced fielders to fight for balance when running down balls. When they did catch one, the ball stung their nearly frozen hands so badly that tears came to their eyes. At home in the last game of the season, in a battle for second place against Marysville, they lost. Down one, the old man was on deck in the bottom of the seventh. Jimmie had singled, Jerry had walked, and Bobby was up. Suddenly, Principal Hill, scrawny and wrinkled now but a track star in his youth it was said, came rushing through the tennis courts and out to the field. "Wayne, Wayne," he shouted, interrupting the old man's practice swings. "I've just been informed that you have been nominated for a $500 journalism scholarship sponsored by the *Everett Herald*. You have an interview in Seattle at the *P-I* with Emmett Watson tomorrow at 10:00 a.m. Congratulations! Now get a hit!" Stunned, the old man said "Thanks" and watched as Bobby laid down a bunt and sacrificed Jimmie to third and Jerry to second. A base hit would score both, Jerry taking a big lead and getting a good jump with two out, and win the game. He stepped into the batter's box. Emmett Watson, sportswriter and columnist for the *P-I*, next to Georg Myers, sports editor and columnist for the *Times*, his favorite writer! $500! He stared at Greg Easterbrook, who didn't have much speed but had a wicked curveball. The old man had waited on the curve in his first two at-bats and had singled to left and lined out sharply to short. Principal Hill was standing behind the backstop. "Rip one, Wayne!" he shouted. The old man knew he would get a fastball on the first pitch, and he wanted it, wanted it so much that he excitedly pulled his head and missed it. He knew he would get the curve next, and he stayed back waiting for it as a fastball sailed right down the middle. "Come on, Wayne," shouted Zee and Bobby and his teammates. Now he knew the curve, Easterbrook's out-pitch, was coming, and he waited on it and waited on it before finally flailing weakly, desperately late, and missing another fat fastball. The Marysville players screamed their approval. Principal Hill turned and walked away. "Tough luck, Wayne," Jimmie said. "Nice try," Bobby said. "It happens, man," Zee said. "Let's go shake hands with 'em, guys," Coach said.

The next morning he drove his Ford to 6th and Wall in Seattle, parked in front of the six-story *P-I* building topped by a 30-foot blue neon globe of the world visible for miles, an 18-foot-high eagle with upstretched wings perched atop it, and "It's in the P-I" in red letters rotating round it. There were three other candidates from Snohomish County who waited with him on folding chairs placed in front of Watson's office door on the sixth floor. They shook hands and identified themselves but were too nervously competitive to talk. Watson came out. "Gentlemen, I'm Emmett Watson," he said, as if they all didn't see his basset hound mug shot in the *P-I* every morning. "I'll be interviewing you for the *Everett Herald* scholarship. Which one of you is Wayne Adams?"

The old man raised his hand.

"Wayne, nice to meet you. Let's start with you. Come on in."

Watson motioned to the single guest chair in the room and swiveled his own desk chair away from his typewriter to face the old man, who was impressed by the view of Elliott Bay beyond the desk. With such a view, who wouldn't be inspired to write?

"Tell me why you're interested in journalism," Watson asked.

The old man sensed that Watson wanted him to reply that he had been called to the profession, that his mission was to find and report the truth, that he wanted to comfort the afflicted and afflict the comfortable, which his teacher Charles Sauvage had said was one of the noble purposes of journalism, but he was unable to do that. He said that he was interested because he had had success in writing for the school paper, that he enjoyed finding different angles and various ways of putting pieces together into a coherent whole, and that he liked getting bylines. Impassive Watson didn't smile, didn't frown. The old man desperately wished that Watson could see the comments Sauvage had made in his string book about his feature on Jack Foster as a Harvard oarsman: "Good English, good organization, punchy writing, complete reporting, has central idea," "I've seen worse in the *Times* and *P-I* many times," "Professional quality," "You have a fine future in journalism."

"And what does your independent reading, your out-of-class reading, consist of? "

The old man said that in the past few months he had read "The Last Hurrah" in the *Reader's Digest Condensed Books*, *The Autobiography of Lincoln Steffens,* and *The Jungle*, both on the rec-ommendation of his journalism teacher, and that he was just get-ting started on *The Grapes of Wrath*. Watson nodded and stood to shake his hand.

"Wayne, thank you for the interview. You'll be hearing from the *Everett Herald* in a few days."

The winner, he heard in a few days, by way of a one-sentence note from Principal Hill delivered to him in Foster's class by a stu-dent messenger, was the kid from Everett High School. Both em-barrassed and relieved, the old man decided that he would not be joining the Fourth Estate. He would be remaining among the commoners.

In May he applied for admission to the UW, where he intended to major in English, not Journalism. Tuition was $60 a quarter, the grade-point requirement for entrance 2.0. His 3.0 would get him in; he would live at home and pay for tuition and books with the mon-ey he earned from his 40-hour per week job, procured for him by his father, pumping gas, polishing cars, cleaning toilets, and running errands at Hopper Chevrolet, and his Saturday work at Safeway. Solveig, with her 3.9 (a B in Calculus), applied for admission to Whitman, where she would major in French and pledge a soror-ity, her expenses, some $6,000, paid for by her parents, although they insisted that she work during the summer by doing most of the cleaning at home and going in to clean the plumbing store on Wednesdays and Saturdays. For the Senior Prom, held in the school gym, they double-dated with Monk and Char, having dinner beforehand in Seattle at Canlis overlooking Lake Union, the old man ordering ground sirloin well-done and Solveig experimenting with frog's legs, which he found surprisingly mild when she shared a bite with him. After the graduation ceremony, held in the school auditorium, they joined their exuberant classmates on a chartered Great Northern train for an all-night trip to Vancouver, B.C., moving from car to car, seat-hopping from friend to friend in the coaches, dancing to the music of a trio playing in the corner of a boxcar decorated in purple and gold for the occasion, munching on snacks in the dining car, then climbing into chartered buses bound for the Hotel Vancouver, where they breakfasted on the top floor in a restaurant with a panoramic view, dozing and chatting in rummy exhaustion on the way home, arriving in Edmonds just in time for the old man to work a Saturday afternoon shift at Safeway. Accompanied by his father, the old man opened a checking account at the National Bank of Commerce in its new building with the drive-through window at 3rd and Main, the bank manager, Ken Gustafson, an old family friend, stepping into an open teller's window to handle the transaction himself. Depositing $100 and opting to sign his checks "Wayne Warren Adams," the old man felt himself for the first time to be an adult. A few days later, Solveig went in with her father and opened an account for $500.

It was a summer of readying, of work, of fun, of love. Every couple of weeks they would drive to the University Book Store on the Ave and browse for paperbacks. The old man read *The Sun Also Rises*, *The Old Man and the Sea*, *The Catcher in the Rye*. Solveig read, in English, *Swann's Way*, *Madame Bovary*, *The Stranger*. They swapped books. Solveig loved *The Sun Also Rises* for its festivals and its rituals, its Spanish mystique, and found the *élan* of Brett Ashley exhilarating, was moved by the way Santiago was at one with the sea and the marlin, his brother, but pained by the obviousness of the Christian symbolism, reveled in Holden's language but was dubious about his sentimental need to preserve purity and the past.

The old man was captivated by Proust's style, the long, looping sentences, was ambivalent toward Emma's romanticism and claustrophobia, empathized with Meursault's discovery of the indifference of the world. On some of their dates, after he finished work and showered, with light even in August lingering late, they went to the Edmonds beach or to Richmond Beach, spread his stained car blanket on the sand, ate tuna fish sandwiches and chocolate chip cookies that Solveig had made, and took turns reading aloud as they worked their way through *Hamlet* (he warming to Hamlet's skepticism and hesitancy, she to Hamlet's eventual realization that the readiness is all), *Antony and Cleopatra* (both stirred by the intensity of the lovers' passion, she admiring, he mesmerized by, Cleopatra's infinite variety, thinking Solveig was a little bit like that) and the French portion of an interlinear translation of *Les Jeux Sont Fait*, spurring each other on to perform, giggling from time to time as they tried to outdo each other in nasality, gargled r's, rounded-lip u's, aspirated h's, and word liaisons, running ending consonants into beginning vowels with abandon in quest of speed and fluidity.

One night a week the old man played league fast-pitch softball on the high school football field with his old baseball teammates. Jerry, who had a devastating riseball, pitched, the old man caught. He liked being in the center of the action rather than a satellite in the outfield, and he could spring from his crouch and release the ball so quickly that, despite not having a strong arm, he was able to throw out most would-be base stealers. Jimmie played short, Bobby was at third, Zee at second, Monk at first. One night Jimmie hit an other-worldly shot over the grandstand. "Truly awesome," the old man said, wanting to get on his knees and bow. Sometimes Solveig would come to the game with some of her girlfriends in her Bel Air and afterwards everyone would go to the Polar Bear for Cokes or milk shakes. Occasionally, after work and dinner at home with his parents, he would drive out to Talbot Park and spend a couple of hours with Solveig and Kjell and Leona, eating popcorn or ice cream sundaes and watching *Perry Mason* ("The guilty party is always on the stand exactly 10 minutes before the program ends," Kjell said), *Cheyenne, Gunsmoke, Wyatt Earp, Have Gun Will Travel, The Danny Thomas Show, The Perry Como Show, Candid Camera,* on their mammoth 24-inch TV screen. *Maverick* was his favorite, Bret so sly and wily, a trickster living by his wit and charm, holding a black belt in mental *jiu jitsu,* using his opponent's strength against him, his very life a game of poker. The old man could only dream of making gambits, of being able to read people that well or of having the stomach to manipulate them as Bret did. "How's work going, Wayne?" Kjell would say. "Good, good," the old man would answer. "We're selling lots of '57s. I'm unloading a boxcar of new ones every week and then polishing them up." "I know Solveig really likes her '56. I got a great deal from Irv Hopper on that one. Maverick would have been proud. How's it going for your dad?" "Oh, fine, fine. He spends quite a bit of time on the showroom floor or at the used car lot out at the county line. And his trio plays dance jobs most every weekend."

"He's so good," Leona said. "I love those New Year's Eve dances he plays at the Legion Hall. He'll jazz up a popular song but he doesn't get so abstract that you can't dance to it."

"Yeah, that's the art, that's the challenge that he enjoys," the old man said.

Every couple of weeks, the old man's mother would ask him to invite Solveig for dinner. She would prepare pot roast with chunks of potatoes and carrots or meat loaf with mashed potatoes. His parents loved Solveig. His mother chatted away about people she saw while working at Safeway, houses that were for sale, gossip she picked up from the weekly meeting of the Sewing Circle. His father said little but continuously beamed alertness in Solveig's presence. Solveig always made it a point to ask him something about music. On the 4th of July she drove down to Edmonds and joined the old man and his parents and grandparents and aunt and uncle for the parade and the picnic and the evening fireworks show while Kjell and Leona went to the Country Club for golf and dinner.

On Saturday nights, they went to a drive-in. On Tuesdays, clocking out for his one-hour lunch break, instead of going home, the old man would hurry out to Talbot where Solveig, who was cleaning house while her parents tended to business at the store, would greet him in her bathrobe for a quickie, then send him back to work with a sandwich of peanut butter and lingonberry jam, a moveable feast to munch on the way. On Sundays, they might lob a tennis ball back and forth at the high school courts in their swimming suits, Solveig's an orange one-piece that resonated with her auburn hair and her faintly bronzing summer skin, then go back to Solveig's to swim in her pool or drive out to Martha Lake to spend the afternoon with classmates. The girls would tuck their hair into white bathing caps and they would all swim out to the raft, dive off the board or jump from the 10-foot tower, then swim back in, dry off, the girls freeing and shaking out their hair, go to their cars for money, buy Coke or Dad's Root Beer and hot dogs at the concession stand, and loll on the grass in the sun and talk about college. Zee was going to play basketball and study electrical engineering at the College of Puget Sound in Tacoma on a combination academic-athletic scholarship, Charlotte and Sylvia planned to room together in a dorm at the U, Charlotte going into Pre-Med, Sylvia majoring in Art, Monk was headed to Whitman for football and Pre-Law, Dave had a full scholarship to study theology and philosophy at Whitworth in Spokane, Carolyn would attend Reed in Portland and study classics. Only the old man was going to live at home, only he was going to become a teacher. And after the talk and the eating and drinking and some frisbee throwing, late in the afternoon, smoldering, the old man and Solveig usually waded out into the lake to the west away from the raft and the plungers and screamers to a spot where two drooping weeping willows obscured them from shoreside observers, walked in up to their chins, spread their feet and dug them into the soft muddy lake bottom, establishing a solid base against the chop of the waves created by gentle gusts of wind, stared deeply into the wild blue yonder and, his right hand working from behind, her left working from in front, achieved shivering climaxes, for the old man, laved by the water, loved by and loving this girl, mind unmoored and adrift in the sky, an almost atonement.

Shortly after Labor Day, Solveig filled her Bel Air with suitcases and books and toiletries and left for Whitman, trailed by her parents, who were going to help her get settled, in the Lincoln. The night before she left, she and the old man went to the Sno-King to see *April Love*. The old man ached. He cherished her, he clung to her, but she was so excited by tomorrow that the sex was one-way.

"You know," she said as he rolled down the window and put the speaker back on its hook after the movie ended, "you kind of remind me of Pat Boone, your cheekbones, your Bryll-Cremed hair parted on the left and combed back from your forehead, your ears at half-flap, your teeth nice in a smile but not perfectly even, your politeness, your wholesomeness, although you have brown eyes instead of blue and you've got those deep dimples that cave in like sinkholes when you smile, and when the state patrolman cited you for negligent driving, gunning it and passing all those cars on Edmonds Way last month, you got off with a $10 fine because the judge knew your dad and your grandparents, just like the cop who caved in to peer pressure and decided to ignore Pat Boone's driving without a license."

"But I can't sing."

"You sang a duet with me in Mrs. Wagner's class."

"Proves my point! Should we drive down to Wilson's?"

"I'd like to, but I really think I should get home, double-check my packing, and get some sleep."

At her door, under the bright porch light, he kept holding her.

Finally she kissed him and said, "Wayne, I love you. I'll call and I'll write. Maybe you can come over for a sorority party later on. And I'll be home for Thanksgiving. Good luck with your classes!" And she pulled away and went inside.

She called two weeks later.

"Wayne, I love my classes! I'm taking French 201 and modern

French literature and Poly Sci 100, plus golf for P.E. because my parents say I need to learn the game. My French lit prof, Simon Weiner, is a cool, suave guy. Very intellectual. I've already had a couple of conferences with him. We've started with Celine's *Voyage Au Bout De La Nuit*, then we're going on to Sartre's *La Nausée* and Camus' *L'Étranger*—guess I have a head start because I've already read it in English—Beckett's *En Attendant Godot* and Robbe-Grillet's *La Jalousie*. The campus here is very nice, small—you can walk across it in five minutes—woodsy, lots of colonial architecture. And so far the sun has shone every day—no morning low clouds that last half the afternoon! Did you know that Walla Walla means 'place of many waters'? It's kind of nice to feel yourself existing in the territory of the Nez Perce. In ninth-grade Washington State history class I learned to admire them and Chief Joseph for their courage and resiliency. They seemed so noble, they really had a sense of who they were. Going through rush was a blast. I pledged Alpha Phi because I really hit it off with most of the girls. My roommate, Joan Davis from Spokane, is very sweet. And so many parties! The Greeks are so active socially, it's a whirlwind. I make sure I get my reading done, though. I intend to graduate Phi Beta Kappa. I finished Céline in five days and I've got a notebook full of quotes. 'A man should be resigned to knowing himself a little better each day if he hasn't got the guts to put an end to his sniveling once and for all.' Ditto for a woman, I say. Weiner quotes Camus: 'The first philosophical question is whether or not to commit suicide.' Well, suicide is not on my agenda, ergo....It's not that I fear the dreams of death, like Hamlet, it's that I want to experience as much of life and learn as much about myself as I can. *'J'espere devinir moi-même avant de mourir.'* Another quote: 'When you stay too long in the same place, things and people go to pot on you, they rot and start stinking for your special benefit.' I mean, I love Edmonds and I love you, our relationship is great and could never rot, but I'm glad I'm having these new experiences now, and I can feel myself growing. Another quote: 'You can lose your way groping among the shadows of the past.' Weiner says that these shadows are illusions, like those in the 'Allegory of the Cave,' and that we must explore the reality of now. Later in life, perhaps, I will want to remember things past and come to terms with my origins, but for now I want to find out what's outside the cave. And I plan to write my first paper on this one: 'Philosophizing is simply one way of being afraid, a cowardly pretense that doesn't get you anywhere,' in which I will contrast the angst felt by the analytical narrator, Bardamu, who is kind of 'sicklied o'er with the pale cast of thought' throughout his night-marish 'journey,' with the sense of wholeness and beauty felt by the intuitive Navajos in *Laughing Boy*. Of the two fictions, the latter seems truer to me than the former. How are things with you?"

"Go-OOd," he said, fighting for breath as his lungs spasmed. "We-ENT down to the U to register last week. My English Department adviser steered me into English 101, Econ 200, Astronomy 100, French 201, and Classics 100—Latin and Greek in Current Use, a vocabulary-building course."

"Oh, that'll be useful."

"Yeah. And then I'm required to take ROTC, so I chose Army, and a PE class, so I chose golf just like you so we can play at the Country Club next summer."

"Great!"

"We start classes on the last Monday of September. I'll be so glad to be done with waxing cars and cleaning toilets at Hopper's. And my Tuesday lunch breaks aren't nearly as much fun as they used to be."

"I hope not!"

"I miss you."

"I miss you, too. Only two months and I'll be home for Thanksgiving."

"Ri-IGHT."

"Wayne, sorry, but I have to go now. I need to get some reading done, and then after dinner I'm going to walk downtown with some of the girls to see a movie."

"Which one?"

"*Love in the Afternoon*, with Gary Cooper and Audrey Hepburn. It's set in beautiful *Pehrhee*. I'd love to spend my junior year abroad, at the Sorbonne. I love you!"

"I lo-OVe you, too."

When school started, the old man drove his Chevy every morning through Lake City to the still-settling gravelled Montlake parking lot next to the landfill dotted with smudge pots burning off the methane rising from the decaying garbage dumped by the dozens of huge trucks that came and went all day and ascended stairs and pathways to the upper campus, a 15-minute hustle to a pressure-filled excitement of new ideas, new possibilities. Was he good enough? Did he belong? "Money is just numbers in bank books," said his Econ professor, Henry Buechel, in an early lecture. How could that be? Did it not have to be backed by something? The astronomy lab was a labyrinth. He could not fathom how to plot azimuths and declensions in the celestial sphere and turned in each week a hodge-podge of wild guesses and hopes. The astronomy professor, Carl Jacobsen, marked all of his work "C"—a more than generous evaluation, the old man felt. "You should have used '*celui*' instead of '*l'on*,' said his French professor, Lurline Simpson, after an assignment to invent an anecdote and recite it to the class. "What's your major, Mr. Adams?" "English." "It should be French." "An excellent paper, Mr. Adams," commented his English professor Marvin Brown on 'Angels in Bitches' Clothing: Greene's Women,' the old man's paper on *The Heart of the Matter* and *The End of the Affair*. The vocabulary class, conducted by a TA, James Robinson, was both easy and stimulating. The old man excelled at memorizing roots and affixes and in making morphological cuts in words and eagerly applied his gained knowledge, as in Brown's class with the Lovelace poem, "A-mar-antha," un-fading-flower, Solveig sweet and fair, too, he thought, in a certain slant of light her hair blooming purplish-red. The ROTC class, focusing on military history, was of no interest to him, but he looked forward to the physical competitiveness of the weekly drill sessions in the Armory, the marching in sync, the crisp pivoting, the precise shouldering and lowering of arms, the smooth sliding of the bolt for inspection. The PE class, conducted on the 9-hole golf course south of Husky Stadium and covering the fundamentals of the swing, various types of shots, putting, and USGA rules, was joy. Even though he sliced an occasional drive or chunked a fairway shot, he was developing a feel for the game and deriving immense satisfaction when he made clean contact, his hopes for playing with Solveig next summer soaring with the flight of the ball. When he had a break between classes, he would go to the Husky Union Building to drink coffee and study. He seldom encountered any of his EHS classmates who lived on campus—waving once in the Quad to Roger Van Dyke and once on the steps of Denny Hall to Sylvia—but occasionally would find at the HUB another commuting high school classmate, Bobby Moore or Annette Bergstrom or Mick Younger, and sit down to smoke a proffered Winston, or a Marlboro from a flip-top box, and audit their complaints about commutes and classes. He ate the sack lunches that his mother made for him—a tuna sandwich, an apple, a banana, three chocolate chip cookies—in the Suzallo Library while reading back issues of the *Saturday Review of Literature*, which he had happened upon one day as he browsed in the Periodical Room and which introduced him to a fascinating array of critical voices and approaches, models whose thinking he began to appropriate and imitate.

In mid-October, Solveig wrote to him on Alpha Phi stationery. "Wayne, dear. I've been so busy. The parties here are amazing! There's just so much playing and studying to do! I see Monk at a party now and then. He's always a mass of bruises from playing football. I hope your classes are going well. I was sorry to hear about the astronomy. I can't empathize with the difficulty you're having in labs, because I'm not taking any science courses right now (although I'll have to sooner or later, and astronomy seems like a good option, given that the Russians have launched Sputnik and it looks like we're going to be in a race for space) but I can and do sympathize. Beuchel may be right about money. When I told Simon Weiner about that, he pointed out that not only money but our whole social contract and all of our personal relationships depend on trust, faith, belief. They're all a kind of fiction. Remember Hamlet: 'Nothing is either good or bad but thinking makes it so.' As long as we agree that the numbers have meaning, or that we share basic values, or that you are who you purport to be, all is well. But when we begin to doubt, things fall apart. Simon is struggling right now with trust in his wife. They have been married for seven years and have two young kids. It's not that she has been unfaithful but that she purported to be interested in his career and in the academic world. She was going to go on to get a PhD in history, and now she seems indifferent to that. She seems satisfied to be a mother and housewife. Simon says he is struggling with his authenticity. He has experienced the dread, the nausea. What does he truly want to do? What kind of life does he truly want to lead? Whom does he truly want to be with? He talks a lot about Sartre, whom we've just finished reading, and says that because humans have free will they are condemned to choose, to create themselves perpetually. But if we have free will, how can we be forced to choose? Is that a valid paradox? Anyway, I really liked the title of your paper on Graham Greene, and your French prof is correct: you *should* be majoring in French, you have a great ear for it, and it would open up many doors for you besides teaching. I'm glad you're enjoying the golf. I am, too, actually. Although I can't seem to develop much of a backswing, I'm getting pretty good at putting. It would be fun to play a round (pun intended) with you! Love you, Solveig."

The old man replied. "Dear Solveig. I've been busy, too. Besides studying, I spend a couple of hours every day in the library reading periodicals and sort of teaching myself literary criticism. I work Saturdays at Safeway, of course, for my spending money. I started playing Wednesday nights in the District 15 recreational basketball league with guys like Jimmie and Jerry Johnson . My game is coming along. I'm taking more shots, driving to the hoop more. I'm gaining confidence. I hit for 20 points last week—I almost think of myself as a scorer, a go-to guy, now! Went to the Princess to see *Designing Women* last Friday night with Mick and Annette. I thought it was pretty good. The way the protagonists, Gregory Peck and Lauren Bacall, were able to work out their differences seemed pretty believable to me. Mick had a six-pack of Oly in his car, so we all drove down to the beach and tucked ourselves into those rocks where you and I like to 'sconce' ourselves to drink it. I could barely even finish one—too bitter! I think Mick and Annette are about to become a couple—they seemed pretty cozy there in the rocks! My classes are fine. I've resigned myself to a C in Astronomy, but I'm pretty sure I'm going to get A's in all the others. Sounds like your French lit prof is really opening up to you. You're on a first-name basis with him now? You have a lot of conferences with him? How did you come out on your Céline paper? I miss you. Can't wait to see you, hold you, at Thanksgiving. I love you. Wayne."

"Hi, Wayne. Wow, I never thought Mick and Annette would be a couple, even though they were in the choir together at EHS and were in a skit at Vodvil. I'm so glad to hear that you're becoming a scorer—I know how important that is to you. I saw *Designing Women* with some of the girls, too, but I wasn't quite convinced that a woman of her taste and sophistication could settle down with a sportswriter. There's plenty of beer available here at the Greek keg parties, believe me, but I don't care much for it either. I prefer Lancer's Rosé, which is also always available along with Thunderbird and Ripple. I've been known to get a little tipsy on Lancer's! Simon Weiner has talked about the subtleties of the burgundies and bordeauxs he gets at the local liquor store. I'd like to try some of those one day. Weiner loved my paper on Céline. He had never read *Laughing Boy*, but he's aware of the concept of *hozoji*, of the beauty of living in harmony with the whole, and he says I did a good job with the contrast and he liked the way that I could empathize with the Navajos and yet provide a sympathetic analysis of Bardamu's angst. I drop in to see him in his office now and then just because he's such a fascinating guy to talk to. He's 35. He's Jewish, but an atheist. He seems so open and vulnerable, and he knows so much about France. He spent a year there, backpacking, riding the trains, staying in student hostels, before he started graduate school at Yale. I think you'd like him. He's kind and gentle, like you. He's very much an existentialist. He fears getting his identity from others, and you're like him in that way. You resist religion, too. My Lutheranism may be fading, and I'm certainly no evangelist, but I believe in wholeness and oneness and the immortality of the soul. We live in beauty, I believe, and I try to live in harmony, in tune, with that. I want to greet each day awe-inspired, open to new experience. Weiner says he must resist the world, face up to himself and to the dread of being responsible for everything he does. To do otherwise is to live in bad faith. From this there is no exit. You're like that with the way you constantly schedule yourself and challenge yourself. You're a perfectionist. I am more accepting of what is, of adapting to, of enjoying, of exploiting (in a good way!) life. I'm more exuberant. Must go now, Wayne. Dinner time at Alpha Phi. Thanks for writing. See you at Thanksgiving. Love, Solveig."

"Dear Solveig. You know, you may be right about my being an existentialist. During my library time I've been reading up on Sartre as well, and I definitely do believe that existence precedes essence. Now that I think about it, it has always struck me that life is absurd, and I agree that we are condemned—by ourselves, absurdly enough—to find a way to believe and act as though it were not. I've always felt that we are responsible for creating ourselves. We are free. It is up to us to decide what to make of our memories, our experiences, our inherited traits. Ironically, though, you are freer than I am. I am controlled by my resistance to being controlled. You bounce off limits with a smile on your face. I need to shape events. You are free to accept them as they happen. I am an inward person, yet other-dependent. I am validated only when others recognize me. You are an outward person, yet independent. At ease in exploring the web of your reality, you nonchalantly validate yourself. God,

I miss you! There's so much to talk about at Thanksgiving. We need to find a time and place where we can be totally alone, for so many reasons! I love you. Wayne."

"Wayne, here's a plan. I'm cutting classes and leaving for Edmonds on Wednesday morning. My parents will be closing the shop early because of Thanksgiving, so we can't meet at my house. Let's meet at the Edmonds beach at 4:30. I'll be coming straight from Walla Walla. Sound okay? Solveig."

"Sounds great! Can't wait!"

On Wednesday, heart racing with hope, muscles aching with dread, the old man drove to the U in rain, knowing that rain at sea level meant snow at Snoqualmie Pass and worried that the accumulation might be enough to delay Solveig. Kjell had placed a box containing a pair of new chains in the trunk of her Bel Air before she left for Whitman, but did she even know how to put them on? The rain soaked his bare head, his car coat (his notebook tucked inside it and pinned against his sweater by his left elbow), his jeans, and his desert boots as he hurried up the hill to Denny Hall.

Shrugging out of his dripping coat as he entered the classroom—Madame Simpson required all to be seated and silent with notebooks open even before the bell rang—and obeying Madame's blackboard direction, he wrote five original sentences using *le subjonctif présent*, having read the assigned chapter at home the night before.

"*Il faut qu'il sois patient,*" "*Il espère qu'elle tienne sa promesse,*" "*Il lui offre un cadeau pour qu'elle sois heureuse,*" "*Il a peur qu'elle ne l'aime pas,*" "*Il faut que nous choisissons.*"

Madame requested each student to read two sentences aloud.

At his turn the old man struggled for breath.

"*Monsieur Adams, je vous attend!*" Madame said.

"*Il faut qu'IL sois PAtient,*" the old man read. "*Il FAUT que nous choiSISSons.*"

"*Et un autre sans 'il faut'?*"

"*Il a peur qu'elle ne l'AIME pas.*"

"*Merci, Monsieur* Adams!"

At the end of the period, he decided that he was done for the day. If Solveig could cut classes, he could too. He went to the HUB cafeteria, drew a mug of coffee from a vat, tonged a maple bar onto a plate, paid for them, and joined Mick and Annette at their table.

"Solveig coming home for Thanksgiving?" blonde Annette asked, exhaling smoke from nostrils and mouth.

"Yeah. I'm seeing her tonight."

"Nice!" Mick said. "Cigarette?"

"Sure. I'll buy a pack next week and pay you back."

"Don't worry about it. You and Solveig getting together for dinner tomorrow?"

"No, she'll be with her family and I'll be with my parents and grandparents and aunt and uncle. But we'll have all day together on Friday for Christmas shopping and lunch and what not, and Saturday my mom's going to invite her for dinner. You guys?"

"We'll get together on the weekend. We're not ready to mingle with each other's families quite yet."

It was too early to go home. The rain had stopped. Maybe the Pass wouldn't be so bad? He descended the hill to the parking lot and drove west on 45th to Highway 99, then north to the Peutz Golf Driving Range. He borrowed a house driver and hit a large bucket, the balls splashing into puddles a couple of hundred yards from the tee. He was not a long hitter but, with the instruction and practice he got in class, he was gradually becoming more consistent, eliminating upper body tension, shortening his backswing, finding a workable tempo and rhythm that allowed him to keep his head still and swing smoothly around his spine, meeting the ball with club face relatively square. His hip turn was too cautious to produce power, but his beginner's banana slice was gone. He found joy in arcing ball after ball, imagining the looks of pleased surprise on the faces of Kjell and Leona and Solveig at EG&C on a sunny Sunday next summer.

Home alone, his mother working a busy pre-holiday shift at

Safeway and his father on showroom duty at Hopper's, he passed the afternoon distractedly reading "The Dead" for his English class, Solveig fantasies frequently forcing him to double back and review a paragraph. Solveig in her Bel Air, hands viced to the steering wheel at ten and two, intently plowing through mountain slush that scraped against the undercarriage, tensely entering the curves that traced the way through the silvery forest, to get to Edmonds, to get to him, Solveig pulling up to the beach, discarding her navy blue coat, her navy blue scarf, running to his Ford through a fury of wind, shoving the passenger backrest forward, giggling, jumping into the back, pulling her black ski sweater with its embossed flurry of snowflakes over her head, her silky hair, her henna hair, her chestnut hair loosening from its combs, tresses confessing, as he climbed over his seat to embrace her, look into her ice blue eyes, unhook her bra, meet her fierce kiss with his own, their mouths each seeking to inhale the other, then drop down to suck her nipples erect in the cold.

At 4:00 he slipped on his coat and went to his car, which he always parked in the vacant lot behind the *Tribune* building. In the glove compartment were a half-dozen condoms which had been resting there for more than two months and a slender white box holding a sterling silver chain bracelet, which he had purchased for $25 at Bly's Jewelry on Main.

He drove down Dayton, crossed the tracks, and parked on the gravelly clay a few yards before sand began. There were no other cars, no other people, in sight. They were gathering at home, laying fires, watching the news, women were stuffing turkeys with stale bread, preparing light meals, Campbell's soup, canned peaches, cottage cheese, sliced tomatoes, everyone saving room for tomorrow's feast. The drab day had lost almost all of what little light it had been able to offer. There was no hint of a sunset, not even an amber tinge in the clouds that comprised the horizon. It began to drizzle. Sporadic gusts of wind rocked the car.

He was alone in pitch darkness at 4:45 when Solveig's headlights washed over him. She parked a few discrete yards away, came to his car in her navy coat and scarf, and settled into the passenger seat next to the door.

"Hi, Wayne!"

"Solveig! You made it!"

"I did!"

"How was the pass? Was it terrible? Was it icy?"

"Actually, it wasn't bad. It had stopped snowing about an hour before I got to Snoqualmie, and then the snowplows had gone through before me, so I just had to pay attention and drive at a sensible pace. It wasn't quite a routine trip, but it wasn't an odyssey, either. I'd have been pretty much on time if I hadn't stopped at the bakery in North Bend to reward myself with a cup of coffee and a jelly doughnut!"

He slid over to her side and wrapped his arms around her. She giggled. He kissed her, mouth closing over her closed lips. He ran a hand across her coat-protected breasts. She gripped it.

"Wayne, let's talk."

"Okay, but before we do, let me give you something."

He opened the glove compartment to reveal the necklace box and the condom he had placed conspicuously beside it.

"No, first let's talk."

"OoKAY, what aBOUT?"

"About you and me."

"U-Us?"

"No, you and me. Wayne, you were the first love of my life, and you are very dear to me. I will always care about you. But things change, relationships metamorphose. Edmonds is nice but there's just so much more world out there. I feel like I can be at home, as long as there are people around, pretty much anywhere. I don't want to be tied down right now. I want to explore, seek new experiences, new relationships."

"AaRE you seeing WEIner?"

"No, not really. We've taken a couple of drives through the

wheat fields to get away from town and talk."

"And mAKE love?"

"No. We just parked and kissed and he held me a little bit. Simon wants me, but I don't really want him. I was flattered by his attention at first, and I like him as a teacher, but I don't feel the connection that you and I had. He's almost twice my age! He thinks he's being authentic in pursuing me, but I think the nausea he's been experiencing is not so much existential as it is just temporary lovesickness. And I certainly don't want to break up a home. I'm going to end it with him, too, as soon as I get back to Whitman."

"So we're ENDed?"

"Oh, Wayne, I'm so sorry, but I'm sure this is best for both of us." She kissed him quickly on the cheek. "*Mes parents m'attend à la maison. Il faut que j'y aille maintenant. Au revoir, mon cher ami. Vous etes très précieux.*"

She stepped out of the Ford, into the rain falling faintly, and in faintly falling rain she walked away. In beauty. It was finished.

[*Merci, mon ami*. I love what you have done with me and with our teenage romance, skewing an ordinary small-town girl as Cleopatra, part Siren, part Jezebel, and the two of us as vanada/adavan/navada/davana, obsessively book-loving young lovers. Revisionist history at its fictional best! Although I certainly had Kim Novak and William Holden in mind at the Canteen—and possibly Dickie did too—we didn't even come close to emulating them. We just did our teenage version of the foxtrot that we were taught in eighth-grade gym class. It's true that you and I practiced our French together, but I recall reading only three other books that summer. Your hand, not mine, was the first to drop below the belt (although I did not demur!), and I was fully dressed when you arrived for our test-prep session, which began promptly after my welcoming hug and kiss. Oral sex was not on our agenda, not even as an *amuse bouche*, then or ever. At drive-ins we did revert to the back seat and bring ourselves to a boil under the cover of a blanket, but by mutual agreement we never risked intercourse. While you snapped to attention, Bobby's purloined condoms remained at parade rest in the glove box. The Martha Lake experience in the shroud of the weeping willows was real but happened only once. Exploring the shoreline as our friends packed up and headed home, we serendipitously found an affordance, but neither of us ever suggested wandering that way again! So were the quickies—for you. You would go off within a minute. I needed more time than was available before you had to clock back in at Hopper's. I had two conferences, and no car rides, with Simon Weiner. I did not betray you. I just dared more real world than you did. Solveig]

C

"Mom, Dad, this is Wayne."

"Hi," hi," "hi," "hi," the three said, smiling and shaking hands.

They were at the Baker house on 45th, a charcoal gray, cedar-sided bungalow with a five-step porch, a westward-facing deck, and a basement. Diane hung the old man's tan, belted raincoat and her black car coat in the guest closet. Her petite mother, Evelyn, wore a green and pink floral print dress, hosiery, and two-inch heels. Her shoulder-length brown hair, turning inward at the bottom like Rosemary Clooney's, had spent some time in rollers. Her deep brown eyes were the prototype of Diane's. Her crew-cut husband, Chet, a six-footer, wore a white Arrow shirt with an open wing collar, a gray and white sleeveless argyle sweater, black wool slacks, and black wingtip shoes. The old man wore tan pleated cotton pants, a dark brown crewneck sweater with a checked button-down shirt underneath, and desert boots.

"Sit down, Wayne, dinner's almost ready," Evelyn said.

He crossed the chocolate-and-beige braided area rug that covered part of the oak floor and sat on the Danish modern couch—dark walnut arms, blue fabric cushions—with Diane, who was wearing a mock-ribbed white twisted tweed "poor boy" sweater, low cut black hipster pants, and black rounded-toe low-heeled shoes.

"So you're an English teacher," Chet said. "I imagine when people hear that they say 'Uh-oh, better watch my grammar'?"

"You are so right," the old man said. "People seem to remember mostly bad experiences in English class—rote memorization of grammar 'rules,' essays returned riddled by a red pen."

"But your classes aren't like that?"

"No, they aren't," Diane said. "Wayne teaches students to be creative and to think incisively."

"Try to, anyway. I like teaching close reading of texts. The interanimation of words. But it doesn't always go the way I want it to. One day I'm Mr. Chips, the next I'm Mr. Peepers. I'm still refining my approach."

"Me, too," said Diane. "But that ITIP class has helped a lot. I'm much better organized now. When the girls come into the locker room to change they check the chalkboard to see what the activity is going to be and who's assigned to get out the equipment, what the day's warm up exercises are and who leads them. After warm ups I'll give some instruction—in basketball, for example, it might be dribbling or pivoting or shooting form—we'll drill for a bit, guided practice, then we'll form teams and play games for half an hour, with me supervising and commenting occasionally. Most girls are okay with P.E. but even the ones who hate it kind of grudgingly accept its value when you keep reminding them of what they can get out of it, what I've taught them to call the five Cs: conditioning, calorie-burning, coordination, competence, and competition. Daddy, have you got some wine for us?"

"Of course. I've got an Inglenook Cask cabernet from one of our trips to Napa Valley. It should be ready. I've had it breathing."

He went to a teak sideboard-hutch in the dining room, where the teak table had already been set, extracted four bulbous burgundy glasses, and poured.

The old man held his glass by its base and swirled the wine, as Diane had taught him to do. Chet smiled. They all nosed in to their glasses, sniffed sharply, contemplated, then took a sip and sucked air over the wine before swallowing it. They furrowed brows while recontemplating.

"Mmm," the old man said. "Good."

"Mint? Tea?" Chet said.

"It's certainly not jammy or plummy," Evelyn said.

"What do you think, Wayne?" Diane asked.

The old man reflected. "Green olive?"

"Yes!" Evelyn said. "I get that."

"I do, too," Chet said.

"So let's eat," Evelyn said. "Diane, help me get things to the table."

They grabbed pot-holders and set out a leg of lamb dotted with chunks of garlic and needles of rosemary tucked into little knife cuts, sautéed red potatoes sprinkled with thyme, crisp slim asparagus spears topped with melted butter and freshly grated Parmesan cheese, and a salad of mixed greens tossed in lemon-scented olive oil.

"Smells wonderful," the old man said. He had never eaten any of those items before. Usually he went out for a pepperoni pizza or a cheeseburger, fries, and chocolate shake. If he ate in, he would open a can of chili and make a tuna sandwich or fry four bacon slices to a crisp, set them aside, fry three eggs sunnyside up in the grease, and lay out two slices of Wonder bread to swab the runny yolk remains with after downing the bacon and eggs. His mother used to cook a pot roast for Sunday dinner or bake a piece of salmon and serve it with lemon wedges, but during the week they ate waffles, or hamburger steak with baked potatoes, or chipped beef on toast with Cedargreen frozen peas, accompanied by a salad of cottage cheese and canned peaches or pears dashed with paprika for flair.

Chet sat at one end of the rectangular table and used a long carving knife to lay out clean overlapping slices of lamb alongside the roast.

They filled their plates. But what was this? Evelyn and Chet extending hands from left and right? He and Diane grasped them, completing the circle. He bowed his head in imitation of the others.

"Dear heavenly Father," Chet said. Dread descended upon the old man. What was he getting himself into? In the old man's experience, no one—not his parents, not his friends' parents, not even his grandparents—had ever prayed aloud before a meal. Aside from his prayer for forgiveness at the Billy Graham Crusade, the old man had beseeched God only three times, each in desperate silence. The first occurred when he was seven and arrived home after attending a Seattle Rainier baseball game with his Aunt Mabel and Uncle Ned, to discover that he had left behind the mitt that he had carried along in hope of catching a foul ball. He prayed to get it back but his mother's phone call to the stadium's lost and found office was fruitless. In recompense, his father drove him the next Saturday to Warshal's Sporting Goods in Seattle and paid for a new Rawlings—an upgrade that was a perfect answer to his prayer. The second occurred when he was eight and his mother lay in bed in the house at 10th and Maple, writhing in stomach pain. He prayed that she wouldn't die, and she didn't. His father phoned Dr. Hope, wondering if he could make a house call. Dr. Hope came, diagnosed the problem, and instructed the old man's father to drive her to Everett General Hospital, where her appendix was removed. The third occurred on a cold Saturday morning in November when he was nine. Zee was away with his family and Monk had chores to do, so the old man wandered down to the high school field to fantasize about playing there one day and to rummage through the grandstand, still littered with confetti and purple and gold crepe paper from the previous night's game, in search of dropped coins or other treasure. As he entered the grounds from the 6th Avenue side, he encountered three cigarette-smoking 15-year-olds cutting through the field on their way to see if there was any action at the beach. He prayed that they wouldn't kill him, and they didn't—they merely pointed their cigarettes and made vague gestures at him, laughing as they passed by.

"We are so happy and grateful to be wrapped in Your loving arms," Chet said. "We thank you for saving our souls. We pray that we may read the signs and follow your guidance every day. We pray for those who are less fortunate than we. We recognize that we are so very blessed materially and spiritually. We pray for the safety of our Marines in Viet Nam. We pray for an improvement in race relations in our country. We ask that You bless our time together this evening and that You bless this food to our bodies' needs. In Jesus' name we pray"—and here all, even the old man, who was shocked to find his lips moving, said "Amen."

Though unnerved by the rite itself, the old man found the words of the prayer unobjectionable. But he was, as always, puzzled by what factors might determine whether God would bestow His grace. Was praying for others actually praying for oneself? Was it, disguised in nudging and wheedling, an arrogant attempt to usurp divine power? How did prayer relate to God's plan? And he wondered about the mechanics of any such bestowal. He was not comforted by the notion that God works in mysterious ways. God could, conceivably, bring manna from heaven, a Berlin airlift without the planes, or multiply an existing supply of loaves and fishes. These would be material transactions that transcended but did not overturn the laws of physics, well within the power of One who could create an entire material universe. But how did God enter the minds and hearts of humans to effect change, hardening some, softening others? What transactive mechanism could possibly be involved? God could conceivably save the lives of Marines and make it possible for them to succeed in their missions by altering the trajectories of the bullets and other explosives employed against them, but how could He effect an improvement in race relations? How could He affect emotion or perception? Could he telepathically and painlessly, unbeknown to the recipients, modify cell structure and neural connections? How could He bless an evening? Could He telepathically release serotonins and endorphins, drugging people to feel good about the way they were spending their time? How could He bless food to bodies' needs? Wouldn't that happen automatically, autonomically, anyway? Or could He augment the digestive process telepathically by formulaically adding or subtracting enzymes, the way iron tablets were best absorbed when taken with Vitamin C?

"So, Wayne, what led you to become a teacher?" Chet asked as they began to eat.

"Probably the example of Jack Foster at Edmonds High. He's a Harvard graduate who always dresses Ivy League style with button-down shirts, bow ties that he knots himself, and slacks with the belt buckle in the back. He was the first intellectual I ever met. Many of my other teachers were intelligent and knowledgeable about their subjects, but he was the only one who attempted to introduce his students to the life of the mind. In his class, which was a mixture of comparative religion and cultural anthropology, he showed us how to ask questions and how to test the validity of the answers. He taught us always to look behind the mask or the veil."

"Did you study Christianity in that class, Wayne?" said Evelyn. "Christianity looks behind the veil, too, you know."

"Yes, it does," the old man said. "Actually, all religions do. We read *The Great Religions By Which Men Live* in that class, covering Hinduism, Buddhism, Judaism, Christianity, Islam, Taoism, and Shintoism. I found the book interesting, and the reason for that I realize now is that it was slanted in favor of an intellectual approach to each religion. In Hinduism, for example, seeking enlightenment—the unification of Atman with Brahman—through meditation rather than through ritual. Or in Buddhism, preferring Hinayana, the smaller vehicle, which sees Buddha as a man, to Mahayana, the larger vehicle, which sees Buddha as a god. Considering nirvana to be a state of mind, a freeing of the soul from the bonds of earthly illusion, rather than a literal place."

"So, more philosophy and less religion?" Chet asked. "What do you think the authors of the book would make of the Hare Krishnas popping up all over Seattle these days in their robes, chanting, dancing, shaking tambourines? Evelyn and I encountered a group of them last week when we went down to the Pike Place Market to pick up some fresh sockeye and a bouquet of chrysanthemums."

"I'm guessing they'd be condescending," Diane said. "They'd praise the enthusiasm and energy but hint that such an emotional approach is quite shallow. They would imply it's an undemanding way to try to harmonize the self with Krishna and achieve Krishna consciousness."

"That sounds about right," the old man said. "They would slight the emotional approach and extol the philosophical."

"You know, Wayne," Evelyn said. "The *Book of Romans* is very philosophical. It's a deep text that practically begs for a close reading. Next month Chet and I are inviting friends for a weekly study of it to be led by a math professor from Seattle Pacific College. We'd love to have you and Diane join us."

"That's a possibility," the old man said. Was his wince visible? "I'll check my schedule."

"There's more wine," Chet said.

"And more lamb," Evelyn added.

"Don't leave me out on the wine," Diane said.

"And I'll take a bit more of each," the old man said. "Everything is really good. To tell the truth, I've never had lamb before. It's like roast beef with more flavor. Grainier, gamier. And"—lifting a leaf on his fork—"what's this aromatic thing in the salad? I really like it."

"That's rocket," Chet said. "We grow it in our backyard garden. Got the idea from *The Unprejudiced Palate*, a book by an English professor at the U named Angelo Pellegrini. You know him?"

"I know of him. But I've never had a class from him."

"He seems very wise. I like his thoughts on cooking and gardening. On teaching, too. 'A teacher affects eternity,' he says. "I guess you'd call him a humanist. I don't think he'd be sold on that ITIP program. Maybe a bit too mechanical for him. Isn't the original meaning of 'education' to 'lead out" or 'call forth' or something like that? Doesn't it imply that teachers have been specially called to light the way to understanding? Wisdom?"

"Well," said Diane, "Pellegrini's probably teaching only a couple of sections a day to about 20 goal-directed young adults who have been schooled in how to be students for at least a dozen years by some hard-working teachers. Let him go into a high school or junior high class of 35 and see how he does without some kind of mechanical or structural framework."

"Oh, I agree on the need for structure and discipline. Fundamentals, goal-setting, all of that. In English class, learning to write clear sentences and present logical arguments in organized essays. In P.E., developing specific skills. But somewhere along the way, in order for it to be truly meaningful, don't you have to touch the soul? Don't the students have to feel turned on? Having gotten their attention, how do you turn them on? How do Timothy Leary or Billy Graham or your man Jack Foster, Wayne, make it work? What is the source of their charisma? Isn't that the $64 question?"

"That *is* the $64 question. Diane and I have talked about that."

"Rhetoric!" Diane said.

"Yeah, I look at it in terms of rhetoric. The ITIP class helps to get you through the day. Sheer survival in the classroom is paramount. Having experienced a chaotic first year of teaching, I would never gainsay that. But to go beyond survival, you need to use all of your rhetorical resources, all of the means of persuasion that Aristotle identified as *logos*, the appeal to reason, *pathos*, the appeal to the emotions, and *ethos*, the appeal to the character or virtue, broadly interpreted, of the teacher."

"I try to appeal to reason by reminding my girls of the 5 C's," Diane said. "I appeal to emotion by giving a lot of positive feedback, praising them and cheering them on as they go through the drills or the games. And I try to be a model to follow by executing the skills gracefully, being enthusiastic, showing vitality, showing I care about them, getting them to care that I care, or on the other hand raising an eyebrow or frowning or staring into their eyes—to the point now that they're not using the excuse that they forgot their shorts or their gym shoes or they need to sit out because of menstrual cramps."

" And I try to win them over, persuade them in the broadest sense of that term, by challenging their critical faculties, responding warmly to their insights, paying judicious respect to comments that I think are off the mark, and by engaging them in various kinds of word play—tactical rhetorical devices within a broader rhetorical pedagogical strategy."

"For example?"

"For example, when the bell rings they know, Pavlovianly, to check the chalkboard for the opening exercise, which usually has to do with rhetoric, grammar, or usage. There'll be a definition and a model to imitate. Things that, in order to become a more perceptive reader or more effective writer, it's helpful to recognize and occasionally employ—balanced sentences, for example, or oxymorons—and things that should be avoided, at least according to the lexicologist Henry Fowler, whose traditional, prescriptive approach to usage I respect. Things like split infinitives and dangling modifiers. While I take roll and kid around with them a little bit, they're writing their imitations. Then I take a couple of minutes to discuss the virtues or vices of the matter in question and call on some to read their creation to the class. 'I think I'll go east of the mountains,' spoke Ann,' somebody came up with for a Tom Swifty, and for ambiguous language illustrated in the form of a bar joke, somebody wrote 'An ambiguity with an urgent need walks into a bar and promptly goes to the bathroom in the hallway.'"

Evelyn laughed. "Sounds like fun! I think I'd be persuaded to get involved in a class like that."

"And then you go on to the lesson or topic for the day?" Chet asked.

"Right. These little attention-getters are a mini-lesson in stuff that I think is worth knowing, but the day's main objective is also written on the board. At first I thought that kind of thing was so corny and so limiting—'Objective: To understand how 'Jabberwocky' conveys meaning through seemingly meaningless language'—but now I see that it really does clarify for students what you're doing and sell them—I used to despise that commercial kind of language, but now I use it unashamedly—on its value. Kids used to wander into class and say 'What are we going to do today?' Now they have an idea from the outset. None of this is a panacea, but the distractions are definitely fewer and the tone of the whole operation feels better."

"So then you and the class would read and analyze the poem?"

"Yeah, I'd hand out dittoed copies and read the poem out loud, talk a little about portmanteaus, and then begin a line-by-line exploration of the text, keeping the kids involved by calling on various ones to provide their interpretations as we go along, helping to make connections between their comments and summarizing from time to time. We're doing a much better job of staying on task."

"That's enough shop talk," Diane said, grabbing plates. "Mom, let's clear the table."

"You two feel like playing some poker?" Chet asked. "It's kind of our favorite game."

The old man looked at Diane, who nodded yes. "Okay," he said. He played occasionally in games hosted by male faculty members, imagining himself to be Maverick or the Cincinnati Kid as he had once imagined being Roy Tucker, enjoying the jokes, the beer, and the snacks laid out on countertops, on average losing a little more than he won, betting when he had a strong hand, too often staying one card longer than he should have when he had a weak hand, seldom bluffing, seldom able to read a bluff.

Diane covered the teak with a plain white cloth, clean though stained at places by coffee and chocolate from previous games that Chet and Evelyn had played with friends. Chet produced a worn deck of Bicycle cards that were bent in the middle from much previous shuffling and doled out to each a dollar's worth of chips denominated as penny-nickel-dime. The old man leaned forward, wiggled his wallet out of his back pocket, and extracted a dollar bill, Diane plucked one from her pocketbook on the sideboard, and Evelyn brought two from the master bedroom. Diane won the cut for deal and shuffled five times, each a crisp, tight rippling, flared them high with an underhand motion, a school of fish leaping, and let them drop to the table in a controlled splash, a pretty performance.

"Five card stud," she said. "Three raise limit. Joker's good with aces, straights, and flushes."

With an ace showing and another in the hole, his pulse accelerating, the old man bet a penny. Chet, with a jack, and Evelyn, with a deuce, called.

Diane turned over her five and said, "I'm out. A penny saved is a penny earned."

She dealt Evelyn a king, the old man a four, and Chet a nine. The old man bet another penny, Chet called, and Evelyn said, "I'll raise it one."

"What are you so proud of, Mom?" said Diane. Was she giving the old man a tip?

"They'll have to pay to find out."

"I'll call," the old man said.

"I'm in," Chet said.

Diane dealt Evelyn a nine, the old man a king, Chet a queen.

The old man looked at Evelyn, who widened her eyes and smiled at him. He looked at Chet, who studied him impassively. The old man looked at his hole card again, trying to fake a tell.

"I'll check to the raise," he said.

"Check," Chet said.

"Three cents," said Evelyn exuberantly.

"No prohibition on check-raises?" the old man asked.

Chet continued to stare at him. "No, I guess we forgot to establish that."

"Then let's make it a nickel," the old man said.

Chet held off for a moment, then set a red chip in the center of the pot.

"I call," said Evelyn.

"Last card," Diane said, and dealt Evelyn a ten, the old man a nine, Chet the joker.

"Bet you don't check this time," Evelyn said.

"No," the old man said with a smile. Evelyn no doubt had her kings. Could Chet have that straight? "Let's make it a dime."

"And up a dime," Chet said quickly. Too quickly. Too aggressively. An intimidator's bluff.

"Too rich for my blood," Evelyn said.

The old man hesitated, looked at Diane pursing her lips tensely, then said "I raise it another dime."

"And up one more," Chet said, "for the final raise."

He isn't Lancy, the old man thought. He doesn't have it. "Call. Aces. You have the straight?"

Chet nodded, shrugged, and turned over an eight. "I got lucky," he said, sweeping in the chips.

"Wow!" Diane said. "What a start. That was intense. What are you going to play, Mom? No peek?"

"You guessed her, Chester—pun intended. Let's just relax after that last hand."

Evelyn dealt round seven cards, face down, to each player. The old man's head pounded. He had been conned, in front of his girl friend, at the hand of his girl friend's father, by a bluffed bluff. The patriarchy was secure. For the next two hours he tried to fight back, immediately dropping out if he had nothing, uncharacteristically bluffing if he showed something that could possibly be construed as strength, winning a few hands but losing many more than that, sipping coffee and commending Evelyn on her rich raspberry cheesecake. Chet had stacks of chips in front of him—over two dollars in all. Diane and Evelyn had less. A single blue chip lay before the old man.

"Well, time to go," said Diane as Chet paid her a rounded-off 75 cents, Evelyn 50 cents, and the old man a dime.

"This has been fun," the old man said, shaking hands. "A wonderful dinner. So nice to meet you. Thank you so much for inviting me."

"Thanks for coming," Chet said.

"It's been a pleasure for us, too," Evelyn said.

Diane kissed each parent on the cheek. "Bye, Mom, bye Dad."

Rather than go straight to Diane's apartment, which she shared with her friend Louise, they drove through steady rain to the old man's place. It was understood that they would have sex.

"I had a good time tonight," the old man said. "The wine, the food, the conversation, the game. I like your parents."

"They like you, too."

"But...."

"Well, yeah."

They excitedly undressed each other in his bedroom and flung back the bed covers. Diane reveled in touching and being touched, in having her surfaces stimulated by his manual and lingual manipulations till she climaxed, but she would not allow him to ejaculate inside her. Brief penetration was permitted, semission was not. Once inside her vagina he had to extract himself in time for her to squeeze him off with a washcloth while both shook with laughter at the absurdity of his gland finale.

[Diane actually let you enter her? That doesn't sound like my sister! Linda]

"I don't want to get pregnant," she had said on their fifth date, when both were letting their hands roam all over each other.

"What about the Pill?"

"I don't think it's safe yet. They say it can cause blood clots and breast cancer."

"What if I used a condom?"

She sighed. "Wayne, I just think it's wrong to have intercourse before marriage. It might be a technicality, but I don't think God would approve."

He sighed in turn and removed his hands from her body.

"But that doesn't mean we can't do other stuff," she said. "God wants us to enjoy our bodies and get closer to each other."

After half an hour in bed, he drove Diane, windshield wipers flapping at high speed, to her apartment. At the door he said, "You know, I was kind of taken aback when your dad said grace before dinner." Rainwater was tinkling through the aluminum downspout that drained the overhang protecting the entry and gurgling into a flowerbed.

"I sort of sensed that. When we joined hands you maintained the lightest touch possible. I felt like I had to squeeze a bit to keep you from slipping away."

"Yeah, I've never been part of saying grace before. To me it just seemed unnatural, odd."

"To me it just seems natural, normal."

"And will you pray tonight?"

"Of course. I need to feel right with God before I sleep."

"Do you actually go down on your knees at the side of the bed?"

"I actually do, yes," she smiled.

"And pray out loud?"

"Sure. In 'Thessalonians' Paul says to 'pray without ceasing' but I confess that I haven't been able to accomplish that. So I do the best I can to stay prayed up by saying many short silent prayers during the day and always praying aloud in the morning when I get up and again at bedtime."

"Fascinating."

"Is it really? It fascinates me that you don't. Communicating with God is paramount to me."

"But how does it work? There are different types of prayers, right? Expressions of adoration and thanksgiving, requests for forgiveness, and petitions for help? Most are mixtures of these elements, but generally the emphasis is on petitions for help. Would you agree with that?"

"Let's put it like this: petitions for help are probably the most frequent, but expressions of adoration and thanksgiving and requests for forgiveness are the most important. It's about first establishing a relationship with God and then admitting your human weakness, your need for help or guidance, and trusting in Him to provide it. Let go, and let God. You talk so much about rhetoric—it's your passion. Well, isn't prayer a perfect example of rhetoric? Using *logos*, *pathos*, and *ethos* to present your heart's desires, to persuade Him, if that be His will, to accept your point of view?"

"But what determines what God will do? Take a zero-sum situation in which two people are praying for opposite results. A gardener's praying for rain and a baseball player is praying for sunshine. Or one person is praying for team A to win its game against team B while the other prays for B to defeat A. Or both are praying to get the same job or promotion. How does God decide which to favor? Or how, in situations that are not zero-sum, as for example when one prays for the survival of a cancer-stricken friend, or when one prays for the success of a relationship, does God decide whether or not to honor the request? Does the relative strength of one's faith in and love of God matter? Is the more fervent believer more likely to be rewarded more often? Does seniority matter? Is the long-term believer, having stood the test of time, more likely to be rewarded than the new believer? Or is the new believer more likely to be rewarded as an incentive to continue with regular prayer? Does frequency matter? Can one's prayer be rejected because one is too needy or too greedy and asks too often? Or, on the other hand, does the squeaky wheel get the most grease? Does the relative 'goodness' of the believer matter? Is the believer who has a heart full of love for humanity and a high ratio of good deeds to sinful ones more likely to be rewarded? Does the extent of the 'miracle-working' manipulation of the laws of nature that would be required to answer the prayer matter? That is, is it more difficult for God to make the sun stand still or to part the Red Sea than to bring in a few clouds for rain or whisk them away for sunshine? Or are all actions equally easily doable for an omnipotent God? Or does it depend on the absolute need of the believer for the prayer to be answered? That is, does the believer sometimes think that the prayer needs to be answered when, seen from God's omniscient viewpoint, it actually does not, either because some other positive development is going to supersede it or because granting it would cause unfair harm to others? Does God have a formula that enables Him to weigh the various positive and negative factors relevant to any given prayer to determine whether or not He bestows His grace? Physicists have shown that mathematics underlies the universe. Is that also true for the 'laws' of prayer?"

"The answer to all your questions is 'I don't know.' You've obviously given this a lot of thought. Way too much thought, I'd say. I'm kind of skeptical of so much skepticism. Is it possible you just have a problem with subordination? God's ways are inscrutable. Wisdom is the fear of God. And faith can move mountains. To me it's simple: I am, therefore I pray."

She smiled.

"Are you aware that you just stood Descartes on his head?"

"Actually, yes, I am. I took an Intro to Philosophy course at the U as one of my electives. But when it comes to wisdom, I get more out of *Bible* study. Which begs the question: shall we do 'Romans' with my parents and their group?"

He did not want to join any group of believers in anything. He did not want to be owned. "Yeah, let's do it," he said. "And thank you for a lovely evening—the dinner, the wine, the poker, the conversation. And the sex."

"Especially the sex," she said.

Both laughing, they couldn't avoid banging their teeth together as they kissed good night, he placing a hand on her breast, she playfully nudging his crotch with a knee.

"Hare Krishna," he said over his shoulder as he ran through the rain towards his car.

"Rama, Rama," she replied.

At home in bed, lying atop a drying trace of semen that had escaped the wash cloth, he re-read the last few pages of *Franny*, in which, over dinner, she tells Lane, her date, who is more interested in his entrée of frog legs than in the idea that is consuming her, that consistent repetition of the Jesus Prayer, even on the part of one without faith, releases a power that synchronizes the words with the prayer's heartbeats, resulting willy-nilly in praying without ceasing and producing ultimately a purified outlook, a new conception of life, and an ability to see God. Though the old man was fearful of expanded consciousness, whether mystically or psychedelically induced, he could not resist an experiment. Struggling for courage, his heart on the verge of fibrillating, he mouthed it three times silently then leaped aloud into "Lord Jesus Christ have mercy on me" at least a dozen more before stopping to evaluate the effect. Mercifully, there wasn't one. He could cling to his self-consciousness. He was intact, pure, uncompromised. No LSD, no LJC for him. Had he seen God, he would have come undone. But the soft, juicy sound of "mercy," its quality unstrained, lingered in his mind's ear. "Mercy." "*Merci.*" See here. He went to the living room, retrieved a Cannonball Adderley LP from the raw-cedar record cabinet he had picked up at Underhill's unfinished furniture store, opened the lid on his portable hi-fi, and dropped the needle on "Mercy, Mercy, Mercy." Bobbing his head, rocking his shoulders, he sang "DUH-duh-duh-duh-duh-duh-duh-duh-duh-DUH" on the repetitions of the chorus. He played the five-minute tune a second time, again vocalizing the rhythm, and on the third intoned "LORD Je-sus Christ please have mer-cy on ME-EE." He felt the tune viscerally, its strolling blues rhythm leading to the potent punctuation of the chorus. He could visualize the better dancers at the Canteen adapting their two-step to it, but in the few awkward shuffle steps he essayed he had no difficulty in knowing dancer from dance.

Back in bed, lights out, the chorus continued to reverberate in his brain. As his pulse gradually slowed, just before he slipped into sleep, it was possible, he thought, saying the prayer again, that brain and heart had synced. But they told him no tale.

[Wayne, no offense, now, but your insincerity, your lack of authenticity, your fear, your closed-offness, your hermeticality, ironically enough, prevented (and still prevent?) the occurrence of the spiritual alchemy typified by Hermes Trismegistus, or Hermes the cunning thief, or the Jesus Prayer. Dave]

[Dave's right, Wayne. You only pretended to let go. Sylvia]

["Mercifully, there wasn't one."? Rather a sloppy use of "mercifully" as a sentence modifier, given that you do not believe there can be such a thing as cosmic mercy. Solveig]

[Wayne, I trust that your account of how you employed ITIP's opening gambit of the Anticipatory Set is an intentional fiction, a bit of poetic license not to be taken literally, for the requisite truth is that the teaching of any particular rhetorical device like hyperbole or stylistic concern like ambiguity would take the better part of a class period and involve much explanation, discussion, guided practice, and feedback. You are just trying to indicate that (a) you found ITIP useful at times and (b) you covered a lot of rhetorical and grammatical terminology, right? Kind of a humble brag without the humble? ☺ Stu]

d

In the late summer of that year they lived in the house on Grandview that looked to the west past other cedar-sided ramblers toward a sliver of the Sound that was mostly hidden by the dense branches of the many firs and hemlocks. Diane was pregnant. They were crazy with excitement. "Isn't it splendid, darling, " she said, "my morning sickness? Such a blessing from God after three years of trying. Didn't we have a lovely time conceiving? Isn't it grand when I'm on top and you've wrapped your legs around me and I glide? Everything we do seems so simple and holy." She was seeing it all ahead, like the moves in a chess game. "Oh, darling, I will be good for you, won't I, because we're not going to have a strange life after all. We're going to have babies and I will quit teaching and be a stay-at-home mom until they start school. There isn't any me, darling. It's God and the baby and you and my parents and sister and our friends and your parents. I am one with the universe, darling, this lovely web of being that is suffused with the presence of God. I believe that all sorts of wonderful things will happen to us. To everything there is a season, and God has a grand plan. And today we will hoe the garden and stake the pea vines and pick cherry tomatoes and basil and nasturtium blossoms for salad for lunch, and after we will make love and I will nap and in the evening we will go to Ray's Boathouse in Ballard for the poached salmon with Bill and Charlene." And they had a fine time, asking the waiter if he had caught tonight's salmon from the Boathouse deck with rod and reel before it could swim through the Locks and thrash upstream to spawn, and laughing, whenever Diane suddenly flinched and gasped, about young Paul or Pauline practicing reverse pivots against the walls of her womb. "Oh, that was a big one, darling." The dill and capers on the salmon and the butter and oak in the chardonnay were lovely. When the waiter was clearing the table, Diane and Charlene walked to the bathroom and the old man and Bill went out on the deck to look at the sun, which was gold-vermilion in its dying. The girls finally came back. "Oh, darling, I'm sorry we took so long, but I've had some silly spotting." Everything turned over inside of him. "I've got it stopped now, though, darling. I won't be any more trouble. We'll go home and I'll put my feet up and rest, and in the morning I'll see Dr. Hope."

In the morning, things began to go badly. Dr. Hope assessed the spotting, which had continued, and monitored the faintness of the fetal heart tones and ordered Diane to stay in bed. And Chet and Evelyn came to visit and brought flaky Napoleons from Larsen's Bakery in Ballard and prayed with her. And Linda and her boyfriend Daniel came to visit and brought *Mere Christianity* by C.S. Lewis. And George and Margaret came to visit and brought Marian McPartland's "West Side Story" album. And the women from her golf group came to visit and brought her a dozen orange Titleists. "Oh, darling, I'm trying to be a good girl. It's so hard to lie still. I want to play golf and go to church and shop for groceries and work in the garden with you and go for walks and make love. If only we could hurry time, darling. But I pray for God's grace." She listened to McPartland's "Somewhere (There's A Place For Us)" and read some Lewis and napped and tried to keep the blood in. He rubbed her feet and fluffed her pillows and played cribbage with her, the board running crosswise on her lap. He made a pot of Earl Grey tea and she put on her mad hat, the red and green Tartan tam that she wore for golf, and they drank the tea together. "Oh, darling, the lavender is so lovely. Just what I needed. Thank you." And he made clam linguini for dinner, their little rambler becoming pungent with the odor of the smashed garlic cloves that he sautéed for the sauce.

And then three nights later it went very badly. She was cramping and moaning and gushing. He called Dr. Hope, who came quickly wearing a long coat and slippers and hurried up the sidewalk in the porch light carrying his black bag. "She's apparently having a miscarriage," the old man said, and Dr. Hope frowned at him offendedly. "We shall see." But when he pulled back the bedclothes there were puddles of blood and traces of tissue and they knew it was over.

"I'm sorry I'm not any good at this, darling. We always wanted three children, and I thought I would have them very easily. But it took us so many years to conceive and then I couldn't hold on to this one."

"We can still have three children. There is plenty of time. Isn't that so, Doctor?"

"Yes."

"You have been very brave, and we will start over again in another month."

In September they returned to teaching school, and in the winter the old man coached basketball, and in February Diane conceived again, and in April she miscarried again, and when she miscarried a third time a year later, Diane went on the pill and they quit trying.

"There is a reason for our failure, darling. It is not by accident. I have prayed on it and prayed on it. We have nothing to be ashamed of. We would be good parents, but that is not the role God has planned for us. He wants us to devote ourselves to teaching and to our students. Don't be so disappointed, darling. We can still have a grand life."

And then the teaching got better. They grew into their jobs. Diane, with her ingenuous and unshakeable belief in a purpose-driven life, enrolled and shone in night classes for a year to become a certified physical trainer and developed and led a coed condition-ing program for the Meadowdale P.E. department, sweetly, relent-lessly, resiliently petitioning building and District administrators to erect an annex to the gym and fully stock it with free weights and other apparatus, then encouraging and assisting athletes, female and male, to develop independent training programs as she su-pervised the weight room after school, not for the money, though she was paid modestly, but for the pleasure, joy, she took in seeing young people build their bodies and achieve their God-given ath-letic potential. Summers the old man studied tragedy and comedy and rhetoric, Aristotle and Longinus and Kenneth Burke, rhetoric becoming more and more the prism and heuristic by means of which he viewed and analyzed the realms of pedagogy and per-formance, his delight astonishing and profound, thinking *grammar the fount and rhetoric the flourish, technical analysis and conscious imitation of such as Hemingway and Faulkner and Salinger and Joyce being Hall marks, the English teacher an embodiment, ava-tar, of an Emersonian mythical self-reliant man who mought could welcome and esteem all comers, the college bound and the likely dropout, the denizen of the Woodway Park estate and the Highway 99 one-bedroom apartment, the jock, the cheerleader, the nerd, the brainiac, the gung-ho, the stoner, the loner, the alienated, and who urged them to employ all of the available means of persuasion, not alone* logos, *ratiocination, rumination, intellection, and noesis* in *sentences enthymemic and* ipso factic, *sublime provender for the leanhungry mind, but also* pathos, *subliminal empathy and sympa-thy knife-piercing the heart, and both imbued, flushed, with* ethos, *a winsome style attesting to, vouching for, the character of the sen-tence maker.*

He began to feel at home, nidified, in the classroom and on the court, teaching Literary Classics and Poetry and Expository Writing and Creative Writing and Freshman English and individual offensive and defensive skills and team offensive and defensive concepts, arriving an hour before school for tutorials, drill sessions, with Doh Song Cho and Vu Tran and Rosario Esposito, who were trusting and patient and steadfast, who with terrific determination and tenacity repetitively produced the short clauses that he asked them to write, noun phrase and modifiers plus verb phrase and modifiers, and sorted out tenses and verb-subject agreement in that stubborn and optimistic fortitude of and with and by which they lived, memorizing spelling rules and shrugging their shoulders and smiling resolutely in the face of anarchy as he explained how "ghoti" could spell "fish," and lagging after practice half an hour with Jodi or Stacy or Sheila to help her get more wrist, backspin, in her free throws like Bill Sharman or quicken her spin move like Earl "The Pearl" or refine her drop step and skyhook like Kareem.

Summarily, dear but restive reader, let us press ahead, all engines full, with this condensed, *Digest*ed one might say, given his "literary" background, version of his pretty unremarkable biography. In the '60s our hero (and we use the term loosely, swashbuckling derring-do an occasional hit but mostly miss quality of his chromosomal makeup), graduated from college and, Phi Beta Kappa key in hand, as it were (you must have noticed by now his ostentatious modesty in all but his prose style), secured a job as a high school teacher, legally evaded military service (drafted after the Berlin Wall went up, he bent over and spread his cheeks, was classified 1A, pondered the intriguing possibility of attending the Monterey Language School after basic training, weighed against it the forced Musketeering gregariousness of barracks life, then sought and received an occupational deferment, teachers at the time being in short supply), had no quarrel with those who turned on, tuned in, and dropped out, although none of those choices held any personal appeal for him, marched once (his hair by this time having begun to Beatle) in blue button-down poplin shirt and desert boots on I-5 across the Ship Canal Bridge with a battalion of Jesus-haired or Afroed Vietnam War protestors wearing tie-dyed tee shirts and sandals, brandishing peace signs, and chanting "Hell, no, we won't go!" (but, never one given to prolonged shouting from high-raised roof beams, once was enough), met and courted (yes, reader, we see you lifting a dubious eyebrow at a word whose use would make our hero wince, owing to its medieval overtones, its infantilizing chivalric romanticism, its gendered rigidity, but, be that as it may, we're just going to have to insist on it, because that is pretty much what he did, opening doors for her, walking on the traffic side of her, pedestaling her) Diane, married her in the red-brick Tudorish-Gothic Wallingford Congregational Church, graying Pastor Swedberg, in a ceremony-planning *cum* counseling session with the betrothed, having noted that the groom-to-be had only once in the year of their going together attended a Sunday service with his prospective bride, asking if he had any faith in the Lord at all, and receiving in reply that he had made one at the Billy Graham Crusade for Christ in 1951, had read the Bible cover to cover, had joined Diane and Chet and Evelyn and their friends for line-by-line exegesis of Romans and both Corinthians, often engaged with Diane in spontaneous, free-form catechism (usually, he did not add, after they had done all they could to satisfy themselves within the sexual protocol Diane had established), and that, though he could not profess a faith, he might be classified, if that would help, as a congenial agnostic (not volunteering his belief that Diane had, in the unconscious, Darwinian, sense, calculated the odds of his being a catch and had bet him across the board, figuring him a lock, if not to win, then certainly to place or show).

Can we move this along, please? Why the specious ventriloquism? We can see your lips move, you know, and you're creeping us out. Can you tamp down the artifice for a minute and tell it like it was, clearly and directly? Let's just do a simple Q and A, okay?

Certainly. Whom the reader loveth, he—I mean they—chasteneth.

But I can't guarantee that I won't conclude our little hand-in-hand skate by suddenly flinging myself into a double Salchow with high hopes of sticking the landing on the outside edge.

Enough already! When did the old man and Diane marry?

August 1966.

Where did they honeymoon?

San Francisco. Jack Tar Hotel, 15th floor, looking out at Bay Bridge, Treasure Island, Alcatraz. Amazed to find phone extension in bathroom. Modern technology! Saw Giants beat Phillies at Candlestick. Juan Marichal vs. Robin Roberts. McCovey homered. Cable cars. Cliff House. Seal Rock. Telegraph Hill. Golden Gate Park. Stimson beach. Yadda, yadda. Hole-in-wall bistro between burlesque theaters in Tenderloin. First encounter with steak *tartare*. Gag reflex in play when waiter broke raw egg over molded mound of roseate sirloin. Girded own loins and waded in. *Délicieux*. Moist meaty mouthfuls zesty with ground peppercorns, minced onion, briny capers.

And Diane?

Steak Diane, flambéed tableside.

How was the sex?

Spring-training-like. Excitedly working on skills. Experimenting with warm up drills, lineups, positions, equipment. Catcher's diaphragm shortened pitcher's delivery and inhibited catcher's framing of pitch. Played doubleheader every day, though not all games went nine innings. Worked out (and in) some kinks. Broke camp, headed north, optimistic about prospects.

Did they have terms of endearment for each other? Dear, darling, lover, sweetie, honey, sugar, baby?

No.

Why not?

He, pathological aversion to cute, corny, trite, sentimental. She, because he didn't.

He didn't fear naked expression of emotion, making himself vulnerable?

That too.

She was teaching at Meadowdale, he at Edmonds when they married?

Yes. In '69 he transferred to new Maplewood High School south of Westgate to become assistant basketball coach. When girls' basketball born in 1972, offspring of Title IX, he won job of head coach. No one else applied.

When did they move to the house on Grandview?

March 1972.

How much did they pay for it?

$30,000. Had dual income of $16,000, counting stipends for supervising activities. Withdrew $6,000 from savings to make twenty-five per cent down payment, with monthly payments of $95 at five per cent interest.

This was to be a halfway house on their journey from apartment in Lynnwood to home ownership in the Bowl?

Yes.

In the '70s, did they become Pete Seeger's suburbanites, barbequing behind a six-foot high cedar plank fence, mowing and trimming and thatching a well-fertilized thick green lawn, tending to flower beds, raising vegetables, DIYing all kinds of home improvement projects?

Yes.

Did they become John Updike suburbanites, joining "sets," coupling and recoupling?

No.

They were never tempted to stray?

They were.

They resisted?

Essentially, yes.

Did they sniff cocaine, puff marijuana?

No.

Did they drink?

Yes. Savored wine daily.

Did they take up running?

Yes.

Did they take up disco dancing?

Yes.

Did they take note of Earth Day?

Yes. Both acknowledged importance of being caretakers, stewards, of earth.

Did they therefore reduce their consumption of carbon and pesticides?

No. Tried not to litter, though.

Did they read *The Greening of America*?

She, no. He, yes.

His take?

Consciousness III fearful retreat from reality of verifiable material, Darwinian character of life to fiction of innocent, technology-free man in harmony with nature, self, and other selves, all paradoxically so equally powerless yet fully empowered that very concept of power rendered meaningless.

When did Diane stop inserting her diaphragm?

After move to Grandview.

It took them three years to become pregnant?

Yes. But would not have put it like that. Diane became pregnant, "they" did not.

To what did they attribute their difficulty?

She, God's plan. He, timing. Statistically unusual, but not impossible, number of ejaculations occurring before ovulation.

Why did they want children?

She, fulfillment of God's commandment to be fruitful, multiply, bring salvageable souls to life. He, to prove he could do it, be creator. Both, atavistic evolutionary urge to perpetuate selves. Force driving through green fuse. Also, sentimental love of children for their own sakes, their sweet vulnerabilities, their adaptabilities, their exponentially increasing capabilities, their multiple metamorphoses, their maturing competencies.

Isn't sentimental love actually subsumed by the atavistic evolutionary urge? That is, we don't value sentimental love in and of itself, we value it because it motivates us to spread our genes?

He would accept quibble.

And even though he believed that the universe is godless and without meaning or purpose, he never questioned the value of creating a child? Of bringing it into the world to experience the mesmerizing, exhilarating kaleidoscope of daily phenomena, the rush of consciousness, become addicted to it, and then cease? Be and then not be? Or of bringing it into the world to experience pain upon pain, a sea of troubles, and then die without recompense? Why?

(a) Aforesaid atavistic urge to perpetuate self. (b) Altruistic wish to enable another to experience rush of consciousness.

What about the pain?

Regrettable. Worth it.

Isn't altruism also subsumed under atavistic urge? Belief in it leads us to spread our genes?

He would accept quibble.

After the seeming finality of the miscarriages, the "sign," how did each respond?

She, with loving acceptance of God's will, determination to follow His plan. He, with myriad of efforts, still ongoing, to be doer, creator, order-imposer.

Did both, despite their disappointment, continue to crave the rush of consciousness?

Yes.

Did fealty of family and friends sustain them?

Yes. With family, holiday, birthday and anniversary gatherings, picnics, poker games, Husky and Seattle Supersonic games. Dancing at Merry Max on Highway 99 to music of George Adams trio, piano, clarinet, drums, George's solos mash up of Teddy Wilson, Art Tatum, Errol Garner, rapid light-fingered right hand arpeggios and trills punctuated by striding left hand chords. "Smoke Gets in Your Eyes",

"Crazy Rhythm," other jazz standards reimagined, transmogrified, yet danceable, fox trot, jitter, swing. Son's turnings, dippings adrenalized as heart soared with filial pride. With friends, colleagues, parties, discotheques, movies, golf outings to Spokane, Bend, OR, weekend getaways to Portland, Port Townsend, WA, Vancouver, BC.

She enjoyed these more than he?

Yes.

He enjoyed them but was never happier than when they went home to be alone together?

Yes.

Once home and settled in, she was ready to go do something else?

Yes.

Did they ever watch together the Rock Hudson-Jennifer Jones version of *A Farewell to Arms*?

Yes. 1976, "ABC Saturday Night Movie," on new 24-inch Zenith color TV in living room at Grandview.

Her reaction?

"Good Lord, that Catherine Barkley is so sappy. What a cipher! I mean, get a life, woman! 'I'm good. I do what you want. There isn't any me. I'm you. You're my religion. You're all I've got. I can't stand to see so many people. I feel very lonely among other people. Don't you like it better when we are alone? There's only us two and in the world there's all the rest of them. I don't take any interest in anything else anymore.' It's great that they're in love, the long row across the lake, the walks in the snow, the drinks in the bars, the fine cathedral in the mist, the sighting of foxes, the two wrapped together in his cape are all very romantic and moving but so limiting. Love should expand her life, not contract it."

His?

Chagrin. Had already seen it in 1957 at drive-in with first girl friend, sated, filled-up, complete, both naked, wrapped in blanket, co-dependent, self-sufficient, everyone else, rest of world, out there, irrelevant to him. Infantilism of long-held fantasy exposed.

Did both nevertheless have tears in their eyes as Frederic Henry walked out into the rain?

Yes.

They began to travel?

Yes. At first, summer jaunts along western and eastern U.S. seaboards. Heartland of little interest. Spring break getaways to Zihuatanejo, Jamaica, Santa Fe, Palm Springs, Myrtle Beach. Later, backpacking trips to western Europe. Visited Europe Through the Back Door, Rick Steves's original store on 4th Avenue, where Polar Bear used to be. Watched videos, bought bags, guidebooks, phrasebooks.

Did he prepare to speak French in France?

Yes. Read *Swann's Way* and Inspector Maigret novels out loud in original.

How did that work out?

Screwed courage to sticking point, struck up "conversations" with *garcons, concierges, conducteurs, inspecteurs, flâneurs*. With terrific determination and tenacity repeatedly produced short in-terrogative clauses ending in *s'il vous plais: Qu'est c'est..., Ou est..., Disez-moi..., A quelle heure..., Avez-vous..., Combien d'argent..., Répetez..., Parlez-lentement....* Felt engaged, worldly. Diane proud of him.

When did they move to the condo?

1985. Bored with yard work. Affluent enough for view spot in Bowl. Looked at offerings all over town for months, settled on up-per unit in just-constructed four-plex at 5th and SeaMont. Crown molding, wainscoting, oak floors and cabinets, wet bar, gleaming white paint, 1300 square feet, sweeping view from every room, walking distance to shops, restaurants, library, athletic club, beach. $150,000 with mortgage of $90,000 after applying proceeds from sale of house on Grandview. Clinked glasses of Heitz Cellars 1974 Martha's Vineyard minty cabernet with Bill and Charlene after lug-ging upstairs boxes and pieces of furniture crammed into rented U-Haul.

Their feelings?

We're home.

Were they or any friends or relatives ever touched by the Aids epidemic?

No.

Did developing theories of plate tectonics and quantum mechanics affect their imaginations?

She, no. He, yes. Age and protean quality of earth, subatomic indeterminacy, wackiness, astounding revelations buttressing gut feeling that life accidental, incidental.

Were they concerned about global warming?

Yes.

Did they do anything to combat it?

No.

Were they early adopters of new technology?

Not vanguard. Second wave. Walkman, VCR, CD player. First computer, IBM PC, 1989. Cell phones, 2000. iPads, 2008. Apple watch (he) 2016.

Did he ever have a perm?

No.

Did she?

No. Kept hair short. Bangs. Used curling iron on sides. Back of neck, increasingly creased, visible.

Did he at one time wear Izod polos and chinos and penny loafers?

Yes.

Did she at one time wear *Flashdance* leg warmers and off-shoulder shirts?

Yes.

When did their parents die?

Margaret, 1975, lung cancer. Chet, 1988, brain aneurism. Evelyn, 1995, stroke. George, 1999, pneumonia.

When did the two retire?

1995.

Their ages?

She, 52. He, 55.

Why retire at such a young age?

Because they could. Pensions fully vested. IRAs and TSAs, enhanced by small inheritances, built up. Been there, done that. Same ol', same 'ol. Enough enough. Time for change. Pass mantle of responsibility. Immerse selves in realm of ludic. Create, recreate.

They began to winter in Arizona?

Yes. Rented condo in retirement community in Mesa. Shoulderless city of 450,000 stretching across wide desert ringed by bare brown mountains. Far from madding clouds. To them, exotic. Stuccoed, tile-roofed dwellings in variations of beige, cream, laid out around golf course, softball field, dog run, tennis courts, pickleball courts, exercise rooms, meeting rooms, swimming pools, spas, wood shop, ceramics room, ballroom. Sun at dawn small round scoop of orange sherbet, at noon huge blinding silver-yellow effulgence dominating sky, at dusk shrinking lemon orb turning wisps of cirrus charcoal, candy apple red. Yards xeriscaped in shards of granite. Angular boulders here, there, for contrast. Occasional dry streamed of medium-sized rocks running from house to sidewalk. Cacti everywhere. Hulking saguaros with creamy blossoms, multi-stalked ocotillos, orange flowers hanging like pennants, prolific prickly pears growing paddles out of paddles topped by yellow, rose, chalices, stumpy, chesty barrels, gnarly chollas, lanky organ pipes, one piece telescoping out of piece beneath it, ground-hugging hedgehog, green agaves leaved like artichoke, fecundly bulbous mammalarias. Color leaping from shrubs and bushes in yards and roadway medians. Brazen burnt-orange blossoms on Mexican bird of paradise. Claret, salmon-colored, blooms on crepe-papery bougainvillea, garnet spears on hibiscus, cerise brushes on fairy duster, blood-orange flags on cape honeysuckle, lavender frostings on sage, hot-yellow, deep gold-vermilion buttons on lantana, white, crimson, peppermint-pink clusters on oleander, cock's comb stems on red yucca, blonde spike on towering phallic century plant, mottled sea-foam green bark on palo verde, mesquite, egg-yolk pom-poms on sweet acacia, lacquered-lavender fronds on jacarandas, orange, blonde, hot-lemon globes of fruit ornamenting hunched dwarf citrus trees. Birds everywhere. Striped Gila woodpeckers rat-tat-tatting streetlight pole, quail, antennae on *qui vive*, racewalking across granite to Diane's bird feeder, turkey vultures riding updrafts, crimson cardinals perching on drooping limbs of sissou tree, curved-bill thrashers shrilly whistling two note "Hey, you!," drab doves dumbly moaning, road runners scampering, cactus wrens, grackles, marshalling, hummingbirds hovering, nectar-sipping. On occasion, other wildlife: coyotes prowling, lizards skittering, long-eared jackrabbits hopping, javelinas rooting, bobcats parading.

Dial it back, now. You're chewing the scenery again.

Sorry.

In Arizona they immersed themselves in the realm of the ludic?

Yes. She, women's golf club, tennis club. Played one or other every morning but Sunday. Church on Sunday morning. Took tennis lessons, reached 3.5 level. Weekly competitive match against teams from other retirement communities. Ponytail canasta or mahjong in afternoons or evenings. Many new friends. Walks, coffees, lunches, Bible study. He, several softball teams, men's golf club, tennis club. Played one or other every morning but Sunday. Played golf alone at dawn on Sunday. Course quiet. Lush fairways greenly beckoning. Run of place. Took tennis lessons, reached 3.5 level. Weekly competitive matches. Together won mixed doubles tournaments twice. Softball doubleheaders thrice weekly. Outfielder. High-average, low-power, hitter. Speedy runner. Annual tournaments, AAA level, Tucson, Yuma, Palm Springs, Phoenix, Las Vegas, Mesquite, St. George. Many championships. Many new acquaintances. Post-game beers.

They were active socially?

Yes. Dinner parties, potlucks, barbeques, drinks on patios, team socials, community pancake breakfasts, hamburger feeds, dances.

Diane liked to entertain?

Yes.

He?

Not.

Diane liked to be entertained?

Yes.

He?

For hour, two.

He never happier than when party over?

Yes.

What were their friends and acquaintances like?

Mostly white, retired, conservative, Protestant, church-going, middle-to-upper-middle class, military careerists, office workers, tradesmen, craftsmen, policemen, firemen, farmers, self-employed business persons, teachers, accountants, ministers, nurses, sprinkling of doctors, lawyers, engineers. Had paid dues, followed rules, kept noses clean, worked, saved, honored flag. Little sympathy for those who did not do same. Oblivious of or antipathetic to notion of systemic inequality.

Where were they from?

Midwest, Rockies, Northwest, British Columbia, Alberta.

Is "Minnesota nice" a real thing?

Quite possibly. Many from Minnesota (also Canada) unfailingly polite, considerate, generous, loath to pry or disagree, loath to foist political or religious opinions on others.

Their feelings upon returning to the Bowl each spring?

Mixed. Both loved ludiculous near certainty of sun, cerulean skies, flooding of light, warmth. Loved desert terrain, extensive vistas, aridity. Back in Bowl, found looming dark evergreen trees, veiled skies, moist chill air oppressive. Gradually attuned selves to lush verdancy, bracing briskness of true home—place where, when you go there, you feel taken in.

Why does he no longer winter in Arizona?

To preserve illusion of idyllic, ludic life with Diane. Also, could not face endless round of social activities without her as buffer, interface.

When did Diane die?

April 12, 2009. Traffic accident, head-on collision, intersection of Highway 99-205th. Drunk driver ran left-turn lane red light, hit Diane coming through. Call at 9:45. Grabbed keys. Shaking. Left Celtics-Lakers playing on TV, left lights on, rushed to Stevens Hospital. Shaking. Diane unconscious in ICU. On ventilator. Nurse attending, monitoring. Skull fractured, face lacerated, swaddled. Dying.

"Oh, darling," he heard her not say, "I'm so sorry I must leave you. We had such a lovely study of 'Revelation' tonight at Rhoda's house on the lake, raindrops bouncing off the water in light reflecting from the windows, God's bounty of beauty, and lifting each other up in our shared awe at God's merciful plan for justice and retribution. We took turns explaining how God has worked in our lives. I said He has given me you, darling, my precious helpmate, and given both of us rewarding careers and lovely lives in the Bowl and romantic escapes to Arizona, blessing upon blessing, with the ultimate blessing, of course, atonement through salvation in Christ, darling. And the chamomile tea and the lemon bars were lovely and brought us such a feeling of communion. And at the end we prayed for the salvation of the ignorant and recalcitrant, that they would see the light, and we were all thinking of you, darling, and for safe travels home."

He did not say anything. He was always embarrassed by the words awe, retribution, blessing, atonement, salvation, communion. They were gratuitous and desperate and untenable, fictive abstractions drawn from discrete temporary adhesions of pulsing quanta named Diane, George, Margaret. You never got away to anything. You were ruled by entropy. Shakily he kissed her cooling forehead and touched her cooling cheek.

"But, darling, didn't I make you a good wife? Didn't we have a fine life together? You do understand about Norm, don't you, as I understand about Hazel? Things change, darling, but marriage is forever. There are days when you hate love as much as you love it. Love is in the gut, the bones. It doesn't look away from the bad things. It isn't perfect, it can be sad and lonely, but we never let the perfect be the enemy of the good. We almost completed each other, darling, and our life together happened for a reason, as my death is happening now for a reason, everything works out fairly, darling, and I am not afraid, the real me is not broken, and there will be heaven enough and no end of time, and it will be grand."

[The Hemingway and Salinger seem close to the mark. Bravo! The Faulkner, however, is forced, overdone. You've crammed a slew of his prose tics into two paragraphs. You've made it parody, not pastiche. I do like the speed of the Q and A, though. Would that more of your self-indulgent stylistic excursions moved along like that! Sylvia]

[The Faulkner could be improved, but its presence is appropriate. As Faulkner created a Yoknapatawpha County, so Wayne is creating a how pretty town. Solveig]

[Wayne, just as I used to enjoy a Rich Little impression, so I enjoy your use of pastiche (and also many of the other allusions—name-droppings, as it were—drawn from the literary tributaries that feed your stream of consciousness). It's fun for its own sake. But I must say, in addition to providing you yet another opportunity to play the versatile virtuoso, I think it's a way of tiptoeing around some pretty powerful emotions. *Tempus fugit*. When will you drop the masks and directly confront yourself? Dave]

[Dave, it's all there. He has indirectly presented his direct confrontation with himself. Yes, Wayne likes to show off, and that may be a flaw. But unlike Rich Little's, which don't go beyond themselves, Wayne's imitations of rhythm, intonation, and diction are liberating and generative. Assuming another's voice loosens his emotional costiveness; going undercover, he uncovers himself. They who have ears to hear, let them hear. Liz Ann]

[Liz Ann, I love that you rise in defense of your rhetoric mentor, but I think that your loyalty to him clouds your judgment. In going undercover, he hides from himself. In his prologue, he says his intention is to make his apology, rehearse his back story, but the mechanism of other voices allows, even induces, him to skew rather than true. He needs to speak as himself, for himself. Dave]

[Does Wayne have multiple personalities? Are we seeing here four faces of Adams? No. On the other hand, are we getting all the information we need? Do we fully understand the Wayne-Diane relationship? No. And my guess is, lacking Liz Ann's miracle ears, we never will. Solveig]

[So ironic that Daniel and I, not Diane, Roman goddess of fertility and childbirth, were the epitome of fecundity, producing three children in four years! Not sure I would attribute it to God's plan but glad the kids were there for you to enjoy and relate to, taking them over the years to the playground and the big climbing rock at the City Park, to movies at the Lynn-Twin, to Sonics games, and to Starbucks for frappucinos. Linda]

e

Because she walked in beauty that his scaled eyes could not see, because the glorious universe was ever expanding from the original outburst of God's love, because she was suffused with God's grace which continuously flowed through her like the neutrinos he talked about, because she was part of the divine plan that had first been made manifest in the Garden of Eden, because her story grew out of the stories of Adam and Noah and Moses and Jesus and Peter and Paul, that she walked on the earth *because* they once did, that they had ascended to heaven and she, an eternally new creation since that magical summer evening in Seattle with Billy Graham, would one day join them there, that God had a special plan for her, of which he had been for so long the most important part and which she could find signs of daily by being open to its working in her and seeking insight through prayer and *Bible* study, by being able to say, from "Genesis" through "Revelation," "This happened and I am part of it, at one with it, I fit in, I matter, it makes sense,

I need not fear death, need not even fear making a mess of this life," knowing that God would test her but never send her more than she could bear, and aching to share her eschatology with a soul mate who would acknowledge that he had a soul, one morning in church she turned and introduced herself to broad-shouldered, bearded Norm standing in sport jacket and tie alone in the row behind her at the one-minute greeting of neighbors following the opening hymns and preceding the sermon, sensed him lighting up as her own pulse accelerated at their handshake, learned her five things about him (divorced, two young kids, liked sports, restored old cars, was an electrician) as he learned his five about her (married, no kids, liked sports, gardened, taught P.E.), turned and smiled and touched his hand again after the benediction, sat beside him the following Sunday, asked if he were stopping for coffee in the foyer where thermoses had been placed atop folding tables, halved a sugar doughnut with a plastic knife on a napkin and shared it with him, rubbing fingers together to rid them of granules when she finished, dabbing her mouth with the napkin and offering it to him, who employed it on his smiling lips and then pocketed it, wondering if he found inspiring Pastor Miles's comment that the Bible has often been used as a manuscript for conformity and not often enough as a manifesto of creativity, that the name of Jesus should conger creativity, beauty, imagination, and wonder instead of rules, laws, conformity, and judgment, skin prickling when he said yes, replying when he asked why she was unaccompanied by her husband that he said religion was not for him, that she still held out hope because as a boy he had been saved by Billy Graham, that she had been hurt when he had read at her request *Surprised By Joy* yet eluded through sophistry springing from willful stubbornness all fine nets and stratagems of belief, refusing to be repelled by the tinniness of non-belief, denying the pure joy beyond mere happiness and pleasure, beyond words at all, of word becoming flesh and God becoming man, resisting the compulsion to enter the blessed depths of divine mercy, afraid of being thought a poached egg, no doubt, yet she loved him and would not give up on him, she had to go home now, he would be expecting her, but would he care to go for a walk sometime and talk about the transformative power of God's love, and the next Sunday agreeing to ride with Norm to Richmond Beach Park after church the following Sunday while he was running a 10K 40 miles away in Monroe, thinking *of course* as she slid into the oxidizing blue '76 Datsun B210 coupe, mandated by alimony and child support, noting with a twinge the skateboards and bag of Nalley's potato chips in the back seat but bearing her barrenness dutifully, excitement growing as Norm drove southward to the beach through sun dapplings in forested Woodway Park, borne forward on the waves of Christian rock, a Steven Curtis Chapman tape, glory unfolding in an assertive, confident, unambiguous beat, parking in the paved lot and walking through dunes, sand getting into her flats and clinging to her pantyhose, to a shoreline firmed by a receding tide, meandering north for a ways and then south for a ways amid tots throwing bread to ecstatically flapping seagulls, kite flyers tugging at strings, Frisbee sailers creating lovely parabolas, clam diggers, sand castle builders, readers and sunbathers stretched out on blankets, picnickers munching, beside the placid Sound, before the dark blue-green Olympics splotched with snow, taking deep breaths, knowing Norm knew it didn't just happen, this order, this beauty, this world and no other except heaven where conditions were just right for life, for the invisible things of Him from the creation of the world could be clearly seen by the things that were made, His eternal power and Godhead so obvious, there could be no excuse, waving an arm from horizon to horizon, saying all around us are holiness and grace, freely given for the taking, new doors of perception mystically opening to the unhardened heart, the unlocked mind, retreating to sit on a thick bleached log gritty with sand, her soul, his too, trembling before God, both declaring that they felt God's blessing, that each had been made and would be forever a new creation, her heart leaping again when he took her hand, a prayer of thanksgiving riding her pulse, involuntarily swallowing as he leaned in to, very lightly, very quickly, kiss her lips, a thundering in her ears blurring her perception, an oozing at her fork perplexing her joy, they should get back, Norm was to take the kids to Green Lake for boarding, mind still swirling as she leaned against his car to pour sand from her shoes, brush it from her feet, listening quietly to Steven Chapman as they returned through the forest, squeezing his hand and saying thank you, it was wonderful, have fun with your kids, see you next week when he pulled up beside her Honda, welcoming him home after the race, how was it, hugging him when, trying not to beam, he confessed to a personal best 39:40, relieved not to get the advance she had been expecting, he too full of himself to reach out, she so very full also, glowing with memories of Norm and the beach, wonderously at one with what was.

f

Because he questioned the privileged place of tragedy among genres in that graduate summer seminar in Parrington Hall, because in his paper on *A View From the Bridge* that he read in mid-quarter to the class he argued against viewing that or any other tragedy as a secular substitute for religion, against Max Scheler's assertion that the tragic is an essential element of the universe itself, an observable property, a glimmering which surrounds certain events, a specific feature of the world's makeup, and maintained that, to the contrary, the tragic is overlayed, not observed, imposed, not discovered, that the alleged glimmering is a fiction, a mirage that disappears when examined at the atomic level, that order becoming disorder is entropy, not tragedy, save that we label it so, and that Eddie, a common man, was a tragic hero who in seeking to do good by his lights instead did evil, resulting in the scarring of four other lives and his own death, as worthy in his blind self-deception, a flaw that was fatal but not fated, of that honorific as procrastinating Hamlet or ambitious Macbeth or rash Romeo and Juliet, and then against a second Scheler assertion that there is no tragedy without transcendence, the hero exceeding the bounds of ordinary human experience, in his blind greatness wreaking havoc, in his downfall expiating his guilt, in the end ennobled, purging us of pity and fear and elevating us to a new, awed understanding of the possibilities of human grandeur and failure, affirming our worth in a way that comedy, with its merely happy ending, never can, maintaining rather that we and our tragic heroes live and die in ambiguity and indeterminacy and uncertainty, our worth unquantifiable, transcendence therefore not a conclusive induction but an axiom imposed by critical fiat, Oedipus Rex and King Lear no more authentic exemplars of humanity than Molly Bloom or Falstaff, neither the tragic nor the comic to be found glimmering in the fabric of the universe, neither form more exalting than the other, whether paradise be lost but partially regained somehow through suffering or paradise be regained through the Bergsonian overcoming of stupidity and rigidity, his an egalitarian stance, and because Professor Frank Jones commended his sturdy refusal to accept whatever the transcendence boys were hearkening after, his tablemate Hazel suggested that they discuss his views further over a bite of lunch at Abby's and, he aflush with seminar success, they walked across 15th to the Ave and faced each other in a booth of burgundy leatherette over BLTs and coffee, she frequently sweeping, her wedding diamond sparkling in the act, her unsprayed long glossy black hair to one side or the other from its middle part, the animation of her chewing and talking impelling it to fall every few seconds over brown eyes goggled by big round black horn rims, asking is the paradox of tragedy, the fearful sense of rightness and the pitying sense of wrongness, the ambiguity, really a reason to dismiss transcendence, on the contrary, doesn't the ambiguity show forth, an observable epiphany, a glimmering we *can* see in the actions of the daring and suffering hero, aren't we lifted to an awareness of a new level of complexity and richness that provides no answers but is for that very reason a kind of triumph, a tragic greatness, whereas it doesn't even make sense to speak of comic greatness, Molly Bloom may be the life force full of affirmations, Falstaff may be large as life, but Oedipus and Lear are far more magnificent, surely entropy, change, disintegration, is part of the warp and woof of the universe, available for all to see, it doesn't require a special tragic vision, it *is* tragic, the tragic inheres in our glorious Promethean quest for a knowledge which can never be quite enough for us, in our damnable Adamic eating of that fruit, tragic transcendence is not to be confused with transcendentalism, it isn't a mystical unity with the Oversoul, it isn't spiritualism, it certainly isn't the comic transformation wrought by salvation and resurrection, it is not independent of the material universe, it is not a state of being that has overcome the limitations of physical existence, it is not a state of being at all but a brief, piercing recognition of our paradoxical embodiment of power and frailty, grinning in the pleasure of combat, enjoying herself and her self, but it seems, he said, floundering in the flood of her passion, flopping his Beatle bangs with a shake of his head, so pretentious, so self-aggrandizing, so needy, to conclude that the ambiguity of a paradox reveals a higher truth instead of an inconclusive mystery, why does everyone yearn to take something positive from tragic ambiguity instead of accepting it as a revelation of our ignorance, but remember, she said, pretentious in its original sense means simply putting forth, asserting, maintaining, nothing wrong with that, and I pretend that a paradox is a positive, a higher truth, thesis and antithesis leading to a more enlightened Hegelian synthesis, tragedy reveals that mankind is a wonder in its potential for daring and suffering, are you so self-hating that you cannot see the glimmer, cannot admit your need for tragic epiphany, and lunch after class once a week became a regular occurrence for them, he wallowing in her volubility, she intrigued, stimulated by his half-baked contrarianism, then walking back across 15th to the upper campus lot where each parked by permit, she was working on her PhD and would start her dissertation in the fall, her husband was a Boeing engineer, they lived in Madison Park, they skied Crystal Mountain together, attended Husky football games, and they would halt at her car, lean against it, the first week he took her hand when saying goodbye, the next he bent forward to kiss her drily on the lips, the third she kissed moistly back, and at their last halting in the fourth he slipped a hand under her untucked blouse and squeezed a pendulous braless breast, both sighing, the quarter at an end, their poignant parting in pity and fear not tragic.

[I sensed that Diane was in turmoil at one point, a certain impatience, a certain desperation, an unaccountable welling of the eyes that she quickly willed away, but she would never speak of it and I knew better than to ask. Linda]

[I think this is the part where we discreetly look away. Solveig]

g

In 2019 the population of the 0.852-square-mile Bowl was just under 3,000, hundreds of tourists, mostly white with a smattering of Asians and a sprinkling of African Americans, swelling that number from 9:00 a.m. to 9:00 p.m. daily. There were other recognized boroughs within the widely-expanded city limits—Westgate and Firdale to the south, Perrinville to the north, 5 Corners at the eastern end of Main Street, and the International District along Highway 99—but the Bowl was Manhattan, minus the skyscrapers, the glamour, the chic, the hustle, the muscle, the wealth, the poverty, the homelessness, the fetid garbage, the grime, the crime. Gerified and gentrified, the Bowl seemed to the old man congested, dense. Although the odd skateboarder jolted over its uneven sidewalks, it was a place for adults, 95 percent of whom had high school diplomas, 47 percent bachelor's degrees. Fifty-five was the median age, and there were as many people over 70 as there were under 20. Pedestrians and cars competed for space. Dozens of two- and three-level condos and townhouses with names like The Commodore, The Mariner, The Ebb Tide, the Reefs, SeaGate, Seascape, and Avalon palisaded the original business district. The median price of a dwelling in the Bowl approached $700,000. Currently, a 2,000 square foot condo with two bedrooms and two baths and a partial seamountain view on Walnut between 5th and 6th was listed at a million, as was an 1,800 square foot townhouse with three bed-rooms, two baths, and "territorial" views on the corner of 7th and Daley next to Civic Field. Eighty-year-old modest ramblers contin-ued to exist—especially north of Bell between 6th and 3rd and in the hollow between 6th and 7th and Dayton and Walnut—but throughout the Bowl—especially along Sunset and 2nd north of Main and in the hills from 7th to 9th—countless original structures had been remodeled and upgraded or demolished and altogether reconceived. No muscular McMansions, no tracts of themed struc-tures, no "developments," nothing Tudor or Georgian or Spanish, nothing a-contextual, nothing faux, just functional, cantilevered glassy multi-levels with decks and patios surrounded by hydran-geas, junipers, rhododendrons, and azaleas. Most of the rebuilds were 2,500-4,500 square feet with multiple bathrooms and bed-rooms, an entertainment room and a vast open space combining a great room, a dining room, and a kitchen with an islanded work-space. Wood laminate or dense carpeting covered the floors, mar-ble the countertops. Ones and zeroes flowed through the walls. Rooms were WiFied, appliances were smart. Electronic devices abounded. Security and climate-control systems could be accessed by device from anywhere in the world. High definition TV content, with hundreds of options, could be streamed as well as delivered by cable or satellite. Though less white (79 per cent Caucasian) than it had been, the population was hardly diverse but—officially at least—it believed it should be. Doubtless there remained many tribal loyalists as well as closeted racists, sexists, and homophobes, but the City Council had created a Diversity Commission to pro-mote an environment that "accepted, celebrated, and appreciated diversity in a wide array of forms"— ethnic heritage, race, sexual orientation, physical ability, religion, and age—although the cost-of-housing barrier muted and mooted the racial and age aspects of the diversity issue. More pretentious, firmly bourgeois, the Bowl had become a hybrid bedroom-retirement community whose economic engine was tourism and whose arboreal, industrial origins were a matter of interest only to aging locals looking for their roots at the Museum or to the odd pedestrian, in need of an excuse to rest in her-more-often-than-his rambling among the plethora of shops and cafes, whose eye might have been caught by one of the historical plaques affixed to various buildings around town. It remained orderly, safe, and clean. There were no gangs or drug pushers, no panhandlers, no visibly homeless persons, no abandoned shopping carts. The town's center, however, was no longer quiet. Coming upon the clot of cars and people circling the fountain at 5th and Main, one who had resided in the Bowl in 1945 experienced the sort of disorientation that a 2019 Bowl resident might experience when first coming upon Times Square. Its people were loyal, hardworking, disciplined, resilient, optimistic, but less modest, complacent, conformist, paternalistic, insular, and unsophisticated. Its residents were less skeptical of big government than they had been. They valued family stability, although half of the adults over 35 had been divorced. They were not looking for handouts. They were generous to charities. They distrusted crusaders and muckrakers but were paying more heed to advocates of political correctness, as it was called by many, or to human rights, as it was called by a slowly increasing number. They were beginning to mull over the notion of white privilege and entitlement. They were beginning to wonder about the existence of implicit bias and systemic racism and sexism. They were beginning to discuss means of honoring the legacy of the Coast Salish indigenous peoples who had gathered berries and basket materials from the creeks and marshes and harvested fish from the bountiful bay itself thousands of years before. A few were even beginning to entertain the possibility of making reparations for slavery and for what they regarded as America's disproportionate contribution to climate change. Many were worried about the direction of the nation's economy. They were concerned

with job loss, outsourcing of manufacturing, unconscionable rewards for CEOs and venture capitalists. Though more affluent than
the generations that preceded them, they suspected that the future might be less promising for their offspring. They assumed that
a family needed dual wage-earners in order to maintain a quality
house and two cars, qualify for the loans necessary to put qualified
kids through college, buy a time-share condo for use as a beach or
mountain getaway and possibly a boat to moor at the Edmonds
marina and, with the help of a financial planner, invest enough in
401 (K)s and other instruments to provide for retirement in their
sixties and funerals in their eighties. They also assumed that both
partners in a marriage would want to work for personal fulfillment.
They had not been taught in the shining three-story grade school
on the hill; it had closed in 1972. If they had grown up in the Bowl,
which was more and more unlikely, possibly they heard at Olympic
View Elementary, a mile to the northeast, or Westgate Elementary,
a mile to the southeast, and at the merged Edmonds-Maplewood
High School on 212th and 76th, new stories about what made them
American: America had been invaded, not discovered, by colonizing Europeans who exploited its native inhabitants and expropriat-
ed their lands, settled by hardy, acquisitive souls with a myriad of
motives, some noble, some mean, governed by white males under
a Constitution written by elitists leery of true democracy, expanded
in territory and influence by a relentless westward movement and
an imperialistic policy of Manifest Destiny but managing to retain a
modicum of integrity by winning the Civil War (which it fought for
both economic and altruistic reasons) and passing the 14th
Amendment, aiding the cause of democracy by helping its allies
win World War I, at long last freeing women to vote, and striking a
blow against genocide and fascism by helping its allies win World
War II. And possibly they heard, in school or in an outlier church
sermon or through the media, that all citizens are equal and should
have but do not have equal opportunity, *de facto* racial segregation
and discrimination are much more common and insidious than

hitherto recognized, Japanese internment camps were abominable, inexcusable, America often fights to make the world safe for capitalism and the American economy, governmental restraint of capitalism is the key to a just and equitable economy, all persons— cisgender. transgender, bisexual, transsexual, gay, lesbian—should be proud of their sexuality and deserve the right to marry and raise children with any person of their choice, parental leave and child- care subsidies should be part of the social contract, living together outside of marriage is a respectable option for all persons, divorce is often beneficial for all parties concerned, all persons are autono- mous, all can make a house a home, all can grow up to be President or a Marine Corps general or a CEO, all can be a pink-collared nurse, a cosmetologist, a legal secretary, failures and successes in life are often a matter not of will power but of chance because one is either lucky or not in inheriting the "right" kind of genes and in being pro- vided with an environment in which the expression of those genes can flourish, lasting happiness can be attained through self-discov- ery and self-expression and by working toward social justice, if one is lucky enough through nature and nurture to be able to realize that.

The town's teeming business district—from 6th to the beach, from Howell to Bell—catered less to the needs and more to the profusion of wants of its people and its visitors. There were no grocery stores on Main. Safeway, The Shopping Cart (which later became Thriftway), and the Edmonds Grocery and Market had closed decades ago, Safeway relocating for a few years in the area that was to become Salish Crossing. The grocery in the strip mall at 5th and Howell, originally an A&P, then Petosa's, had become Ace Hardware. Shoppers seeking to stock pantries and refrigera- tors had to drive up Edmonds Way to the QFC at Westgate or up Maplewood Hill to Haggen's at 76th. There were no gas stations in the Bowl—commuters had to pump their own gas at the Kwik and Clean at Westgate or the Texaco on 196th and Olympic View Drive—nor was there a bus station, although county buses did come into the downtown area and the Sounder commuter train connecting Everett and Seattle stopped twice a day. But there was almost everything else for the body and the psyche. There were dozens of restaurants, with a variety of cuisines and ambiences, scattered throughout the Bowl. One could grab a simple maple bar or bear claw at the Edmonds Bakery or, a half-block away at 4th and Main, munch on Salt and Iron's small plate offerings of bone marrow, grilled fennel and octopus, speck, seared pork belly, and *chevre* and honey gorgonzola *dulce*. Alcoholic beverages were readily available. Engels' Tavern continued to exist as Engels' Pub, the Up and Up had become the '50s-style bopNburger, and the Sail Inn had upscaled into Rory's Bar and Grill, featuring 23 craft beers. There were two craft breweries, a distillery, a wine bar, a wine shop, a wine-storage facility for oenophiles who lacked micro-climate-controlled space at home, and nearly every restaurant offered an intriguing wine and beer list. There was a cheesemonger. There was an ice cream parlor, a frozen yogurt shop, a gelato shop. There were several women's clothing boutiques, including Sound Styles, Whim Sea, Rebekah's, C'est la Vie, Rogue, and Saetia. There was a footware store and several jewelry stores. One needed the digits of three hands to count the number of hair and nail salons. Eyelash extensions and eyebrow microblading were available at the Vanity Lash Lounge and Lashes by Louie. One's physique could be recontoured, and one's unwanted hair removed, at the PUR Skin Clinic. There were all manner of places, such as Innate Radiance, Innate Health, to assist in achieving, or maintaining, wellness—spas, massage therapy parlors, yoga studios, Pilates studios. Oxygen therapy was available at Ohana Hyperbarics. There was a naturopathic dermatologist and a naturopathic health center and a vitamins and herbs store. There was a model and talent agency, a counseling center and a chiropractic therapy clinic. One inclined to look could find here and there a psychic, an astrologer, or a holistic healer offering to help with spiritual exploration. There was an animal dermatologist, an animal hospital, and a place to buy natural pet-food.

There were home decor stores, a kitchenware store, a toy store, a rocks and minerals store. There were two travel stores: The Savvy Traveler and Rick Steves's Europe Through the Back Door. There was a store that sold new books, but the one that sold used books was holding a closeout sale and was due to be replaced by a sushi bar. There was a print shop, a dry cleaner, a consignment store, an optometrist, an audiologist, a pharmacy, a mortuary, a construction company, a place that sold flooring, a machine center, an auto repair shop. There was Christopher Framing and Gallery, Aria Studio and Gallery, Christina's, Art Gallery North, Zinc, the Cascade Art Museum, and Cole Gallery. There were several art studios and jewelry workshops, and the Papery and the Art Spot offered art supplies. The Edmonds Theater featured recently-released movies. There were eight banks and multiple lawyers' offices, real estate offices, insurance offices, and offices for financial planners and tax consultants. The town was brighter, more beckoning, the old gem getting regular polishing from business and municipal leaders who did so want it to be loved. In the central business section, public walkways and business interiors had been made wheelchair accessible. At 5th and Main, seven towering pin oaks provided a bower of shade in spring and summer, *feuille morte* pangs of beauty in the fall. Volunteers cleaned the beach and the streets, bright red, blue, or green umbrellas could be borrowed from streetside bins to fend off rain showers, and a new public restroom was available on 5th north of the fountain. Murals, officially sanctioned and commissioned graffiti painted by sublimating Kilroys seeking to express their version of the beach town's zeitgeist, were scattered throughout the business district: an impressionistic sunset with a white sailboat adrift in a sea of orange, blue, and black streaks reflected through striated wisps of cirrus clouds, Bunyanesque lumberjacks superimposed on a clearcut hillside, an anthropomorphic leviathan ferry boat swallowing cars as the whale might have Jonah, a pathos-laden rendering of a rusting, peeling tugboat, a shaken-snowglobe flurry of huge wet snowflakes falling on bundled-up winter visitors to the fishing pier, a glimpse through wispy leafless alders of a white-blue Sea with a low bank of light clouds clinging to it beneath a butterscotch sky, a surrealistic Main Street scene juxtaposing a contemporary SUV parked in front of the Edmonds Theater behind a '40s woody station wagon with continental kit parked in front of a 5 and 10 cent store. From early spring to late fall stuffed flower baskets, dazzling densities of purple, orange and red blossoms, hung from street poles. At every corner, concrete planters overflowed with an eclectic mixture of dense green shrubs and brightly blooming annuals. At night, lights strung from fascia boards fostered a festive feeling.

The town offered its residents much more than movies for entertainment. The community no longer rallied around high school sports, but the Edmonds Boys' and Girls' Club and the Edmonds Youth Club provided a multitude of organized activities for kids of all ages and genders. Although the Old Settlers' Picnic was now attended only by a tottering few, the 4th of July Parade, minus the softball games, still drew large crowds, as did the lighting of the Christmas tree. But there were so many more community events, blends of commerce, entertainment, and culture, that drew people out of their condos and hillside homes. There was the Waterfront Festival with its rides and games, the Scarecrow Fest with imaginative effigies scattered all over town, the Haunted Museum, the Trick-or-Treating Event with hundreds of joyful identity thieves— from Frozen Princesses to male transvestites—clotting the streets in a crush of colorful costumes, the Edmonds Jazz Connection Festival, the Classic Car Show, Heritage Day. There were *pétanque* tournaments at Civic Field. Every three weeks there was a Thursday evening Art Walk among galleries luring patrons with wine, appetizers, and music. Throughout the year the Driftwood Theater on Main above 9th offered plays featuring local amateur actors. The refurbished old high school building at 4th and Daley was now the Edmonds Center for the Arts, its balconied auditorium providing a home for the local Cascade Symphony and a venue for traveling jazz, pop, and folk artists. During the summer there were Sunday afternoon concerts in the City Park and lunchtime performances by live music groups at Old Milltown's Hazel Miller Plaza. There was the Saturday Summer Market, scores of canopied booths on a blocked-off section from 6th and Bell to 5th and Main, featuring local artisanal food products—humanely raised beef, chicken, and pork, free-range eggs, organic produce, troll-caught fish, gluten-free baked goods—and handicrafts. Hundreds of shoppers questing an authenticity and purity and community not to be found in supermarkets, or even Trader Joe's in Lynnwood or Whole Foods further out in Alderwood, happily Alphonsed and Gastoned each other while traipsing and snacking and filling their reusable bags, street musicians—here a bluegrass band, there a flautist—further elevating their moods. Biggest of all were the annual Edmonds Arts Festival at the Anderson Center and the Taste of Edmonds at Civic Field, three-day-weekend affairs to which out-of-towners descended by the thousands.

Emerson transcendently declared that every natural fact is a symbol of some spiritual fact. John Muir, when he gazed upon El Capitan, sensed the presence of a spirit with which he could become one, as did Thoreau when he mused upon Walden Pond. The old man, beholding the Bowl poignantly mid-way as the ferry shuddered back to Edmonds from Kingston, looking down and up all the streets, all the days, cherishing both what he saw and remembered, seeing no green light, sensing no spirit, no oversoul, no Platonic realm of fixed perfection, thought instead of bouncing, swerving, transmigrating atoms, hooking up, breaking apart, a ceaseless, mindless, accidental process of creation and destruction which not even the fittest, most adamantine, could survive, himself, his town, this world, this universe in flux, Sea, trees, clouds, rain.

[I think I need to see this grave new world. Solveig]

3

Songs of the Answerers

a

Good afternoon, friends, compatriots. What a pleasure it is to greet you here in the Plaza Room of the Anderson Center, formerly the school where I attended grades one through eight from 1945 to 1952. These walls speak to me of a town where people once lived lives of quiet self-determination, free of excessive restrictions. They practiced good manners, unburdened by the constraints of political correctness. Free of virtue-signaling restrictions, of gasping at straws, they tossed their used plastic forks and Styrofoam cartons into their metal garbage cans. They decided for themselves how and where to store their firearms. If they had a tree on their property, they cut it down or left it standing, as they saw fit. The City Council sought to meet the needs and interests of the residents, not the tourists or the mercantile elites. People knew their neighbors, helped their neighbors when asked, but respected their individual freedoms, and the town grew organically, from the bottom up, as everyone exercised those freedoms. The Council was accountable and transparent; it listened to the people. It was not bent on manipulative, top-down social engineering. Those were halcyon days. I loved that old town. But now, looking at the

Council's misguided attempt in recent years to control our minds, I fear that the old Edmonds is slip-sliding away. Oh, I don't doubt that the Council means well. All do-gooders do. As far as their ideals go, I come to praise, not to bury. Equality, fraternity—these 18th century revolutionary words stand for honorable principles. The Housing Strategy Task Force, the Climate Change Goals project, Indigenous People's Day, the Safe City designation—these are all, all honorable inventions. 'Twere best no one speak ill of them here! But, friends, let us not forget that they come at a cost—that cost being the loss of that other—and the single most important— revolutionary ideal: liberty. Today's City Council, even as it enshrines equality and condemns paternalism, paternalistically seeks to manufacture what it envisions as utopia, when in fact there is much disagreement among its electorate as to what constitutes utopia. Its zeal, its Messianic belief that it knows best, leads it to treat its constituents as children. But we are not children, and we do not need to accept the Council's paternalism. We can and must call upon the Council to demonstrate a more nuanced understanding of the complex issues before it.

For example, is the so-called need for affordable housing in Edmonds a real thing? Do we need to subsidize affordable housing with jacked-up property taxes and kickbacks to construction companies? Is everyone entitled to live here? How crammed do we want to get? Already traffic in the Bowl backs up at intersections, the sidewalks are jam-packed, we can't find a place to park. And increased numbers are bound to mean increased crime—it's a statistical inevitability. Do we really want more condos displacing houses, more drab low-cost apartment buildings, more mother-in-law apartments, more ADUs? Do we want to erase single-family zoning? Single-family zoning is responsible for so much of the Bowl's charm. Do we want to become Kirkland? Or Ballard? What's wrong with having a single-family house on a lot, a bit of space for a lawn and a couple of flower beds? Must density be our destiny? If we wanted density, we'd move to Manhattan. Why should we bear the burden of paying to make room for more people who have no stake in Edmonds and who might not love it the way we do? Now, friends, this is not in any way an argument in favor of segregation by age, race, income, or any other means by which people can be categorized. I say "No" to discrimination, "No" to redlining, "No" to affirmative action, "No" to special treatment of any kind. I argue in favor of a free market, one that grows organically. Ideally, perhaps, the Bowl would reflect the demographic makeup of America; realistically, it cannot. Let the market work its magic without manipulation by the Council. If gentrification is the result, so be it. Everyone is welcome here, but no one is *entitled* to live here. The utopian dream of a racially and economically diverse community should not be implemented artificially by *diktat*. If Bowl residents in particular, and Edmonds residents in general, skew older, whiter, and richer, that's the way the market works.

I ask you also, how much should our little town's Council concern itself with reversing climate change? How much can we affect the big picture with our local actions? Climate change is a matter for nations to deal with, not tiny communities like ours. Only a concerted national effort led by Congress—an imposition of carbon taxes so severe that they would cripple our economy and restrict our mobility—can hope to make a difference. Even so, without an alliance of many nations working on the problem, there is little hope. Think locally but act globally. And even then, is that what we really want? Do we want to revamp our whole way of life? Do we want to be unable to drive to Seattle to watch the Seahawks play or fly to Arizona to visit our dying mother undergoing hospice care in her senior community? Do we want to bundle up in parkas inside our homes during the winter? How much are we saving the environment from degradation by banning plastic utensils and plastic bags? Is it even measureable? How cost-effective is recycling? These are all feel-good nostrums that mostly succeed only in restricting our freedom. And not only that, but isn't it possible that some of our climate change is due to the vicissitudes of our solar

system—solar flares, for example, or variations in the earth's tilt—
that have been occurring since it clumped into being and that we
can do nothing about? Isn't it at least conceivable that we should
use our human ingenuity more to *adapt* to the effects of climate
change than to try to *reverse* it?

Now certainly it is fitting that the Council has instituted
Indigenous People's Day in October. The Coast Salish people who
inhabited our land before we did deserve our recognition and respect. But Indigenous People's Day should not be a replacement
for Columbus Day. Both holidays are important and both should be
celebrated in the same month. Columbus is the symbolic representative of the Europeans who came to this land and turned it into
a prosperous democracy that—in spite of its flaws—has been and
continues to be a beacon of hope to the oppressed throughout the
world.

And we are, and should be, proud to call ourselves a Safe City, a
city where legal residents of all races, ethnicities, creeds, and sexu-
alities are made to feel welcome and secure. A place where hate
crimes and hate speech are punishable to the full extent of the law.
But by the same token, let us always make sure that we honor that
most sacred freedom enshrined in the Bill of Rights, freedom of
speech. Let us respect the uttering of unpopular views even though
we might condemn the view itself. And let us never take the further
step of becoming a Sanctuary City that violates federal immigration
laws. Such law-breaking would not only be wrong but would add to
our overcrowding and also run the very real political risk of our being denied federal grants to improve our local infrastructure.

Now that word "infrastructure" brings me to one last concern:
the Council's proposed $27 million environmental excrescence
called the Waterfront Connector, a concrete bridge supported by
concrete pillars stretching over the railroad tracks from the intersection of Sunset and Edmonds streets and extending through
Brackett's Landing Marine Park to Main, blighting our landscape
and our seascape. A fiscal, ecological, and esthetically brutal

monstrosity, a scene stealer that would dismay residents and repel tourists. There have been promises of state and federal grants to help with the exorbitant costs, but those will not come close to covering the total bill, and you know what that means: higher local taxes for you and me. The irony is that a bridge is not even necessary. Emergency fire and medical aid for the beachfront can be provided much more efficiently and cheaply. We already have a fireboat, Marine One, to deal with our very rare waterfront fires, and for a fraction of the bridge's cost we could build a small triage health facility on the beach side of the tracks to deal with the very few waterfront medical emergencies that occur when stopped trains have blocked the access roads at Main and Dayton. We could even put a heliport on its roof to facilitate medical evacuations. Among all the possible ways to tear the gown of our charming little town, the Waterfront Connector would be the most unkindest cut of all. It would forever be our expensive, ugly, soul-sucking albatross, its erection the thin edge of a wedge that insinuates itself into our community and leads to zoning changes that would result in both tacky accessory dwellings and high-rise buildings, destroying the unique character of our place . I for one say that we should not try to become a diamond as big as the Ritz, we should be content simply to remain this sparkling little gem.

b

Good afternoon, sisters and brothers and others. I greet you here in the Edmonds Convention Center, but what I have to say is not conventional. We are in a time of crisis, both local and global. I grew up in our pretty little town in the '40s and '50s, oblivious to the very real existence of oppression and inequality. Naively, I believed that all men—yes, men!—were equal and that all could rise, socially and economically, as far as their characters and abilities would take them. I believed that all women were equal to each other, although not equal to men, and that all could rise, socially and economically, as far as their looks and personalities would take them. I thought that was the natural order of things. I was unaware that inequality—racial, sexual, economic— is systemic. White male privilege was so taken for granted in our culture as to be invisible. I had no idea that the system was rigged. Nor did I see that the system had been built upon the destruction of indigenous peoples and their cultures. Decades later, after I became a cardiac surgeon at Virginia Mason Hospital on Pill Hill in Seattle, I gradually woke up. I began to see how money and skin color affected one's ability to get quality health care. I began to see how gender affected one's professional opportunities for responsibilities and advancement. And there, as I gazed down occasionally at the perpetual chokepoint where I-5 narrows to worm its way through Seattle, I became increasingly aware of humankind's responsibility for climate change.

Today, I would not say that I am 'woke'—but I am more awake than I used to be, and in my wakefulness here is the Edmonds that I daydream of: a town that rediscovers its soul, a town that values inclusiveness, a town that offers diversity and density and affordable housing, a town where people are civil, yes, but not at the expense of fighting for what is right, not a town where a plea for civility (a foolish civility is the god hobblin' little minds!) is a weapon used by the patriarchy in defense of the *status quo,* and a sentimental plea to preserve quaint picturesque charm through single-family zoning serves actually as a NIMBYist Trumpian wall to screen out the *"declassé,"* a town that not only accepts but warmly embraces and enthusiastically encourages cultural and demographic changes (to paraphrase Shakespeare, sweet are the uses of diversity), a town that provides a safe space for undocumented immigrants, a town that celebrates indigenous peoples, a town that cherishes the environment and battles climate change, a town that realizes that for each species lost a piece of our soul is washed away, a town where every child has a roof over their heads, a town where senior citizens can age in place, a town that treats the homeless and the addicted with compassion, a town where every street is safe for pedestrians, a town that is working to improve the infrastructure and housing options in its International District.

And, in order to turn this dream into reality, here is what I think we need to do: remove height restrictions for condos and apartment buildings—but not for single-family McMansions—and allow the building of multiplexes and ADUs on single-family sites, subsidize contractors who are willing to build less expensive apartments, provide property tax relief for seniors and the disabled, build a homeless shelter, maintain our green spaces and our tree canopy, reconstruct the Bowl's dilapidated and dangerous sidewalks, improve disability access to sidewalks and buildings, exchange our gas-powered, polluting, city-owned vehicles for EVs, establish a parking area outside the Bowl and run shuttle buses downtown to reduce congestion and shrink our carbon footprint, encourage the establishment of bike-sharing and scooter-sharing businesses in the Bowl, encourage additional businesses to join the environmentally-conscious EnviroStars program, support the proposed ban on plasticware and Styrofoam, encourage recycling, provide funds to fully restore the Edmonds Marsh and improve salmon habitat, support the building of the Waterfront Connector because every life is precious and we must never disdain those who find themselves on the "wrong" side of the tracks, move Council meetings to the neighborhoods— Firdale, Five Corners, Perrinville, the International District— subsidize low-cost multiple-unit housing along Highway 99, reduce the speed limit there, and add median barriers and sidewalks and crosswalks, and last, but not least, preface every Council meeting with a statement recognizing and honoring the indigenous peoples from whom we took this land. Let us repay our debt to them by striving to achieve true equality. Let our future atone for our past.

C

Hi, everyone. It's wonderful to see you all here in the foyer of the Edmonds Center for the Arts, this beautiful Art Deco building

Bruce Evans

where I once attended high school. The contest for Position 8 is remarkable in that it features three candidates who are 80 years of age, longtime residents, and old friends and classmates. What are the odds? Each remains physically active and mentally alert, each is energetic, each still cares about what Edmonds was, is, and will become. I am proud to be in this race with such good people as Char and Monk, and I am confident that whoever wins will represent our townspeople (and octogenarians everywhere) with distinction. There are, however, some important differences among the three of us. Here at the old EHS, where I was senior-class president and a co-captain of the football, basketball and baseball teams, I learned the values not only of leadership and competition but of cooperation and compromise. And these values were reinforced by my professional experiences. After graduating from CPS in Tacoma, I went to OTS and served four years in the Army, then came back to Edmonds to work as an electrical engineer and project manager for Boeing, helping build 747s at the Mukilteo plant. I was all about team-building. The deterioration of civility in public discourse today, both nationally and locally, hurts me deeply. It tears at the heart and soul of our relationships. I am an independent who cares about people, not politics. I am not tied to any special interests or factions. I am neither progressive nor conservative. The positions I take are based not on ideology but on a genuine concern for the happiness of all. I want to bring all voices to the table, make sure that all points of view are heard, and make decisions that will satisfy a majority. I am not taking a stance in advance on issues such as the Waterfront Connector, affordable housing, climate change, Indigenous Peoples' Day, and so on. I'm about remaining calm, putting politics aside, and working out agreeable solutions to agreed-upon problems. All opinions are valid. There are no absolute rights and wrongs. It's true that Edmonds is more than just the Bowl, but it's also true that the Bowl is the heart of Edmonds. Yes, we must preserve our history, but we must also adapt to the present and anticipate the future. Yes, we must change—but not precipitously.

Our town's identity and character are indeed very special, but they cannot be preserved in amber. My goal will be to elicit full and frank discussions of the issues and then vote on the basis of what I think a majority wants. My opinions, my druthers, are not worthier than anyone else's. We're all equals. If it were practical, I'd refer all Council motions to popular vote, but since it isn't, I intend to vote for what I think will make the most people happy. That's as close to democracy as we can get.

[Monk's got my vote. Charlotte scares the bejeezus out of me! Maloney]

[I'll hold my nose and vote for Char. Liz Ann]

[I won't hold my nose—I'll inhale deeply and vote for Char! Sylvia]

[I suspect that Edmonds isn't as liberal as the 2016 Presidential polls indicated. Monk is going to win. Solveig]

4

A Noiseless Patient Spider

"Eeigle, schmeeweigle, steeigle," at eight wandering alone through the Maple Street neighborhood, down to Zee's or Monk's, writing cursively in the air with index finger, Palmer method, all loops and swoops, as instructed by Shakespeare, Miss Gwendolyn, third-grade teacher, and speaking in tongues, rapt in the sounds, floating in a warm bath of non-sense, playing with verbal feces, kid language, id language, his mother ice-creaming her hair at the kitchen sink, urring cake batter with a blender, id the entity in identity, immersed in the delicious irresponsibility of daydreams, a Blanc check, Si, Cy, Sue, okay you're a taxi, to feed his nightmares, who's on first, take my wife—please, but how the elephant got my jammies on I'll never know, reprieved from the repression of linguistic constraints, semantic and syntactic requirements suspended, upended, content manifestly absurd and latently too, meson-like bouncing freely and decaying rapidly in a linguistic chaos of condensations and recombinations, id expanding into idea, wormholing wit (woot, woot) forcing new connections, finding new doors, new odors, of perception, the mood subjunctive not indicative (as if!), transactive only in its resistance to authority and its phallic display, an inebriating chalice in wonderland bearing tequila mockingbird to him throned above the beach on his bench at 80, still enjoying an active lex life, lost in himself in the vacant vast surroundings, anarch of all he surveyed, dopamiened, mind ababble in a slurry of words made fresh, dragonbite of himwit falling on deft ears: a granma's anagrams, Alan and Lana both anal, distant star, Garbo, shooting star, LeBron, rock star, Alex Honnold, Japanese apprentice pastry chef passes doughnut-making test with frying crullers, Asian game store has Chinese checkers, ethics board finds Rachel Schlurr guilty of hate speech, odd, a venial memory speaks bearing a pale rezemblance to a story by Bokanov (we know our Vladimir liveth, abracadavera, he is risen), he says you're a...a poet, classicists, having a Latin common, infer that Dante painfully discovered a basic empiricist principle, seeing his Bea leaving, yet managed to attain a divine comity, surrounded by a slew of murderers our impassive faces mark us—oh, really, us?—as Stoics, abso—bloody—lutely, and now they're beating up liberals, those cucksockers, and my periodontal problems have me on an erosional molar coaster, Flunked your essay test, eh? Yes, words failed me, my talk sick masculinity, my girl friend's genes make her look phat, and she loves to do cartwheels and somersaults, Tumbler? Yes, I do, her body is Rubenesque and her breath smells of sauerkraut but she pursevers, that woman who's continually putting back the bag that keeps slipping off her shoulder, lobal warming the hot-ear sensation a man may feel when talk turns to his peckerdildos and m'lady's maladies, menstrual shows, becoming blue over red states, though sometimes God stops spots, Dog, Go ogle a porn website, oh, cripes, Suzette, we're tired of pancakes, so, quiche, Lorraine? eggs, Benedict?, Ze-zir salad, Caitlyn? enough isn't, all by his lonesome, idiosyncratic, so be id, let id be, futile felicity, finally, bringing no atonement, no salvation, no news for modern man, God's spell checked, tao lost in tau, Mnemosyne ultimately marooned in a clump of beta amyloids, Kilroy's inscription fading with time, the old handwriting on the wall, he had to wonder: Humans have invented some 6,000 languages, but do an infinite number of languages exist in God's mind (and wouldn't that make the number finite?)? Does God know an infinite number of, and infinite number

of combinations of, sounds and morphological and syntactic con-
structions? Is there a Proto-Theo-Lingo from which they have devolved? Does God think in an infinite number of languages
simultaneously? Does He, like Wittgenstein, know only what He has
words for, or does He think digitally, in ones and zeroes, or does He
not need language or numbers to think? Can there be language
without sounds or signs of some sort and bodies to make or receive
them? Is He just pure consciousness wherein thought is language-
and number-free and thought and action are one? Do all possible
uses of all languages already exist in God's data base? Can any human use of language ever be original in the sense that God hasn't
already imagined it? Did Shakespeare only write what God had already conceived? Can God ever be surprised by language usage or,
having already imagined an infinite number of *Finnegan's Wakes*,
can there be for Him literally nothing new linguistically under the
trillions of suns in this universe? Lord, don't stop me if you've heard
this one, but if, in a wrinkling of Your brow, with the intent of creating life, you produced a quantum fluctuation in the void and con-
cocted the singularity from which this universe ballooned, whose
effulgence on this rarest, sunniest, bluest, greenest of April days
from my vantage here at the base of the Bowl gleams from the flapping white wings of windhovering seagulls, this morning's minions,
from the whiteness of the churning ferry *Spokane* and its silver
wake, from the billowing white sails of surface-skimming sloops
and the powerful white cabin cruisers plowing their white-edged
furrows, from the snowy eastern slopes of the Olympics, and fills
me with in—fucking—effable joy, was a singularity, and that particular singularity (not a pleonasm), the only option You had? Must
any universe be exactly like this one? Must each and every singularity compact to the same density? Must each and every singularity
inflate to some two trillion galaxies? For life to exist, must each singularity produce exactly the amount of matter and energy and dark
matter and dark energy that exist in this one? Could you have
downsized or supersized your singularity? Or gone in another

direction altogether and made the universe steady-state? Or cyclic, a Big Bouncing from expansion to contraction to expansion to contraction *ad infinitum* rather than the one-way rush to disintegration implicit in the Big Bang? When you made the singularity, when you gave the Word, were You constrained by the natural laws of physics and chemistry that scientists have since discovered? Have there always been, so to speak, legal limits to Your creative options? Must E always equal mc^2? There's nothing You can do about it? Could you alter the speed of light if you wanted to? Are the prevailing laws the only laws that are possible? If so, where did they come from? If not, why did You impose them? In birthing the universe, could You not have come up with a quicker, cleaner, cold-fusion process? It couldn't have been done without all that heat and radiation? You had to explode a myriad of stars in order to make the elements that constitute me? It had to take 13.8 billion years for me to come into existence to sit on this bench here in the Bowl? What would You have been doing with your time—would there have been any time, or would there have been nothing but time?—prior to forming the singularity? Where were You when You when you did it? Where are You now? Are You to be found in every quirking quark, as a pantheist would claim, or standing idly by contemplating the harmonious operation of Your clockwork, as a Deist would maintain, or Schrodingerianly part of and apart from everything until You exercise an option? Whence came You? Were You before You were? How is it that You are immortal? Could You commit suicide if You wanted to? If not, why not? In any case, if, as my Christian Scientist grandparents believed, man is ultimately not material but spiritual, why is the material even necessary? We are such stuff as stars are made of and we can't be anything else? If You can separate soul from body at death, why create bodies at all? Why not make all experience an out-of-body experience? Why not settle for ethereality without materiality? The supernatural without the natural? Metaphysics without physics? Universals, not particulars? Heaven, not Edmonds? Timeless essences, not disintegrating Adams? Why not just one plane instead of two? Wouldn't that be more economical, more elegant, more pleasing to Occam? If all matter, including people, is nothing more than molecules behaving according to mathematical rules, why not be satisfied with the rules alone? If all things are number, if number is a preexisting ideal of which things are mere copies, why could not You, and any spiritual beings You might choose to create, be satisfied eternally contemplating the ideal? If the music of the spheres is an interplay of numbers, why do we need to see the spheres? Why do we need to hear the notes? Or is spirit, like music, feeling, then, not sound, a hyperlinking, self-transcending feeling of love and awe at the sensed immanence of God, a sublime, mystical joy found in the apprehension of a super-symmetrical yin/yang unity of the ideal and the material, realizable only through an exchange of electricity between neurons? Can we divine the existence of beautiful concepts, such as matter and energy being always in flux and transformable into each other at the quantum level, change without change, unceasingly, only by discovering their embodiment in the physical world? We can't *be* without ubiety? We can hear a fly buzz when we die but, absent some blooming of metempsychosis, not after we die? We cannot come by Caesar's spirit by dismembering Caesar? Without skin we lose touch not only with the world but with our self? Like atoms and electrons, we exist only in so far as we interact with an environment? No body, no feeling, no ecstatic insight? No body, no spirit, no soul, no self? At death, must the soul be given a new body or be transplanted into another body in order to continue its existence? Is resurrection or reincarnation requisite? Does the new body need oxygen and aliment? Does it excrete? Will it want sexual gratification? Does it have the same color that it had on earth? Does the social construct that is race deconstruct when the original body does? Does the new body have the original one's gender or genderlessness? Does it have the same brain and same memories? If it suffered from dementia, will it remember what it didn't experience? Will it speak the same language(s) that it did on earth? Is there a celestial Esperanto to serve as *lingua franca*? If so, how will facility in it be acquired? Or is there a celestial Google Translate that automatically converts language into the listener's preset preference? Does the new instantiation occur instantaneously with death? Can there be no state of being apart from material being? Or is there a provision for temporarily placing the soul on ice, a period, for Divine judgment perhaps, between the cleaving from one body and the cleaving onto another? And if Your ultimate Big Bang purpose was to create life and to place, at the top of a great chain of being, humans, why? You are, after all, perfect. For what reason was your self-sufficiency insufficient? Boredom? A disdain for the monotonous contemplation of mere abstractions? A pragmatic need to exercise Your omniscience and omnipotence by turning numbers and laws into things and beings? But, knowing everything and being able to do anything, wouldn't that exercise soon become boring too? Loneliness, emptiness? An aching need to be revered, adored? Graciousness? Delighted to the nth degree by the joy of consciousness and bubbling over with love, You chose to make it possible for other, though lesser, sentient beings to experience that delight to, shall we say, the mth degree? And, why, if some version or other of Christianity is true, did You choose to present the theory and practice of it piecemeal through revelation and scribes? One might question Your pedagogy. Clearly, Your classes have ever been unruly. Just as today some overwhelmed teachers expel students for eating in class, swamp them with meaningless assignments, separate them for talking and take away their cell phones for texting, play favorites, in some schools as a last resort even send them to the principal for physical punishment, so You expelled Your primal pupils for eating forbidden fruit, drowned all but the ark types in a flood, destroyed a tower to prevent people from sharing language to enrich their knowledge and power, privileged some as pets by making a covenant with them at the expense of all others, and rained fire and brimstone when all these methods of discipline failed. The entire *Bible* is a compendium of poor lesson plans. You have often seemed unprepared, winging it. Yes, Adam and Eve were born immaculately (discounting that mud for Adam and that bloody rib for Eve) in that they had no nature, no instincts, no genetic inheritance, and no nurture, no previous experience, no cultural history, no lore handed down by parents and community. Certainly it was a challenge to teach in *The Blackboard Garden*. All the more need, then, to craft a solid lesson plan. Marshalling the resources of rhetoric—*logos, pathos, ethos*—You should have won their hearts and minds with an anticipatory set and a clear statement of Your objective. You should have established Your authority at the outset, rather than assuming that they would love and respect You and accept Your word as law. Lecturing and hectoring, without motivation, illustration, and feedback, seldom lead to that change in behavior we call learning. Formal instruction, based on precept and admonition, and informal instruction, relying on unconscious imitation, must be supplemented by technical instruction. Rather than simply standing at Your dais in that open air classroom and offering Adam and Eve dominion over all the creatures of the earth and seas and admonishing them, on pain of death, not to eat of the fruit of the tree of the knowledge of good and evil, as if this would suffice to teach them to live in harmony with You and the animals and each other, You could have won their attention by retarding the pull of gravity and goosing the push of dark energy for just a nano-second and then, as for a nano-second they felt themselves infinitesimally rise involuntarily into the air, along with the tree and some vibrating fruit, and their flesh ever so slightly begin to uncongeal and their mouths almost open to shriek, returning the forms to their norms, smiling and making soothing sounds while catching a sparrow beginning to fall from its wobbling nest. Having narrowed Your students' focus, You could then have stated the lesson's objective, in infinitive form and from their point of view: To understand that they will have dominion over the earth and all its creatures, bask in Your love, and achieve immortality if they refrain from eating the fruit of the tree of the knowledge of good and evil. You could have

clarified the objective by explaining what it means to have dominion (possessing and exercising the poet's power to name, the horse-
whisperer's power to control), to bask in God's love (being
shot-through with feelings of joy and exaltation, unburdened by
conflict, angst, or guilt, rapturously warbling songs of innocence),
what immortality is (first a definition and then, for illustration, with
Eve as witness, *tout à coup* slaying Adam with a rabbit punch and a
moment later resurrecting him, then slaying Eve with Adam as witness, checking for specific behaviors in the process ((screams, wails,
moans, sobbing, gnashing of teeth, swooning, sighs of relief, wide
smiles, tears of joy, hugging)) as evidence of their understanding,
asking each to verbalize what they had learned from the explana-
tions and demonstrations, reinforcing with praise (("Good, good,"
"Save the mark," "Right on," "Yes!")) whenever possible, correcting
gently (("Not quite," "Sort of," "Can you think of another way to say
it?" "How do you define that term?" "Can you provide an example?")) when necessary, then going over to the tree in question,
warning that they must never touch it, warming them to You by
humorously cautioning them not to bark up the wrong tree like that
best friend they recently named *Canis lupus familiaris*, pointing out
how its bark and leaf structure differed from that of other trees,
identifying its fruit, explaining what "eating" meant (any piece,
however small, no matter how attractive and delicious they might
find it, taken into the mouth, swallowed or not), asking each to
paraphrase in their own words what You had just said, having them
demonstrate their understanding by taking a safe bite of fruit from
a different tree, trigger-warning them that You had a deep-seated
need for them to prove their love for You by resisting temptation
and that their fidelity and obedience would surely be tested by a
jealous, devious creature, a serpent perhaps, which lurked in the
Garden and would use its rhetorical wiles ("It's soo delicious, soo
nutritious, and, best of all, in eating it you will become like God") to
inveigle them to ingest the magical but forbidden fruit, cautioning
them to steel themselves, reiterating that if they failed to do so

they would be cast out of the Garden and cursed to an excess of brow-sweat toil and childbirth pangs, asking if they had any questions, answering those they had, then asking each to summarize in their own words the trigger-warning and its consequences, following that with a pop-quiz (Could they just touch the tree as long as they didn't eat the fruit? No. Could they take a bite of the fruit provided they didn't swallow it? No. Would they be pardoned for eating the fruit because they revered You and wanted to become just like You? No. Would they be given a second chance if they made a little mistake and took just a little bite? No. Would they be given probation or put on a from-work release program if they behaved well after leaving the Garden? No. Would their lives always be full of pain? Yes.), bringing the lesson to a conclusion by asking them to restate its objective in their own words once more, then, taking nothing for granted, popping back frequently to review and re-teach as necessary. You could have. But all along You knew it was a mug's game, didn't You? You and John Keating, John Novak, Gabe Kotter, Harvey Lipschultz, Jaime Escalante, Pat Morita, Mickey Goldmill, Frankie Dunn, Mr. Chips, Miss Dove, Miss Brooks, Miss Jean Brodie, Sam Mussabini, Charles Kingsfield, Richard Dadier, and Wayne Adams all know that no educational theory, no matter how philosophically and psychologically sound, no matter how meticulously put into practice, would have succeeded in achieving your objective. Knowledge and power sell; ignorance and innocence remain on the showroom floor. Humans bristle with psychological reactance. Capricious, captious, perverse, they resist the blandishments of seemingly advantageous restrictions or requirements that impinge on freedom and autonomy. They must play with fire.

A shadow fell over him.

"Wayne Adams?"

He turned to his right. A handsome, round-faced woman, deep-set dark eyes, teeth even and white, not entwined with each other or mottled like those of most of his coevals, inky hair, twisted into

Mobius strips by a curling iron, extending past her shoulders, bangs almost touching her eyebrows. Wearing a long-sleeved, scoop-necked, ankle-length beige dress with thin brown vertical stripes, a straw boater with a wide brown ribbon circling between its brim and crown, white running shoes, no socks. Was this Marie Osmond?

"Yes?"

"It's Sylvia Vose."

"Sylvia! Really? How are you?" He stood to shake her hand. He noticed through blurred peripheral vision that Sunset had been coming to life during his raptivity. Cars were creeping north from Main, out-of-towners stopping to park and love on the view. Pedestrians—solitary senior strollers like Sylvia or, their kids safely off to school, twosomes of fit young mothers chattering effortless-ly, joyfully, as they set an eight-miles-an-hour pace in their bright nylon shorts and tee shirts with matching headbands, their sweat jackets off and tied around their waists—had begun to populate the sidewalks. Hammers were pounding and saws screeching as ren-ovating carpenters were getting to work adding rooms and decks and balconies to a couple of '30s or '40s bungalows along the east side of the street. He set his iPad under the bench. "Please sit down and join me. I don't think I've seen you since our 25th reunion at the Landmark Inn in Lynnwood. We had one dance together."

"I remember. We did a little non-descript slow dance before you and Diane started flying all around the floor doing your disco stuff. I was so sorry to see her obituary in the *Edmonds Beacon* online 10 years ago."

"Yes, thank you."

"It was a car wreck?"

"Yes. Out by Echo Lake on old Highway 99. She was on her way home from a Bible study about 9:00 p.m. when a drunk driver crossed the center line and hit her head on."

"How awful."

"Yes. She never regained consciousness. Died at Stevens Hospital a day later."

"I'm so sorry."

"Yes. I still miss her. She strengthened me. But what about you? You told me during our dance that you and your psychiatrist husband Roger lived in San Francisco? You had a couple of kids? And you had just opened a little tea parlor *cum* art gallery?"

"Yes. I'm surprised you remember that. Well, a few years later Roger fell in love with his pretty receptionist and, truth to tell, I had a little fling with a young man who worked for me. Roger and I ended up divorcing, and Benjamin and Megan stayed with me. Roger married his receptionist, my young man soon escaped my cougar clutches, and I reassumed my maiden name (it's nice to see you wince at the utterance of that phrase). I've had a few male friends over the years but no long-term relationships. I discovered that I rather like being unencumbered. Ben and Megan are now in their fifties, Ben in Alaska and Megan in Utah. Together they've given me five grandchildren whom of course I adore. And Megan's daughter will make me a great-grandmother in October."

"So Sylvia returns to Sylvania for what— a brief visit? To see your brother and your cousins and a few old friends?"

"No, I'm back for good—if that word can be applied to an 80-year-old! Last year I finally sold my tea parlor/gallery, which was doing pretty well what with the tech boom in San Francisco but was also becoming way too much work, and when I did I began to feel an urge to get back to the old home town. I realized that here I could still dwell amid low clouds, hills, marine air, drizzle, cool temperatures, saltwater vistas, and gentrification, with the added benison of trees, and all made more poignant by the infusion of childhood and teenage memories. I've been settling in for the past month now."

" From 'Baghdad by the Bay' to *The Gem of Puget Sound*."

"Speaking of Clouds!"

"You remember Ray?"

"Of course. I used to read *The Tribune Review* from front to back every Thursday. I loved the 'Social and Personal' section. Gretchen

Meyring used to call my mother every week to find out where her sewing circle was going to meet."

"As you may remember, at one point my parents and I lived in the apartment above the *Tribune* office on Main, in what is now Glazed Amazed, a ceramics place. The floor used to shudder when that heavy linotype press thundered every Wednesday night. And my dad and Ray's son Ken were high school classmates. They played in a lot of bands together over the years."

"Yes, my parents used to go to the dances your dad played at the Seattle YMCA and the Lake City Elks' Club and The Merry Max Dine and Dance out on Highway 99. They'd been friends with your dad since grade school."

"Our families used to do a lot of things together. Picnics at Echo Lake. All that potato salad and blackberry pie. That huge log separating the wading area that we daringly swam under like navy frogmen on our way out to the raft. Poker games at your house or our house. You and your brother Vernal and I would play Monopoly on the living room floor, then fall asleep on the rug about 10:00 and our dads would wake us at 1:00 a.m. for the scrambled eggs that our mothers were making."

"I remember best that fifth-grade summer when you moved down to 4th. We spent a lot of time on our own running around in swimming suits at that beach down there."

"Sometimes I just sit on this bench and overlay a visual from the late '40s."

"The boathouses? Andy's and Jim's and the Edmonds with those tracks running about 50 yards out into the water so boats could get launched at low tide? They were always busy. Most everybody rented boats for fishing in those days—couldn't afford to have their own. The Edmonds Yacht Club was years away from existence."

"We certainly rented. At first, when we lived up on Maple Street, it was just a rowboat. On windless Sunday afternoons my dad would row us north to Brown's Bay and we'd fish for silvers with worms and pop gear. Later he saved up enough to buy a little five-horse

Evinrude and we'd get up at 3:00 a.m., my mom would make Spam sandwiches with lots of mustard and fill thermoses with coffee and cocoa, and we'd go out to Possession Point and troll with herring and dodger. The Sound was just gunwale to gunwale with kicker boats in those days. We caught more dogfish than anything, but we usually managed to get one or two humpies that my mother would bake for dinner."

"And the creaky old wooden ferry dock with its smell of creosote, the cars in line from the ticket booth and then back to the north on Sunset. Nothing like this wide concrete pier with the pedestrian overpass. No highway bypass extending from Edmonds Way to those holding lanes south of Main. No cops directing traffic. No two-hour waits. But what I remember most is the one sawmill that was still left down there south of the dock where the beach park is now. That sweet cedar smell in the sawdust and the smoke. And the massive log boom that we would wade out to at low tide and dive off."

"Into that 'scrotum-tightening sea'."

"Scalp-tightening for me! Did you hate the iciness of the water as much as I did?"

"More. But I kept doing it because in my dreams you were my girlfriend."

"Really! You didn't have a crush on Solveig?"

"Not until our senior year. In our sixth-grade summer, when you and I and Gary and Solveig and all our friends were old enough to go bean-picking, riding in that big old tarp-covered truck with the benches in the back that they crammed us into for the trip to the fields in Redmond, I'd scramble to wedge in next to you so we would be thigh-to-thigh and I could graze your breast with my elbow when we made a sharp turn."

"#MeToo! Objectivized sexually, even then! I was hardly aware of your moves, though, because I had a crush on Gary and was always sneaking peeks at him."

"Gary's running for City Council now, you know."

"Yes, I do know that. And Charlotte and Monk, too!"

"And they always attend our class reunions. As do I. Did you get your invitation?"

"I did. And I'm going to come. I'm excited to reconnect."

"Great! You can join us in singing."

"Singing?"

"Yeah. We always sing the *alma mater* after announcements and before we eat, but for this, our 80th year on the planet, I wrote a remembrance of our grade school and high school days that Gary is going to help me deliver, and also an Edmonds version of 'How About You?' as rendered by Frank Sinatra in his '56 LP 'Songs for Swingin' Lovers.' May I?"

"I guess."

"I liked the Bowl in June
How about you?
I liked how Mathis crooned
How about you?

I liked a pep assembly
With a big game due
Chocolate malts and cherry Cokes
Car coats and moron jokes
How about you?

I thought drive-in movies a treat
How about you?
If, that is, viewed from the back seat
How about you?

I liked the Wireless
And the Vodvil too
Desert boots and Mary Janes
Crew cuts and flowing manes
How about you?

I liked Jack Foster's class
How about you?
And giving Principal Hill sass
How about you?

Racing up and down 99
In a chopped Ford '49
Was crazy to do
But I liked it
How about you?

I liked watching 'Cheyenne'
How about you?
And being a Rainiers fan
How about you?

Packed team bus rides to Arlington
Where we seldom won
I'd never rue
'Cause I liked them
How about you?

From '54 to '57
With all our hormones revvin'
The time just flew
And I liked it
How about you?"

"Well how about that? My excitement mounts! But right now I have to finish my walk and get home because I'm expecting a phone call from my daughter. I prefer not to walk and talk—it's too distracting."

"And where is home?"

"Just over that way. I can see it from here. I bought one of the condos in that relatively new Pine Street development on the hill that used to overlook Union Oil."

"A great spot."

"I feel some entitlement guilt, but God help me I do like that place. I'm close to the water, I can watch waves spilling themselves on the beach, I can see past Whidbey up the Sound to Hat Island and beyond that to Mt. Baker. If I turn slightly to my right I look over the marsh and the bird sanctuary—the swallows, the crows, the blue herons, the goldfinches—and up at all of the town—the houses and business buildings and tree-covered hills—the cradle of my life, my *omphalos*. I gaze out, and then I gaze within."

"So you meditate."

"I do."

"And what else?"

"I walk, read, watch stuff on Netflix and HBO Go."

"Like what?"

"Like *Orange Is the New Black*, *Schitt's Creek*, *Veep*, *Silicon Valley*, *Arrested Development*, *Curb Your Enthusiasm*."

"Some of my favorites."

"And I shop. I've always enjoyed prowling boutiques, craft shops, consignment stores, used-book stores. I maintain an extensive email correspondence with San Francisco friends. Thursday I'm going to visit the Edmonds Cemetery and look at the graves of my parents and some of the other Edmonds old-timers."

"I haven't been to the Cemetery since my dad died in '99. Both of my parents, my paternal grandparents, and my dad's sister and brother-in-law are buried there too."

"What about Diane?"

"Diane is not buried anywhere. We both willed our bodies to science and opted for cremation years ago. When I asked where she'd like her ashes scattered if I should happen to outlive her, she said, 'Surprise me. I'll be watching you from afar, you know. I'll be up in Heaven, having the time of my death.' She believed strongly that her soul would be given a new body after her old one died. So late one afternoon, after the Science Care people were through with her and a few days after the memorial we held for her at the Hilltop Presbyterian Church, attended by a throng of her former colleagues and students and fellow church members and Lynnwood Golf Club members, I put her urn in my golf bag and walked on as a single at the Lynnwood course that we had played together so often for years. I imagined her watching me as I hacked my way from hole to hole. After I bogeyed the 12th, a 100-yard par 3 that she loved because she made so many birdies there, so often just knocking her 7-iron stiff and sinking the putt, I looked in all directions to be sure no other players or the course marshal could see me, then scattered her ashes beneath the maple trees back of the green."

"And said a little prayer over them?"

"No. And Diane would not have expected that of me. She and I had different views about prayer."

"Wayne, why don't you join me at the cemetery on Thursday?"

"You know, I could. Thursday's my day off."

"Day off? You're not still working?"

"Oh, no. I mean a day off from softball practice or weightlifting or shooting baskets. After I retired from teaching, I discovered the amazing world of competitive senior softball. I played a few years in the local Edmonds league, just thrilled to be playing at all, forever *homo ludens*, you know, then at 60 got involved in a couple of Seattle leagues and hooked on with a traveling team comprised of guys from Tacoma, Renton, Bellevue—all over the area. Gary was content just to play in Edmonds, but I wanted more. From April to October I'd play weekend tournaments throughout the west— Kelowna, Wenatchee, Olympia, Salem, Eugene, Concord, San Jose, Santa Barbara, Palm Springs, Phoenix, Mesa, Las Vegas, Mesquite, St. George, Denver. I kept up the pace as we progressed through the age divisions—60, 65, 70—but when we hit 75, with the ranks thinning due to infirmity and death, we began to cut back. This year, in fact, I'm going only to one tournament—St. George. And I'm now playing again only in the Edmonds league, which itself is becoming a very difficult challenge because there are no age divisions—just

55+. Five years of age makes a significant difference in speed, strength, coordination, endurance. Twenty-five is downright scary. So that's why Gary and I practice on our own three days a week. The Z-man and I are still reliving our childhoods. In our minds we're still the Maple Street All-Stars."

"Well, I want to relive my childhood by visiting the cemetery. So what do you think? Want to meet me there on Thursday? 10:30?"

"Let's do it."

[Wayne, your "mind ababble in a slurry of words made fresh" section is at best puerile, at worst sexist and racist. I would advise you to leave it out. Charlotte]

[Wayne, old buddy, I find your lesson plan parody as much a satire of ITIP methodology as of God's pedagogy. Bill]

[Sorry I interrupted your "raptivity," Wayne. But was it really getting you anywhere? I find meditation more rewarding than wheel-spinning. Sylvia]

[Wayne, your questions run the gamut from Solomonic to sophomoric. In regard to the possibility of God's thinking without language, "mentalese" (with its aural tease of "mentalease") might be the word you are looking for. An omniscient subject needs no language, no logic, no brain. It knows immediately and eternally. God never does mathematics. In regard to why there is a material world, something rather than nothing, and why people are material beings rather than spiritual essences, I subscribe to Leibniz's Principle of Sufficient Reason. For every truth, there must be a reason why it is so and not otherwise; and for every *thing* there must be a reason for that thing's existence. There must therefore be an explanation for the existence of the world, whether we can find it or not. This teleological explanation does not have to posit or imply the existence of God. "Un-things" (such as mathematical entities and logical laws discoverable by human reason) might furnish an answer to the mystery of the world's existence. I, of course, am partial to a theistic explanation. Dave]

5

Uncut Hair and Mothers' Laps of Graves

He parked on 9th, which was called 100th W. outside the Bowl, and waited on the sidewalk before the cemetery's primary entrance. A ghostly gray, cool morning—onshore flow again—with the possibility of afternoon sun. He was wearing his New Balance shoes, black jeans, and a gray hoodie zipped up to his jugular. Fists jammed into hoodie pockets, he gazed out at the cemetery, a sunken, mostly open six-acre rectangle bounded by tall evergreens on the west and south which shielded it from a Westgate strip mall and a housing development, by lightly-trafficked 15th on the north, and by busy 9th/100th on the east. A narrow blacktop service road ran east-west, another north-south. Except for an elevated Columbarium plaza with waterfall erected in its northeast corner in 2006, the cemetery, founded in 1891, remained true to its modest origins. Its sward, green but not lush, littered here and there with wind-blown fir and pine cones, was kept unevenly trim with tractor-mower and weed-whacker. Somewhere in there lay the bones and scraps of burial suits and dresses of his grandfather and grandmother and mother and father.

The old man was the last surviving member on both his mother's and his father's sides. His mother's parents, her brothers and sisters and their offspring, who all lived in Seattle and with whom he had lost contact by the time he reached middle age, were gone.

His Edmonds grandfather had died of prostate cancer in 1965. He had fought the illness, not knowing what it was because he would not consult a doctor, by praying and reading *Science and Health*. His grandmother, trapped between faith and fear, finally begged, when his grandfather could not get out of bed on his own, to let her take him to the emergency room of the newly-constructed Stevens' hospital, just south of the new high school on 76th. He was terminal. They put him in a double room and hooked him up to oxygen and an IV. The old man and his father and Diane visited the next day. They found little to say. They mentioned that the Seattle Rainiers were off to a good start. His grandfather was taciturn, resentful, could not look them in their eyes, ashamed that he had failed his faith, had let Satan in by succumbing to the illusion of ill health. After a few minutes, they left awkwardly. At 4:00 a.m. the old man received a call from his mother. Once visiting hours were over and the nurse had made her bedtime check, his grandfather had pulled the IV from his arm and the oxygen from his nose and willed himself to die. His grandmother went to live with his parents. At family gatherings on holidays and birthdays everyone sat in painful silence as she repeated stories about her childhood and her life with Bertrand, her autonomic system humming along without "her." When her dementia became too much for them to cope with, they put her in a home in Lynnwood, where she soon died of congestive heart failure. His mother, who had suffered for years with ulcerative colitis, atrial fibrillation, migraine headaches, and osteoarthritis (three surgeries on her knuckles retarding the clubbing of her hands just enough to enable her to continue, agonizingly, to punch the keys on the cash register at Safeway), died at 55 in 1975. In March she had become apathetic, had no appetite. She began calling in sick, saying that she'd go back to work the next day but never doing so. In pajamas and robe, with a crooked index finger she'd dial her call from the wall phone in the kitchen, then retreat to lie on the couch all day. She said she had the flu. The old man and Diane came every few days to the old two-story house on

Wharf Street in north Edmonds, which had a glimpse of the Sound between cedars and the large waterfront split-level owned by a state legislator, and talk about what they were doing—cultivating their garden at their house on Grandview, playing in couples' golf tournaments, planning a summer trip to Europe. She brightened at their visits, smiled at what they had to say. She herself said little more than that she felt as if her body was encased in cement. She wasn't vomiting or coughing, she was just inert, too tired even to smoke her Pall Malls. The old man would coax her to take a few bites of Jello or ice cream by spoon-feeding her. She so welcomed his attention, his touch on her shoulder. His father could not get her to eat more than a bite of toast or poached egg, although she would drink the coffee he brought to her from the percolator that was always plugged in. One day she banged her shin on the coffee table and her skin shredded and peeled away from the flesh. His father took her to the ER at Stevens where a doctor examined her and promptly admitted her to a double room. X-rays revealed that she had advanced lung cancer. The pain came on within days. They put her in a private room and gave her morphine shots. The old man and his father visited her every night for a week. On what turned out to be the last night, they came in to find his mother and a friend from work hugging each other, her friend appending consolatory pats. The tears in their eyes released a flood from the old man's as well, bringing a tiny, grateful smile to his mother's lips. When the friend left, his mother called "Shot" to a nurse who had popped her head in, then resumed her forlorn mien. As the morphine took effect, his mother fell asleep, breathed very deeply, exhaled, then lay without inhaling for half a minute. The old man did not know what a death rattle was. Could this have been one? At last she took another deep breath, exhaled, and lay seemingly breathless again. The old man's father looked at him and said, quietly, "Did you think she was gone?" "I did." They remained in the room for half an hour. "I suppose we might as well go home," his father said. "Yeah." "She'll be unconscious for hours. They'll call us if...."

"Yeah." "Why didn't you stay?" Diane said when he got home. "She must be near the end." "She could hang on for quite a while, and I've got school tomorrow." At 3:00 a.m. his father called. "Wayne, Mom's gone," he said, and then sobbed gutturally. The old man had never heard such sounds coming from him. "Dad, do you want me to come over?" "No, there's nothing you can do. I'll be all right." "Why don't you go over there?" Diane said. "He needs you. You need each other. You can take bereavement leave tomorrow." She got out of bed and embraced him. He hadn't known how much he wanted to be held. He did not go over that night, but he did take bereavement leave the next day and met his father at Beck's Funeral Home to make the arrangements. More than 100 people crowded the mortuary chapel—coworkers and spouses, Music and Art Club friends and spouses, Sewing Circle friends and spouses, Edmonds merchants and spouses. A Presbyterian minister that Diane knew gave a restrained eulogy, outlining his mother's life, she who believed in an undefined God and wanted everyone to go to church though she herself never did, and speaking of rewards to come. Although his father could play the piano for an audience, he was unable to speak to one. The old man, however, had spent parts of the three days before the funeral preparing an elegy which he recited at the grave, the mourners hunched in heavy coats against a cold wind, after the minister's final brief prayer and before Steve Beck said "This concludes the service, folks."

My mother lived in throbs of pain
Her tissues taut, her joints aflame
Yet that did not her love deter
And she gave us more than we gave her.
Now, earth, into your lap we place
This tough, tired lady for your embrace
And make of you a last request:
Pillow her in eternal rest.

His father had died of pneumonia at 82. After the old man's mother's death, his father continued to live in the ramshackle house on Wharf Street for another 10 years. For a few months he actually seemed brighter, more alert, engaged. When the old man would telephone, he would often get, if not no answer, a busy signal. His father continued to teach piano to a few students at Mills Music in Bothell and to play the odd dance gig, but increasingly clubs were dispensing with live bands in favor of cheaper DJs and recorded music. Most sold off their pianos; his father was forced to buy a portable keyboard and lug it along to the few jobs that he did manage to contract. In time he seemed to lose confidence in himself. He began to let things go. He made only token efforts to keep his bathroom and kitchen sink clean and to sweep the kitchen floor, ignoring the powdery dander accumulating on furniture and sills and the film from the two packs of Winstons he smoked daily that was gradually opaquing the windows. Once a year the old man Pledged and Windexed for him. Dropping by occasionally for a cup of coffee, the old man would renail a loose plank he noticed on the deck or get up on a ladder to change a dead light bulb in an overhead fixture. When he found himself taking on the chores of weeding around the shrubbery and mowing the lawn, the old man began urging his father to sell the house to an interested developer who wanted to demolish it and rebuild it. The thought troubled his father—to erase his house was to erase him—but eventually he came round to conceding the advantages of leaving the drafty, creaky place and moving back to the Bowl. He bought a one-bedroom condo unit with a wide view in an older building on Alder on the hill above Old Milltown. Diane helped him pack. The old man rented a U-Haul and did most of the lifting and carrying. His father worked less and less. He mostly stayed in the apartment, studying the activity on Puget Sound through binoculars, watching sports on TV, and reading the Seattle newspapers, *The Reader's Digest* and, although he seldom bought anything, *Consumer Reports*. Diane invited him to dinner every two weeks. His father would regularly bring mail-ordered Omaha steaks for Diane to broil and she would always have prepared his favorite, angel food cake with chocolate frosting, for dessert. After dinner the two men would watch a televised game together while Diane made phone calls or went for a walk. Other nights his father drove to the new China Palace at 5th and Walnut, to Clare's Pantry at 3rd and Main, to Portofino's on Olympic View Drive, or to Jimbo's on 196th in Lynnwood and dined alone. To give them an activity in which they could spend time together, the old man offered to begin bowling with him in a Tuesday night league at Robin Hood Lanes in Westgate. His father had been a bowler for years, but the old man had only bowled a few games as a lark with friends or with Diane. Immediately the competition excited him. The first few nights he used a house ball and, doing what came naturally, threw it with a back-up spin. The rare strikes that he got were misfires pulled left that happened to back into the Brooklyn pocket. His father had his own ball and threw a skidding hook from an upright five-step hopping approach, braking suddenly to a stop on a stiff left leg, not sliding into it, and landing the ball on the lane with a thunk. He averaged in the 150s. The old man read *The ABCs of Bowling*, borrowed from the library, and observed closely the various bowling styles on display in the league matches, amazed at the skill and power of the surprising number of bowlers who averaged 200 or more. He bought a ball at the alley pro shop, had it drilled to fit his hand and weighted to hook. He decided on a simple four-step approach, staying low with knees bent, starting one board left of center and throwing his ball over the second arrow to get it to break into the one-three pocket. Tempo was crucial for him. If he didn't rush to the line, if he started his arm swing as he took his first step, if he kept his arm relaxed and released the ball smoothly at the end of the swing, if he kept his eye on the arrow, if he followed through, he could throw a hooking, working ball with fair speed and accuracy. He was thrilled by the visual and auditory triumph of the powerhouse strike, pins blasting backward with *éclat*, was tantalized by the agony and ecstasy of the mixer, unexpected strikes, unexpected splits, pins crazily tripping up or flying past one another on balls that were light in the pocket but driving hard, and galled by the pocket hit that left a solid 10-pin. The result of every shot could basically be explained by the laws of Newtonian physics—speed, spin, angles, and coefficients of friction—but those laws could not be exploited to his satisfaction on every shot, and always there was the possibility that they would be subverted by quantum uncertainties. In his first year he averaged in the 160s and gradually improved until, in his fourth year, he peaked at 190. He and his father would acknowledge each other's good shots wordlessly, with a smile, a nod, and a high five. The night in 1990 that their team won its lone league championship, the two of them bought their teammates a round of beers and nachos in the alley's bar and snack shop. It was the only athletic triumph of his father's life, and he proudly displayed the championship trophy on top of his piano in his condo. In 1999, after they had dined together on Sunday and bowled together on Tuesday, the old man's father called on a Saturday in February and said, "Wayne, I'm sick. I started coming down with something when I came home from bowling this week." He was coughing, shivering. He lacked the energy even to dress himself and go out to eat. The old man brought him tomato soup and plain red Jello from the deli at the Westgate QFC, but he was unable to eat them. "Dad, you've got to see a doctor." "At 8:00 o'clock? It's too late. Take me to Dr. Hope tomorrow." "You need help right now. I'll take you to Stevens." "I don't want to go to the hospital. I want to stay home." "We have to go, Dad." The old man dressed him, uneasy about helping him into his boxer shorts. In the car the two were silent, listening to the Husky basketball game on the radio. When the ER doctor diagnosed pneumonia and ordered him to stay, his father panicked. "Let me go home, take me home, I want to go home," he insisted. "Dad, you have to stay. It's the only way you can get better." "I can take medications at home. I promise I will." He kept trying to get out of bed, his gown flying open, but the old man restrained him. Finally, nurses tied down his arms and inserted an IV and a catheter. The next morning, after glucose and saline and a steady dose of antibiotics, he was better—and even more bitter. He kept wiggling, agitating, trying to loosen his bindings. "Untie me. Take me home. Let's go. I'll be all right. Let me up. I have to go to the bathroom." "Dad, you're on a catheter." "Amazing stuff, those antibiotics," the pulmonologist, Dr. Alan Barnett, said. But on the day after that his condition began to worsen rapidly. They put him in the ICU. The old man visited twice a day. His father was morose. The old man told him that, when they did get the pneumonia cleared up, he would have to go into a rehab facility for several weeks. "Oh, cripes," his father said, "it's not worth it." Those were his last words. Immediately he feigned sleep and invited death to overtake him. Two days later the doctor moved him out of the ICU and into a private room, where they kept him sedated and waited another three days for him to die. About 30 people—a couple of adult former piano students, some fellow bowlers, some coeval Edmonds old-timers like the Hamiltons and the Andersons, and Zee and Janice, Monk and his second wife Sandra, Diane and her sister Linda, and a few that the old man did not recognize—attended the funeral at Beck's. The old man employed a minister from a list provided by Beck's, furnished biographical details, and asked him to present a religious-reference-free *curriculum vitae*. His father had, at the request of the old man's grandparents, occasionally filled in as substitute organist at the Christian Science Church, and he kept a copy of *Science and Health* on the bookshelves that held his *Digest* collection, but otherwise had evinced no interest in religion. He and his father had not once discussed the subject, a fact about which the old man was exceedingly glad. When the minister finished, the old man stepped forward to the lectern which sat on a table that also held his father's old portable hi-fi turntable, his metronome, and a plain white LP sleeve. He extracted from the sleeve a 1974 recording of the George Adams trio live at the Lake City Elks and played "These Foolish Things," a five-minute track on which his father soloed extensively, lyrically and tenderly, as if from deep within, Teddy Wilson-like clean right hand single notes alternating with gentle two-hand chords, his tour de force, the old man thought, tears welling. When the beauty died, two tears from his left eye having waterfalled onto his glasses as he bent to cradle the tone arm, he warbled for the dead one:

My father was a slim, shy man
Whose feelings you might think he'd banned
Until his fingers touched piano keys.
Then how eager he was to please
To bob and shudder, shout and moan
And take us with him, no longer alone.

He set the metronome to ticking and invited the mourners to pass by the open casket.

At the gravesite, following the minister's spare "ashes to ashes, dust to dust," a slight, acne-scarred woman with shoulder-length gray hair approached the old man. "Wayne, I'm Maureen. I was a friend of your father's in the '70s. We met at the Lake City Elks when he was playing regularly there. Sometimes we'd have a drink together after hours, you know. Then we kind of drifted apart. But I was so glad to hear that recording. It brought back many wonderful memories. I loved his solos on that old beat up grand they had. I didn't go there to dance, I went to listen to him."

As his stomach dropped, he thanked her for coming. So it had been an affair, an infusion of passion, a remission from the quotidian, that had given his father a brief new life, even as, for of course she must have known, it stole his mother's from her.

He turned back toward the street and saw a waving, smiling Sylvia, who had just pulled up in her sea green Prius, its homely aerodynamic forward slant proudly humble.

"Hi," "Hi," they said on the sidewalk, exchanging brief hugs and back pats.

She was wearing black cotton pants, a black cloth trench coat, and sneakers with oversized soles for stability.

"I thought we'd just wander across the grass in a clockwise direction, note some of the names out of our past, visit our parents' graves, then sit for a few minutes by the Columbarium," Sylvia said.

"Okay," the old man said. "'Wandering over the beautiful uncut hair and mothers' laps of graves.' Which is not, we must concede, growing among black folks as among white. We were—and are still, in the Bowl—a very white enclave. Do you think there are any blacks at all buried in this cemetery?"

"I doubt it. Tree-cutting whites kind of took this whole lovely area from the few Native Americans that were here and then your grandparents and mine arrived and unwittingly (let's give them the benefit of the doubt) erected economic and cultural barriers that discouraged people of color from moving in. At least we recognize our privilege now, and I know that the City Council has formed a committee to promote diversity, but certainly well into the future we will continue to experience the incredible lightness of being here."

[The myth of the noble savage seems to be essential to many "enlightened" *weltanschauungs* today. I would remind you that the sedentary Coast Salish hunter-gatherers who preceded us whites developed an inegalitarian society structured on the basis of hereditary nobility. They were patriarchal, sexist, and bellicose. They were territorial, kept slaves, hoarded luxuries, and flaunted their wealth in ostentatious potlatches. Monk]

[No society is perfect. In any case, the perception of a few flaws in Native American tribes, who were so wonderfully in tune with their environment, in no way justifies their brutal treatment and the criminal expropriation of their lands by whites. Charlotte]

"Well, you, maybe. Me, not too likely. I'm sensing time's winged chariot hovering near."

"I'm not your coy mistress, you know."

"No, no, of course not. These days sex only embarrasses me. I was having trouble even 10 years ago, when Diane was alive. She would KY up expectantly, but an hour after taking Viagra my stomach was cramping, my bowels were rumbling, and I had achieved only a flaccid sensitivity. Today, if I entered a Seinfeldian contest, I would win, hands up. I'm the *condottiero* of my condo. Or is that TMI?"

"There's no such thing as TMI. I'm interested in everything. What I meant is that I'm not shy, I don't play hard to get, and I'm not owned by anyone. But is it just old age bringing time's Uber, or are you referencing your multiple myeloma?"

"Multiple myeloma. If you live long enough—if something else doesn't kill you first—it's inevitably fatal. So in the offing, prior to my offing, are chemo and radiation, wretched retching, fatigue to the marrow. But at this moment I feel fine. I'm taking massive doses of calcium and Vitamin D to strengthen my bones against the inevitable crippling onslaught of osteoporosis that the cancer produces. I had an infusion of Zometa last month to kill off some of the surplus of cancer-causing white blood cells that infest my bone marrow and will have another in a couple of months. I have energy. I have a goal."

"To win gold at the Huntsman Senior Games!"

"Yes! Why don't you come with me?"

"Hah! Except for swimming, I've never cared a thing for sports."

"You wouldn't have to care about the games. You could just immerse yourself in the beauty of the landscape—the mesas, the buttes, the iron-rich red cliffs, the lava fields, the white rock mountains, the canyons. And, of course, in the pathos of aging, desperate old men casting themselves as characters in a theater of the absurd."

"For the moment, let's just immerse ourselves in the homely beauty of this landscape."

"Sure."

They stepped off the service road and onto the uneven grass. Most of the older graves were marked by gray flat cement plates or gray stubby cement headstones with laconic inscriptions: names, dates, relationships ("mother, sister, friend," "brother, son, grandson"), husbands and wives and sometimes children lying side by side beneath the simplest of home pages. Many of the newer ones were mini-monoliths: three-foot tall sculpted pieces of granite, obsidian, or terra cotta, personalized with inset colored lithographic headshots of a smiling deceased surrounded by bas-relief etchings (a tennis racquet, a music staff with a treble clef and two measures of quarter notes), fraught with engraved outpourings ("God took her home, it was His will, but in our hearts she will live forever," "We miss, remember, and mourn you"), farewell hashtags from the bereaved. Cautiously, paying attention equally to their footing and to the graves, he sometimes grabbing her elbow, she sometimes grabbing his, one stumbling on the uneven two-inch concrete curbing that outlined some of the graves, the other miscalculating a drop step into one of the many declivities produced by the earth's heaving here and settling there, weaving in and out among the maze of graves randomly while working clockwise generally, the yard's only visitors at that hour, far from the madding crowd, all quiet except for the faint swish of tires on 100th to the east and the claxon caws of crows in the hemlocks to the west, noting plastic vases of plastic orange-red dahlias and plastic yellow daisies, here and there a real rosebud decaying, and sporadic plantings of small, fading American flags, stepping over unraked clumps of yellow-brown grass recently sheered and seared by a weed-whacker, walking among millwrights and sawyers and merchants whose premises they had frequented, and clerks and bus drivers and mechanics and teachers, like Joyce Koerner who in fifth grade had taught them about Hernando De Soto and Ponce de Leon and John Jacob Astor and Jim Bridger and read to them Caddie Woodlawn stories, and like Teddy Albert, their young charismatic high school choir director with the wavy hair and the bold grin, his prominent bicuspids tangling with his incisors, and secretaries and housewives and helpmeets, past pioneers and the sons and daughters of pioneers, many of whom had been active in the businesses and service clubs and city administrations that had defined community parameters in the '40s and '50s, past others who had blushed unseen, by the old man and Sylvia at least, mute Miltons perhaps, nearing the Columbarium they finally came upon, within 20 feet of each other, the graves of George Clarence Adams, Margaret Elizabeth Adams, Edward James Vose, and Violet Gladys Vose.

"Ah, George and Maggie," Sylvia said. "I always liked them. But your dad was really shy."

"Yes, he was. And that was okay with me. We had a good relationship because we both kept our distance. He tried jobs like selling cars and giving piano lessons to supplement his income as a musician, but he was not very successful because it was so hard for him to marshal his rhetorical resources. He would wait for days in the showroom at Hopper Chevrolet for that special customer who had already made up his mind to buy. He could successfully teach piano only to students who were self-motivated to practice. My mother finally got so exasperated that she took a job checking groceries at Safeway. She always wanted us to be richer and to have a better house and to be noticed in the community. But to me his diffidence was a welcome quality. We could talk freely about sports and jazz, and neither one of us ever wanted to get personal or spiritual or metaphysical. I felt he was always proud of me, but he never pushed me into anything, even music. Three different times I started in on piano lessons with him but I never lasted more than two weeks because I would neglect practice to go out and play ball with Gary and Monk and the guys."

"And your mother was always so social and active. Kind of like my mother in that way. Going to Sewing Circle every week, Music and Art every month, serving as Cub Scout den mothers, arranging birthday parties for us kids and Halloween and Christmas parties for the adults. Sometimes, if things got too quiet for her, my mom would lift the phone off the hook on the wall, give the operator a number to put through, tell one of her friends or sisters or cousins that she'd be dropping by, put both me and my brother on the front bench seat of our round-backed '48 Ford so she could extend a protective arm in case she had to stop short, and away we'd go, the mothers chit-chatting and drinking coffee for a couple of hours, the kids left to figure out a way to play together."

"And your dad?"

"Kind of in between your dad and Maggie and Vi. He drove bus for the STS for years, of course, and that was a good role for him. I rode with him sometimes in the summer—kind of an early take-your-daughter-to-work thing, I guess. He had a little patter with the riders, he could tease and joke a bit while he steered with his left hand and clicked change from the coin changer on his belt with his right or reached up and ripped off a transfer from a pad clipped to the dashboard. He said he always enjoyed the little interchanges. I could tell that he liked the power of calling out place names authoritatively—"Lago Vista, Wallingford"— and that he felt he was performing a valuable service in getting people to their destinations. But at home he was pretty quiet and it was my mom who ran things."

"Mine too. My dad was the titular head of the house. He kept the books, paid the bills. He loved cars, and although my mother thought it unnecessary, he bought a new used one—strategically avoiding the heavy first-year depreciation, you know—every four years. A '50 Ford in '51, a '54 Studebaker in '55, a '58 Chevy in '59. He sold that one to himself, when he worked at Hopper's—one of his rare commissions! But my mom was the family's engine. She organized the fishing, the bowling, the picnics, the trips to the Husky games. She was the one out looking at real estate—vacant lots, spec houses, recent listings for sale or rent. She was the reason we moved eight times before I got out of college and went to live on my own. She was the one who declared when I was in grade school that I was going to go to college—which no one on either side of my family had ever done—and made my dad buy a $250 savings bond to finance my freshman year. And she was the one who decided to cash in that bond when I was in high school and apply the money toward a down payment on a new house with a peek-a-boo view on Hummingbird Hill!"

"Does that explain why you commuted to U-Dub and I lived on campus? You had to live at home and work part-time to finance your own education, whereas my parents had just enough money to get me into a dorm?"

"Exactly. Fortunately, in 1957 we could get into the U with just a 2.0 g.p.a., and tuition was only $60 a quarter. After graduating from high school, I sold my '49 Ford convertible for $500 and downscaled to a $200 '48 Chevy coupe, worked summers on the school district grounds crew, and during the school year boxed groceries part-time at Safeway. I got by."

"I had it a little easier. I didn't have to work during the school year, but I chipped in $400 a year to my parents for my education. Summers I took a lot of baby-sitting jobs and worked weekends clerking out at the fruit stand on Highway 99 near Lake Ballinger."

"So let me ask you, were our families typical, and if they were, were we actually living in a matriarchy wink-winking at the Biblical and cultural myth that father Ozzie knew best while Harriet provided the true wisdom and grit and glue for her family? Were women sexploiting their husbands, offering them a missionary position (at least I can't imagine my mother exploring any other alternatives) twice a week to gain control of the family?"

"Not at all! Don't give me that 'hand that rocks the cradle' business. Don't give me that *Our Town* nonsense about women voting indirectly by influencing their husbands before the 19th Amendment came along. Any 'control' that women exerted in the '40s and '50s devolved to them circumstantially. Women assumed the responsibilities of child-rearing and insuring domestic integrity and coherence because men either abdicated them or delegated them. Women had no real authority. They might have appeared to be leaning in, to be empowering themselves, to be surreptitiously assertive without asserting, to feel an inner potency and worth, but they were only doing what their husbands in effect commanded them to do. They had little real authority at home—they were paper-tiger mothers—and none at all in the outside world. They were oppressed by a social construct whose administrators were men—who, incidentally, in a different way, were oppressed by that construct, too. Men were not allowed to be tender, nurturing, expressive, emotional."

"They suffered from toxic masculinity?"

"Yes."

"And who was responsible for the construction of that construct?"

"Men themselves! From the testosterone-dominant prehistoric caveman times, cartoon apeman types brandishing a club in one hand and dragging a nubile female in an off-the-shoulder animal skin outfit by her long ratty tresses in the other, from the original male-dictated division of labor—men the hunter-warriors, women the child-bearers, home-fire-tenders, and berry gatherers—to the days of big-cheese farmers in the dell 'taking' wives ('hi-ho, the derry-o,' we all pat the bone), to captains of industry and finance, Dayly life with father, Clarence laying down the laws of efficiency to Lavinia, and everything cheaper by the dozen, don't you know, down to George and Edward wearing the pants, Margaret and Violet the housedresses."

[Reader, I understand your vexation but hope that by now you've willingly suspended your disbelief and become tolerant of the many lengthy polished pronouncements that come so trippingly off the tongues of Wayne's characters in various colloquies. *Les lecteurtrices moyen sensible* must remember that this is a closet novel whose reality is virtual, at best. As Cabinet Secretary Sir Humphrey Appleby in perhaps the greatest of all sitcoms, the BBC's *Yes, Prime Minister*, says of his habit of putting his idiosyncratic stamp upon (*i.e.,* falsifying) the minutes of Cabinet meetings, the minutes should say what, upon deliberate reflection later, the Prime Minister would have liked them to say, so Wayne would have us accept as spontaneous the crafted Algonquian eloquence of his characters. In real-life conversation, I well recall from our high school days, Wayne himself is quite the hemmer and hawer. Solveig]

"But haven't we made progress? Aren't things getting better for women? They can openly love, live with, and marry other women.

They have equal opportunities in the military—there are even some female generals. They are becoming scientists, engineers, surgeons, CEOs. We've had Margaret Thatcher, Golda Meir, Angela Merkel, Indira Ghandi, Benazir Bhutto, Aung San Suu Kyi, Theresa May. We almost had Hillary Clinton. Women *are* becoming empowered."

"Wrong! The exceptions prove the rule—and that rule is still made by men. 'Empowerment' is a buzz word that comes too glibly off the tongues of both men—even some Republican men!—and women. The implication is that women are responsible for their own oppression, that there is something wrong with them, that they need to improve themselves, that they need to stop apologizing, be assertive, submit a compelling resume, negotiate a raise, fight for respectability. Any version of feminism based on a feel-good self-help philosophy misses the point and does more harm than good. "

"The point being?"

"That they are not to blame for their lack of power and relevance, the system is. Social constructs are based on warped, unfair assumptions about authority. Women remain drastically under-represented anywhere that genuine power resides, especially in business and politics. Hillary had no chance in 2016. The election was rigged—not by any specific person or group, any chicanery or skullduggery, not by the Russians or the FBI, but by a systemic oppression of the mind. Hillary was a good candidate—experienced, tough, compassionate, dogged—but she was done in by a world view that dates from the caveman—or Adam and Eve, take your choice—that men were meant to rule."

"She did win the popular vote."

"But not the electoral vote, and the electoral system was constructed by a male-created, male-dominated federalist society fearful of true democracy."

"And she did have some flaws. She was duplicitous, evasive. She danced around issues like Benghazi and her private email server."

"Trump's flaws were infinitely greater. But he's a man; he gets to write off his debts."

"And there was racism—the revenge vote against Obama. And xenophobia, tribalism, nationalism, a changing economy roiling the working class, Clinton fatigue, frustration with politics as usual, desire for change, a fresh face."

"All explained by adherence to the male power structure."

"Sylvia, such single-mindedness!"

"If by that you mean such determination to cut through obfuscatory clap-trap to get at the truth, I agree."

"And such vehemence!"

"If by that you mean such self-respect, then I agree. I'm standing up for Maggie and Vi, who were not allowed to be free."

"They couldn't have been happy in their traces? They couldn't have heard and responded to the call of the domestic?"

"Right! And American slaves were happy on their plantations, and prisoners are happy behind their bars."

[Amen, sister! Charlotte]

The old man groaned. "Sylvia, can we go over to the Columbarium and sit on the steps now? My sacroiliac is seizing up. I can walk for an hour, I can play softball for three hours, but I can't stand still for more than five minutes without fidgeting in sciatic pain. I'm impressed with the way you maintain a poised, balanced stance."

"As you may have noticed, I have a solid base. I've got some heft all the way down. I'm grounded. Your legs are too skinny to support your slumping, top-heavy torso."

They walked to the stairs beside the fountain, the old man gaining brief relief by leaning his right hip against a railing, and contemplated the sleek 10-foot tall sweeping marble-topped rectangular structure of granite-faced niches, some engraved and occupied, some not. They studied a color-coded board demarking sections and prices, which ranged from $1,950 to $4,950, the most expensive ones centrally located at eyelevel, the cheapest ones relegated to the wings at floor level.

"It's a nice idea," Sylvia said, "even though it reeks of classism.

Saves space and encourages cremation, which is better for the environment than burial. That's where I'm going. I bought in on my last visit to town a couple of years ago. I've found my last niche. My spot is right there." She pointed chest-high, just left of center. "Have you decided how you want to be disposed of?"

His sacro bit him again. "I'm definitely going to be cremated. Now, do I want some kind of monument, some temporarily permanent record that I was here? So long lives this, and this gives life to me? Or do I want to be scattered in anonymity, like Diane?"

"I think there's something to be said for leaving a visual reminder of your existence—for the sake of others, if not yourself. Haven't you enjoyed strolling through these archives today, remembering, rethinking, refining perspectives? Even if we stipulate that a marker won't mean anything to you—that neither your body nor your soul any longer exists and neither will ever cohere again—couldn't it be meaningful to your younger acquaintances and to some of your former students who might pass through and be prompted to reflect upon their personal histories, or something you said or did, some example you set? Or, failing that, at least be another useful *memento mori*? Wouldn't it be, in a way, *rude* to leave no trace of yourself, to vanish like a Snapchat?"

She smiled and directed him to turn and sit on a debris-free step beside the clattering fountain. He roamed his eyes over the stiller town, smiled to think of rude forefathers out there as well, tried to visualize a woman giving birth astride a grave or a grieving visitor lustfully honoring the Sabbath in that theater.

"Sylvia, did your parents die happy?"

"Well, my dad died suddenly of a heart attack at 65, but I'm sure that, as a Christian and a male, he found life to be meaningful and enjoyable. My mom died at 85 in the Edmonds Landing assisted living facility on Dayton. By then her memory was pretty much gone—so let's say she had the happiness of an infant whose physical needs are taken care of by others. But in her prime, even though she was oppressed in a way that she was either unable to see or unwilling to call out, her religion would have made it impossible to convince her that she was not happy. And, in spite of my objections to male domination, I get that."

"My parents—and grandfather, too—decidedly did not die happy; they were happy to die. No raging against the dying of the light for them; they most kindly stopped for death."

"And for that you...what? Pity them? *Resent* them? *Disdain* them?"

"Disdain? No, never, I have too much love for them, too much pity and compassion, no, wait a minute, pity implies condescension , who am I to offer it like alms, compassion is empathy, rapport, so too much pity, yes, but not in a good way, I'm not entitled to it, and, hauntingly, not enough compassion, I should be a bigger person, and yes, you put your finger on it, a little bit of resentment, a haughtiness, why didn't they fight harder, unwarranted because I have not yet experienced the physical and emotional pain, the readiness for death, that they did."

She nodded. "Yes. I wouldn't be too hard on them. The end does not necessarily unjustify the means. The denouement of the last act, even if tragic or tawdry or tepid, does not render meaningless the experienced richness of the complications and ambiguities of Acts I through IV. Or, to put it in your sports terms, you can enjoy the vicissitudes of a game, all its ups and downs, your own good plays and errors, even though you ultimately lose it. Being is its own excuse for being."

"Or possibly the *only* excuse for being?"

Sylvia looked away from him. Were they done?

"Sylvia, it's almost noon. Should we go have lunch somewhere?"

"I suppose so. I *am* hungry."

"One of the waterfront restaurants? Arnie's? Anthony's? Fresh halibut, fresh salmon, fresh tuna? Or Spud, down by the tracks? Takeout fish and chips?"

"How about Chanterelle?"

"Sure. An unpretentious but eclectic menu. In the century-old

Western storefront building. Meet you there, then. Maybe we'll get lucky and find spots in the city parking lot behind the restaurant."

The old man followed Sylvia as she passed QFC, turned right on 104, and merged into heavy traffic. Some of the cars took the swooping bend sinister toward the ferry dock when the road Yed to provide two descents into town, but they went straight ahead, passing tall firs and hemlocks and coasting down 5th, the Bowl and the dark Sea and Whidbey opening before them like an invitation. They slowed when they reached the old man's condo, traffic backing up as drivers and their passengers deliberated over restaurants and darted their eyes in search of parking spots. Sylvia shrugged and waved and took the last remaining space when they pulled into the small city lot off 4th, and the old man smiled, turned left down the alley to Dayton, went to 3rd and then almost to the City Park before he found an opening that he could nose into, enabling him to avoid the embarrassing fits and starts, tries and retries, of an octogenarian parallel parker. He locked the Santa Fe and jogged back to Chanterelle, breathing easily. Sylvia waved to him from a dark corner table in the back as he came through the Main Street entrance.

"At least *you* got lucky," he said. "Every restaurant in town is busy at lunchtime these days. That's okay with me, though. I think I need these kinds of noisy places. The clutter and clatter of life. The hurly-burly. Here you get a mix of tourists and locals, a lot of them seniors our junior looking for moderate prices. Remember when there were just three diners in town?"

"Sure. Brownie's on 4th, Bud's Cafe and Tuson's Grill on Main."

"My family used to splurge once in a while and eat at Brownie's or Bud's. I would order a hamburger steak, well done, and French fries. My parents would get chicken-fried steaks with mashed potatoes and gravy. They'd have coffee, I'd have milk. None of the entrees cost more than 95 cents. We never went to Tuson's because it was too pricey."

"My family did go there now and then. Dad and Mel Tuson were good friends. Sometimes he'd walk over there in the afternoon for coffee and he and Mel would roll the dice to see who paid."

"I'm curious," the old man said after he had activated the flashlight on his phone to help him decode the faint, blurry menu script and they had ordered from a not-quite middle-aged pony-tailed brunette waitperson wearing a black tee shirt and black slacks, the brie and pear quesadilla (about 400 calories, he guessed, though not many of them protein) and a diet Coke for him, the Montrachet chicken salad with goat cheese and a vodka martini for her. "You say you meditate. You gaze inward. I remember seeing you on Sundays at Hughes Memorial sitting with your parents in pews up front while I sat with Gary and Monk and the Maple Street guys in the back, and I know you were awed by Billy Graham at the Seattle Crusade in 1951. May I ask? Do you still believe in Jesus as your personal savior?"

She patted her hair with her left hand, gently traced one of its twisting Mobius strips. " My views have been tempered by the eastern religions over the years. I believe in some Christic experience suffused with Buddhist and Taoist elements. I believe there's a universal draw to inclusion. There is a spiritual force outside us to which something inside us is compelled to respond."

"Ah, Sylvia, that inclusive 'us.' I don't think I've ever felt that compulsion."

"Wayne, that's awfully hard to believe. I think you're in denial. But my own personal Jesus, you were asking? I think we all personalize our spiritual quest, whether we call it Christ, Lord, Teacher, Love, Mystic Law, The Tao, or the Ineffable. We call out at moments, we ask protection, we wish blessing and love. We feel a pull. We crave completion. Atonement."

"So we're filled with longing and then fulfilled by belonging? Atonement has always scared me, Sylvia."

"What, the quiet knowing of oneness that is our true nature? Getting out of our own distracting, egotistic way?

"What I fear is that apart from my own distracting egotistic way there is no me. My distractions define me. They are my ballast. I have to cling to them. If I let go, I disappear. I agree with the Buddhists that existence is suffering, but I cannot accept that the objective of life is to end suffering and that the way to end suffering is to cease clinging. To cease clinging is to cease. The Buddhists posit that cycles of reincarnation eventually lead to nirvana, a state beyond desire, beyond suffering, a timeless realm where the concept of a distinct existence disappears, where no one is any one and any one is no one. That does not work for me. I don't want to lose my identity in something larger than myself."

"Are you sure? I think we all seek refuge in authentic atonement."

He was having trouble hearing—the high ceiling, the hard surfaces of the tables and the suspended metal light fixtures, the clinking of plates being gathered by the bus persons, the full house of chattering, gesticulating patrons. He raised his voice to encourage Sylvia to do the same.

"Most, maybe, but the authentic *me* seeks refuge not in atonement but in independence. I am not blessed with a 'be' attitude. The mind of the authentic me doesn't want to be quiet. It wants to use today and yesterday to prepare for tomorrow. It wants to churn, to multitask, to run a bunch of apps simultaneously. Rewind, fast forward. Rewind, fast forward. Keep those synapses snapping. The authentic me defines itself by its inevitable failures when it attempts to transcend limiting expectations. The authentic me is always short-shrifting the instant, is never fully in the moment. The authentic me is always saving the jam for tomorrow's bread. I can remember the past, I can imagine the future, but I can't grasp *now* because it's already gone. I find that whenever I try to cherish the moment I am conscious that I am losing that moment while simultaneously failing to use that moment to prepare myself physically or mentally or emotionally or financially for the next one. To be in the moment is essentially to be longing for it, trying but failing to cling to it, in despair at its transitory nature."

"But every moment," Sylvia said, her volume rising in sympathy with his, "has an infinite number of half-lives in which we can dwell. Now is all there is. As Wittgenstein said, eternal life belongs to those who live in the now. You make time run not by acting frantically but by slowing down. You sink into the moment; you sync your heartbeat to the rhythm of now. There is no better preparation for the next moment than to be fully in this one. Wayne, if you are longing, desperately trying to cling, you are not in the moment. You may think you are, but you are not. You are confusing living *in* the moment with living *for* the moment. You are not your thoughts. The thing is to observe them without either grasping for them or pushing them away. You can only live in the moment if you are unaware of the moment. You are totally absorbed. Your self-consciousness evaporates. Be becomes finale of seem."

Their drinks arrived. Although the Coke came with a straw, the old man chose not to unwrap it. They raised glasses in a silent salute.

"Yeah, I've always loved that line, and Sylvia, I do see how what you say can be possible—and wonderful—at times. In a dark theater rapt in a movie and wrapped in surround-sound. Immersed in the labyrinth of a crossword or cryptic puzzle. Lining one into the gap and racing around the bases—nothing else exists at that moment. And basketball—the fluidity of my favorite game! Pivoting, jumping, gliding, sliding. Mindful of where you are, of where everyone else is, sensing where and when to move, no distinction between action and thought, thought unmediated by language. Active but at peace. In your body but detached from it. Okay, I'll concede that. But, although you *seem* to be detached from your body, it be not detached from you, and it keeps reminding you through muscle fatigue and shortness of breath and jarring collisions that you are indeed an *other,* apart from all others. It also reminds you that without its electro-chemical system there is no you. You are *an* other but also *not* other than your body. As you age, your autonomic system without your permission begins to take a little time off, its internal housekeeping becomes less meticulous, you need iron and vitamins, you begin to outsource your production of testosterone or estrogen, your immune system begins to see you as a terrorist, your cancer is forming, your arteries are filling with plaque. The authentic me is a briefly useful fiction whose tale ends idiotically in a narrative violation as the body disintegrates and the self vaporizes. Lose yourself to find yourself, we are so often told. I cannot agree."

Sylvia raised an eyebrow. "So, Macbeth, how would you put it: to loose yourself you must bind yourself?"

"Maybe—if I thought a paradox were any kind of a solution! A true paradox is an unsolvable conundrum, like Zeno's Achilles never able to catch a tortoise that's been given a head start or an omnipotent God making a stone so heavy He's unable to lift it. It is not an ersatz transcendence. If a senior playing softball is like a dog walking on its hind legs, then a paradox may be the last refuge of a scoundrel."

"Wayne, I'm not sure whose words you are alluding to in that odd little *modus ponens*—Pepys, Ben Franklin?— oh, it's Dr. Johnson, isn't it?—but clearly you are bent upon looking through every glass starkly. You are not a body of atoms, you are consciousness. Consciousness is the experience of *being* an organization of atoms merged with the all, *of* the world, not looking *at* the world. Your sense that there is a you looking out through your eyes at a world that is separate from you is indeed a fiction. There is no stable self that is carried on from one moment to the next. Spirituality is the moment-to-moment realization that the conventional sense of self is an illusion, and it is achieved through meditation. Meditation is simply paying attention. Meditation is living in the moment. The point is that if you truly stay in the here and now you will not experience the fear of losing this moment or of being unprepared for the next. You will simply *be*. To quote Rumi, 'You wander from room to room hunting for the diamond necklace that is already around your neck.'"

"To me that kind of paradoxical Rumination is just an easy escape. Paradox is where you go when your dreams bang against adamantine facts and logic."

She leaned forward. "Or is paradox where you go when you divine that appearance is not reality? When you have the insight that a person is not a self-sufficient entity and does not exist as the controller of the body and the mind? When you quit clinging to dualism? When you realize there is no distinction between phenomena like thoughts and emotions and the mind-awareness which reflects them? When you see immediately into the reality of things unhampered by heuristics? When you see that nothing exists essentially? That you need only let your ego go? Form is emptiness, emptiness is form. You cannot achieve happiness unless you're not looking for it. To improve your performance, stop thinking about it. If something is bothering you, move toward it rather than away from it. To make the most of time, lose track of it. Know that you don't know. Don't just do something, sit there. Keep coming back to the now. To ecstatic equanimity, rational exuberance, detached engagement, relaxed intensity. These paradoxes are reality. To deny them is to live in alienation."

"Alienation, it seems to me, *is* reality," the old man said.

She leaned backward. "A self-willed illusion, I'd say."

They paused to sip their drinks. The old man dabbed his napkin at the sweat that had begun to pool on the table from his overly-iced Coke. Sylvia, using only her pretty teeth, cleaned the toothpick of its olive and chewed it slowly.

"So meditation leads to spirituality and spirituality leads to what? Serenity? Bliss?"

"Yes. Ridding the mind of the distractions of thoughts leads to atonement."

"And atonement is by definition a state of serenity or bliss?"

"Yes. Existential suffering is entirely the product of your thoughts. Negative feelings like anger, panic, or depression are mere illusions that vanish when you examine them closely. That which is aware of sadness is not sad. That which is aware of fear is not fearful. Awareness is the antidote to suffering. By rewiring your brain through meditation you can become free to return to your right mind. Free to become one with what is. You can keep bouncing back to bliss."

"And there is no possibility that maybe you have deluded yourself?"

"No. The delusion *is* the self."

"And emptiness is fulfillment! Sylvia, I am just too superficial and literal-minded to accept that. I can stop by woods, but I can't fully enter them. My little force does think it queer! To me, emptiness is loss. I'm a clinger, a clutcher, a grasper, trying to resist the emptying out that accompanies age by keeping current on the one hand and by inviting memories to refresh themselves on the other. My memories and my thoughts are extraneous, illusionary distractions? From what? Perhaps so on those occasions when I am trying to maintain a rigorous, disciplined *train* of thought, but what is to be gained by always defaulting to the mindlessness of mindfulness? That's serenity? That's bliss? Or is it dementia? Is it death? Sometimes for me bliss is just riding the stream of consciousness, seeing where it takes me, even into painful places, playing with language and memory, consciously dreaming, ego intertwined with id, polylinguistically perverse. My thoughts break down barriers and, briefly, liberate me. That's as close to *dolce far niente* as I can get."

"But that doesn't last, either, does it? And it's more diversionary than satisfying, isn't it? The human mind is a wandering mind, and a wandering mind is an unhappy mind. The ultimate wisdom of enlightenment cannot be a matter of having fleeting experiences. Real freedom must be coincident with normal waking life. It grows from direct insight into the unconditioned reality that lies behind all manifest phenomena. When you look closely for 'I,' the feeling of being a separate self will disappear."

Beaming, their waitperson appeared tableside with a plate in either hand. "Here we go! Careful with the quesadilla—that plate's hot. Ground pepper on the salad? Enjoy! Can I get you anything else? Refill on the Coke? Another martini? "

"Yes."

"Yes."

And she was off.

The old man mopped up more condensation from his glass. "So I think, therefore 'I' am not? It seems to me that pure consciousness apart from the five senses of seeing, hearing, smelling, tasting and touching is a spiritual fantasy. The mind is not independent of the brain."

"But consciousness is the light by which the contours of the mind and body are known. Consciousness itself *is* free. We need to break our identification of the self with thought and allow the continuum of experience, pleasant or unpleasant, to simply be as it is. Through meditation we seek to recognize that which is common to all states of experience. It isn't a matter of thinking new thoughts. It is easy to think that something like this martini—which, incidentally, is delicious—is just an appearance in consciousness. It is another matter to recognize it as such prior to the arising of thought."

She emptied her glass.

"And is the martini helping you to expand or alter your consciousness?"

"Of course. And I'm hoping the next one will open yet another door to reality."

He smiled. "Diane and I used to enjoy wine most every night—something reasonably complex but affordable. And I still do. I'm excited by the sensory thrills that wine can provide. There's something synesthetic about it. You can have fun pretending for a moment that you are tasting color, smelling feeling. Diane would occasionally have two, but I generally stop at one glass. I cling to Apollonian clarity, fear Dionysian ecstasy. It's just too scary to feel myself beginning to dissolve and flow."

"Scary? You should try LSD."

"Mmm. This brie-pear thing is soft and good. Sour cream, sweet acid. You have?"

"Yes." She scraped some goat cheese onto her fork, then

stabbed through a couple of spinach leaves into a toasted walnut. "I became friendly with a painter whose so-so surrealistic works I was showing, an accountant by day but an adventurer by night who got me into yoga and tantric sex and then LSD. When you're on acid, your brain is flooded with signals that crisscross between the various regions. It mixes up the sensory modalities, muddling you with the things you see, feel, taste, hear. In certain areas of the brain activities get ramped up, in others they get suppressed. A portion of what you feel as your self overflows into the outer world, into objects, which begin to live, to have another, deeper, meaning. You and the pizza you are eating are no longer separate entities. You *are* the pizza and the world beyond the windowsill. You lose track of which is which. As the ego dissolves, you experience the oneness of all living things. It is sublime. Time dilates. You feel great. You feel eternity in the moment. You feel atonement. Unless you don't."

"Here we go!" Their waitperson swooped in with fresh drinks, set them down, mopped up the sweat puddles in front of the old man, carried off the used glasses.

"You had some bad trips?"

"Shattering. Terrifying hallucinations that I thought were real—bugs and snakes coming at me, streets churning and melting. One time I had the illusion that I could fly. After a few of these I realized that this was self-torture and was not for me. Psychedelics can open up forms of consciousness that lie beyond rational consciousness. They can raise you to new heights of awe and understanding—or plunge you into the abyss. For me they were just too risky and painful. Meditation is a safer route to waking up from the dream of the self. The painter and I did not stay together, but I have remained committed to meditation."

"It's a key ritual in your 'religion'?"

"Yes. Meditation and prayer."

"Prayer?"

" Not prayers of supplication, not prayers to a god, but the unspoken, ecstatic outpouring of love and joy, a silent speaking in tongues, when I feel myself to be at one with what is. My personal religion has long been done with any obsession with 'sin,' and 'cross,' and 'suffering.' There is far too much man-made, male-dominant culture masquerading as religion. Un-Christian Christianity. Un-Muslim Muslimism. Jews who have wandered far from how the chosen are to love. Rules, creeds, orthodoxies are not a cup of water to offer someone thirsty. Saving, being saved, should be the beginning of our conscious relationship with cause and effect— our growing toward the light. Not amassing wealth and power. Not dominating. Not forcing. Not proselytizing. Not colonizing. And definitely not enslaving."

"I'm with you on the proselytizing, colonizing, and enslaving, but striving, seeking, winning—these are the very essence of life. Nature's red, in truth and law. Doesn't a basic irritability underlie all living substance? To live, mustn't both animals and plants interact with and dominate their part of the ecosystem, however small it may be? Mustn't animals eat each other or plants, and some plants eat animals?"

"So your motto is prey, eat, live?"

The old man laughed and raised his dripping glass in salute. "Yes! Because even the glorious lilies of the field, though they don't spin, are actually toiling madly all day to feed themselves through photosynthesis, and their little roots are competing with alien roots to take in water and other nutrients as well. Don't viruses like Sars and Mers and H1N1 parachute into our apertures on aerosols and try to set up camp in our cells? Don't the very bacteria in our guts constantly jostle for supremacy? All life forms fight to exist, and all defend their own territory with things like weapons, or thorns, or hard shells, or poisons, or camouflage. Don't most kinds of reproduction demand some form of domination and submission? Doesn't even the apparently amiable splitting of a cell imply some violence? Isn't it true that for most living things to survive, some other living thing must die or at the very least be exploited? Mustn't life wrest its existence from its environment?"

"To what end?"

"To a dead end. Because (a) you'll often fail and (b) even if you succeed you are compelled by a biological imperative to continue striving until you and the essence of you—your memories—die. There's just one damn thing after another. You never achieve a final victory. And—okay, I see I'm going to have to grant at least one paradox—even though it ends your suffering, dying is the worst failure of all. That's the human condition, which is unacceptable to most of us—a fact that is also part of the human condition. If we as individuals are mortal, and if our universe and therefore our species are mortal, as the second law of thermodynamics implies, our life does not matter, but we must pretend that it does in order to keep on, although keeping on, Godoting— in either quiet desperation or in raucous aspiration— is pointless."

"Wayne, this is stupid stuff—and I'm not just saying that because you're eating your vittles fast enough and I'm melting into my martini! You, the self-proclaimed inventor of the HSQ, keep trial-ballooning these nihilistic ideas that verge on horseshit—but, fortunately, the vodka vitiates your passive-aggressiveness for me."

"Martinis do more than Milton can?"

"Sometimes! If life's a bitch and then you die, never to exist again in any way, shape, or form, would it not have been best for you never to have been conceived?"

"One passive-aggressive quibble before you proceed. There was no 'I' before conception. 'I' wasn't hanging around somewhere waiting to be conceived and given human form. 'I' did not exist until one of my father's sperm cells, after the big bang of his ejaculation, willy-nilly, who knows why (size, shape, Usain Boltish quick-twitching flagellum, serendipitous position at the head of the pod when the gun went off?) penetrated what happened to be my mother's egg cell of the month. And 'I' would not have come into existence had any other sperm cell from what turned out to be my father penetrated any other egg cell from what turned out to be my mother. In the strictest sense, it couldn't have been best for 'me' never to have been conceived, because 'I' wasn't. 'I' wouldn't have been happier if 'I' had not been born. 'I' would not be better off if 'I' had not been born."

"It's a moot point, Wayne."

"So let's moot it."

She leaned forward again. "No, I mean you might be technically correct but that's of little relevance to my argument."

"Which is?"

"If you truly believe that existence is meaningless, you should have long ago asked yourself what Camus called the most fundamental of existential questions—'Shall I commit suicide?'—answered in the affirmative, and done yourself in. If you truly believed, like David Benatar, the anti-natalist avatar, that to bring a child into a world of suffering is immoral, you would not have sought so fervently to conceive with Diane. Your actions belie you. You don't have the guts to be a nihilist or even an Aristotelian who truly excludes the middle between belief and nihilism. Your seeking, doing, and making imply that, at the very least, even if you are not eternal, and even if you do not achieve transcendence, your life has value in itself. You have a self capable of having experiences, something that the never-conceived never will."

"Quibble: there are no never-conceived."

"Again, moot."

"But you are favorably contrasting our existence with nothing. There can be no contrast because there is no middle to exclude. You provide an A, existence, but no non-A."

"The non-A is nothing."

"Yes."

She slouched backward. "Wayne, if you're going to Abbott-and-Costello me, then I'm done."

"No, please, Sylvia, sorry. I love to hear you talk. My point is that we have no way of knowing whether this existence is meaningful or not because we cannot experience non-existence."

"Regardless, I am confident that nothing, in this context, *is* something—and that we *do* experience existence as rewarding. We relish sensual pleasure, we enjoy emotional relationships with people, we have the satisfaction of exercising our mental and physical powers in all kinds of tasks and projects. In all of these ways we feel ourselves become a part of the whole."

"But aren't all of these also ways in which we sense ourselves apart from the whole? There is that rush of life's phenomena, the blooming and the buzzing, which I readily admit I still crave and cling to, but what about our experience of sensual pain, our all-too-often bad relationships with people, and the frequent frustration of discovering that our mental and physical powers are not up to the tasks we put them to? Do these not lead to alienation from self and world?"

"Not if we see that they are all parts of the whole, a synthesis of A and non-A, a higher middle ground. The meaning of life is to give life meaning."

"Please! Let us put an end to paradox!"

"Sorry, can't be done. We must embrace the fictions of paradox as the answers to the absurdity of life. You're more than a little stunted in your spiritual growth. You remind me of that Stephen Crane creature in the desert, holding his heart in his hands and eating of it. If asked if it was good, you would reply..."

"'It is bitter—bitter, but I like it because it is bitter and because it is my heart.' True. So true."

"Whereas I believe in altruism. I believe we should eschew bitterness and savor love with open minds and open hearts. Mindful people are more joyful, more serene, more attuned to a shared humanity. In their caring for others they are rewarded with the release of serotonin and dopamine in the nucleus acumbens, imbuing them with the wonderful sense that life is worth living. Merging with something greater, being in the presence of enormous beauty and goodness, is heavenly. To be truly alive is to feel one's ultimate existence within one's daily existence."

"So altruism is actually an expression of selfishness."

"Look who's resorting to paradox again!"

He shrugged. "You're right. Guilty."

"But sorry, not sorry?"

"Yes. Because I believe that it is for selfish reasons that humans feel love and behave ethically. In the overall scheme of things, we and our genes have a better chance of surviving if we don't colonize, if we don't enslave, if we practice the Judeo-Christian Golden Rule and the Confucian Silver Rule, treating others with love and respect because we wish to be treated with love and respect, refraining from harming others because we wish not to be harmed. The release of the feel-good hormone oxytocin when we behave ethically is an evolutionary development. We have, over eons, learned to reward ourselves with it when we do the 'right' thing. We become addicted to it, we behave in ways that give us our fix, and gradually our survival rate improves. We have developed a compassion gene to further the success of our selfish gene. Steven Pinker's *The Better Angels of our Nature* has a bootload of footnotes documenting the decline of violence and mayhem through the ages. Disguised as altruism, our selfishness rewards us with longer and less painful lives. And with that, as we conclude our day together, you trying to find one more drop in your martini glass, me eating my heart out, I'd like to say that, in spite of the occasional dumpling of horseshit that each of us has dropped, I have truly enjoyed our lunch. Certainly the Coke's caffeine helped, but for me the analytical sparring spurred my pulse, released a surge of adrenaline, and heightened my awareness of myself as a being apart. I loved the competition. I'm wired!"

"And certainly the martinis have helped, but for me our talk, our analytical sparring, has paradoxically served as meditation, leading me to feel again the bliss of atonement. I'm all dopamined up, and for that I thank you."

"The only problem is that in the hours and days to come, my delight will give way to rue, the old *esprit de l'escalier*—why didn't I say this, why did I say that?—and I will be haunted at odd moments by my failures. Whereas you, I imagine, if you sense the encroachment of any rueful thoughts at all, will simply peer at them closely and find that they were never there."

"I expect so."

Their waitperson appeared tableside and picked up the old man's plate, clean except for a couple of fugitive pastry flakes. "How was it? Everything okay? Finished with that salad, ma'am? Coffee? Dessert? Blueberry cobbler today."

The old man and Sylvia looked at each other.

"I think we're fine," the old man said.

"Two checks, please," Sylvia said. "We'll go Dutch. Or is that a slur?"

"It could be. Linguistic usage changes with the times. Originally I think the expression referred unpejoratively to Dutch doors that divide down the middle, but now it might imply selfishness or cheapness on the part of the Dutch. Best not to use it. I'm sure that Charlotte—and for good reason—would accuse us of being 'tone deaf' if we did.

[Damn straight! Charlotte]

As kids we All-Stars used to squabble up and down Maple Street, accusing each other of being Indian givers, of welshing on a bet, of gypping somebody or jewing somebody down. Wouldn't do that today. No way, Joe. And certainly just remove 'niggardly' from your spoken and written vocabularies, because too many people know only what the word sounds like and not what its original meaning is."

Smiling gamely, their waitperson looked at the old man confusedly.

"Separate checks," he said. "And everything was great. Thank you."

Two days later, he posted on his blog:

Epitaphs for the Digital Age

Wandering through the Edmonds Cemetery recently, lonely as a Wordsworthian cloud and feeling an Ishmaelian November in my soul, I was first startled and then oddly cheered by the changing nature of today's tombstone inscriptions. Apparently many are now taking the electronic revolution all the way to their graves, as evidenced by the following examples:

As F8 would have it...

From the Cloud to the clods

What app from Hell did I mistakenly download?

Not what I anticipated when I hit Control-Alt-Delete

I suppose no one wants to join my Group now

I was counting on McAfee to prevent this

Any chance it's just buffering?

Wish I could say I'll be back in a GIF

I should have left a trail of Cookies

Is it too late to be Saved?

[Talk about whistling past the graveyard, Wayne! Gary]

[Yes! I think this might score a 90 on the HSQ. Carolyn]

[Wayne, how do these mock epitaphs even grow out of our visit to the cemetery? I think they trivialize our experience as well as the lives of those buried there. Moreover, they are all laments, regrets, ruings, plaintive expressions of your fear of death. They are pseudo-hip, pseudo-flip. They belie your thoughts on the lives and deaths of your parents and grandparents. In spite of the many pleasures we experience on earth, few want to go through this life again. In the interest of fairness, here is another take:

No more passwords to remember

At last I'm spam-free

I'll never be hacked again

I've Escaped

I'm in my Favorite Place.

Res(e)t In Peace! Sylvia]

[Wayne, I do enjoy the topics you bring up for discussion but

---

often doubt your sincerity. You decry the invoking of paradox as a kind of weaseling, then fall back upon it when you encounter a contradiction you can't resolve. You say that nature is red in truth and law but ignore the benevolent intricate symbiotic interdependence to be found in nature's ecosystems. You celebrate the rush of life but then conclude that consciousness of it leads to alienation. You quibble over moot or inconsequential points. Cavalier caviling seems to be becoming an emergent feature of your lex life. Dave]

6

The Learned Astronomer

I n mid-April, encountering Facebook Messenger's red alert, he
opened this:

"Hi, Coach! Hope you'll pardon my Holmesing in on you
through Facebook. I recently learned from my niece Delaney, who
knows LaTasha at Starbucks, that your peripatetic self still roams
around Edmonds (comma here or not? I say not—simple compound
((fun with oxymorons, just like we had back in your classes!)) noun
clause direct objects with no interrupters, right?) and that your
athletic self still plays senior softball. How wonderful! For the past
two years I've been volunteering two days a week at the Edmonds
Historical Museum. Granted, I don't drink coffee, but still how could
our paths not have crossed, because I always park on 4th between
Dayton and Walnut and walk over to work. Or did they metaphori-
cally—or might that be virtually?—through LaTasha? Three degrees
of separation? I live in the Seaview area with my partner (no comma here either, because the two nouns are in direct apposition with
each other; they are one and the same, and I love her) Jennifer. I
graduated from Stanford with a degree in Library Science, took a job
as an assistant librarian at Bothell High School, met Don Hamilton,
an orthopedist, when I blew out my ACL playing pickup basketball,
married him, had two boys in quick succession, went back to work,
divorced after the boys left for college (mutual consent—we both

wanted someone else), retired six years ago. Coach, may I be so bold as to suggest we get together one of these days—an informal lunch, maybe? I'd love to catch up with you."

They found an unoccupied bench along the path of gray brick pavers that wound south past the human-made dunes of green grass and the plantings of native bushes and grasses—blackberries and cattails and wild rose hips and Northwest myrtle and fireweed—of Brackett's Landing Park, south of the ferry dock and just north of the totemically carved Friendship Tree, a gift from Hekinan, a sister city, its bas-relief firs and salmon and ladders and Japanese characters splattered with white seagull droppings, and opened the takeout bags of fish and chips they had purchased at Spud on the east side of Railroad Avenue. Slender iron rods, painted the blue-green of verdigris, comprised the seat and backrest of the bench which, he noted with pleasure just before sitting down, bore a commemorative plaque recently purchased by Patty Warfield in honor of her parents, who, the plaque revealed, liked to sit on a log at that spot near the Edmonds Sawmill and watch the sun set during their courtship and where also, a generation later, the mill gone and the beach anyone's for the taking, the old man and his girl friend Solveig liked to park in his '49 Ford and stare at the sinking sun while swallowing nervously and furtively stroking each other below the waist. A placid May Day, the light marine haze of late morning evaporating before their eyes, the air warming into, a glance at his watch told him, the low 60s, windshields on yachts winking into visibility. The old man, in his Classics cap, gray hoodie, long-sleeved, zippered, forest-green polyester Pebble Beach golf shirt, black jeans, and new black and white Under Armour low-cut sneakers with flexible cloth uppers that yielded to his swollen, tingling, neuropathic feet, contentedly inhaled odors of iodine, vinegar, and hot grease. Liz Ann, wearing a cardinal red ball cap embossed with a white S, light blue jeans and a white sweatshirt with a striking Japanese character silk-screened in black on the chest, larger than life at six feet and probably 180 pounds, up 40 from her high school playing weight, kicked off her sandals and extended her long legs. "I see you're looking at my feet," she said. "I have two perfectly normal goddam feet and I don't know why you're staring at them."

"Bless you," the old man said. "You remember."

She lifted her cap and shook out her long cornsilk hair, which on the basketball court she had worn in a pony tail and whipped in a defender's face when backing her down in the post. Middle age had creased her forehead with two horizontal wrinkles and trenched a furrow between her blond eyebrows, but her eyes were still bright blue. "Of course I do. I was really intrigued by that story, although it was decades before I realized why I identified with Seymour and bananafish. I remember so many things. I loved your classes, Coach. The Maplewood English Department offered a cornucopia of electives in those days, and in my four years there I took all that you taught—Literary Classics, College Prep Comp, Humanities, Creative Writing, Growth of the Language, Semantics, Poetry. When I went to Stanford, I kept a jar of honey on my desk, like—I mean as!- you did in your classroom. You'd invert it now and then so we could appreciate the golden bubble rising from the bottom to the top. Beauty in the mundane, like the red wheelbarrow glazed with rain-water beside the white chickens. When we came into your room for class you had us trained to look at the chalkboard, read a definition, and imitate a model while you took roll, such as 'Hyperbole—The use of exaggeration for rhetorical effect. He's so cheap that he puts grocery store discount coupons in the coffee shop tip jar.' In a fun way you covered so many things, depending on the subject matter of the class, different rhetorical devices like oxymoron, synecdoche, tmesis, litotes, anaphora, pathetic fallacy. Or different 'infelicities,' as you called them, comma splices, dangling participles, split infinitives, pleonasms. You charmed us by playing with our names. When Toby raised his hand you'd say 'Toby or not Toby, what is the question?' You'd look at April and say 'Oh to be in English now that April's here.' You called Joy 'a thing of beauty forever,' and whenever Sarah offered a comment you'd declare 'Thus spake Sarah Schuster.' I, of course, being partial to Shakespeare, was 'the Elizabethan.'"

He looked toward the L-shaped fishing pier to his left, anglers casting baited lines over the railing in long arcs.

"This is embarrassing to recall. It was an indirect way of expressing my affection for everybody. I mean, I couldn't just say 'I love you guys,' now, could I? But I was also seeking to ingratiate myself for purposes of manipulating you. It was part of my classroom management. Bestowing a nickname—"

"An eke, or also, name, etymologically, you taught us."

"—is at least as much about controlling as it is about endearing. I was just a kinder, gentler Donald Trump."

"But we loved being wooed that way!"

They extracted and set on the bench their drinks—a diet Coke for him, an unapologetic sugared one for her—and cardboard holders of fish and chips, thimble-sized plastic containers of tartar sauce, and wads of napkins, spread the empty paper bags on their laps as placemats, and balanced the food on their quads.

"So, no ketchup on the fries?" the old man said. "Nor I. I want that salty, greasy, crispy fry to mush up in my mouth unmasked by sugary citrus."

"Me, too," Liz Ann said. "I eat it plain with relish."

The old man raised a fry in salute. She smiled, her teeth like a sample from an ear of white corn, except for the upper left canine, which had been smacked by an opponent's swinging elbow in a battle for a rebound—the officials made her leave the game to swab the blood from swelling lips—and ever after had leaned upon its premolar neighbor. The increased fleshiness of her cheeks and the onset of jowls made her long nose less prominent than it had been in high school.

"The character on your sweatshirt—what's the translation?"

"'Freedom.'"

"Well, I'm glad you felt free to hit me up on Facebook. It's such a pleasure to reconnect. Do you have a lot of Friends?

[Ooh, Wayne, at Pendant we would say that that (infelicitous juxtaposing of relative and demonstrative pronouns, you'll retaliate!) is a pretty cheesy *segue*. I've noticed all along that transitions are your *bête noire*. Peevishly, you sometimes give up and take the corny way out. Solveig]

"Probably not in comparison with most people. Maybe 100."

"I'm about the same. None of my family members is alive any longer, but I have a Facebook connection with some former colleagues, students, players, softball teammates, childhood friends. Unlike you, I don't post much, but I do enjoy being able to keep tabs on others without incurring any obligation to relate directly to them. Now and then I'll hit 'Like' at some cyclist's selfie taken in the midst of the Emerald City Bike Ride, or of some traveler's hilltop picture of tile roofs in Croatia with the blue Adriatic below, just to show that I'm not dead yet and that I endorse their going and doing and adventuring and accomplishing. Once in a while I am moved to say 'Congratulations!' or 'Sorry to hear that' or 'Get well soon.' And it's intriguing to note who among my Friends feels compelled to make religious or political comments. My former students run the gamut from agnostics to evangelicals and reactionaries to antifas. You, for example, make it quite clear that you are a lesbian who abhors Donald Trump."

"Yes. Let the word go forth!"

They broke off pieces of fish and dabbed them in the tartar sauce, which the old man thought could use a bit of dill or fennel.

"Such a frabjous day in the northwest wonderland," she said. Seagulls screeched and scavenged the beach as the tide receded. They swooped and flapped, soared and celebrated, their soprano squealings coming in epistropic units of three that the old man assumed must have some grammatical or rhetorical significance. Three preschool girls in two-piece swim suits chattered and slalomed and twirled among the gulls in the sloppy sand at the water's edge, their lotus-positioned young mothers watching from blankets spread back on the drier sand. "With their slithy toes are they gyring and gimbling in the waves? Should they beware the Jabberwock?"

[This one's a little better. Solveig]

"'Tisn't quite brillig, but yes, they should. We all should, right? At least according to your interpretation."

"I know! We had so much fun with that poem. That day's anticipatory set activity was on portmanteaus, then you read 'Jabberwocky' aloud, which gave us a feel for the tonal changes in the poem, and put us in small groups to explicate the text. After much discussion and digging in dictionaries, my group concluded that the poem exemplified the archetype of the quest and that the Jabberwock symbolized man's (as we said in those days) foe: the kind of crazy talk, jibber-jabber, jubjubbing, turgid, burbling, whiffling, bantering, inaccurate, imprecise, obfuscating, fulminating, bullshitting nonsense to be found everywhere—in boroughs and groves, in homes and rathskellers. Or, today, in the mythomaniacal tweets of Donald Trump. Because you were always on us about our diction, like—I mean such as—'disinterested' means having no stake in, not uninterested, and 'decimate' means killing one in 10, not destroying or killing a large proportion of—and our sentence structure—comma splices, dangling modifiers, lack of parallel construction, circumlocutions—we decided that the hero was the adolescent you, and that the poem was a portrait of the English teacher as a young man wielding his trusty verbal sword, his red pen, to dispatch misleading or infelicitous language."

They pulled in their feet as a puffing male jogger in shorts and tee shirt hurried by.

"Well, I tried. Forging in the smithy of my editor's role the uncreated linguistic conscience of the human race. For a number of years I did graduate work at the U in the summer—seminars in Tragedy, Transcendentalism, Victorian Poetry, The Modern English Novel, but also courses in Rhetoric and Linguistics. I was aware of the move from traditional, Latin-based grammatical analysis to structural linguistics and transformational grammar. The notion of grammar as an intuitively understood system of rules for generating sentences intrigued me and affected my teaching of sentence rhetoric, but I stayed with the traditional approach and terminology when it came to a formal study of grammar in my classes. I was excited by the debate over *Webster's Third International Dictionary*, and in principle sided with the descriptivists rather than the prescriptivists. I enjoyed browsing the *Dictionary of American Slang*, and now I always check the *Urban Dictionary* online for the word or phrase of the day. It's lively, creative stuff. Let the dictionary tell us how language *is* used, not how it should be used. Couldn't agree more! But I was also very much a devotee of Henry Fowler and his *Dictionary of Modern English Usage.* I liked the notion of making judicious linguistic selections based in part on logic, in part on esthetics. Whose logic and whose esthetics? Admittedly, those of editors and professors, mostly white and more than 50 per cent male, privileged to impose their preferences."

She shifted to sit side-saddle and looked directly at him for a moment. "But it was helpful to know that such preferences and considerations exist. Sure, there might be a little bit of Stockholm syndrome involved, some identifying with your masters and keepers, some wish to be accepted by them, but I like knowing that for some people a thing can be only unique, not 'fairly unique,' or that it must center on, not 'around,' or that something is as good **as** or better than, not 'as good or better than,' that something is one of the few, not 'one of the only,' that you push the *edge* of the envelope, not the envelope itself, that to beg the question is to assume the truth of a conclusion without providing logical support for it, not to raise or invite a question."

"And I think, when you were heading off to college and career, such knowledge probably had some practical value, too. The college profs used to care; nowadays, I doubt it. My reluctance ever to split an infinitive would not even register on most of them, let alone their students. Some of the stuff I taught would be regarded as nit-picking at best, discriminatory at worst. Times change, language changes. Words are memes. When their 'misuse' is copied frequently enough, in spite of the efforts of old gatekeeping epime-miologists and usageasters like me to stop their spread, when they go viral—a term that has itself gone viral and that I use here in a purely descriptive, non-pejorative sense—they acquire new meanings, new uses. Thus 'incredible' now means 'fantastic' at least as often as it means 'unbelievable,' 'fantastic' means 'wonderful' much more often than it means 'fantasy-like,' 'wonderful' means 'terrific' way more often than it means 'inspiring wonder,' and 'terrific' means 'incredible,' 'fantastic,' or 'wonderful' 100 times as often as it means 'terror-making.' We're a more informal society than we once were. Our text messages and tweets are short bursts of simplified spellings and emoticons. We value equality and tolerance, we disdain privilege and bias, so we are modifying our pronoun usage. We now use 'they' as a singular, gender-neutral pronoun to refer to a person whose gender isn't known or to one who does not identify as male or female."

"You used to drill us on pronoun-antecedent agreement—for example, 'It's time for everyone to turn in *his* assignment.'"

"I did. And now 'It's time for everyone to turn in his assignment' is regarded as inappropriate because it reflects not only patriarchal domination but gender insensitivity, since not everyone falls neatly into 'his' and 'her' categories. 'It's time for everyone to turn in *his* **or** *her* assignment,' while not quite as patriarchal, nevertheless reflects gender insensitivity, and is cumbrous besides. Although it's like pouring poison into the porches of my aged ears, I concede that 'It's time for everyone to turn in *their* assignment' solves those problems."

"So 'To each their own'?"

"Yes."

"But isn't there a grammatical-semantic incompatibility in that phrase? 'To each their own' grammatically solves the power and gender problems but semantically implies that 'To each their own' and 'To each his own' are equally acceptable, when that isn't exactly what you mean."

"Good catch, Wittgenstein. The interanimation of words! A linguistic expression is often more complicated than we at first assume. I won't give 'To each their own' my imprimatur just yet, but I am looking upon a liberal use of it—that is to say 'their'—favorably! And I hope that the next pronoun change in English will be the eradication of 'whom'. I am far too often reading, even in the *New York Times*, utterances like 'Whom better than Alexandria Ocasio-Cortez to lead the nation into the future?' I cringe when people use 'whom' in the nominative position in an attempt to sound learned or proper."

"So for 'whom' the bell tolls?"

"I hope so! For many years I devoted much of a class period to the 'who/whom' conundrum, but I now contend that 'who' should become everyone's default pronoun, filling both nominative and objective roles, because figuring out when to use 'whom' is just too complicated for him or her or them."

"But not for I! I can still do it, Coach. Give me a chance!"

"Okay, try this." He set his half-empty container of fish and chips beside him on the bench, took a pen from a pocket, and scribbled over the greasy Spud bag 'Who/whom shall I say is calling?'

She borrowed the pen to use as a pointer. "To determine whether to use 'who' or 'whom,' you always told us to ask ourselves 'What's a nice pronoun like you doing in a clause or phrase like this?', figure out the grammatical function of the word, then decide which of its forms is appropriate. So: 'I' is the subject of the main clause, 'shall say' is its complete transitive verb, 'who/whom is calling' is a noun clause serving as the complement, the direct object, of the main clause, within that noun clause 'who/whom' is the subject, thus 'who' is the correct form and the sentence should read 'Who shall I say is calling?'"

Flushing at her performance, she handed the pen and bag back to him.

"So I haven't lived in vain! You are able to range beyond your intuitive knowledge of the deep structure of English to demonstrate an analytic knowledge of its surface structure. I have educated you, led you out of the shadowy cave of ignorance and into the light of day."

Liz Ann lifted her eyelids. "Don't mock the naming of parts! I love parsing! From *pars orationis*, 'parts of speech,' right? The ultimate goal of education, in my opinion, should be the Delphic 'Know thyself,' but no knowledge, including that of grammatical analysis, is irrelevant to the achieving of that goal. Everything that you learn should be incorporated into your understanding of yourself and of your relationship to the world and the universe."

The ferry *Puyallup* approached the dock, its horn, sounded a single time, resonating like a baritone sax. Its idling engines hummed and gently churned foam as passengers streamed down the elevated walkway toward Railroad Avenue and cars and trucks clunk-clunked across the raised iron threshold and onto the pier.

"Liz Ann, I agree. I marvel at the very existence of language, at its crowd-sourced emergence from the brains and mouths of our tree-hugging and cave-dwelling ancestors who somehow, over millennia, found ways to put sounds into patterns that majorities in clans or tribes came to accept as meaningful. I've always loved to study grammar and to teach it. In one sense it's just fun, mental gymnastics, like a crossword puzzle, but it's also deeply satisfying to know that language *has* a structure that can be analyzed, that we can make conscious this aspect of our unconscious, that its study can lead to insights about the nature of the mind and of learning. And it's certainly helpful to have terminology with which to talk about the linguistic usage of others—whether in literature or in routine transactional communication—and to aid in your own employment of the medium. Grammar intertwines with rhetoric as you seek to establish a voice suitable to your persuasive purpose. Out of the black, willy-nilly, inchoate ideas and images, words and phrases and clauses, pop into your conscious mind, and then, based on your knowledge of diction and sentence structure, you go to work revising them according to your rhetorical needs. So you decide to say 'they,' rather than 'his' or 'her,' in hopes of persuading your audience that you are a 'woke' person, fair and decent, and to say 'The solution was unique' rather than 'fairly unique' for the sake of precision and economy, knowing that those who are aware of the difference will, shibbolethically, appreciate your discernment, while others will not even notice it. And you decide to use, let's say, a periodic sentence because you think holding the main clause in abeyance will focus attention on what precedes it and create an intriguing suspense."

"I remember those periodic sentences. And the loose! And the balanced! You gave us a lot of models to imitate! We'd write sentences for homework and then share our results in our discussion groups. What was that concept you talked about—the generative rhetoric of the sentence?"

[Uh-oh, a little more Velveeta here. Solveig]

"Yes. In the early '70s Noam Chomsky's notion of the grammatical principle of embedding or recursion and Francis Christensen's notion of sentence form itself as the generator of ideas inspired me to teach elements of style in a way that, I hoped, would help each student develop his or her or their own. Style is the person themself, I might say in a bit of Buffonery! I have always been averse to the plain style advocated by Strunk and White in their popular little manual. I am attracted to distinctive styles—the hardness of Patrick White, the softness of Malcolm Lowry. I love textural richness, density, variety—in part, I admit, as an acrobatic verbal selfie, sheer unapologetic narcissism, a demonstration of the writer's ethos that may prove appealing but runs the risk of appalling, like a behind-the-back pass or a reverse layup when neither is necessary, but primarily as a way to provide rhythm and texture, the jazz-like riffing of subordinate clauses and phrases after, before, or in the midst of the main clause adding to or qualifying meaning. Christensen argued for what he called the cumulative sentence (essentially what traditional rhetoric called a loose sentence), a main clause followed by any number of subordinate clauses and phrases, each one shifting down to a lower level of specificity, detailing the detail that preceded it, providing examples, implications, qualifications—codicils, you might say. The form itself is liberating. It generates ideas by stimulating your powers of observation and analysis. You examine your subject with more alertness as you seek to add layers of meaning. With enough practice, you internalize the structure, you rewire your brain, as we say (probably all too often; that's definitely a meme that's gone viral) these days. And, of course, the principle applies to the practice of periodic and balanced sentences as well."

Out in the middle of the Salish Sea, pleasure boats bobbed on the wakes of a black jumbo freighter heading south to Seattle and a white, many-windowed cruise ship, *The Argosy*, riding high and sassy as it glided toward the Inside Passage to Alaska. Liz Ann's phone text-pinged inside her jeans pocket. She ignored it.

"Well, it was certainly fun. The guys in my group came up with some pretty hilarious stuff. Parodies of you, for example. One of the non-obscene ones that I remember is 'Wayne raised both eyebrows halfway to his receding hairline, like Fosbury at the top of his flop, his eyes widening in horror, as if he'd just heard someone start a sentence with 'Hopefully' instead of 'I hope'.' I know that there was carry-over to my writing in college, and I've forever maintained a love of word-play, but I think that above all your stuff led to my becoming a better reader, helping me to work my way through the syntactic mazes of Proust and Shakespeare."

"It pleases me to hear that. In my undergraduate days I was heavily influenced by the New Criticism of Cleanth Brooks, I. A. Richards, and others, and I used to devour *The Saturday Review of Literature* along with my tuna fish sandwiches at lunchtime in the UW library. In my teaching I cared little about the history of literature—trends, cycles, developments, biographies of writers—but very much about textual interpretation, close reading. "Just give me the text," one of my profs used to say, and I was in full agreement. That kind of analytical skill, teasing out the meaning of metaphors, digging for the relevance of allusions, detecting and appreciating intended ambiguities, disambiguating unintended ones, is valuable in understanding Proust and Shakespeare but also the *Bible*, the *Constitution* and other legal documents, and even the dense, dull language we're asked to wade through these days before we adopt apps on our electronic devices. And surely, in these Trumpian times, it can help us distinguish among real news, fake news, and real fake news, make us more discerning, less gullible."

To the north the alto whistle of a freight train screamed its warning, and soon they heard its wheels clicking over the joints of the tracks behind them. The iron rods of the bench had for some minutes been biting his back and butt. He stood for a few seconds, rotated his shoulders, wiggled his hips, then sat again.

"And this concern with the interanimation of words affected the way I taught prose style. Certainly the approach has its critics—the anti-formalists, the anti-behavioralists, those against the part-to-whole method. They find such exercises a-creative, a-rhetorical, artificial, stultifying, and particularly inapplicable to expository writing, where the emphasis they say should be on organization and logic and clarity. But I think that imitating a form can stimulate creativity. In basketball for example, we used to drill on dribbling to a two-foot jump stop and then making a front pivot or a reverse pivot to get off a shot. We'd do it several times without a ball, getting the footwork, the rhythm and the balance, then with a ball, then against a passive defender, and finally against an aggressive defender, each time with the requirement that the player make a front or reverse pivot to free herself for a shot."

"I know. And it worked. The step-through move became a major part of my offense."

"Right. You incorporated it into your game. You learned the skill through formal instruction and guided practice and then, in scrimmages and games, began to see-feel-sense—some combination of perception and intuition—where it could be employed for what we might call rhetorical effect, a telling, freeing move that enabled you to score or to assist someone else to score with a pass."

"And that was true also of all the other drills we did—the head fakes, ball fakes, step-backs, bounce passes, overhead passes, baseball passes, crossover dribbles, spin dribbles, behind-the-back dribbles, bank shots, hook shots, all types of layups. You used to talk about *Funktionslust*—the love of exercising skills that we're good at. It's as if they became extensions or expansions of ourselves. In time we just flowed into them, or they just flowed out of us, in response to a need."

" Yes. And, similarly, writing exercises can enhance perception and, given enough repetition, lead to fluidity. Even punctuation exercises play a role here. Being required to write sentences employing a colon or a pair of dashes forces you to see that what goes after the colon or between the dashes must in some way augment or add specificity to what precedes the colon or surrounds the dashes. Sentences requiring a semi-colon make you balance or contrast independent clauses. Imitations can lead to an expanded, more versatile style—a grammar of moves generating a rhetoric of motifs—which you can adapt to any occasion. On the other hand, I also believe that at times students learn better if they work together to discover and develop ideas, Googling the teacher only occasionally for assistance."

"That's why you often put us in groups."

"Right. And usually it paid off, as it did in the analysis of 'Jabberwocky.' But not always."

"Sometimes you never know," she said with a smile.

"I always know I like *that*, though." He returned her smile.

"Were you thinking of 'Invictus'?"

"Exactly. When I asked you to rank in order of artistic quality 'Invictus,' 'Now Sleeps the Crimson Petal,' 'God's Grandeur,' 'The Emperor of Ice Cream,' 'Stopping by Woods,' and 'Batter My Heart, Three-Person'd God,' I was mostly concerned about what standards you came up with and how you applied them to your evaluation of the poems, not the actual ranking itself. Based on the Romantic assumption that the young are all classicists—"

"Ahem."

"—and the Platonic assumption that at least some learning is remembering—summoning innate ideas of the true, the good, and the beautiful—I expected you to focus on unity, structure, rhythm, diction, precision, freshness, richness, subtlety, surprise. I expected views to vary, with one exception: 'Invictus' had to be last."

"And we all rated it first!"

"Indeed you did. You were not troubled that Henley bludgeons the reader with the vague, the general. He offers no fresh imagery, no specific detail, no indication of why he should be in pain, what menaces he faces in this life or the next, no reason for us to believe that he is the master of his fate and the captain of his soul. Now, Henley himself in fact suffered from tuberculosis and had a leg amputated as a consequence. Details about dealing with that, familiar words used unfamiliarly, idiosyncratically, could have resulted in a good poem."

"But you must admit it had unity, structure, and rhythm. And most important of all, even though it wasn't subtly expressed, it had a rousing theme. We were high school kids, Coach! We were used to competing in various sports against other schools, with the pep band playing the theme from 'Rocky' during timeouts to inspire us. As a coach, in tight situations, you weren't so subtle yourself: 'Suck it up!' 'Bust a gut!' 'Dominate!'"

"I know. Under pressure, my imagination failed."

"But the trite, the expected, was what we needed. The one time you said something different—'Why don't you break your backs, girls?'—we got totally confused and a little offended and almost lost the game. How did we know, until you told us in the locker room afterwards, that you were alluding to Stubb's motivating words to his oarsmen when chasing whales in *Moby Dick*? Anyway, we could all see that the other poems were more intricate, and we liked them, but the one that most spoke to us was 'Invictus.' We longed to believe that we were masters and captains, and we warmed to meaning that was blatant, not latent. So maybe the young are not entirely classicists. Or maybe they need to have their memories jogged a little bit by a teacher who prompts them to delve deeper—which is what you did when you asked us to discuss our criteria and justify our rankings. Once you got over your initial disappointment, you turned it into a good lesson. You didn't convince us to change our minds, but you got us to think, you discomfited us, you planted a seed. It was definitely a factor in the gradual evolution of my own esthetic standards."

"Nice of you to say so. Like a coach helping her team regroup after a disappointing performance, you turn defeat into moral victory! In any case, education in America has long been such a fraught issue. Since at least the early '50s, when I started reading stuff I found on the coffee tables of my parents and their friends—*Look, Life, Colliers, The Reader's Digest*—articles on education, sex, and food have been the staples of popular magazines. Most will agree that education is of the utmost importance, but not since the days of the one-room schoolhouse and the *McGuffey Reader* have we had anything but short-lived consensus on purpose or process. We bounce back and forth from John Dewey to Robert Maynard Hutchings, from Jean Piaget to Rudolf Flesch, from Maria Montessori to Alan Bloom and Benjamin Bloomberg. We see, we saw, we gee, we haw, we pitch, we yaw. As we do with religious doctrine and practice, we disperse into squabbling factions whenever we discuss objectives, curriculum, and pedagogy because they so grow out of our own slant on the meaning of life and the nature of personhood. So we say that the purpose of education is to liberalize, to open eyes, to free the mind, to teach critical and creative thinking, to transform the culture, to develop a lifelong love of learning, or we say it's to teach the three R's, to prepare for the world of work, to sort out according to ability, to develop specific vocational skills, to transmit the culture, to pass on the core values of democracy and capitalism, such as patriotism, discipline, work-ethic, competitiveness. We say that the curriculum should grow out of the needs and interests of the student, or that there is a certain body of knowledge and skills that must comprise it. We say that the student is a discoverer who learns by doing, or that he/she/they is a vessel to be filled. We say that the student should learn to read through the Whole Language method, looking and saying, or through an intensive study of phonics, sounding out words. We say that the student best learns history or science or mathematics by acting like a historian (examining primary sources), a scientist (collecting data, forming and testing hypotheses), or a mathematician (drawing principles—theorems, for example—from the study of a specific problem) or that the student should be told, via lecture, textbook, or film, the facts of history, the laws of science, and the principles of mathematics. We say that the teacher is a guide or that the teacher is an authority."

"And I followed all this cycling and recycling of philosophies and methods with my boys from kindergarten through high school, and of course in my career, beginning as an assistant and eventually becoming head librarian, providing resources and support for all of the various programs and practices, from the days of the card catalogue, *The Reader's Guide*, microfiche, cassette tapes and overhead projectors to the arrival of desk-top computers, cell phones, and iPads. I always loved learning and wanted to be involved in education, but I knew that teaching was not for me. I didn't have the presence for it. Being a librarian felt just right. I could work with kids without having to be their daily model. And I could control a microcosm holding within its 5,000 square feet a fair sampling of the world's knowledge, wisdom, and artistic expression. Its seafoam green walls, industrial-gray padless carpet, and metal stacks were my home away from home, my baby. Such a rich and satisfying Gestalt: the entire universe put in order by Dewey Decimals and Google. And I was the guide to the galaxy, assisting with a myriad of approaches adopted and abandoned, sometimes re-adopted and re-abandoned. Programmed learning, cooperative learning, mastery learning. Basic academic competencies, the 3 Rs. Business letters and the five-paragraph essay took priority for a while, then journaling and exploring writing as a process. Speed-reading, using your finger as a pacer, à *la* Evelyn Wood, one year, free reading the next. At Bothell, at the end of every second-period class, students and teachers—even the librarian and her student-assistant staff—would remain in the room for an additional 20 minutes and read whatever they liked: comic books, magazines, newspapers, novels, self-help books, anything except assigned texts. I remember there was a lot of blushing and giggling when my girls passed around an underlined copy of *The Sensuous Woman,* giving apparently no thought to the demeaning nature of its basic premise—though I must confess I found the presentation of tongue exercises useful in my relationships with both Don and Jennifer! For a while we had homogenous classes, then grouping into basic, regular, and honors. Then along came the Advanced Placement Program and International Baccalaureate. There was a concern over learning styles—visual, auditory, kinesthetic. We went through phases of more homework and less homework. We evaluated students against each other according to state or federal norms on standardized tests, and against themselves based on things like personal portfolios. At the elementary level we developed Individualized Educational Programs for the physically and intellectually challenged and special programs for the gifted. And of course there was No Child Left Behind and, just as I was on the verge of retiring, here came Common Core and STEM and crazes for charter schools and home schooling."

"Yes, in education we must admit that we have a richness of embarrassments. But do you know where I come down in all this?"

"Squarely in the middle?"

"Exactly! Somewhere between Miss Dove and John Keating. Early in my career I read Rousseau's *Emile* and A.S. Neill's *Summerhill* and John Holt's *How Children Fail* and *How Children Learn* and was warmed by their Romantic belief that the curriculum should grow out of the felt-needs of the students, but whenever I stepped back into the classroom it seemed to me that there was not world enough and time. Waiting for intrinsic motivation to kick in too often results in failure to launch. Extrinsic motivation—competition, grades, praise, fear of failure—is a necessary counterbalance. I think we need to synthesize the thesis of the student as vessel with its antithesis of the student as discoverer. Reading is far more than decoding letters and sounds, but skill in decoding with facility and accuracy is prerequisite to being able to move from text to subtext, for achieving levels of interpretation, for grasping symbolism, metaphor, irony, ambiguity, and paradox, for being able to read or write anything beyond the plain style. I'm all for a heavy dose of phonics for beginning readers."

"I'm grateful that my sons got that at Seaview Elementary in the '80s."

"And reading and writing surely require more than a rich vocabulary, but I'm convinced that a study of Latin and Greek roots and affixes, if pushed to the point of application, can improve one's reading and writing both."

"The word-attack skills! When we'd come upon an unfamiliar word in a poem, you'd jump up in a karate stance and say 'Hah! Hah!' while making chopping motions with your right arm, and we'd know to break the word down into root and affix. 'Cornucopia'—'cornu,' horn, 'copia,' of plenty. "Legerdemain'—'leger,' light, 'demain,' of hand. And, of course, my favorite, 'education'—'e,' out, and 'duct,' to lead. To lead out of ignorance is still the best, most comprehensive meaning of the word. I believe we go to school to become as free of ignorance—of the world and of the universe, of ourselves and of others—as possible. Education liberates. The aim is to become, in the Emersonian sense, Man (or, better, Person) Thinking. Thinking critically about oneself and everything else."

"I so agree. Even the vocabulary lists I used to test you on in College Prep Comp had merit, I thought, because I required you to select from them five words to include in your weekly essays. It sounds so artificial and sterile, so inorganic, but it works. You found a way to use them, and the words became your own. There is a place for rote learning, for memorizing. One mark of the educated person is being able to remember and regurgitate stuff. The greater your knowledge of roots and etymologies, the greater your appreciation of the interrelations between words. The more material you have at your disposal, the greater your potential for critical and creative thinking. And through the process, no matter the subject or the method—a formal lecture, a technical demonstration analyzed and presented step by step, with question and response or other active involvement on the learner's part, or in free-flowing group discussion—underlying all, imbuing all, like the background beat provided for jazz soloists, is the informal imprinting, on the student's psyche, of the teacher as meme, modeling, as you say, Person Thinking. Given all of our embarrassments, our gullibility, our susceptibility to the next short-lived placebo or Hawthorne effect, all of our approaches and programs that do not survive, are we getting anywhere? I actually think so. We inch our way along. We've crawled out of the sea, we've evolved lungs to replace our gills. Although we're still squirming forward by wiggling our tails and fins, we do know more about how to teach. Our pedagogy, our methodology, our knowledge of the principles of learning, have improved. Give me a learner long enough on motivation, and a place to stand, and I can mold the world! But mold it to what? This is where we run into conflict, and probably always will and probably always should. Pendulum swings seem to me both inevitable and healthy. When it comes to philosophy and curriculum, we will always need to correct our corrections."

"Well, correct me if I'm wrong, but I think it must be about 12:30, and I have to work a shift at the Museum at 1:00." She checked her phone. "Yep, 12:33."

[*Et tu*, Liz Ann? Solveig]

[Just imitating my mentor! Liz Ann]

"Coach, this has been such fun, and I feel that there's much that we haven't touched on. Like basketball. And lesbianism! We should do this again."

"I'd love to. But let's change the venue. How about a beer just across the tracks at 190 Sunset?"

[This is what you resort to to (I know, I know) thicken the plot? Solveig]

"Great. I love their courtyard!"

The old man collected their trash and put it in his Spud bag. He walked her back to her silver mini-Cooper in the Spud parking lot. His Santa Fe sat next to it, his gym bag on the passenger seat. He would lift weights and shoot baskets at HSAC before heading home.

"Little car for a big girl," she laughed. "It's so dexterous that whenever I'm in traffic I feel as if I'm back on the court making quick moves."

They hugged. A bit of breeze wafted a few strands of her lemon-scented hair into his face.

As she opened her door she said, "Hey, Coach, I fear we are in danger of losing the subjunctive mode. Is it on its last legs, as it were?" She grinned.

He smiled. "No doubt."

[Wayne, I appreciate your thoughts on educational philosophy, curriculum, and methodology. I share some of them. You obviously did some excellent work as a teacher, and I'm happy to learn that many of your students responded positively to you. But this dialogue is just a bit too Socratically smug for me. Like Socrates' pupils by his side in the *agora*, Liz Ann is too agreeable, too eager to accept this sorites here and that enthymeme there. I half expected her to step up onto that verdigris bench and intone 'Oh, Captain, my Captain!' Surely many of your students did not enjoy your exercises in sentence rhetoric, surely many did not become close readers and original stylists. Dave]

[Right on, Dave! I refused to join the cult of Wayne. It wasn't fun, it was boring. I hated being part of those smug little groups. That's why I smashed one of those vertical windows that open like a door and broke into his classroom one night and poured beer over his desk and wrote 'FUCK YOU WAYNE!' on the chalkboard. So now you know who did it, Wayne. Maloney]

[That was you, Lonnie? The window was boarded up for days, and the damn carpet smelled like beer for a week. Not appreciated! Liz Ann]

7

Urge and Urge and Urge

May 15, opening day. The Classics versus the Hot Shots, game time 8:00 a.m. The old man got out of bed at 4:30, unable to feign sleep any longer. Beside the bed he stretched calves, quads, hamstrings, glutes, adductors, lower back, tris, rotator cuffs, did planks and pushups, balanced, then went to the toilet to review his swing thoughts—load, see, snap: a trip of the hips round the spine to bash, at three, on the ball—while depositing a mound of stool, made black by iron supplements. He rubbed Icy-Hot on his sacroiliac and put on his uniform: long-sleeved black undershirt, crew-neck jersey, white with black pinstripes, CLASSICS arched on the chest in black, black 21 on the back, black ankle-length softball pants, white socks, black windbreaker, black cap logoed with a white C. In the kitchen he worked through his pills, this once almost oblivious to the view, feeling his pacemaker responding to the spur of his surging adrenaline. His heart had been rewired; had his brain?

He breathed deeply and said, "Good morning, Alexa. What is the temperature?"

"Good morning, Wayne," Alexa said. "The current temperature is 49 degrees. Today, expect a high of 64."

"Lexa, what is the question of the day?"

"Today's question is from the topic of general knowledge. It is worth five points. The term 'Renaissance Man' is another way of describing which type of person: (a) polymath (b) Philistine (c) sycophant (d) periodontist?"

The old man guffawed. "Oh, Lexy, be Sirious!"

"I'm sorry. I did not understand your answer."

"Polymath!" he responded, his belly still spasming.

"That is correct. A polymath is a person of wide-ranging knowledge or learning, like a Renaissance Man. You have earned your 61st general knowledge badge and five points. You are among the 45% of users who answered this question correctly. You have a total of 1,436 points. You have earned a bonus question. Would you like to answer it now?"

"No, thank you." After such an easy win, a true laugher, why risk defeat? Why not just ride this buoyancy all the way to the game? That wasn't being superstitious, was it?

To keep his legs fresh, he drove down empty 5th to Starbucks, helping himself to a primo parking space at the corner of Main, and arrived at the door just as LaTasha was unlocking it.

"Wow, looking good, Wayne!"

"Thanks, LaTasha. The Kid from Edmonds is ready to play."

"You're in some sort of senior softball league, I take it?" said a regular following him in, one to whom he had never spoken but had occasionally nodded, a youngish senior, 65, maybe, recently enrolled in Medicare, maybe, gray crewcut, dynamic grin, aerodynamic ears, penetrating, glasses-free eyes, 5'10"-180, maybe, weight on the balls of his feet, bouncing with vitality. Some seniors, the old man had observed as they waited in line at Starbucks or gazed from sidewalks at shop windows or rested on exercise machines at HSAC, virtually cancelled themselves, letting their mouths gape and their eyes, behind glasses, glass over, death-toward-being seemingly their default being-toward-death.

"Yeah. You interested? Teams are always looking for younger players."

"No, thanks. Those days are gone. At my age I'm just

concentrating on my golf game."

He ordered an egg-feta-spinach wrap for the protein, an 8-grain roll for the fiber, and a *grande* pour-over of single-origin Columbia Narino Supremo for the menu-touted notes of dark chocolate and black walnut, scanned, anapestically took the roll and his iPad and sat down to eat at the far corner table with view of the street. He broke off a clover leaf of the roll and stuffed it into his mouth. Stale, dry, disappointing. But not an omen. There were no such things as omens.

His phone chimed an arpeggio. He tingled in hope, braced himself in dread, as he also did each of the half dozen times a day he checked his email. He craved affirmation, wallowed in its bestowal for hours, but feared its fettering obligation to respond, to summon his rhetorical resources, to affirm the affirmer, to wag his tail appreciatively, to admit his need. A text-message from Liz Ann: "Good luck today, Coach!" "Thanks, Liz Ann," he tapped in reply. As it whooshed away, a second text, from Sylvia, rang in: "Just read your recent blog post on aging—disappointing!"

Then three beeps from the microwave. "Here you go, Wayne," LaTasha called, setting a cup and a plate on the counter behind him. "Your wrap's ready. And your pour-over, too."

No longer buoyant, he trudged over to get them, trudged back. Sylvia had disdained his piece on epitaphs and now the one on aging. Damn! He opened his wrap. Syl, Wayne be frontin', now don't you be huntin' for sumpin' that's really nuttin'. He took a small, hot, juicy, faintly sour bite, hit the simplesite.com icon for his blog, and opened "*Wabi-Sabi*."

You know, dude, said a white freshly bathed naked octogenarian to his altered ego as he put on his bi-focals and leaned forward to peer into the wide mirror backing the sinks in his bathroom, every time I do this I think *Look away, you're hideous.* From forehead to ankle, in various places to varying degrees, the exitless maze of my Byzantine skin is puckered, seersuckered, scored, chevroned, tildeed, trenched, crinkled, parenthesized, hashtagged, rippled like lake water agitated by the drippings from a rower's oar, fanned out in creases like stylized sun rays, pebbled and sunken like a deflated leather basketball, or corrugated like ET. *Ouch.* Its elastic gone, it folds, it droops, it jiggles. It's crepey, it's creepy. It's dreggy, it's drecky. It's *de trop.*

Venerable one, replied his altered ego, you are blinded by your sight. You hold the mirror up to nature, but you don't see reality. What you see is what you don't get. Slip through that looking glass. Go East, old man, to the land of *wabi-sabi.* Unclench. Cling not to anger, disgust, remorse, sadness. Let go of your pinched Western esthetic. As you gaze at yourself, find the beauty in decay. The patina of age is lovelier than the bloom of youth, a desiccated raisin more profoundly pleasing than a plump grape. The warping of time gives birth to the sublime. The symmetric, the pneumatic, the smooth, the firm are far too easy to love, like snow-capped mountains, moonlit lakes, Neil Diamond songs. Don't mourn lost September morns; rejoice in the continually metamorphosing embers of November. The metastasizing of flaws is fascinating. Impermanence and entropy are liberating. The tarnished, the hoarfrosted, the withered, the scarred, the nicked—the soul trembles before the austere glory of the authentic. Keats was half right: truth is beauty. The imperfect is the tense of life. The rough is itself the diamond. To a fully opened eye, the tangled spaghetti of Maggie Smith's facial wrinkles rocks; Clint Eastwood's crags make his day.

Dude, I'd like to believe you, I really would. You mean well. You're a loyal altered ego carrying out your dream job— that is to say, your job of dreaming. It's why you exist. I eye the glass, you offer the reconciling gloss. You speak of the union of soul and oversoul, of atonement with nature, of transcendence. But I call that wobbly-sobby. Your view is refracted through a rosy prism of spiritualism, whereas I can only see through the glass darkly. My view is superficial, my interpretation literal. There is no hidden meaning. The attempt to expand consciousness by whatever means—meditation or psychotropical drugs or speaking in tongues—and the

Platonic quest to find the ideal, which is the real, behind the real, which apparently is not, are equally vainglorious. Appearance is reality. We are animated matter. We age. We begin to disintegrate. We lose whatever beauty we had and with it our vigor and power and control over our environment and ourselves. *An aged man is but a paltry thing, a tattered coat upon a stick*, and no matter how the poet spells his name, there's no yeast to leaven our decline. We become irrelevant. We die. We fully disintegrate.

Executive ego of mine, even if we stipulate (as we certainly should) that our flesh has an Ozymandate to die, and even if we grant (as I'm arguing we probably should not, because hiding in the hideous I perceive an awestruck "o" and a reverential "deus") that seeing is believing, that there is no ideal behind the real, the continuous kaleidoscoping of the epidermis on its journey from birth to earth is wonderful in the most literal sense. Become your own seeing master and teach yourself to behold the marvels of the journey. It's not a matter of ratiocination or drugs or ecstatic frenzies. It's a matter of attention, repetition. It's simple classical conditioning. As a cheese eater, you progressed from flavorless Kraft slices to nutty and ever so faintly sulfurous emmental to peppery pecorino to the lushly rotting blue ammoniacal veins of Gorgonzola. With painting, you gradually discovered many varieties to savor, from the picturesque to the poignant to the painful to the pathological. Botticelli's "The Birth of Venus" and Monet's "Water Lilies" are gorgeous, but you also found provocative rewards in Bosch's "The Garden of Earthly Delights," Dali's "The Persistence of Memory," and Picasso's "Guernica," not to mention the geometric distortions of "Les Demoiselles d'Avignon" and his other Cubist works. You've investigated the Ashcan School's exploration of life's seamy side and have looked at the dirty, brutish, raw "Outsider Art" in vogue today. You've learned that grotesque and gruesome are not in themselves ugly. You've seen that grotesque and gruesome can grow on you.

I certainly have. That's the problem that I've painfully pointed out.

Yes, they've become you—but with practice you will see that they also *become* you. Google facial closeups of such momentary monuments of magnificence as Charlize Theron, Melania Trump, Gisele Bundchen, Sofia Vargara, Matthew McConaughey, Brad Pitt, Channing Tatum, Bradley Cooper. Study them daily. Sooner than you might expect, their monotonous callow blandness will come to seem chilly, not cool. Google facial closeups of molderers who have eschewed Botox and silicone, like Maggie and Clint, Dame Judy Dench, golf commentator Judy Rankin, Willem Dafoe, Nick Nolte. Study them daily. Sooner than you might expect, you will warm to their textured, tortured tissue. Use Netflix to look back at Miss Jean Brodie in her so-called prime, her vapid face like plain tofu, its insipidity a stark contrast to the mien of the Dowager Countess. Then go back to your bathroom mirror and give yourself a chance to rejoice in reality. Everyone, including yourself, deserves a fair seeing.

You know, dude, that just might work. Maybe what you're saying is not so wobbly-sobby after all. I'm going to give your aversion-immersion therapy a try. How I'd love to be able to dive into a deep pool of narcissism again!

"Sylvia," he texted, "thanks for reading me. Our talks have complicated my thinking, for sure. But, tho it's a struggle, Imma cling to my superficiality!"

Self-cajoled, feeling the game again growing within him, too amped to dig into the *NY Times,* he simply sat and munched the wrap and sipped the coffee, which seemed to deliver, in addition to the dark chocolate and black walnut, a whiff of the peat moss that every spring he and Diane used to spade into the wet clay earth of the gardens at their L-shaped two-bedroom cedar-sided rambler with attached garage on Grandview in North Edmonds, a half-mile from the Bowl. Following the lead of Chet and Evelyn, they spent hours each week from spring to fall cultivating vegetables and flowers. In the big garden of their fenced back yard, their vegetable love growing, they planted Bibb lettuce, Swiss chard, rhubarb, bush beans and peas, beefsteak tomatoes, cucumbers, cabbage,

broccoli, cauliflower, zucchini, pumpkins, beets, carrots, Finnish potatoes, parsnips, shallots, garlic, oregano, tarragon, rocket, cilantro,
basil, parsley, sage, rosemary, and thyme. In the beds along all sides
of the house they grew tea roses, rhododendrons, azaleas, and
blue hydrangeas. In late winter they buried bulbs for daffodils and
black tulips; in the summer they set out lemon marigolds and pink
and red impatiens in that space. In the front lawn, which the old
man kept trim with a gas-powered rotary mower, they planted two
dense lilac trees, purple bloomers, fifteen feet apart. He and Diane
were doers, together. He mowed, she raked. He hoed, she staked,
propping up heavy tomato stalks, realigning rose bushes after prun-
ing them back to five-leaf clusters. He set out the soaker hoses for
the vegetables, she tended the flowers with her watering can. She,
like her father, filled an emptied MJB coffee can, procured from the
old man's parents, with water and dropped into it one end of a
long cotton sock, placing the other at the base of a cucumber plant,
which then drank long and slowly. He, like Almanzo Wilder, followed
the same procedure with milk and a pumpkin plant. The cukes
emerged with thin rinds and moist flesh, the pumpkins swelled to a
size ideal for the jack-o-lanterns which each carved to place on the
front porch in October, hers always better executed, with eyeballs
and angled noses and articulated teeth, his with four gaping holes.
They harvested vegetables together, they cooked dinner together.
They bought Pelligrini's *The Unprejudiced Palate* and cooked their
way through it, learning to mince and to bone, to make frittatas and
risotto and *pasta e fagioli* and polenta and rabbit stew and roast
chicken with tarragon. They progressed to Julia Child, their love
of inner organs—sweetbreads, liver, tripe, kidney—blooming, and
then, browsing one day in the Edmonds Library, when it was part of
the new civic complex between 5th and 6th and Bell and Edmonds,
where the Christian Science church and Sunday School buildings
had once stood, discovered Elizabeth David, whose precise prose
suited the detailed simplicity and gumption of her gastronomy,
admonishing them neither to embroider nor to cut corners with

ingredients or execution. The old man admired the integrity of her approach but was not above sloughing and bluffing, his mincing and dicing sometimes verging on chunking, his deboning characterized by some sawing and ripping, his measurings ballparkish. He liked to suggest substitutions—garlic instead of shallots, walnuts instead of almonds on the *haricots verts*—and additions—chicken livers in the *cassoulet*. "Just follow the recipe and do it right," Diane would say. "Everything is there for a purpose." Her touch was sure, her work exact. After reading David on bread-making, she quickly became adept, punching down with authority, kneading tirelessly. Each week she provided a new, textured loaf—wheat, rye, pumpernickel, or sourdough made from a yeast strain that she kept in the refrigerator—so aromatic when pulled from the oven that the old man would immediately have to cut himself a ragged chunk. At dinner, she would close her eyes for a brief silent prayer, he would take a sip of wine, and then they would commune over the food, blessing it with attention. Each summer they took on a home improvement project. Together they tore the old composition shingles off the roof, rolled out new sticky tar paper, installed new flashing around the chimney, and covered the whole with thick cedar shakes, she lining them up and he nailing them in. Together, wielding brushes, they repainted the fading barn-red siding charcoal gray and trimmed the window sashes in white, he laboriously scrubbing face and hands with turpentine at the end of the day, then dumping his spattered clothes into the garbage can on the patio, she emerging virtually unscathed. Together, they laid oak parquet flooring over the old linoleum in the kitchen and dining room, she measuring the tiles and spreading the glue, he cutting and laying the pieces in.

The old man cherished and envied Diane's competence—she could miter baseboard corners without using a box—and was occasionally irked but more often tickled by her certainty, her impatient, impulsive directness. She knew what she wanted. If she noted black spots on the leaves of the roses, within the hour she was off to Wight's Nursery in Lynnwood to get a lethal spray. When she telephoned someone, she demanded bluntly "Is Susie there?", never bothering with a preambling "Oh, hi, John! Hey, how are you? This is Diane. Does Susie happen to be around?" In stores, she moved quickly, darted with assurance, made instant decisions— this book, those shoes, that cantaloupe. Circling a rack of hanging blouses at the Aurora Village Nordstrom, she would authoritatively dismiss the unsuitable ones with a deft swipe of her left hand, clanging one hanger against another. The old man could seldom buy anything on a first viewing. He needed to check other stores, other models, other brands, get all the specs, sift the information for a few days. Clothes, running shoes, softball bats, golf clubs— were they affordable? If affordable, was that the way their money should be spent? If so, which option was best? He dithered. When he saw an intriguing book at the Edmonds Bookshop, he would heft it, check the blurbs, randomly sample a few paragraphs, consider the price, reshelve it, and return a day or two later to pay for it. "If you want it, get it," she would say. "I can't today," he would reply. "I'll think it over." It took him a week to give himself permission to buy the Robert Fitzgerald translations of *The Iliad* and *The Odyssey* that he coveted. Cars, appliances, house wares—she was ready to buy at first sight if something looked and felt right. Often enough, he ended up agreeing that her instinctive choice was the right one for them. Thriftily, she would pull from a pocket and reuse a tissue on which she'd already blown her nose, but her heart told her that the best way to save money was to spend money. Reward cards from Starbucks, Walgreens, Target, and Safeway filled all the slots in her wallet, and she was compelled to take advantage of discount coupons that arrived in the mail. A dollar off the foot-long turkey-ham sandwich at Subway? That would be her lunch for two days. Twenty per cent off any purchase at Kohls? She'd need a new pair of running shoes within a year anyway, so best buy now. Two dollars off a two-pack of three-pound jars of Skippy peanut butter at Costco? Buying three saved six dollars and provided the security of a year's supply. She kept pantry and closet shelves full; they never ran out of bananas, tuna fish, band aids, light bulbs, or batteries. She loved to be on the go. She had weekly outings with her golf group, her tennis group, her Canasta group, her Bible study group. Idling at home, she would leap toward a ringing phone in excited anticipation. She was up for anything—a coffee stop, a trip to the library, a run, a movie, a ball game, a walk on the beach, a ferry ride. Although the old man was compelled to keep up with the world and to improve something—knowledge, skills, conditioning—every day, he also needed several timeouts to gather himself, draw inward, rest, sort out thoughts and emotions, invite inspiration. He liked schedules. Once a week, he would dust and vacuum, she would do the laundry and clean the bathrooms. But on what day, at what hour, would she run the washing machine? When the hamper was full. Should he wear a pair of pants one more day and chance being without it for the next week because she suddenly felt it an opportune time to do a wash? That was up to him, a risk he must run. What time would they have dinner? When they were hungry. Eventually they compromised: she would do laundry at some time on Mondays, they would eat dinner between 6:00 and 6:30. In the kitchen she moved aggressively, single-mindedly, oblivious to him. Absorbed in her task, she turned from mincing board to stove decisively, crashing into him if he had made the mistake of moving into her path. When the dishwasher was full, she ran it, even if the noise forced him to jack up the volume on the TV. When she unloaded the washer or set the table, she banged and clanged silver and crockery, full-speed ahead. Nothing at that moment existed but that task. The old man, when learning to drive, had been taught by his parsimonious father to consider the comfort of his passengers by accelerating slowly and smoothly and decelerating gradually and gently, letting the engine's compression do the work, in the process saving gas, brake linings, tire tread. But Diane, behind the wheel of a car, was all quick accelerations, speed shifts, sharp turns. She would race up to red lights and make sudden stops that bent torsos over seatbelts. On the freeway, in the midst of heavy traffic, she continually changed lanes, moving from left to middle to right and back again, needing to find a way out of the maze, her turn signal blinking her irritation. On the golf course, she fumed at slow-playing groups ahead of her. "Hit the damn ball," she would implore them *sotto voce*. She never took practice swings or lined up putts, just played quickly by feel. She craved perpetual motion, poor antsy dear (so to speak). *Mais zoot alors! Qu'est que c'etais le temps?*

[*Pour ainsi dire*—love it! Solveig]

6:45!

His heart thumped. Time to move! He grabbed his iPad, set his plates quietly on the counter, tossed his cup in the trash.

"Good luck, Wayne," LaTasha said. "Keep your eye on the ball!"

"Thanks, LaTasha. I'll try to harness my neurotic neurons."

He stepped into the unisex bathroom, which smelled reassuringly of antiseptics, took from his jacket pocket a plastic Walgreen's bag containing a coiled catheter and a nitrile glove, and drained the coffee from his bladder.

Leaving the Bowl, he drove out Snake Road to the Meadowdale Playfield five miles north. His car thermometer registered 52 degrees. The old man's team, the Classics, and its arch-rival, the Hot Shots, had dominated the Edmonds Park and Rec Senior Softball League—which consisted of players who lived in Shoreline, Edmonds, Terrace, Lynnwood, Everett, or Marysville—since its inception in 1993. One or the other had won every championship but two in the league's 26 years. The Ancient Mariners, the Olde Timers, The Codgers, the Sunshine Boys, the Good Ol' Boys, Forever Young, and the Legends occasionally succeeded in recruiting some young, under-60 talent, but most of the good newcomers opted to play for the established winners, the Classics or Hot Shots. A majority of the players—all of whom were white except for Nate Inouye, a Hawaiian, and Wes Watanabe, a Japanese—had played high-school baseball; a fair number had played fast-pitch or slo-pitch softball during their working lives and wanted to continue with the sport after retirement. This year the Classics had brought in two new 56-year-olds, Johnny Merlot, a fleet outfielder, and Gordy Goldsmith, a bow-legged shortstop with excellent range and a powerful arm. Five players were in their 60s, three in their 70s. The old man and Zee were the oldest players on the team and in the league. Because of their relatively slow reaction times, they alternated on defense at the less demanding positions of second base and catcher. The several dozens of others who had comprised the league when they began playing in '95 were now dead, or physically unable to perform, or had sensed that their teams no longer wanted them as their skills declined. The old man had gone to the funerals of many players—victims of cancer, strokes, heart attacks—over the years. In 2004, one of them, a stubby, left-handed, tobacco-spitting pitcher, Kenny (King) Cole, had collapsed on the field while delivering a pitch, members of both teams gathering around in a prayer circle while summoned EMTs administered CPR in vain.

At the three-field complex, he parked, changed into his softball shoes, and headed for Field 1, which was bordered on the west by towering evergreens. There was no rain, but the skies were low and the clouds mean, the air heavy and moist, almost wringable. His eyes began to flood. He hung up his bat bag, dapped with Zee and the manager, pitcher Larry Miller, a 70-year-old 200-pounder who was beginning to find it a challenge to hustle to second base for two-out force plays when the middle infielders were playing deep to improve their fielding angles. "Great day for a game, hey, you two octos?" Larry said. "As long as it's not actually raining, any day is," the old man said. "We're ready to go." He and Zee had been practicing together three times a week for over a month. They played catch as their teammates straggled in, then took the field, an emerald green carpet with henna-colored base paths and pitching circle and white foul lines, to shag balls for batting practice, the Hot Shots occupying an adjacent field for their warmup. In his excitement to hit, to test his new skills against competition, he fought for breath. When his turn came to take 10 practice swings against Larry, he visualized proper rotational mechanics—load, see, snap—and then

had an almost perfect session, spinning the ball deep from left center to right center. With the old man and Zee alternating at second
base, the team ran a brief defensive drill, Larry hitting grounders to
the infielders and calling "Take one" or "Take two," or fly balls to
the outfielders and calling which base to throw to, then jogged in
to the aluminum bench behind the dugout screen.

Larry posted the lineups written in black felt pen on an erasable
board.

Hot Shots	Classics
LF—Dick Dodge	RC—Merle Oberon
SS—Buddy Budnick	LF—Johnny Merlot
1B—Chuck Metcalf	SS—Gordy Goldsmith
LC—Doc Holiday	3B—Tommy Thompson
RF—Rabbit Watson	C—Billy Fontaine
LC—Guy Fletcher	RF—Vern Rapp
C—Tim Clark	1B—Dale Hills
3B—Frank Baxter	2B/C—Wayne Adams
2B—Jim Montgomery	C/2B—Gary Zylstra
P—RJ McCoy	P—Larry Miller

"Okay, guys," Larry said. "Tommy will lead us."

They made a tight cluster and joined hands. "Lord, we thank
You for the blessing of good health that enables us to play this
game that we love. We realize how fortunate we are. We pray that
You will watch over us as we play today and keep all players on both
teams safe from harm."

"Amen," everyone, even the old man, chorused.

There were 15 spectators— a few wives bundled up in ski
jackets and holding kazoos, a couple of pre-school grandchildren,
a passerby who had stopped for a rest while walking his German
Shepherd—in the bleachers when the game began. The Classics
jumped to a 5-0 lead in the top of the first. Fleet Merle, a place hitter, lined a single up the middle, Johnny grounded one through the

hole between first and second, Merle racing to third, and Gordy, a left-handed swinger, drove one deep into the gap in right center for a triple. Three batters, two runs. Legendary third baseman Tommy Thompson, the cleanup hitter with the boxy butt and thighs like telephone poles, the one guy actually capable of hitting a ball far enough to strike the chain-link fence 300 feet away, the league's best player even though his COPD forced him to suck oxygen from a bottle nestled into a pack on his back, inexplicably popped out to the pitcher, a weak fizzling fart, but Billy walked and Vern smashed a one-hopper that bounced off the shortstop's chest, moving Billy up to second and allowing Vern to reach, Gordy cautiously remaining at third. Dale, first-pitch swinging, flew out weakly to short left field, Gordy again unable to score. The old man swabbed the tears from his left eye and stepped into the box, legs quivering but mind focused. "C'mon, Wayne, we need you right now," Larry yelled, partly an encouragement, partly a demand. "Spin it, Wayne," Zee said, taking practice swings in the on-deck circle. Staying true to his protocol, turning his back on the thoughts of failure that kept trying to insinuate themselves into his consciousness, he took ball one as Hot Shots pitcher R.J. McCoy tried to tempt him with a short pitch. "Good eye, Wayne, good eye." He took another ball, slightly inside. He steeled himself not to swing until he had taken a called strike. If he swung at a pitch just because he liked it, because it looked hittable, he knew he would be too early and would transfer his weight prematurely, forcing him to slow the swing down and to contact the very bottom of the ball and thus to pop up the way Dale had. Once he had a strike, he was prepared to swing at the next pitch if it was at all near the strike zone. He would say to himself, "This is my pitch," then as RJ released it he would say "Wait, wait" (without the second "wait" he would be too early). When it dropped to a level that would enable him to maintain his balance yet swing as hard as he could, he would stride aggressively into his rotation, his head remaining still, and say "Hammer it," like a woodsman sinking an axe into a tree, as he threw the bat into the ball. He got the strike, the ball plunking the middle of the plate. He was ready. The next pitch was on the outside edge, perfect for going to right. He waited, waited, high-stepped toward right field and hammered a rising line drive which flew over the first baseman's head and down the line, rolling almost to the fence before the outfielder could catch up to it. Adrenaline gushing, he raced past first and then slowed and stopped at second as the runners all scored ahead of him. The five-run limit! "Attaboy, Wayne," "Great start," "Clutch hit," his teammates were yelling and screaming as he jogged to the dugout to get his glove for defense amid a flurry of high-fives and daps and shoulder claps. In the stands Bernice Rapp, Margie Thompson, and Gloria Fontaine, who came to all the games, stamped their feet and blew their kazoos. "Nice hit, Wayne," the young leadoff batter for the Hot Shots, Dick Dodge, acknowledged as the old man went behind the plate to catch Larry's warmup pitches. "Thanks," the old man said. "Got lucky." "Hope I'm that lucky when I'm your age," Dick said.

The old man's euphoria subsided as the Hot Shots, in their red jerseys, white pants, and white caps, responded with a barrage of hits in their half of the inning. Three straight singles loaded the bases, and a fourth scored their first run, bringing up Jack "Rabbit" Watson, the fastest player in the league. "How you doing, Wayne?" he said as he stepped into the box. "Good, Rabbit. No pressure on you, now." "You got that right. Pressure is when your Social Security payment doesn't come in." Rabbit took a strike, then a ball. His foul tip on the third pitch, like a struck match instantly blown out by the wind, was too quick for the old man. The ball grazed his unresponsive glove and caromed off his right shoulder. Bernice, Margie, and Gloria groaned. His teammates said nothing. Stunned, he picked the ball up from the dirt and tossed it back to Larry. He should have caught it. A 70-year-old would have caught it. They'd have kept Rabbit from running if he had caught it. On the next pitch, Rabbit lofted a deep fly over Johnny's head and raced around the bases, gripping his cap in his right hand, his silver hair sweat-stuck to his scalp, his arms pumping, his legs churning, to score. An inside-the-park grand slam! The Classics trudged off the field while the Hot Shots roared out of their dugout to greet Rabbit at home plate. Five runs. Ah, runs. They keep crowding you up, the old man angstromized. They keep crowding you up.

"Sorry, guys," the old man said in the dugout.

"Forget about it," Larry said. "Our turn to score now."

But they went down one-two-three, Zee lining out to third, Larry grounding to second, and Merle flying out to right center.

The old man and Zee switched positions on defense. Repeating his mantra—"Down, down"—he had no trouble handling the first ball that came his way, a dribbler that he gobbled up smoothly. The Hot Shots then put two singles together, and the next batter hit a hard grounder three steps to the old man's right that he managed to backhand. He checked the glove twice to make sure the ball was in there, then, amazed and relieved, threw it to Gordy covering second, who threw it to first for the double play, Bernice, Margie, and Gloria responding with more foot-stomping and kazoo-blowing and his teammates shouting "Nice job, Wayne!" "Great play, Wayne, you're like a vacuum out there!" "You mean because nature abhors me?" the old man said with a smile.

After four innings, the score was Classics 11, Hot Shots 10. In his second at-bat, the old man, maintaining mental equilibrium, had smashed a line-drive single up the middle, Zee had followed with a hard top-hand ground ball between third and short, and both had come around to score on successive hits. Leading off the fifth, the old man turned on a pitch and lashed a double down the left-field line. Three for three! Zee moved him over with a grounder to second base, Larry popped out to the shortstop, and then the old man scored on Merle's sacrifice fly to left-center before Johnny ended the inning with a groundout. But the Hot Shots immediately tied up the game in their half, and neither team scored in the sixth.

"Okay, guys, our time, let's hit, here we go!" Larry said in the dugout as the seventh began.

Gordy lined an inside-out single to left, and Tommy walloped a line drive that rattled the chainlink fence in left-center, Gordy moving to third easily and Tommy chugging into second, his chest heaving as he sucked from his oxygen bottle. Johnny trotted in to pinch-run for him, the small crowd applauding the big man's feat, and Tommy walked back to sit on the bench and dap with appreciative teammates who came over to congratulate him. The next batter, Billy, flew out to shallow left, neither runner able to advance. Vern lined out to short, the runners again holding, but Dale then patiently worked RJ for a walk. Bases loaded. Bernice, Margie, and Gloria kazooed raucously.

All right, the old man thought. *Les jeux sont fait.*

"Okay, Wayne, just like before," Larry said.

"Like you can, Wayne," called Gloria.

"No pressure, Wayne," the catcher, Tim Clark, said.

"Rabbit told me that pressure is when your social security payment doesn't come in."

"What does he know about that? He's a retired Air Force colonel. He's been on a fat military pension for the last 10 years."

The old man laughed, acknowledging the wry in the catcher. He visualized his rotation as he stepped into the box. Load, see, snap. Speak, hands, for me! The first pitch was a perfect strike in the middle of the plate, tempting to hit, but he took it, following his protocol. The next would be his. Wait, wait. It came in on the inside edge, and he waited, but then, overcome by an urge to lunge at the ball, didn't wait, rushing his snap, speaking out of turn, his shoulders opening up, his head moving with them, his eyes pulling off the ball. He chopped a grounder to third, the worst thing he could do. The third baseman scooped it up, stepped on third to force Johnny, then threw home to get Gordy. Never, never, never hit a grounder to the left side with runners on! You stupid fucking idiot, he said to himself as he ran fruitlessly to first. His mind had betrayed him. A neurotransmitter had faltered. Agenbite of dimwit!

"Don't worry about it, guys," Larry said. "Let's just hold 'em and go extra innings."

But in the bottom of the seventh, Rabbit led off with a single and one out later scampered home with the winning run on Tim's double. The Hot Shot wives tooted their kazoos when the two teams met in the middle of the infield to shake hands.

"Good job, guys," Larry said as they put their bats and gloves in their bags. "It was anybody's ball game. And we play them three more times. We'll get our revenge."

"Good hitting, today, Wayne," Zee said. "Looks like you're pretty well rewired now."

"Not that last time. We should have won that thing. Something came over me. I choked in the clutch."

"So, you want to swing by Starbucks on 220th and get a single-origin coffee from their Clover machine and maybe decompress a little?"

Suffused with shame and desperation, the old man said, "No. Thanks, Bro, but I need to go straight to Harbor Square and pound the hell out of some machines for about an hour while the fire in my gut burns off some of its fuel. This hurts even worse than when I struck out against Easterbrook in high school. I'll see you at our next game on Thursday. And be sure to let me know if I can help with your campaign."

[The Lord giveth and the Lord taketh away. Blessed be the Name of the Lord! Tommy]

[Wayne, I was cheering for you all through "Wabi-Sabi," so proud of your growth—and then it all went to hell in the last sentence as you succumbed once again to lookism! Charlotte]

8

To Turn and Live With Animals

When, in disgrace with fortune and men's eyes, Wayne, white man, stared from his Morris chair at the bleak, black Sea and all alone bewept his outcast state, when he imagined that he could turn and live with animals, so placid and self-contained they seem, always at one with their breath, centered, grounded, authentic, whole, blissed with ignorance, never sleeplessly examining their lives, never whining about their awkward swings, dropped balls, fizzled throws, their failures of concentration, never plagued with the mania of owning things or of establishing and maintaining reputations, never kneeling Confucianly to their ancestors, never worshipping Christianly an intercessor, gradually it occurred to him that he was selectively imaging meditative, cud-chewing bovines scattered among daisies in a fenced, grassy pasture, contentedly belching and farting methane while koantemplating the sound of one cow crapping, these images that he stared at long and long bringing him tokens of his Buddhist, quantum self, reminding him that everything changes, nothing endures, the profoundest question being not what does life mean but how does one stop suffering, the profoundest answer being by doing nothing, by letting go of self and other fictions, fictions, like everything, no matter how seemingly exquisite, being nothing, by and by it occurred to him also that the placidity of unfenced animal existence in the wild is the real fiction to let go of, animals being fettered not free, their lives fraught with turmoil, constantly in peril from predator and privation, constantly on the *qui vive*, ears, eyes, noses, and heat sensors pricked, avoiding, evading, attacking, competing for food, for mates, for status, establishing pecking orders, kick-bite orders, alpha and beta hierarchies, staking out urine-scented territory, building nests, ever paying allegiance to their atavistic instincts, their physical placidity an illusion, their mental placidity ineluctable, and he exulted that he *could* long, daydream, think abstractly, examine his life, no, he would not choose to live like an animal, not even the king of the jungle, let alone a domesticated cow, he would choose consciousness, choose suffering, choose the ultimately meaningless search for meaning, not the lobotomy of self-renunciation. Get over himself? He could not, nor, truly, could any human whose mental faculties were intact, full awareness of the world impossible without an intervening 'I,' a consciousness of self that emerges unbidden from the bubbling of the brain, the enlightenment of atonement an illusion, suffering and joy the double helix of life, and vowed that he would be at the batting cages when they opened in the morning.

[Wayne, I am dismayed by your beliefs that animals are fettered, not free, and that abstract thinking is the *summum bonum* of life. The instincts you malign as fetters are actually liberative; they enable animals to act freely, genuinely, in harmony with themselves, uncontaminated by thought or self-consciousness. Humans, on the other hand, obsessed with self-consciousness, lack authenticity. They are oppressed by thought, crushed by the constraints of the very culture they have invented, slavishly confined by batting cages. Charlotte]

[Imma agree (so fun to say, but am I culture-appropriating?) with Char that wind-swift thought, the power of ratiocination, is a mixed blessing. There is something to be said for being a bee in a hive, an ant in a hill, instinctively fulfilling a social role, operating without internal conflict. OTH, I agree with Wayne that without self-consciousness, there is no joy. The self-harmony we attribute to non-humans is meaningless because it is not something they experience. The enlightenment of atonement is a worthy fiction available only to humans—and can be achieved without paying penance in batting cages. Dave]

9

Riddle Song

From the wide estuary of 100 coevals populating the Plaza Room at the top of the Anderson Center, classmates, perhaps half of them accompanied by still-existing helpmates, dressed casually in jeans, tennis shoes, long-sleeve blouses, cardigans, and flannel shirts, having at various times during the past hour gone with the flow, fought their way upstream, swirled in a tight eddy, and been pushed into a sparsely populated backwater, having bear-hugged and pair-hugged and dare-hugged those whom 60-plus years ago they had cliquishly or shyly ne'er-hugged, having patted and gripped and chattered and nodded and frowned and narrowed their eyes and widened their eyes and sympathized and empathized and congratulated and commiserated and acknowledged and remembered and wondered and expressed great joy and satisfaction that all who were there were there, having been welcomed by Eric Ericson and Olga Thorsdottir, having applauded the delivery by the old man and Zee of "Remember When?", their scripted reminiscence of childhood and adolescence in Edmonds that concluded with the old man singing his revision of "How About You?", having lifted dinner plates from the catered buffet table and speared tiny paprikaed meatballs and small squares of teriakied salmon and scooped bow ties of pasta from chafing dishes and covered any empty spaces with a floret of crude broccoli and a ball of watermelon or honeydew, having sat at tables of eight to eat with favorite friends or at least compatible acquaintances, having stood to sing the alma mater, having lined up to serve themselves slabs of white-frosted chocolate cake bedecked with "EDMONDS TIGERS CLASS OF '57" in cursive purple and gold, a group who had all been members of Jack Foster's Cultural Heritage class and used to swim together at Martha Lake—Sylvia, Dave, Charlotte, Zee, Monk, Carolyn, the old man—slung pullover ski sweaters or short ski jackets over their left shoulders, stepped outside, and drifted past the huge concrete planter filled with junipers and a dwarf red Japanese maple and white-blossoming azaleas to the panoramic southwest corner of the open rooftop.

Monk, who had been senior class president and whose chunk of cake contained the "I" of the "TIGERS," waved at the tattered June sky lidding the Bowl, the Sea, the Olympics. "Awesome," he said. A typical unsettled late spring day, temperatures riding up and down the 60s as the sun, now gibbous, now crescent, waxed and waned behind zephyr-propelled puffs of lustered cumulo-nimbus and scattered jagged bars of black cirrus. The classmates took turns holding each other's plates and slipped on their sweaters and jackets against the breeze-chill factor that worsened during the waning. "I love the action, the kaleidoscope, the nacreous glow, the apocalyptic purple haze. Pushes my God spot, opens my doors of perception."

"The safest, healthiest way to do that," Sylvia said.

"Clouds cover more than three-fourths of the sky here 226 days of the year. Most of the rest are partly-sunny, defined as 40-60 per cent of the sky cloud-covered. We get maybe 30 bright, totally clear cerulean days a year. 'The bluest skies you've ever seen are in Seattle?' No, Perry Como, that's nonsense. Should be 'The bluest skies you'll rarely see in Seattle.' And you know what? That's okay with me. My stint in the navy after law school at the U-Dub took me all over the world. I saw spectacular Indian Ocean dawns and Polynesian sunsets, but I was so happy to get back here to the clouds and the drizzle and the hesitant sun, to the coolness, to the moss and the evergreens, to the subtlety, to the modesty, and set up a family law practice in the Bowl. Enjoyed your little revision of 'How About You?', Wayne, but why is it that there is no good song about Seattle, and no song at all about Edmonds, no 'I left my heart,' no 'Do you know what it means,' no 'Some folks like to get away,' no 'Do you know the way,' no 'A foggy day,' no 'Meet me in St. Louis,' no 'I love Paris,' no 'Chicago, Chicago,' no 'I'm from Big D,' no *Arrivederci, Roma*?' We can't be proud of our modesty?"

"Maybe not—although the Puget Sound region is often re-ferred to as 'God's Country,' by locals and visitors alike. In the case of Edmonds, it's probably just a numbers game. The town has been in existence for only 130-some years. Not enough people have yet lived or visited here. There's been no one yet with the inclination and drive to produce a song. Maybe when a few million more have had the Edmonds experience, a bard will emerge."

"Nah, I think it's got to come from someone who lived in Edmonds during the middle decades of the 20th century. Someone autochthonous, a native son or daughter who knows the town's soul. So you'll work on it, Wayne? Edmonds as God's Country?"

"Ha! I'm the wrong guy to go soul-searching. And, unlike my dad, there's no way I could write a tune. I think we're going to have to settle for Bing Crosby's 'Black Ball Ferry Line Up in Seattle' with the vague views and the chuggin' and the bells and whistles and the local-color Native American names. It's catchy, it's kitschy, it's prob-ably the best we're ever going to get about Seattle or Edmonds."

"And what about celebrities? Has any kid from Edmonds ever gone on to light up the firmament? Besides Rick Steves?"

"As far as sheer name recognition goes, Rick has got to be our brightest light. He's known worldwide. Handsome Americans fol-low his guidebooks everywhere. But we also claim Ken Jennings, the 'Jeopardy' genius, and Jay Park, the singer-dancer. Jerry Gay won a Pulitzer in photography, and Dave Hamilton pitched a lot of games for the Oakland A's in the '70s."

"And, don't forget the women," Sylvia said. "Rosalind Summers starred in the Winter Olympics, Bridget Hanley had a key role in 'Here Come the Brides,' whose theme song, Monk, just so happens to have been 'The Bluest Skies You've Ever Seen Are in Seattle,' and Anna Faris is very well-known for her acting and comedy."

"Oh yeah, there's Jason Miller, too," Monk said. "Trump's former political strategist."

"Oh my God, please spare me!" Charlotte said.

"In any case," Monk said, grinning and swallowing a last mouthful of cake, "it's not a very big constellation, is it? Modesty rules there, too."

Though none of his classmates was famous, the old man had noticed at reunions over the years that several of them had come to resemble facially someone who was. Monk was Larry of the Stooges; Zee, Pierce Brosnan; Sylvia, Marie Osmond. And though they weren't doppelgangers, spit and images of, Susie Richards, with her chipmunk cheeks, dark eyes, and toothsome smile, was Mary Tyler Moore, satchel-mouthed Margie Bennett, with her quick, clever smirk, was Carol Burnett, narrow-eyed Charlie Richardson, with his prominent cheekbones, tiny ears, and ironic smile, was Richard Gere, Lloyd Cross, with his long face, hollow cheeks, and brutally large lips, was Lee Marvin, and Brian Tucker, with his wire-rimmed glasses, thinning hair parted on the left and combed to the sides, and his aquiline nose, was Harry S. Truman.

Monk set his empty plate on the edge of a concrete planter. Tugging his phone out of a front pocket of his blue jeans, he said "Hey, let's commemorate the occasion with a group-selfie for Facebook and Instagram. 'Old Tygers Still Burning Bright!'"

"Good idea," Dave said. "Everybody huddle tight in some semblance of fearful symmetry."

"Yeah, show our cameraderie," the old man said.

They clumped together. Monk extended his long right arm and triggered two shots in landscape with his thumb, then checked his work. "Looks great! The smiles will pass for genuine. I'll post when

I get home and email everyone copies, too."

They gave themselves some elbow room.

"So," said Charlotte, who, with her plum lipstick, nose that delved so steeply that her nostrils were scarcely visible, onyx eyes, high forehead, and gray spiky butch hair wasn't anybody's ghost— or, wait a minute: was she an aged Amy Walter?—"do you people ever wonder, looking at all this gorgeosity, what might happen in the event of a serious earthquake? What if the North American plate and the Juan de Fuca plate that run along the Pacific shore from northern California to Vancouver Island were suddenly to clash and the ensuing subduction produce 'The Big One,' the 9+ on the Richter scale that many seismologists are promising us?"

"Remember the 6.5 of '49?" Zee said. "5th grade? We were all right here in this building. In the cafeteria, having lunch. The linoleum floor rippled right under my feet. The tables jumped. The food trays glided. The milk cartons sloshed. I held my breath. It must have lasted at least 30 seconds."

"I screamed," Sylvia said.

"But a 9+, Char?" Monk said. "That would be quite a show! Too bad none of us are technologically competent enough to produce an augmented Virtual Reality version, a synesthetic fusion incorporating 3D and *Brave New World* feelies and *Li'l Abner* smellovision. Imagine the immersion! The rooftop we're on now dropping down a floor as the foundations of the old Anderson Center crack and crumble, us toppling and tumbling and shrieking."

"When we manage to get to our feet," the old man said, "we look out to see condos quivering. Cars falling into sinkholes on 5th. Wires snapping everywhere, gas mains exploding. And now here comes a tsunami racing up the Strait, hurling the ferryboat over the dock, waterfront-visitors suddenly double-taking and running up Main only to get swamped by a roiling flotsam-jetsam stew of yachts and sailboats and logs and pilings and buoys and cars and sidings and broken windows and garbage cans and directional signs, then bum-rushing the Center here, taking our legs out from under us, icily swamping us, before hurling us gasping into the maelstrom as it surges on, its saline residue burning our eyes, puckering our lips, until finally being tamed by the elevation, beaching us at 9th and lodging the ferry in a new dry dock there."

"So we're dead? Concussed or drowned? I'm not seeing the humor in that," Charlotte said, scraping up a last bit of frosting with her fork.

"'Fraid so. But we're immortalized on VR. The only other place we're immortalized in literature, to my knowledge, is in *On The Beach,* when the submarine on its reconnaissance mission surfaces in front of Edmonds and finds all the streets empty. I felt a warm glow when I read that section years ago—an affirmation of the Bowl's existence."

"But," Charlotte resumed, "we're not really concerned about possible ecological disasters? We're taking it lightly? *Que sera*? Nobody's mentioned politics tonight, yet three of us classmates are running for Position 8 on the City Council. We're the elephants on the rooftop. Everyone is being scrupulously silent, but I feel compelled to speak out. I think we need to get on top of this and so many other issues. I want to see Edmonds do more planning—stronger building codes, buried power lines, designated escape routes, bulkheads against high tides, water collection basins, designated upland refugee shelters at the Driftwood Theater and Edmonds-Maplewood High School. We may not get a tsunami worthy of augmented VR, but we certainly might get flooding and cracking and crumbling and fires and panic."

"I'm with you, Char," Sylvia said. "And certainly, with or without an earthquake, climate change is going to affect our waterfront. We've got to prepare for rising sea levels. By 2100, Sound waves may very well be lapping at the feet of Starbucks on 5th. Gary, is that something you'll take seriously if you're elected to the City Council?'

"Of course. I don't feel a sense of desperation, but I think we need a plan."

"Monk?"

"Apocalyptic earthquake? No. I'll take my chances. In fact I'll take my *great-grandkids'* chances. Climate change? Climates have always changed. Sea levels have always changed. The tropics have migrated. Glaciers have come and gone."

"So you're a climate change-denier? What else? You're an anti-vaxxer, too?"

"Ha. No, I'm neither. I just think that there may be multiple causes of climate change, the sins of industrialization being only one of them, and that, regardless of the causes, the consequences may not be as dire as predicted, but even if they are, human ingenuity will come up with workarounds either to combat them or to adjust to them when and where necessary. I love nature. I was an Eagle Scout and an avid hiker and backpacker. I've trekked in the Andes and the Himalayas. Until about 10 years ago I was all over the Olympics and the Cascades every summer. I found beauty and awe there, felt to a certain extent the kinship of all living things. But I don't have a romantic view of the natural world as once a paradise now despoiled by greedy, capitalistic humans. I love the whole complex web of civilization, our internal combustion engines, our cars and jet planes, our freedom, our mobility."

"But this freedom comes at the cost of life!" Charlotte said. "We're making the planet uninhabitable. We've got melting ice-caps, disappearing shorelines, loss of habitat, dying ecosystems, a million species at risk of extinction, searing heat, droughts, wildfires, hurricanes, floods. People need to be reminded at all times that they are ruining the earth. Read Bill McKibben and Elizabeth Kolbert."

"I have. They are hyperbolic Jeremiahs."

"No, they are spot-on. I could imagine Wayne using their work to teach rhetoric. Their writing is factual and logical, it is full of passion, and it fairly bristles with ethical character."

The old man grinned, shrugged, and wiggled temporizing fingers.

"We in the industrialized west created this mess for the rest of the world," Charlotte said, "and it's up to us to make reparations. And we do that by starting locally. But environmental concerns are only one among a myriad of issues, all of which fall under the rubric of 'Equality, Fairness, Justice' that headlines my campaign. You know, Wayne's not the only one who rewrites songs. When I found out that he was messing around with 'How About You?' it occurred to me that I could create a campaign song for myself based on John Lennon's 'Imagine.' Would it be all right if I debuted it for you now?"

"Please do," the old man said.

Charlotte smiled, took a breath, gathered herself, clasped her fingers at her abdomen, and sang softly, sweetly, shyly:

Imagine Edmonds heaven
Allow yourself to see
No hell around us
Only harmony.
Imagine all the people living equally.

Imagine there's no homeless
It isn't hard to do
No racism or sexism
No homophobia too
Imagine all the people sharing equally.

Imagine no elitists
No corporation speech
No patriarchs to defeat us
Respect for all we teach.

Some may say that I am dreaming
But I know I'm not alone
I hope you find my views redeeming
And will seek with me to atone.

There was a brief silence, then Monk said, "Char, that was lovely."

"It was indeed," Zee said. "Are you going to sing it at your campaign appearances?"

"I think so."

"Then, Monk, we've got a problem. Its pathos is likely to appeal to both Boomers and Millennials."

"The arrangement of notes does indeed kill us softly," Monk acknowledged. "Give Lennon credit for that. The appeal to the ideals of the superego is pure Char. I think the only way I can combat that is to appeal to the ravenous id. She goes high, I go low. No offense, Char, but I must seek to attract the votes of those who are looking for a cure for the common scold."

Charlotte faked a smile. "Monk, I'm proud to be a scold. What this world needs is more common scolds."

"What this world needs," Zee said, "is more common sense and compromise."

"And what I think our little colloquy needs," said Dave Williams, a contact-loving, hard-nosed football lineman who went on to play at Whitworth and then to study at Fuller Theological Seminary in Pasadena and eventually become a professor of psychology at Big Sur Theological Seminary and whose father once pastored the Edmonds Baptist Church, his brows lifting above his black horn rim glasses, "is to let the campaign go and return to Monk's reference to his genetic God spot, which I take to mean an intuitive religious sense that enables us to cope with our instinctive fear of death. As Ernest Becker in *The Denial of Death* makes clear, we are desperately trying to deny not only that Jonathan Swift's Celia, but Cecil and all the rest of us shit, for the shameful anus and its smelly product symbolize the fate of all that is physical: decay and death."

"Now just a darn minute here," the old man, waggling an index finger, nasally jimmystewarted. "I completely agree that thanatophobia is universal and instinctive, but I'd like to put in a good word for shit. Though often rotten-egg foul, sulfuric, its smell is sometimes bracingly acerbic, with hints of broccoli or Brussels sprouts or menthol or eucalyptus, and once in a while even pleasantly rose-petally sweet, its colors run a mini-spectrum from light mocha to sepia to taupe to black, and its forms a wide variety ranging from marbles to French fries to bananas to logs to *Starry Night* coils to field-plopped cow pies to the chunky vegetable beef soups or scarcely viscous *consommés* of diarrhea. Salvador Dali in fact used to make proud note of those days on which he turned out what to him was a structurally perfect stool. Such beauty needs no excuse for being."

"Yes, yes, Wayne, a terrible beauty is born, we get it, but for our purposes the emphasis is on 'terrible,' because our shit means that we are mortal. When I look at this gorgeosity and fear someday losing it, I don't think Apocalypse, I think of its aftermath, heaven. I take an idealist approach to the eschatology of 'Revelation.' Mere anarchy being loosed upon the world and the ceremony of innocence being drowned provide a bracing allegory of hope. It's about warring within yourself to discover and define what heaven is for you. The Beast can be, variously, your raw, demanding, unrepentant ego, or social injustice, or the State. The Second Coming is your recognition and acceptance of Christ and all that he stands for. The Final Judgment we impose on ourselves in so far as we do or do not choose to dwell in a spirit of atonement with him. All of this before us, much as I love it, is just the tease of a greater beauty to come, a mere imitation of what will eventually be a realized ideal."

"So there's no Lake of Fire? No being 'Left Behind?' Sylvia said.

"Well, there is and there isn't. In my view, the Lake of Fire exists within one's soul. As Milton's Satan discovered, you yourself are heaven or hell. As for being 'Left Behind,' I think one is left behind in the same sense that I was left behind in calculus class by Monk and Zee and Char and some of the other class brains. There were some subtle appreciations, some sublimities if you will, that I just didn't get. I suspect that there'll always be a Bell curve of salvation. One's allotment of grace is whimsically acquired. As particles that interact more strongly with the Higgs field experience more resistance and behave as if they have larger masses, and those that interact less strongly experience less resistance and have less mass, and those that don't interact at all, like photons, have no mass, so it is with grace. There's no accounting for the interactions."

"So heaven's not a place?" Sylvia asked. "I could certainly subscribe to that. And why is it me stacking the dirty plates and forks to return to the caterers and not one of you men?"

"Well, it is and it isn't. I think holistically. I believe that science and theology can be integrated. It's not because we are irrational that we accept what can seem on the surface to be incredible religious doctrines. Wayne's man Chomsky, *pace* John Locke and the *tabula rasa,* posits the innate existence in humans of a language organ that can access the deep structure of a universal grammar. Similarly, I posit that humans have a religion organ that can access inborn cognitive templates that run deeper than mere cultural conditioning. Just as we have an intuitive linguistic sense of transformations, recursions, and embedding, so we likely have an intuitive religious sense of the supernatural. Monk spoke of having his God spot pushed, and I think that's very accurate. Anyway, Christianity is not necessarily in conflict with science. The *Bible* is not outdated and unscientific but its exegesis must include a careful study of its historical context, its overall shape and design, and its use of literary techniques like symbolism and allegory. In 'Genesis,' for example, one can find gender fluidity. God first created an ungendered human in God's image. The first creation comprises both male and female, and only later splits into two separate genders, with the rib being a metonymy or a synecdoche. Male-dominated Christian sects co-opted and weaponized the story to aid them in the subjugation of women—good point about picking up the plates, Syl. You must bring that kind of thing to bear to show that the *Bible* can be used as a guide to political participation, ecological conservation, and cultural correction, and that it also has room for science—for the Big Bang, entropy, evolution, quantum mechanics, even for the possible validity of string theory."

"Amen!" Charlotte said.

"Wouldn't that be eisegesis?" the old man said. "Bringing in a preconceived idea of its meanings? Like believing that the U.S. is a Christian nation and then looking for references in the *Constitution* or the *Federalist Papers* that could support that interpretation?"

"Well, yes and no. I think it's more a matter of being open— open to the possibility of non-literal meanings. I think a reader must bring all possible resources to bear. Isn't that what Kenneth Burke said in regard to the job of the critic of literature?"

"Yes, it is," the old man said. "I guess I'm just quibbling over what it means to be open. Being open to a deconstruction of the Bible that harmonizes it with modern science is a little different from looking for ways to harmonize the two. It seems to me that a kind of confirmation bias is at work in the latter, like a Supreme Court justice viscerally in favor of the right to abortion scouring the Constitution to find a right to privacy or one in favor of allowing unlimited corporate campaign contributions digging for a way to consider corporations as persons."

"Or like a non-believer scouring the Bible to find scientific im-probabilities or historical inaccuracies?"

"Sure, okay. Like that."

"And is this the sort of thing you teach—besides the fact that women shit!—at Big Sur?" asked Carolyn, a former Director of Human Resources at Blue Cross.

"Well, remember that I'm 80 and Professor Emeritus now, and I never did teach theology directly, but it is the sort of thing that informs my teaching in the one class in clinical psychology that I conduct each semester. Right now I'm especially into teaching mindful meditation as a way to develop empathy and compassion. Empathy and compassion are intuitive states that can be cultivated and strengthened through practice."

"Brain rewiring," the old man said. "I work on that a lot. Concentration, repetition. Trying to improve my softball swing, my reactions to ground balls, my balance."

"Mm, more like brain emptying or flushing. You take a chunk of each day and just live in the present. I give each student a mantra and ask them to repeat it in their heads for 20 minutes, allowing thoughts to pass through like birds across the sky, and fall into a deep state of rest. It's like an ocean—there is brain wave activity at the top but silence at the depths. The mind is alert but in a non-directed way. You have thoughts but not at any level of meaning. Concentration here is counter-productive, over-controlling, anal. You nourish the mind so that you don't have so much struggle and stress in life. It can be done anywhere, even in the midst of activity and distractions, and it energizes you, makes you more resilient, while it also quiets you, clears your mind, frees you to develop per-spective. You sleep better, you let small things go. You develop your sense of compassion, which leads to a better understanding of oth-ers and improves your ability to counsel or minister to them."

"I'm a big believer in meditation," Sylvia said, "but Wayne calls it the mindlessness of mindfulness."

Dave laughed. "So I've read! That's Wayne, all right, enthusi-astically pooh-poohing enthusiasm. But much madness is divinest sense to a discerning eye, no, Wayne?"

The old man smiled. "That's what she said."

"Mindfulness is only a tool, a means to free yourself for some-thing greater."

"Like the contemplation of truth and beauty?"

"Certainly that's one possible outcome of becoming mindful. The holy spirit of joy can proceed from the contemplation of truth and beauty. When you smelt out your impurities in the cauldron of becoming, a plenitude of possibilities opens up for you."

"I certainly feel that way," Zee said. "Science and spirituality are complementary, not conflicting. Our contemplations of the cosmos stir us. We don't so much worship because we believe as we believe because we worship. We tingle as we approach the grand mystery, as we gaze at the material and find the ethereal. Wayne and Monk and I used to lie out at night in our sleeping bags, and I would feel myself letting go, disappearing into that ocean of stars, falling into infinity, merging with the absolute."

"That was my experience, too," Monk said. "Call it our bright night of the soul."

"Not mine," the old man said. "The Whitmanic pressing close of bare-bosomed night, mad naked summer night, night of white hot stars, chilled me. Apparently lacking that genetic urge to become part of something bigger, I became hyper-conscious of being apart from something bigger."

"Whatever your experience might have been, Wayne," Dave said, "I reiterate that religion is not just bad science masquerading as good. The 'irrationality' of religion is, paradoxically, a rational reaction to the mystery of the universe because it has evolutionary value. It has room for science but it transcends science. Science seeks to describe the laws of the universe, religion seeks to give them meaning. Religion seeks profundity, delves deeper, beneath the material, and discovers the unseen moral order that imbues everything with significance. Even if it's wrong, it's right. It's what enables us to survive."

"And I," the old man said, "would deem your effort to make science and religion compatible not so much rational as rationalization—what my wife Diane might have called squishy, washy-wishy. You take science and...and—"

"Culture-appropriate it?" Dave said.

"Weaponize it?" Charlotte said.

"Gaslight you with it?" Sylvia said.

"Yes, yes, and yes," the old man laughed. "I love it when we get all argy-bargy on each other! What I was getting at is that Diane always fearlessly excluded the middle. At those points where science clashes with the Bible, only one can be right, and for her it was the Bible. One of her favorite quotes was 'Blessed are those who have not seen, and yet have believed.' She was an acolyte of Francis Schaefer, a believer in the literal inerrancy of scripture, an originalist, a strict constructionalist made of Calvinized steel. She didn't meditate, she prayed to a literal God Who was physically there ready to reward or rebuke her. She believed in total depravity, predestination, limited atonement, irresistible grace, and the perseverance of the saints."

Dave smiled. "Certainly Diane's literal approach, eliminating ambiguity, is a legitimate, if restrictive, way to transcend and find meaning and spiritual fulfillment, as indeed is that of religious sects who speak their fiction to power, like the Hassids, Wahabis, Amish, Jehovah's Witnesses, Seventh-Day Adventists, and on and on. You can find purpose, and with it peace and joy, within the confinement of such microcosms. Actually, though, if we include the middle, as I think we should, Diane's belief in irresistible grace can be seen to fit in quite nicely with my Higgs field analogy. And the Calvinist insistence on predestination can be seen to harmonize with one current theory about free will—namely, that 'you' don't have any. Certain studies involving the pushing of buttons seem to show that choices and decisions are already made before 'you' are aware of them. 'You' do not decide the next thought that 'you' will think. 'You' are not the boss of your brain. The conscious mind has its origins in the unconscious. 'You' no more initiate events in your prefrontal cortex than 'you' cause your heart to beat. The feeling of having free will arises from your moment-to-moment ignorance of the prior causes of your thoughts. Our choices seem free only because we do not understand how they emerge from antecedent causes funneled through the laws of physics. There's just a whole lot of intriguing, intertwining possibilities when it comes to psychology and the varieties of religious experience. Too bad Jack Foster is gone now. It would be fun to have him here participating in our little discussion. My conservative Baptist dad was the first to model religion for me, of course, but Jack's openness and wide-ranging sympathy for the world's major religions are what I have most tried to imitate."

"I think we all were influenced by him," Charlotte said. "One calm August evening after graduation, in the midst of the Pacific high pressure system that sets in for a few weeks each summer, when Monk and I were going together, long before I realized that I was gay, Jack invited us to sail with him on the boat he kept at the Yacht Club. He spoke about being able to sense and find a wind that I certainly could not feel. He was sort of a boat-whisperer, able to make minute adjustments in the sails to overcome or exploit inertia. The doldrums did not exist for him."

"He was quite the oarsman, too," Monk said. "He was the stroke on the Harvard varsity eight, you know. I still remember Wayne's story about him in the *Wireless*. He talked almost mystically about rowers with strokes free of all excessive motion, perfectly at ease with themselves in the midst of intense effort and synchronized with each other, their whole greater than the sum of their parts, experiencing the ultimate rush, a kind of emergence, when the cox upped the stroke count and the boat took off."

"Yeah," the old man said. "He detested the noise and smell of motor boats and the self-indulgence of their operators, but he loved the magic of moving himself on water by shell or sailboat. That's when he had his Zen moments. And, Dave, I concede that often I do not decide the next thought that I will think. I have no control over my nocturnal dreams, a bit of control over my daytime reveries (I can sometimes squelch them or give them a direction or, as I often do, just welcome them and wallow in them), somewhat more control over specific memories that I wish to call forth. If you ask me to form a syllogism, I believe I can direct my mind to produce an 'All A is B, C is A, therefore C is B' scaffolding, although it's true that whatever terms I use to flesh out the premises will have come to me mysteriously. I don't know what my memory will say, but I can, unless I have severe dementia (and at that point I am indeed not the boss of me) command it to speak, as old anagramming Bokanov did. 'It just occurred to me' is an expression that could well precede most of the clauses and phrases that I think or that I utter. But my executive self, a necessary fiction, I believe, can choose to accept them, reject them, or modify them. It just occurred to me to say that I'm the decider, the buck stops here. And my executive editor, having started to cross out the line, thinks the better (or worse, depending on your opinion of George W.!) of it and writes *stet*. I suspect Jack would agree with me that if we conclude that, contrary to appearances, we actually lack free will, owing no doubt to some personal algorithm of genetic inheritance and acquired experience, then we must also conclude that we are not responsible for anything that we do. We can be neither praised nor condemned for our behavior. Either we're depraved on account of being deprived, like a Shark or a Jet, or we are in thrall to the disease of affluenza, like Ethan Couch. Cultural norms and statutory laws become irrelevant. If I am not the boss of me, I should never be subject to prosecution, punishment, or even shaming. And I don't have to admit that I am a sinner in need of Christ's sacrifice. Christianity has no meaning without free will."

"But," Dave said, "is it not generally assumed in Christianity that we are all sinners because of the original sin of Adam and Eve? We are held accountable for that. And do we not often say, after some kind of personal success, 'All glory to God?', thereby demonstrating that our achievement was God's doing, not our own? In religion as in life, puissant paradoxes abound. The proponents of this no-free-will theory, like Sam Harris, claim that it is actually liberating. They say that the fact that nature and nurture determine whether you will choose vanilla ice cream rather than chocolate leads not, as one might expect, to fatalism and a sense of either futility or irresponsibility, but to a sense of hope and possibility. Your moment-to-moment ignorance of the prior causes of your thoughts provides a sense of freedom. You are more free because you recognize that you are less free. Everything about you seems less personal and indelible. Acknowledging that there are background causes for your thoughts and feelings allows for greater creative control over your life. Realizing that you are being steered by, shall we say, a greater—or at least an unknown—power can allow you to choose a more intelligent course. There's no telling how much you might change in the future. Learning new skills and forming new relationships may radically transform your life."

"So we are more free because we recognize that we are less free?" the old man said. "Squishy, very squishy. I'd give such chop-logic a 90 on the HSQ."

Dave smiled. "Anyway, by a magic that we don't yet fully understand, billions of electrical signals move around in a brain, and a self-conscious mind emerges. It's like the emergence that Monk alluded to in regard to Foster's rhapsodizing about the whole being greater than the sum of its parts. Emergent structures arise via the interconnected actions of many undirected, autonomous entities. Other examples include the shape and behavior of a flock of birds or a school of fish, weather systems, economic markets, the world-wide web, evolution, religion, and the development of languages. The self is not an isolated property of what's inside your cranium but an emergent property of your whole mind-body integration. We don't know why minds emerge from the neural networks in our uniquely wired brains, we don't know how we acquired the particular algorithms that guide us, and we don't know why we have the sensations, emotions, and thoughts—the stream of conscious-ness—that we do, but we are borne by them into a realm of potent potential."

"Now when you say 'mind,'" Sylvia said, "you seem to mean not only consciousness, the self, but the soul, the spirit, the *atman*. Are they all synonyms? Because to me, consciousness and the self, emerging as they do from the brain, are transient. They die when the body dies. But the word 'soul' connotes something eternal, transcendent, woman united forever with the Trinity, say, or *atman* united forever with Brahman. You seem to imply that some sort of resurrection or reincarnation, some material body, is necessary for the soul to continue to exist. Are you positing an eternal body-soul duality?"

"Again, yes and no. Certainly I believe in immanence. The spiritual permeates the material. The divine is manifested in the mundane. I am pantheistic with a lower-case 'p'."

"As am I," said Sylvia. "I believe that we are in something big. It's in the very air we breathe and the light we see. And I believe that something big, something numinous, some spark of divinity, of the formless Tao, of the source of life, is in us."

"But I also believe in transcendence," Dave said. "It may well be, as most traditional Christian views have it, that we are resurrected in the flesh. Alternatively, if—extrapolating from modern science—the soul is the unique hormonal-synaptic signature integrating brain and body through a complex electrochemical flow of neurotransmitters, conceivably it could be reduced to information-laden ones and zeroes and uploaded into other-than-you substrates, like machines or cloned biological replicas. Or there just might be a transcending, superseding spiritual realm where souls and consciousnesses exist ideally, Platonically, independent of materiality. The possibilities are provoking."

"Yes," said Sylvia. "My Buddhist-tinged spirituality is as amorphous and mysterious as your Christianity, Dave. There is some us-ness that will merge with the all after our parting with this physical existence. And we tap into our eternal us-ness, our soul, when we let the chatter and the knee-jerk reactions go by. When we clear our minds, the unknowing frees us to know."

"Many people also find," Dave said, "that meditation opens them to the value of helping others, of making others happy. Studies have shown that often the more you give to make others happy—love, assistance, material goods, even just simple attention—the happier you yourself become. As Jimmy Durante sang, 'Make someone happy, make just one someone happy, and you will be happy too.'"

"I don't doubt those studies," the old man said, "or Jimmy Durante either. It's in our self-interest to be altruistic. Doing a good turn daily, as we learned in Scouts, Boy and Girl, can prompt an oozing of dopamine and perhaps put us on the path to a Merit Badge, both of which I am in favor, but am I the only one who thinks the formula smacks of a pyramid scheme? The song implies that everyone is sitting around unhappy waiting to be made happy, and that at least one of those is waiting to be made happy by *you*. And yet, if the sentiment of the song be true, those people should be not sitting around unhappy but actively working to make someone else happy in order to make themselves happy, not relying on you to do that for them. Further, following the implication of the song, you yourself should be sitting around unhappy, simultaneously waiting for an unhappy person to come along and make you happy while yet working to make an unhappy person happy yourself. The concept of making someone happy in order to make yourself happy while someone else is making you happy in order to make themself happy dizzies the brain, with the promise of emotional reward depending on ever-increasing investments of solicitousness and vulnerability, lest the whole thing break down and the participants be left happiness-bereft and forced to start the make-someone-happy cycle all over again."

"Really, Wayne? Resorting to *reductio ad absurdum*?" Dave said.

"Who's chopping logic now?" Sylvia said. "Our beloved make-bate of a classmate *does* have a tendency to Waynesplain, to wallow in sophistry and pettifoggery. For most, the more people who agree with us, the more we're convinced we're right. For Wayne, the fewer who agree with him, the more he's convinced he's right."

"Be that as it may," Zee said, "if Diane was Calvinized steel and Dave and Sylvia are pure protean possibility, I guess I must be pig iron. I was saved by Billy, too, you know, and I have retained a quietly simmering faith. I believe that Christ died for my sins and that I'm eventually going to a real place called heaven, where I will probably be given a new body, although I'm not sure about that. Was the universe created in six days? No. That's metaphorical. Did Jesus rise from the tomb on the third day? Yes. That's literal."

"Okay," Charlotte said. "So Sylvia and Dave think that heaven is and is not a real place, Gary thinks it definitely is, and Wayne apparently thinks that the very concept is a chimera. I'm with Sylvia and Dave. Monk?"

"With Zee."

"Carolyn?"

"With Gary. I think Wayne's problem is that he is unable to imagine existing on a higher plane, an ineffable realm, at one with God, loving Him, communing with Him, basking in His glory, contemplating truth and beauty, and also being at one with all other resurrected beings or disembodied souls and loving them as well. We can imagine heaven as that place where we are at last ourselves, where we feel taken in, accepted, free of the needs and insecurities that haunted us throughout our earthly existence. Wayne can only conceive of heaven as a continuation of high school. He wants to be a perennial sophomore."

"Carolyn, you are so right," the old man said. "I can't imagine atonement, I can't imagine just *being*, brimming with love and saturated with grace, I can't imagine disinterestedly contemplating truth and beauty, just ratiocinating and appreciating like a madman, beholding the sublime, for any prolonged period of time. Whether I stare at a starry night or *A Starry Night* or a building whose form oh-so-Wrightly follows its function or the faces of people I love, I cannot remain long in a bath of wonder, joy, and awe. I am self-obsessed, time-centered, analytical, control-oriented, individualistic. I am an action, not a state of being, verb, my past imperfect, my present tense, my future conditional. To live is to act and to act upon, to fend off, with what Ernest Becker would call my 'character armor,' death, to secure and dominate my minuscule portion of the universe, even if I share it literally and symbolically with other people and symbiotically with bacteria and viruses and parasites, to keep breathing and keep eating as long as I have consciousness. I can't be without doing. Life is strife. To me, stasis, such as is apparently found in Heaven, is inconceivable. I crave process, not completion. I doubt that the prisms through which each of us view the world— our gender, race, ethnicity, socio-economic class, formal education—that unique fusion of implicit biases that is us—could ever fully dissolve in the afterlife, causing everyone to see 'reality' in the same way, but if that *should* happen, in my opinion it would not be a good thing. Let's say that in heaven everyone is happy, in no need either to administer or receive the Jimmy Durante anodyne. And everyone is equal economically in the Karl Marx-Thomas Picketty sense. And everyone is dreamily free, appreciated for the content of their character, in the Martin Luther King sense. And everyone is equally privileged (or equally unprivileged) in the Peggy McIntosh sense. We've all achieved the speed of light and time has stopped. What now? Is that all there is? Work of any kind would be point- less, because one would have no physical or spiritual needs. Play of any kind would be pointless, because one would have no need for re-creation, no need to discover an already discovered self. Love would be pointless, because one would have no need either to give it or receive it. We're left to bathe in sublime awe somehow at one with and yet less than and separate from God, contemplating truth and beauty, lovely equations like Euler's identity, say, ecstatically reveling as our medial orbitofrontal cortexes continuously fire and flare."

"You know, Wayne," Dave said, "maybe you won't have to throw the baby out with the sublime bathwater. As I suggested a minute ago, the soul might be digitizable and downloadable. It might be immortalizable. We are clearly moving in that direction. Can you hang on until 2029?"

"For the arrival with a shout of Ray Kurzweil's Singularity, you mean? Ten more years? I doubt it. Probably both me and Kurzweil will be erstwhile by then. But I admit that the possibilities of Transhumanism have excited and fascinated me."

"Well, they have me, too," Dave said.

"As Wayne well knows, they appall me," Sylvia said.

"And me," Charlotte said. "I'm no Dr. Jekyl. At the base of Transhumanism is egotheism, solipsistic self-love, narcissistic long- ing for a transcendence of the human body, the quest to make an infrahuman. It's human-racism. It's immoral. It's unthinkable.

It's a consumer culture's ultimate dream of turning humans into commodities."

"And it's inherently unfair," Sylvia said. "It favors the privileged—the educated, the rich, the Alpha dogs who have the awareness and the means to turn themselves into cyborgs, to take advantage of things like cloning and cryogenics."

"So you two are bioluddites?" Zee asked. "You're against implanted pacemakers and defibrillators and nanomedicine and bionic prosthetic limbs?"

"Well, of course not," Charlotte said. "I used to implant pacemakers for a living. I strongly favor the use of devices that can improve the length and quality of life. That's not playing God, it's using God-given intelligence to make life better."

"I do, too, of course," said Sylvia. "I think what Char and I resent and resist is the Promethean hubristic belief that humans can supplant God and live in awe of themselves. Although I'm not a Christian, I would argue that Transhumanism is the Antichrist, the mark of the Beast."

"I see Transhumanism more as syntheism," Dave said, "humans working with God, as we understand him, interning, for eons, probably, before ultimately achieving theosification. The Mormons have always believed in the project of becoming gods, you know, and a few years ago some of them formed the Mormon Transhuman Association. They believe that God and his works are subject to natural law, and they seek exaltation through scientific knowledge. We hear all these remarkable conjectures these days. We could map and download the human brain onto a collective server, thus achieving universal immortality. We could live forever inside a mass virtual universe, without the limitations of our physical bodies. The parts of our brain that generate visceral sensations could be digitally manipulated to make it feel exactly as if we were still alive. Our minds could become the Internet. We could become the Cloud. Our brain avatars could automatically access all the information that exists in the virtual world, so we would all know everything there is to know. And then, Wayne, you could be at one with all the resources that exist. You could become Becker's answer to the crippling denial of death, an artist who transcends the repressive limitations of culture and becomes the father of himself. You would be free to *do*, not just be, in the workshop of a virtual and eternal high school. You could make art or create new universes to your heart's content."

"And is that all there is? Becoming God or the Cloud? Isn't even that pointless? Art would be irrelevant because as God we would already know all possible literary uses of all possible languages, all possible ways to combine all possible materials into things like paintings and collages, all possible ways to combine all possible musical notes into songs and symphonies, all possible ways to achieve expression through all the possible movements of dance. We would already know the abstract laws and the material representations of all possible kinds of universes. We would already know all of the possible ways life can be life and people can be people, all the possible ways they can organize and comport themselves, all possible topias, utopias, and dystopias. Anything we did would be like filling in a second copy of a crossword puzzle that we've already solved. A lot of learning is a dangerous thing. It's exciting for mere humans to play softball game after softball game because we don't know how each will turn out. We don't know how we ourselves will play, how our teammates will play, how our opponents will play—there is an infinite number of permutations and commutations, an infinite number of unpredictable butterfly effects. A softball game is unalgorithmicable. For the same reason, it's exciting for mere humans to make art, or tinker with technology, or work to build or tear down a society or to strengthen or remake a culture. We are such stuff as make dreams. To our limited minds, there are so many unknowns, so many possibilities, so many hypotheses to form and test. Perfection is sterile. The simulacrum, the simulation, is everything. The mimetic, not the ideal, is the human plane. We are cave people drawn toward the light whose only hope is never to emerge fully into it. The most we can ask of life is that it be a perpetual high school where we matriculate, just keep taking course after esoteric course, but always fall short of 1600 when we take the SAT."

"Wayne, you've got Peggy Lee on the brain," Sylvia said. "One moment everything isn't enough for you; the next, it's too much."

They all took a moment, possibly to be in the moment. This was possibly the last moment they all would ever be together. The air was cooling, the breeze becoming wind. Dark clouds were massing to the west. In a few minutes water and mountains would vanish into thick air. They shivered and stamped their feet. The old man gazed downward to the busy Bowl, people in cars and people on foot hobnobbing transactively, intent upon getting and spending. It was not, could never be, until those final moments when he was overcome by physical pain and exhaustion, too much with him. Like an earlier, unrelated American Adams, to his life as a whole he was a consenting, contracting, party and partner. He gazed outward and gave himself over to the fallacious pathos of a concupiscent Sea baring its swelling bosom, of an Olympic range offering its ample flanks, to an elusive sun. He felt in tune, if not at one.

"Well, people, I need to be going," Charlotte said.

"Me too," Carolyn said.

"It's time," Dave said.

That instinct of the aged, to get home before dark, was kicking in.

In their farewell round of hugs, they pulled each other in tight, squeezed hard, pounded backs a second or third time.

"See you at the 65th," the old man said.

"And you'll write an Edmonds song for us?" Monk asked.

"I'll write something."

[I am trying to wrap my head around what Wayne is saying. Humans search for meaning. See Viktor Frankl. But meaning is not to be found. On the one hand, if we are not immortal, our lives are meaningless. After 10- to-the-10th-to-the-68th-power earth years have passed, there'll be no trace of our genius or our genes or of any systems with which they have been affiliated, perhaps no trace of anything at all. On the other hand, if we were immortal, if we became God or the Cloud, our lives would be meaningless because omniscience and omnipotence paralyze. Can you imagine existing in a state of sterile perfection for 10- to-the-10th-to-the 68th Groundhog Years? Whether we were in, or out, of any moment would be of no moment. We would be *blasé*. Why even bother? Therefore there is no God because why would there be? Carolyn]

[Carolyn, might I suggest you lie down with a cold compress on your forehead? Your brain must hurt after those synaptic contortions! Dave]

10

The Handkerchief of the Lord

Teammates—for in the brotherhood of senior softball we are all teammates, no matter what uniform we wear, Hot Shots or Classics or Old Timers—on this stormy day we gather under our oversized golf umbrellas with their perky red and white, blue and white, green and white panels vibrant beneath the low charcoal cumulonimbus clouds here in the Edmonds Memorial Cemetery where so many of our forebears are laid, in this rare June air—for all air is rare we've learned with age to understand, no one more so than the man we lay to rest today, Tommy Thompson, who played with his nose plugged into a bottle of oxygen nestled into a pack on his back— needles of rain paradiddling our shields and clanging rim shots on Tommy's casket as it waits to be lowered into the ground, banging the drums rapidly, the rat-tat-tatting forcing me to stentor my voice, as water puddles on the clay-based ragged turf beneath our feet and creeps up the edges of our shoes, to celebrate the life and play of our prophet, our taciturn Tommy, the epitome of *homo ludens*.

For life, our evolved intelligence tells us, is absurd, and we are absurdly condemned by that selfsame intelligence to try to make it surd, to attune ourselves to an atonal universe incapable of caring or not caring whose unkeyed melodic and harmonic and rhythmic inflections reverberate ambiguously, the inferred music of its spheres inaudible, the vibrating strings of the M-theorists ditto, detected background cosmic radiation from the Big Bang indecipherable static. Entropy, not purpose, is intrinsic to the universe. Meaning is willfully superimposed by us. Plato and Pythagoras may have guessed right. All may be number, beautiful number, and abstract ideas may be the reality notioned by branes. The universe is mechanistic, but its laws are abstractions. Water is water only by virtue of number: two molecules of hydrogen, one of oxygen. Card games are a hierarchical competition of numbers, the cards themselves merely a mnemonic to help our limited memories keep track of values and sequence of play. Language and music are an ordering of sounds and silences that produce meaning and feeling. And we ourselves, teammates, are number, an arrangement of atoms into cells in brains that, mysteriously, have self-consciousness. Emerging from and operating under the laws of physics and biology, our brains have become capable of understanding some of those laws and have become "us." Incomprehensibly, through the activity of uncomprehending neurons, we comprehend. We have an abstract self that grows out of but is not independent of our bodies. The self is not a soul that exists apart from or transcends or outlives the body, the self emanates from the brain and is wholly dependent upon it. It dies when the brain dies. But while alive, the self, conscious and intelligent, yearns. It yearns to know, it yearns to do. It yearns to act rationally, it yearns to act authentically. It yearns to understand itself and the universe. It yearns to explore and exploit the universe. It yearns to express itself. It yearns to replicate itself. And, yes, it yearns to survive. It yearns to be immortal. It yearns in spite of its recognition that its yearning is absurd in a universe of quantum indeterminacy where matter and energy are both wave-like and particle-like, where evolution depends on random genetic mutations, where position and momentum are subject to Heisenbergian uncertainties in the midst of the overarching stark certainty of entropy. You and I, teammates, can't help yearning to improvise a tune in harmony with our selves.

While the universe vibrates, dances, in super symmetry, we, any one, some one, no one, yearn to dance and sing in concert with our own vibrations. "Trust thyself," Emerson said, "Every heart vibrates to that iron string." Now, teammates, I know what you, glad and big like Tommy, are thinking: "There is some shit I will not eat. I'm not taking that entropy crap. I'm not taking that Darwin crap. I'm not taking that indeterminacy crap. I'm not living and dying for nothing. Life is not absurd. A sufficient number of events in the *Bible* have been verified to validate what the heart intuitively knows: life has intrinsic meaning. The music of the cosmos is not atonal. Meaning is not for the nonce. It is fixed and eternal. God created the world and man and sent his Son to be crucified to pay for man's sins, that whosoever would believe in Him would have eternal life. I accept Christ as my savior. He atoned for me and I am at one with Him, in tune, in harmony, beamed up. There is an interconnection between what's inside of me and what's outside of me. The boundaries of my self, my soul, are porous and diffuse. I flow into the universe, it flows into me. I utter truth in the face of the falsehood of meaning-lessness. Woe comes to him who, stupidly or willfully, fails to get square with the Lord. Delight comes to him who does not waiv-er but ever stands forth for the Lord." And, teammates, I have no doubt that Tommy would say that too, 6' 2" Tommy, 220-pound Tommy, Tommy with the flowing shoulder-length gray-streaked hair and the full gray beard, long enough at the chin to knot into it, in a forward-facing mini-ponytail, that distinctive silver ring he sported, Tommy who launched drives into gaps and bravely took balls off his beefy chest at the hot corner with that oxygen pack on his back, coping with the COPD caused by years of smoking Camels, Tommy sucking it up, each of his inspirations an inspiration for us, Tommy who went to church every Sunday unless he was at a soft-ball tournament, who read his *Bible* every day, who closed his eyes in silent prayer before he tore into that cheeseburger with onions that he purchased at the concession stand between games, Tommy who had given up a need to control, Tommy who sought to control his attitude, not nature, Tommy who gained control by not seeking control, Tommy for whom free will and determinism were perfectly compatible, Tommy who prayed for events to happen as he wanted them to but who also wanted them to happen as they did happen, that being God's prerogative and plan, all glory to God, Tommy cultivating grace and gratitude, Tommy happy as could be by being willing to be happy as he was, Tommy transcending himself, connected with truth, with God, flush with the Holy Spirit. But teammates, on this I hope we can agree, as we hear that rolling thunder to the southwest near Richmond Beach and reflexively hunker lower in anticipation of additional bursting clouds blowing our way: in the realm of the ludic, it matters not whether you are a believer or an atheist, a Christian or an existentialist. It matters only that you are a player. For just as play is the seed of culture, intrinsically motivated children absorbed in means, not ends, in process, not results, incidentally, accidentally, learning social skills and values in the flow of their invented games, it is also the blooming treasured outcome of culture, we aged in our second, even third, childhoods finally free again to play for the sake of playing, our re-creation entirely unserious but intensely absorbing , a self-chosen, self-directed, authentic pursuit of a sublime Gestalt, an act of self-exaltation in which we pass from our solid, stolid state to an ethereal vaporous state before condensing again into that kind of solid form that we other solid forms huddle in the wet to inter today. Whether we live on after our lump of clay is lumped with the clay, or whether we don't, while we are here, let us play. Let us create leagues and teams, let us keep standings, let us don colorful uniforms, and let us grab bats and balls and gloves and make a world for ourselves within the agreed-upon pleasing geometric constraints of chalked lines on fenced-in green outfield grass and red infield dirt, square white bases angled 65' apart like the points of a diamond, and within the legalistic constraint of the rules of the American Softball Association. And let us try, each batter, to the best of their creative ability, to journey from home and return safely to home, evading Scylla and Charybdis and

Circe, and, each defender, to rub out the wily voyagers, each of us on either side chiming in to create the rhythm of the game.

Ah, teammates, I'm sure that Tommy knew nothing about Zen. He was Western to the core. But more so than any of us, on the diamond Tommy had the proprioceptive awareness of a Zen archer, a Zen surfer, adaptively attuned to affordances, absolutely present, factoring in the position of the sun, the speed and direction of the wind, the inning, the score, the number of outs, and the whereabouts of baserunners, reading the stance of the batter, his grip, two-handed or overlapping, the angle of his bat, the trajectory and location of the pitch, noting the presence or absence of a leg kick, the timing of the swing, early, late, or on the dot, the dominance of top hand or bottom hand, and also the angle of the swing, anticipating, flowing, seizing his opportunities. In motion, no matter what his arms and legs might be doing, he was always centered, balanced, true. The big man was pure grace. Teammates, I admit that in the field, moving for a ball, I lack at times that precious sense of where I am. My center fails to hold. Confused by the anarchy of my loose limbs and the cloudiness of my deteriorating vision, I lose focus, I may bobble a ball or throw it weakly or wildly off legs that are askew. But Tommy, in spite of his girth and that pack on his back, could always bend at the knees while his feet slide-stepped or crossed-over, could watch the ball into his glove, his hands quickly and gently receptive of even the hard half-volley suddenly at his feet or the smash down the line that he snared backhanded, shrugging the ball up as he smoothly crow-hopped and, without reflecting, without trying, actually, arrow a throw to the appropriate base. He and his glove were one, he and the ball became one, a union of perception and action, intention and realization, such was his total immersion in process. And at the plate, he and the bat too were one, his composite Mikan Freak merely an extension of feet and legs and core and arms and hands, his stance comfortable and ever so slightly open, his weight shifted to his right hip yet stably balanced, the Freak pulled back and cocked toward the pitcher, back leg and front side thus spring-loaded, his relaxed overlapping grip a natural burl that the bat seemed to grow out of, his eyes on the ball as it leaves the pitcher's hand, an alert but self-effacing automatism, passive as the pitch rises then begins its descent, initiating his leg kick, winding his hips, not directing the swing, waiting for the swing to take him by surprise at that supreme instant when the ball is most vulnerable to being maximally re-directed, then with violent equanimity, his head still, his eyes communing with the bottom half of the dropping ball, driving off his back foot, unwinding his hips, transferring his weight to his front foot, swinging around his spine, his lead arm pulling the lagging bat through, allowing it to reach peak acceleration at the point of contact, his lashing wrists releasing all his stored-up energy and launching the ball in a long parabola deep into the gap in right-center or left-center, letting go of the Freak with his right hand, his shoulders at last opening up, his head turning for balance, his eyes following the arc of the ball, and continuing the momentum of the swing with his left hand in an extended follow-through that only ends when the bat taps him on the back. And which do we prefer, in our ways of looking at the batter? The beauty of inflections, or the beauty of innuendoes? Tommy swinging, or Tommy just after, tracking the gorgeous flight of the ball? Both, I'd say.

Now, teammates, having noticed that the two representatives from Beck's Tribute Center standing by in their black raincoats and black fedoras, as decorous and disciplined a pair of undertakers as one could ask for, have for some time been shuffling their feet and twiddling their fig-leafed fingers, and that family members and assorted friends are eyeing in alarm the water level climbing up their shoes, I will jump quickly to my peroration. He was autotelic, teammates. Immersed in play for its own sake. Rebelling against meaninglessness. Vibrating, animating unlived lines, wringing a music of his own from them. That was Tommy, right up to the myocardial infarction that ended his life last week. What more, other than more of it, could you ask of life? Lost in the supreme fiction of the ludic, autonomous, unmotivated by fears or hopes, threats or rewards. Shrugging off his few fielding errors, his rare mistimed swings of the bat. Quietly ecstatic, joyfully settled. Taking pleasure in what he did best, inexpressively reveling in *Funktionslust*. Ah, teammates, if only. You and I, alas, are heterotelic. We get rattled. Extraneous thoughts intrude. We choke. We lose our rhythm. Angst is the very ground of our being. We can never completely trust ourselves. Our hearts quaver timorously rather than vibrate vigorously. We can never be pure and ingenuous like Tommy. Yet, absurdly, we are condemned to yearn to be so, to continue playing softball into our 80s, to keep striving for the unattainable bliss of becoming insepa-rable from our song, our dance, our swing, and in this Sisyphean endeavor to be like Tommy, teammates, we rebels must imagine ourselves happy.

11

A Uniform Hieroglyphic

Mavericks, as the twelve of you sit before me on the dressing room benches in your white sleeveless V-neck uniforms with the purple numbers and trim, knees bouncing, ponytails bobbing, gum snapping in excited anxiety, dreadfully ready to take the floor of the Tacoma Dome for the state championship game against the South Valley Wildcats from Yakima, time-trapped mortals, perhaps two of you bleeding and one perhaps three worrisome weeks late, about to plunge, in wild hope and fear, into an entropy-defying time out of time that you yourselves will create, refusing to accept the universe as it appears, from your mundane macroscopic perspective, to be (cooling, changing), and what you, even in your tender teenage years, appear to be (changing, dying), and equally unsatisfied with, not knowing what to do with, what I think is closer to the truth, the physicist's quantum alternative, an unseen microscopic reality of a ceaseless swarming of quanta in a web of relations in which nothing *is* but what is not, objects and space and time being the constructs of your ignorance, the reason why there is something rather than nothing the result of your inability to see that the universe is, ultimately, process, a dance of molecules, what are called things nothing more than long events, a stone a complex vibration of quantum fields that holds itself in equilibrium before disintegrating, a person a network of cells in a eb of chemical processes and social relations, time not a smooth flowing from past to present to future but a relative measure of the fitful passing of heat from warmer bodies to cooler ones, a fluctuation of discrete jumps in which one event can actually occur both before and after another event, pointils that from your distant point of view you blur together and perceive as order becoming disorder, not conceding even for a nano-second that the world needs to be understood in its becoming, how things happen, rather than in its being, how things are, insisting for example that an earth amenable to life must have been designed for you because you exist rather than that you exist because earth is amenable to life, insisting that time is one-directional and fraught with emotion, believing keenly that death is woeful loss, not merely a disintegration of an equilibrium, an undoing of homeostasis, convinced that your hearts are ticking time bombs, rebelliously yearning for clarity, order, purpose, immortality, for the madness of art, for your own sakes, Mavericks, throw yourselves gallantly into this glorious game tonight, cause each intense moment to matter, shape spacetime with your now choreographed, now improvised, particles and waves of movement, bend it with your pace of play, your extra passes, your ball reversals, your post entries, your screens, your cuts, your stop-and-go dribbles, speed it up with your fastbreaks, retard it with your delay game, even bring it to a halt with your timeouts, and prevent those South Valley girls from shaping it their way with your defensive pressure, give them no space or time to execute, swarm them, climb into their bras, deny dribble penetration, bump cutters off their routes, cut off passing lanes and angles, jump-switch, trap, harass the ball with your predatory hands, dive for it when it's knocked loose, contest any shot, box out boisterously when it's released, explode for the rebound, turn game-time into time as you long for it to be, not just a winding down to death but motion made distinguished use of in a space where anticipation, imagination, deftness, agility, strength, effort, and courage bring exaltation, at-one your bodies with the motion of the universe by rehearsing its rhythm and balance in your own joyful, quark-like spurting and stotting and gliding and bumping, become one with it by exploiting its laws even as you yearn to defy those laws, to outpace the speed of light, to escape the clutches of gravity, to expunge the enervation of entropy and gloriously transcend your human limitations. Go now, and become your ideal selves, he might, upon late-life reflection, have said.

Liz Ann returned the paper to him and smiled, her crooked left incisor angling leftward jauntily.

"Good thing you didn't," she said, "or we would have been too puzzled to compete."

She stared eastward into the cerulean. A warm Sunday afternoon in July. Amid a dozen other, younger, lolling beer drinkers in pairs or fours, the males in shorts and tees, most of the females in torn denim short shorts and halter tops, the old man and Liz Ann sat side by side in slatted Adirondack chairs in the umbrellaed courtyard of 190 Sunset at Salish Crossing, embosked from the acre of cars in the asphalt parking lot by densely planted concrete flower beds bursting with the orange-red-yellow beaming faces of nasturtiums, the tight raspberry-apricot buds of Tropicana tree roses, and the white asterisks of jasmine, all climbing libidinously up and around a yellow-green fullness of leafy dwarf vine maples and Japanese maples. Summer in Edmonds—this year, exceptional even in this age of climate change, wanton sprees of multiple 85-degree days engorged with sunshine from 5:00 a.m. to 9:00 p.m., a gracing, if such intentionality were possible, of the Bowl and its denizens, who bathed in the glory of warmth and light, ripeness being, for the moment, all. The old man, having weathered the eras of jean shorts and cargo shorts and plaid shorts, wore simple plain black cotton shorts that stopped an inch above his knees and an untucked, collared, blue-white checked shirt that hid most of his neck wattles. Liz Ann had on light blue jeans and a black tank top that revealed, on her substantial upper arm, just below her left shoulder, the vertical black and white tattoo of a domino.

"The tattoo new?"

"Yes. I finally decided to get some ink. I've always liked the sleek look and feel of dominoes."

"And the one pip?"

"Means I'm odd, I'm queer. But I do like what, in your contorted way, you're getting at, in that paper. I assume it's for your story? The ultimate existential dread that spawned the artistic motives for why we played. Whether they grew out of our macroscopic view or the physicist's microscopic view, whether we saw entropy as death or change, whether we had, most of us, been coaxed to see life as Christian comedy or, maybe one or two of us, secular transcendent tragedy, or, none of us, absurd chaos, we all yearned, none more so than our coach I dare say, both to exploit and to reverse-engineer the laws of the universe, to remake life according to our heart's desire, frail humans seeking to become autonomous controllers, creators."

They sipped their pints of Brackett's Landing IPA, alcohol content 8%, one of Brittany's and Justin's Harbor Square brews. The Old Man held the fruity hops in his mouth for a few seconds while four single anomalous flavors played in succession on his tongue and palate and then resounded as a chord in his nose when he swallowed and exhaled. Orange! That was one of the noms. And pineapple! Lime, yes. With a dash of pepper? And was that last thing a hint of banana? Or butterscotch? The ale was like a rainbow popsicle, exotic treat of his youth, Mrs. Bienz poking her sausage-roll curls deep into the freezer chest at her Confectionary to find one for him in exchange for a nickel. As with prose, as with jazz pianists, so with beer and wine: the old man enjoyed all styles, from spare to rococo, but was most delighted by the bold, the gaudy, the peacockian. The clean, crisp malt of a simple lager, the sturdy chocolate of a stout or porter, would certainly be welcome on his tongue—but not quite as delightedly so as the sparkle of this IPA.

"Sorry to drift off for a second, Liz Ann. Was I moaning? I'm just enjoying this ale in this sun so much."

"It *is* good," she said. "But in a frou-frou kind of way? Kind of busy, kind of frilly? Or is that the lez in Liz coming out?"

"Not at all! Well-put. Frou-frou is apt. And I'm wallowing in it unashamedly. An old New Critic who just wants the text, not the background, I'm skeptical of the concept of *terroir*, the romantic blood-and-soil fiction that a wine conveys an expression of the ground and climate from which it came, as if you could taste the very limestone or chalk or schist or clay or rainfall or sunshine that conditioned its provenance when actually what you taste is the winemaker's more or less artful concoction from the sugar and tannin and acidity in the grapes that grew in that particular *terroir*, and no way this brew we're drinking, made from hops and barley grown in eastern Washington and malt and yeast from who knows where, expresses Harbor Square, whose *terroir* is asphalt on a bed of clay, but damned if it doesn't perfectly match the giddiness I feel on these rare summer days in Brackett's Landing when we are briefly freed from our gray oppressive regimen of clouds and clamminess. A big fruit-forward jammy wine like a cheap Bogle red blend, $7.95 at Costco, can cheer me in the same way, leaping on me like an exuberant young Saint Bernard, shaking his body against me, rubbing his head on my crotch, licking my hand, demanding attention, saying love me."

"Okay, if that's the way you're going to go, all smiles and similes, I'd say that chugging this ale is like being showered with colorful confetti or glittering pixie dust. A happy quaff for this occasion, agreed, but I need something sterner, more reticent, more disciplined, for my daily drink. You know, Coach," she teased, "replicable studies have shown that as we age, our ability to taste diminishes, it takes stronger and stronger stimuli to impress us, more spices, more exotic flavors."

"Maybe so, but I swear that if this ale had existed at the time, I'd have had about three schooners of it after we won that championship game."

"Oh, really? So what *did* you do? After you grabbed me from behind in a bear hug and said 'Liz Ann Mann, I love you!' and we all galumphed up and down the court and hugged each other over and over and you talked to the newspaper reporters and we cut down the nets and were presented that huge trophy and the band serenaded us with the alma mater and we sat for team and individual pictures, our parents all firing away with their Konicas and their Polaroids, and then mingled on the floor for half an hour with families and friends, all of us already so unbelievably drunk with the pleasure of triumph after achieving the ultimate—I mean, state champs! I was staggering and swaggering on that for weeks—and went back to the locker room for your final speech, in which you thanked us for all we had given you and said how much you admired our courage and how proud of us you were for coming back to win?"

"Well, my wife and Coach Baylor and his wife gathered up our team's bag of basketballs and the first-aid kit and the scorebook and the statistics and the video that our managers had produced for us, and I lugged the trophy, and we headed for our car, which was sitting lonely in that vast empty parking lot at 10:00 p.m., then drove back to 13 Coins in Seattle for a late-night pasta (I had the tortellini with thyme) and Schramsberg Brut."

"So you were drinking the stars?"

"I was so high emotionally already that it certainly felt like it. I do like the twinkle in the mouth that champagne produces, but the twinkle attracts so much of my attention, it's so amusing, that I can't concentrate on the other values of the wine. Give me a rich, oaky, buttery (yes, I said it) chardonnay in preference to its bubbly counterpart most any day. But two bottles of champagne were certainly called for that night, and Bill Baylor wouldn't hear of anything else. And Diane and Charlene loved it. What about you?"

"Most of us rode back to Seattle with our parents and met at Farrell's for burgers and ice cream—still following the school district's Athletic Code, you know—no smoking, no drinking, no drugs. But the next night, Saturday night, we all went to a celebration kegger at a big house in Woodway Park and got wasted. Brenda, your heady, crafty point guard, was falling-down drunk. We had to carry her to the car to get her home."

"Was this a one-off?"

"The falling-down part, yes. The drinking, no."

"For all of you?"

"For most of us. For most of the athletes of both genders in all of the high schools in the District in all of the sports. A small number smoked cigarettes, a small number used marijuana, but probably 75%, at least by the time they were juniors and seniors and going to weekend parties, drank. It was the thing to do."

"So I assumed, actually. Over the years, the principal would occasionally get a report of a player drinking and we would call her in to question her. When we got an admission, we would suspend her from the team for the season, as per the Athletic Code. And I myself caught a couple of girls smoking, one at Harbor Square Athletic Club, just tossing a butt away after getting out of her car, gym bag in hand, going in for a workout as I happened to be jogging by, another with cigarette between fingers ordering fries at McDonald's at Westgate when I stopped by for a diet Coke. But I always figured that we—the Superintendent, the Athletic Director, the principals, the coaches—were deluding ourselves. Everyone agreed that kids should not smoke, drink, or use drugs, and most wanted to believe that the athletes bearing the school colors on the fields and in the gyms were sterling exemplars of asceticism and probity, eschewing alcohol and sex, but in fact they were sterling exemplars of real teenagers experimenting with new pleasures while demonstrating competence and in some cases excellence in athletics and academics."

"Well, yes, we had priorities, we had goals, we were under control. Of course, mistakes were made. As you surmised, Miranda, our shooting guard, was three worrisome weeks late and pregnant on the day we won the championship. But when the pregnancy was confirmed, she and her boy friend, very sensibly I thought, agreed that they didn't want to marry each other, and she chose to carry the baby to term and give it up for adoption."

"Yeah, I remember that tempestuous Miranda once came into the training room in her practice shorts before one of our evening practices, climbed onto a table to have me tape her chronically sore ankle, sat back, spread her legs so she could hang the bad ankle over the edge of the table, and in the process unwittingly sent me a whiff of the aroma of female sexual arousal. She had obviously just been with her boyfriend. And she had a great practice! Full of energy and concentration, really into it."

"Sure! One of the values of participating in athletics is that you learn to compartmentalize. I loved my classes, I loved basketball, I wanted to be a great student, a great player, and I also enjoyed a weekend party."

"And what did the game mean to you? Did you think of yourself as an artist making order out of chaos with the material of your own body?"

"Not at the time, but later, yes. As a little girl I always liked using my body—running, jumping rope, tumbling, climbing on the Jungle Gym. In third grade I started playing Youth Club basketball for mostly social reasons—my friends were doing it. I found that the games interested and pleased my parents, especially my dad, who had played in high school. He attached a backboard and hoop to the shake roof of our garage and we'd play on the driveway, dribbling and shooting layups. I was impressed with the way he could dribble behind his back and shoot jump shots. He gave me some pointers but didn't really push me. Of course none of us girls had any skills to begin with, and our games were a chaos of turnovers, with final scores like 8 to 6, but I began to see that with my strength and coordination I was one of the better ones out there, I scored a basket almost every game, and my dad was always so excited when I did. Looking back now, I realize that it felt good to throw my body around in competition, do something physical, assert myself and achieve a tiny bit of dominance. I have since come to realize that I was unconsciously reveling in the chemical rushes elicited by a myriad of electrical impulses passing between my contracting muscles, my moving joints, and my brain.

"The next summer I went to the Youth Club's basketball day camp with Brenda, played on the driveway with my dad, and began to get better. Within a couple of years I was playing in two leagues, Youth Club in Edmonds and Little Dribblers in Lynnwood, and going to day camps, and then in middle school I started going away to week-long camps at WWU in Bellingham and PLU near Tacoma. As my skills developed, I began to feel proud of my body, to control it and take control with it, to gain sensual pleasure in moving gracefully, pivoting and sliding, jumping explosively, banging into other bodies, the bracing pain of a minor collision and the satisfaction that you gave at least as good as you got, even masochistically welcoming the hot sting of a floor burn and the hyper-ventilated flaming of the lungs, the sucking and gasping, after several whistleless trips up and down the court. My Youth Club coach used to keep a paper bag in his pocket for me to breathe into when I pushed too hard. I loved being put to the test, showing what I could get my body to do, it was an end in itself, although of course I loved winning and loved being an integral part of a team, loved being part of the Maplewood Mavericks, loved being part of that championship season."

"Loved scoring the winning basket as the final buzzer went off?"

"Well, yes, there was that!"

"We got off to such a terrible start in that game, and I blame myself for that. I think I prepared us on the Xs and Os. We went over their personnel and their plays and how we were going to defend them, where we would provide help, when we would double-team the post, we knew how we were going to attack their half court and full court defensive pressure, clearing out to prevent traps and looking for backdoor cuts and give-and-gos and shuffle cuts off of screens. We had it analyzed, but we were not emotionally ready. I had done my task analysis but was too intimidated by the universe to provide you with a bold anticipatory set. Not only did I not give the pregame speech about entropy and art, I also failed to Henry the Fifth it."

"Band of Mavericks? Once more into their breeches? But that wasn't you. Entropy and the Battle of Agincourt were not topics that you could comfortably invoke before an audience. Your pregame oratory was long on *logos*, short on *ethos* and *pathos*. You got very calculating and analytical and understated. You seldom breathed fire, seldom pumped us up. But we figured that was part of the plan. You always said that emotion didn't last but knowledge and technique did. The same was true in our huddles at timeouts. No matter how dire the situation, you would pull a piece of chalk out of your pocket and start diagramming stuff on the floor as you knelt before us, staying very technical, not ranting and raving. We thought it was because you were keeping your poise."

"It's because I was scared. The chalk was my prop, it gave me the illusion of control, as if I could diagram my way out of any problems. I've always craved success, wanted to be a maker, a doer, but always entered any stage with fear and trembling at the audacity of my hope. How dare I dare? I can't breathe, my lungs spasm, I choke in both senses of the word, please let this cup pass from me, constitutionally I'm an underdog, prepared to fail stoically, it's agony to get an early lead, such pressure to hold it, such despair if you don't, I'm at my toughest, sharpest, when coming from behind, then my heart soars, you hit me in the mouth, okay, good, I deserve it, you're better than I am, you are in tune with the universe and I'm not, but now, goddam it, I'm pissed, and yes, relieved, grateful, thank you, I'll show you now, I'm gonna fight back, I don't care how fucking good you think you are, I'm capable too, maybe not tuned in but clever enough to exploit the universe in my own way! Those, Liz Ann, are my notes from underground."

"So interesting to see this side of you! You're being vulnerable! Opening up! Or are you? I mean, in your 20-year career you won 387 games and lost only 121. You went to State 14 times. You had a first, a second, two thirds, and six other placements for trophies that are still displayed in the Edmonds-Maplewood gym. Possibly you're conning yourself and trying to con me? When I was playing, we had lots of games where we started strong and stayed strong. Many times we blew our opponents out. You can't have been scared every game."

"Every game. Well, there was one exception. One season, back in the '70s, Clover Park of Tacoma was killing everybody. We met at State and they blew us out by 50. I didn't worry a bit going in, and I didn't worry a bit afterwards. I had scouted them and knew there was nothing I could do about it. But with every other game, I felt that winning or losing depended on me, that it was incumbent upon me to find a way to win with whatever players I had, and that I was a failure if I didn't. So I was a failure 120 times."

"But all those times you were named Coach of the Year by the Seattle Times or the Everett Herald or King TV? That didn't give you confidence?"

"That only made things worse. My self-imposed expectations kept rising, and my self-confidence kept falling."

"If so, you covered it up well. You always seemed to be in charge. We players always believed in you. Did you ever get any criticism from parents?"

"Not to my face, although I'm sure there was plenty of ranting out of my ear shot. An anonymous letter one time from someone who said I was playing the wrong people. Wanted his daughter to get more playing time, no doubt. And, your senior year, one long, anonymous, rambling message on my answering machine after we lost that District playoff game to Anacortes and had to come back through the loser's bracket to get to State."

"Miranda's mom? I can see that. She voiced opinions about a lot of things."

"But she was right. We fell apart in the second half, and I was responsible. We had gone 20 and 0 in the regular season, won the Western Conference, and bussed up I-5 to Mt. Vernon and its beautifully maintained old gym—the same one in which I had played in the '50s, with the built-in wooden bleachers and the long foyer with pictures of Bulldog players going back to the '30s—for our first District game, matched against the lowest seed. The trip was pure nostalgia for me, awash in memories of all those I had taken up Highway 99 with my buddies when playing for Edmonds, that same *faux*-relaxed joking and chattering among the players until we got to Everett, then the quieting as Coach Baylor and I moved through the bus to review defensive assignments with certain players, then the setting of the sun and the settling in of silence as we crossed the Stillaguamish River, those special solemn moments of unity, an unspoken avowal that for 32 minutes of game time we would live and die for each other, in the enchanted realm of the ludic."

"So what happened? They switched defenses and we didn't adjust? Because we were killing them in the first half, moving the ball, everybody scoring, flying around on defense."

"Yes, they went to a match-up zone, which I did not recognize. And the great, shameful irony was that in years past I had employed that very defense and had actually taught it to their coach, Cathy Lockhart, at a clinic the previous fall! We ran the regular stuff we used against a 2-3 when we should have been back-screening and reversing the ball to Miranda for 3-pointers, and sending multiple cutters through the lane, and working you and Janelle in a high-low post two-person game against single coverage. But I just choked, panicked, couldn't think clearly, and they came back to tie and then win in overtime. It was entirely my fault. And that wasn't the only time. There were other games over the years where teams kept changing defenses and I was two or three possessions behind in recognizing the change, so we were in the wrong offense half the time, and twice in state tournament games we got ahead and the opponent threw a run-and-jump full court press at us, which I read as a zone press, failing to stay calm and mentally step back and analyze coolly, stunned by tension, just sticking with my first impression and never adjusting our offense, hoping for a miracle. Enchanted realm of the ludic, my ass! Not those nights."

Liz Ann laughed. "Don't be so hard on yourself. You coached 500 games. There were bound to be a few clunkers. For the most part it *was* enchanted. Anyway, we proceeded to win all our loser-out games, giving us the District championship, then went on to win three in a row at State."

"But the first one, against Spanaway, we almost lost. Again, my fault. We had a far superior record, we knew that on paper we were better, and I let you go into the game over-confident, in love with yourselves after winning District and going 23-1 overall. I was scared, as always, but failed to recognize that this time you guys lacked respect for our opponents. Our pressure man-to-man was listless, we were a step slow, they caught us out of position, they slashed through us, we were preventing nothing. Finally I realized at halftime that we were unprepared mentally to apply pressure and force turnovers. We had to back off, go to our sagging man-to-man, seal the key, and rely on their poor outside shooting. We barely escaped with the win."

"Yeah, I'd kind of forgotten that. But that's on us as much as it is on you. We were more responsible for our lack of emotional readiness than you were."

"Maybe so, but it never felt that way to me. We showed again the lack of emotional preparation the next night against Hoquiam in the semi-finals. We're all staying at La Quinta, near the Dome, so in the afternoon we drive over to the PLU gym, where we have a walk-through and do a little shooting. Our opponents, on the other hand, choose to spend their day lunching and shopping at the South Center Mall. We know exactly what Hoquiam will do—run the Flex on offense and on defense set up a full-court zone press after scores and fall back into a 2-3 zone. We review all the baseline screens and down-screens in the Flex. We have the pattern down pat, we are ready to anticipate and get through the screens, and then we get into the game and they run the offense very fast and set physical screens that jar us and open up cutters for layups or short jumpers, just knock the wind out of us. It's all thought and no emotion. We are timid, we are tentative, we are slow, we are soft, they jump out to a 10-point lead, their crowd is going wild, ours is groaning, I'm stunned, it's all my fault, why can't we stop them, they do the same thing every time. We're all in shock. Finally, I call time out and shout at you over our band blaring the theme from 'Rocky' to switch all the screens and smother the cutters, my chalk jabbing Xs and Os and arrows and loops and swoops on the floor. It's just enough to get you competing. You start anticipating and banging and denying, and their coach screams to the refs about fouls not being called, and they're no longer scoring at will, and we begin attacking on offense, now we're not content just to get the ball down the floor against their press, we get the ball to the middle aggressively and quickly reverse it and look for someone open cutting toward the basket, and we catch them, then gradually pull away."

"So we struggle because we either lack respect for our opponents or we fear our opponents?"

"Yes."

"And that's your fault? Even after all your preparation?"

"Yes, because in the process of preparing you I infect you with the virus of my own insecurity, my fear of failure, my lack of swagger, my inability to make the leap from wish to will. I mean, what happens the next night against West Valley in the championship game?"

"*La meme* damn *chose*?"

"*Oui, la meme* damn *chose*! Again we have our afternoon walkthrough. We know that a large part of their offense is the fastbreak, that we need to have floor balance and sprint back hard any time the ball changes hands, even if we score, because they're inbounding or outletting instantly and pushing the ball hard every time. We know that in their half-court offense they like to go inside to their All-State post player Michelle Aikens, she's 6'2", college prospect, the UW wants her, she's very strong, has dynamic moves, and if she's doubled and can't get her shot she kicks the ball out to the player left open by the double team. We know we have to push her out as far as possible, front her if she's low, deny her from the side if she's high, pressure the passers, deny entry passes as much as possible, and help hard from the weak side when she does get the pass, with the next nearest defender looking to close out fast on the inside-out pass to the open shooter. I repeat all this in my pregame speech. I utter no myth-making remarks about the ludic or about basketball players as existential rebels or artists shaping spacetime with their bodies, at-oneing themselves with the rhythms of the universe, I am just too damn matter-of-fact, prosaic, I don't dare the poetic, my speech never takes flight, I fear the fate of Icarus, I can't give myself over emotionally to the occasion, it's too risky, I fear the corny, the sentimental, fear speaking freely, fear playing freely, bleakly fear that the road of excess leads to the hovel of comeuppance, I dream that the dream is impossible, the stage, the moment, is too big for me, I James Dean it, and again we get overwhelmed in the first quarter, inundated, the score is 15-4, they're throwing baseball passes the length of the floor for layups, they're all over us on defense, anticipating, tipping balls loose, attacking, playing with *élan*, Aikens is pivoting right through our double-teams, their fans are roaring their pleasure, full of blood-lust, yelling 'Git along, little dogie,' when I stand up to give direction, their cheerleaders are sassing us with their green and gold pompoms, their coach, Mike Gunderson, is up on every one of their possessions, clawing his paws like a wildcat, flapping his arms like an eagle, exhorting them to fly down court, raising his fists in triumph after every basket, he stalks the sideline, he owns this stage, he's in his element, I am so pissed at that guy—"

"And we are, too, we want to kill those bitches."

"—I call timeout, their band is taunting us with 'More Than a Feeling,' the South Valley girls are laughing and high-fiving each other, I'm yelling, you can barely hear me, my chalk breaks into two pieces, I'm so angry at myself—"

"And we're just as angry at ourselves—"

"My chemicals are surging now, I shout 'Get back on defense' and draw vectors showing motion, 'Stop the ball, push out, pressure, deny, double hard, recover, close out, seal, on offense protect the ball, get a step and penetrate with your dribble, ball-side wings go backdoor, point guard run a give-and-go, weakside wings run your shuffle cuts hard,' and we begin to stem the tide, we're awake, we're aggressive, Miranda pokes the ball loose and goes full-court for a layup, you and Janelle clamp down on Aikens, twice in a row Brenda passes to you on the wing and runs the give and go, you hit her on the cut, there's no help and she gets layups, you pass and post up, get a return pass, turn and face, dip into your grammar of moves, select a step-through, and score over Aikens, Janelle grabs a miss by Miranda and puts it back, suddenly it's 15 to 14, and Gunderson calls timeout, his players are looking what-the-hell"—

—"fuck—"

—"at each other, we're exuberant on the sideline, we've actually seized the moment, our band is rocking 'Celebration,' we're exhorting each other to keep up the intensity, and we play even the rest of the half and go into the dressing room with the score 25-24. And what's my mood at this point?"

"Relief?"

"Yes, relief! Relief that we haven't totally embarrassed ourselves. Relief that we are respectable. That we belong on the same court. That we came back. And what should it have been?"

"Bodacious audaciousness?"

"Yes! The game was ours to win if only we dared to do so. But I of course was out with my now-shorter piece of chalk, again Xing and Oing. You players were upbeat, spirited, and I proceeded to bring you down with talk of tactics and strategy. I needed to be more holistic, less analytic, needed to display a swashbuckling persona, needed to connect with your spirits as well as your brains."

"We did start slow again in the second half. But was it your fault?"

"I think so. We're down 39-27 after five minutes into the third quarter. The South Valley girls have their mojo back. They're slapping hands, they're bouncing on the balls of their feet, their ponytails are flying, Gunderson is raising a claw or slam-dunking a make-believe ball after every one of their baskets, their fans are screaming 'Sit down, Big Maple!' when I get up to call another time-out so we can rest and regroup. I get the chalk going, but it's all a sham. There's nothing new to add. I say, 'Guys, there's 11 minutes left, plenty of time to come back. We can do it.' But I don't really believe it. Did you believe it?"

"Actually, yes. At least Brenda and I did. But not just because you said it. We had played against some of those girls at camps and in summer leagues. They were good, but we knew we could compete. We belonged out there. Everything you said about the Xs and Os was right, and we were just frustrated that we were not making it happen."

"Because I was not providing the spark, not inspiring you by stealing a torch of fire from the gods and brandishing it?"

"Only a wee bit. We knew you were inhibited in that way. We knew that you would always try to model grace under pressure. You could never invoke 'Invictus,' right? Never bring yourself to say that we were the masters of our fate?"

The old man shrugged. "No. Never."

Liz Ann laughed. "Because that's too uncouth for you, both too pretentious and too plebian, too heavy-handed, too coarse, too vulgar. And yet the concept is so you, isn't it? You don't believe in the existence of an entity that permeates the universe and works upon its human inhabitants, whether it be called destiny, predestination, divine providence, karma, or kismet."

"No. Fate is simply what happens. Fate is entropy."

"And yet you yourself are all about using the will to heroically exploit the various complex vibrations of quantum fields that call themselves 'Edmonds' or 'Wayne Adams,' to determine to some extent what happens, to determine fate. All your efforts to train, to rewire your brain, to sort yourself out in your blog, to be a maker, a doer, a controller, to fashion the essence of your existence, make it clear: in spite of your protestations to the contrary, striving to become the master of your fate is what most absorbs you in life and provides your *raison d'être*. Coach, it's time to come out of the closet and admit that in addition to loving mushy French fries and popsicle beers you love 'Invictus' !"

"Never! I will concede that I *seek* to master, or create, my fate, but in the fell clutch of circumstance I lack that invincible derring-do, my will, my concentration, fail me. And, theme aside, never will I concede that 'Invictus' is a well-wrought poem. It is pure fustian! I will confess, however, that I'd like to have one more popsicle beer. Can I get you something?"

"Do Brittany and Justin make a pilsner?"

"I think so."

He took the empty glasses inside and brought back two full ones.

"Try this."

The afternoon remained beautiful, the flowers remained radiant, the deep sky remained cerulean ("Okay, Perry Como," the old man thought, "I'll give you this one."), the beer garden remained crowded, the men's resonant baritone guffaws and the women's tinkling giggles continuing to express tipsily their joy in the day.

"How is it?"

"A nice change. Disciplined. Reticent. Neither runny nor chewy, just agreeably firm with a very slight bitter bite."

"And my IPA continues to titillate me. I'm starting to lose my edge. Where is my self? I'm going all *sfumato*. My margins are bleeding into this garden, this sky. By the time I finish it, I'll be a pantheist! Good thing I'm walking home, not driving. The exercise will help to sober me—if I can keep my balance."

"Well, I'm driving out to Seaview, but I'm not concerned. Since I weigh more than you, I can metabolize more alcohol."

"So, where were we?"

"Trying to determine how we were able to win that game. Coach, we did it by transcending you. We knew we had to be responsible for motivating ourselves. Any failure of will would be our fault, not yours. We all believed in the paradoxical co-existence of fate and free will. We believed that we had a role to play in achieving our fate, which was flexibly predetermined, had parameters, yes, but they were elastic. It was written in the stars, but we had to fulfill it with our actions. We could become what we were meant to be, champions. This is quite sensibly how people get through life, Coach. No matter how strait the gate, they believe they will manage to squeeze through. Die? Heaven awaits. Experience adversity? Overcome it. That the South Valley girls thought the same thing was irrelevant. We compartmentalized. Those chicks were going down!"

"You *were* amazing from that point on. You found an inner grit that almost brought tears to my eyes. You grimly, methodically stalked them down. You executed precisely at both ends of the floor. Your defense was aggressive, physical, seamless. You shut off their fastbreak, made them set up, then prevented them from getting the ball inside. They made a few baskets from outside, but you executed your fundamentals, boxed out, and rebounded all of their misses. Your offense took advantage of their pressure, their gambling, their overcommitting, with backdoors and give-and-goes. You backscreened for easy lobs to cutters. You were gaining on them, outscoring them at a rate of two to one. They were confused, they were getting hesitant, unsure how to defend us. Our fans were ecstatic, theirs were groaning, Gunderson was on his feet, clasping his hands together, imploring his team to apply even more pressure, and then with a half-minute left, you slipped the backscreen you had set for Brenda and took her bounce pass to the basket for a layup, with Aikens fouling you from behind for a three-point play to tie the score at 51. The South Valley girls go into shock. Gunderson calls time out to set up a play. Our band is playing 'Thriller.' In our huddle I pull out the chalk and draw a half-court with a big A in the low post. "They're gonna go to Aikens," I say. "Push her as high as you can. Deny. If she does get the ball, double hard from the weak side. No matter what happens, if they score or not, call time out when we get the ball back." They bring the ball up court, swing it to the side, and there's Aikens, making herself big, all ass and elbows, but you've nudged her out a couple of feet so she can't just make a simple power move, and when they float the entry pass over Brenda's outstretched arms, Janelle comes flying over from her girl on the weakside and tips it free, and in the mass scramble for possession the ball caroms off a South Valley girl and bounces out of bounds at the baseline. Twelve seconds left! Our fans are roaring. Gunderson pounds a fist into an open hand. You call time out. I diagram a play. They've been pressing man-to-man all game, so we'll have Janelle take the ball out and Brenda and Miranda will back screen you and Christine. You'll turn and fly down the court and, if you're open, Janelle will hit one of you with a long baseball pass for a game-winning layup. If you're not open, Janelle will pass to Brenda or Miranda and they will push the ball up and get whatever shot they can, with you and Christine looking to rebound. It turns out you and Christine are not open, because Gunderson switched to a zone press, to guard against a deep pass and to avoid fouling, so Janelle inbounds to Brenda, who weaves her way through passive defense to our free throw line, where in her hurry she puts up an off-balance shot that bounces off the rim, but you hurl yourself into the air over Aikens and rip the ball down, then go up quickly with a little floater that drops through the net as the buzzer goes off and bedlam sets in. You gave me a state championship, Liz Ann."

"No more so than you gave us one. We couldn't have done it without that chalk! You were always winning no matter who was on your team. And you had a chance at another one with a different bunch of girls five years later."

"True. If I hadn't choked it. We were up by 10 with three

minutes to go, playing fast and loose, playing with *brio*, probably the best basketball a team of mine ever played, and when Walla Walla called timeout in despair and confusion, instead of exhorting my girls to seize the day, I seized up, my heart shriveled, I played not to lose, I drew inward, I wasn't looking to shape space-time, just hoping not to be swallowed by a black hole in the next three minutes. I told the team to hold the ball on offense, play keep-away, kill 20 seconds of clock before looking for a shot, told them not to pressure or gamble on defense, above all not to foul, and they lost their edge. The girls went passive, tried to be too careful, our point guard dribbled a ball off her own foot trying to go nowhere, our best scorer let a pass sail through her hands out of bounds, Walla Walla sensed our passivity, applied insane pressure, bullied us, bumped us, hacked us, poked the ball loose, got a couple of breakaway layups, we're up by six, we finally get a call from a ref when a defender knocks our point guard down lunging for the ball, we make the free throws, the only points we get in these last three minutes, but they come right back and knife through us for layups or short uncontested jumpers, the last one coming at the buzzer to give them a one-point win, and my girls come off the floor looking at me with heartbreak, as if they'd let me down, when really it was the other way around. In the locker room, amid the tears and the sobbing, I apologized for my failure of will. "You guys are probably the best team I've ever had," I said, "and we should have just kept attacking and won going away. I am so sorry to have held you back when you have given me so much."

"Oh, so sad," Liz Ann said. "But certainly your decision was respectable, defensible. You see it all the time, at every level. Get a lead, milk the clock late in the game, don't shoot the ball too early, make them foul you, play a prevent defense, don't take chances, don't stop the clock by fouling. And though it doesn't work every time, it often does."

"Yes, but it was the wrong decision for this team. They needed just to be themselves, play balls-out. I, on the other hand, needed to cling, to hold on to what I had. Their will was to win, my wish was not to lose."

"In that, you were like a lot of other coaches. But, over the years, didn't you find that defeat has a richness and resonance all its own? As change or entropy often does? Didn't it produce a depth of feeling? Didn't it give you perspective? Didn't it make you better able to sympathize and empathize with others? Didn't the humbling, paradoxically, lift you up? Didn't the pain, the suffering, teach you to cope, help you to develop inner strength? Didn't the sharing of the agony of defeat create a bond with your players? Weren't you, all in all, a better person for it?"

"Well, yes, a grudging yes to all those questions. Granted, not to experience loss in life is to be not human. Not to experience loss in life is to be shallow, incomplete. It is to be innocent of reality. It is to be Adam and Eve before the Fall. It is to be Gautama before he became the Buddha. To experience loss is to gain knowledge, and gaining knowledge is good. That said, there is so much rationalizing going on in the framing of those questions, so much spin, so much alchemy, so much desperate attempt to turn loss into gain, with even an absurd implication that the more we lose the more we gain. We're having it both ways. If we win, we win. If we lose, we win. As you say, it's quite sensibly how people get through life. But I would rank such utterances pretty high on my HS/BS quotients. As Mae West and many others are alleged to have said, 'I've been rich and I've been poor, and rich is better.' I've won and I've lost, and winning is better."

"But not winning all the time. And surely being rich is better only because she had experienced the deprivation of poverty. And winning is better because you have experienced the torment of defeat. I know you are not one to believe that the tragic and the transcendent inhere in the very fabric of the universe—you made that quite clear when we read *Hamlet* and *Macbeth* and *Romeo and Juliet* in Lit Classics—but most literary critics do, and as I take my final swig of pilsner and empty this glass, I am tipsy enough to visualize you as a tragic hero seeking greatness but falling short and in the process revealing the glory of what it means to be human."

"I like it! 'The timorous tragedy of Coach Wayne Adams, his fatal flaw a lack of swagger, his epiphanic life showing that a lack of pride goeth before a fall.'"

"Sure, I'd read that. A mash-up of tragical-comical-historical-pastoral. Besides, it's not like you lost all the time. In fact, you won most of the time. Maybe you shouldn't be crying in your IPA."

"Definitely should not. Am not. Just unwilling, in spite of this enchanting ale, and the resplendence of the weather, and the deep pleasure I take in your company, to be co-opted by even the most wonderful people."

"Speaking of wonderful people, I need to get back home. Jennifer will be expecting me. She's warming up a fig and gorgonzola pizza from Epulo, and then we're going to watch something on Netflix."

"*Invictus*? *Hoosiers*?"

"Right! No. *Carol* for the fourth time. We love the texture—the dim lighting, the low camera angles, the lumbering of the heavy old Packard, the terseness of the storytelling." She tapped the back of his right hand as it rested on the wide arm of the chair. "Thank you for the beer and the talk on this lovely afternoon. Basketball has meant so much to me."

"And me."

"And has this been therapeutic?"

"We shall see."

[Hey, Coach, I didn't understand one bit of that paper you asked Liz Ann to read! And did you ever stop to consider that all those diagrams you were making on the floor with your chalk were upside down to your players? Very hard to follow—sometimes I didn't even try! But don't worry, Coach, I was into the game and always gave 100%. Thanks for all your Xs and Os, but I played more on feeling and instinct. I usually just knew what to do without thinking about it. And if I didn't, that was OK too! Miranda]

12

Great are the Myths

August 10, championship day, the Classics versus the Hot Shots in a one-game playoff. The teams had finished the season in a tie, both going 19-2, the Classics losing twice to the Hot Shots but beating them once, the Hot Shots losing once to the Classics, and once, inexplicably, to the last-place Ancient Mariners. At 7:30, the sun, a happily frequent refulgence in this climate-changed summer, toasting the skin on the back of his neck (71 degrees already, a glance at his watch told him) and bouncing brightly off the emerald and henna carpet of Meadowdale's Field 1, the old man, having performed his pregame home and Starbucks rituals, clad in black cap, white pin-striped jersey sans undershirt, black shorts, and black , neuropathy-countering, compression socks, windmilled his Mikan Freak with either hand alternately, loosening up, then rehearsed a few swings, feeling his form—load, see, snap—before taking BP. For him it had been a boom and bust season, uplift followed by recession, uplift again followed by depression, his batting average in the high .700s early, falling to .500, climbing back to .600, dropping to .450, then steadily rising to .650. He had continued to memorize his swing. In addition to team batting practice, he hit once a week at Civic Field with Zee, farewell gestures of homage in the months before work crews were to begin fashioning the space into an elegant multi-purpose park. He had been, and remained, happy with his physical rewiring. His grip and hip rotation and bat snap were sound and automatic. His muscles remembered. He had not been happy with his mental rewiring, his timing and focus. The wires of his concentration too often short-circuited. He choked. He panicked. He swung too early, he swung too late. He pulled off the ball, he fell away, he flailed or hacked. He failed in the clutch, he failed when the team had a big lead and there was little at stake. His craven need to succeed, he, a lifelong scoffer at paradoxes, had finally admitted to himself, caused him to fail. Not always. He had a game-winning RBI single against the Codgers, he had rally-extending doubles in comeback wins over the Old Timers and the Legends. Manager Larry Miller had moved him to the bottom of the order when his average tailed off, elevated him slightly when he seemed to be regaining his groove. And he *was* regaining his groove—by not trying to regain his groove. By imitating the late, great Tommy Thompson, the apotheosis of a mindful softball player, seemingly always able to realize his intentions.

When Zee had finished rattling his 10 short line drives and hard top-spin grounders, the old man stepped into the batter's box, where he loaded his body and emptied his mind. After falling to .450, his career abyss, he had in desperation abandoned his old hyper-conscious approach. He was no longer tinkering with mechanics. He was letting go. He was hitting holistically now. He had no swing thoughts. Thought was his enemy now. He faced the pitcher in an angst-free Zen state of no-mind, obviating any insinuating fears of failure, precluding any stress-induced premature firing of neurotransmitters. His heart did not race, his stomach did not crater, his jaw did not quaver. He settled into the moment, embraced it, embraced the joy of presence, how wonderful to be here! He chillaxed, accepting himself, allowing reality to connect with him. He was in a relationship with something beyond himself. He! Him! Sylvia and Diane would be stunned, would feel vindicated, would be tempted to wag a finger and say "Mm-*hmm*." Gone were the inauthentic bad faith sins of self-doubt and self-correction. Being and doing, he had sensed at last, were a Taoist yin-yang unity. He could be and do, do and be, simultaneously. At the plate he was attuned to the vibe of the pitch, not just with his eyes and his brain but with his whole body, the highest expression of human capacity. He was not in his body, he *was* his body, ready to adapt, to read and react as naturally as a cruising bee diving into the welcome nectar of a flower or a coiled snake launching itself toward a fat mouse. He was swinging by feel, balanced, smooth, free of tension. He no longer automatically waited for a strike. Balls and strikes were irrelevant artificial constructs. He trusted his innate sense of pitch-worthiness and swung at the pitch that felt right. He no longer said "Wait, wait." A mantra was a distracting imposition. The right timing came through intuition uncontrolled by reflecting intelligence. Attuned to the pitch's affordances, he calmly regarded its parabola, felt it come into his presence, patiently stayed with it all the way, even through the temperate violence of his hip rotation and stride and wrist snap, and catapulted it, with a velocity unexpected from a man his age and size, in trajectories that streamed over the infielders and between the outfielders. Not always. There were instances when he unaccountably tuned out, swung at an inauspicious pitch that was a bit too short, a bit too deep, too far inside, too far outside , swung a little too early or a little too late, swung over or under the ball, instances when his attention had strayed, resulting in dribbling grounders, feeble popups, sleepy flies. But these he dismissed with a shrug or a chuckle (you can't be perfect, he could now accept), confident that he could slip right back into the moment when next at bat, waiting, watching , whaling, unburdened by thought.

Larry's first pitch was short, uninviting, offering no affordable access. The old man let it go. "Sorry, Wayne, that slipped," Larry said. The next 10 were all swing-worthy, and the old man lashed them from left to right, according to their affordability, with the exception of one that he got on top of and beat into the ground, prompting him to nod and smile in self-forgiveness.

As he pivoted to return his bat to the third-base dugout, a voice from the aluminum bleachers behind home plate called, "Nice job, Coach!"

"Liz Ann! My God! Didn't expect to see you here."

She was wearing a cardinal-red Stanford baseball cap and large, round, pink-rimmed sunglasses.

"Saw the announcement in the *Beacon*. Had to come. Couldn't miss it. Love seeing you in another championship game. What's going through your mind—entropy or the Battle of Agincourt?"

"Neither. I'm seeing with my third eye, now. I'm thinking without thinking now."

"You? Mr. Chalk Jock? Playing spontaneously, without fear? Incredible!"

"I'm a new man."

The Classics took a short infield practice after everyone had hit. As usual, the old man and Zee were to alternate at second base and catcher. He took his ground balls attentively, feelingly, wordlessly, shrugging them up. His "Down, down" mantra had been wiped from the hard drive of his mind along with his "Wait, wait" mantra. His shuffle steps were quick and smooth, his crossover pivots sharp and balanced, his throws, seamless motions that started from his feet and ended with a crisp wrist snap, direct and accurate. His teammates were up, confident. There was positive chatter all around. "Nice job, Wayne," "Attaway, Zee," "Great range, Gordy." "Good arm, Pat." (After Tommy's mid-season death, the old man, with Larry's approval, had again asked Pat Dahl to join the team, stressing their need for a replacement. Pat had agreed, on condition that his wife Darlene, who ran a part-time catering business from their home in Emerald Hills, had lettered in fast-pitch softball at WWU, and kept fit by running weekend 10Ks and playing tennis at Harbor Square, be allowed to join as well. Reluctantly, Larry had consented. After just one game in which he rotated Darlene as an extra through the outfield, the league permitting unlimited substitution, Larry had installed her as a starter in right-center, relegating Merle Oberon to the role of pinch-runner. They hadn't been the same team since. They had been better.) Larry then hit a few balls to the outfielders. The old man and Zee took turns covering second on throws from left and left-center. "Great peg," he yelled as Johnny threw him a one-hopper from deep on the foul line. They went out for relays on throws from right-center and right. Darlene was 5'7", a firm 140 pounds, round-faced, lithe, electric, her black ponytail, threaded through the space at the back of her adjustable cap, swishing whenever she moved. She overthrew him on her first ball, the old man getting off the ground about four inches, to no avail, and she screamed "Motherfucker!", her teammates trying not to laugh and glancing at the growing crowd embarrassedly.

"Sorry, Dar."

"Not you, Wayne, me. I flat-out missed you."

" Dar, don't hold back, say what you really mean," Larry yelled, to the amusement of the crowd. "Try another one."

Darlene raced to her right and snagged a line drive with her extended glove just a foot off the ground, jump-stopped, pivoted, and roped a throw that the old man quickly relayed to Gordy at second.

"Beautiful, Darlene," Larry said.

They were ready. They jogged in to their dugout while the Hot Shots, wearing white caps, red jerseys, and white shorts, walked over from their practice on Field 2. They gathered to read the two lineups that Larry had posted in the dugout.

Hot Shots	Classics
LF—Dick Dodge	RC—Darlene Dahl
SS—Buddy Budnick	LF—Johnny Merlot
1B—Chuck Metcalf	LC—Billy Fontaine
LC—Rabbit Watson	SS—Gordy Goldsmith
RC—Guy Fletcher	3B—Pat Dahl
RF—Doc Holiday	RF—Vern Rapp
C—Tim Clark	1B—Dale Hills
3B—Frank Baxter	2B/C—Wayne Adams
2B—Jim Montgomery	C/2B—Gary Zylstra
P—RJ McCoy	P—Larry Miller

"Hey, this is what we've been waiting for," Larry said. "The game of the year against our good friends and arch-rivals. It's our time. We know we can beat these guys. We miss the great Tommy Thompson, our special player and our special friend, but I know he's with us today. He's looking down right now and smiling upon us." They tightened their circle, raised their right arms, made a bouquet of their hands. "Lord, keep us all safe today, and may we play in a manner that honors You."

"They've got us twice so far. Now it's payback time," Darlene said, bouncing on her toes. "Stomp 'em!"

They laughed and brought their hands down in unison, shouting "Amen!"

The old man looked at the growing crowd. There were perhaps as many as 100 people present, Bernice and Margie and Gloria, of course, and other teammates' wives and some of their adult children with their children, another contingent of 40 or so in support of the Hot Shots, a few curious players from other league teams, and Mary Bright, the Parks and Recreation director, with the championship trophy next to her.

Larry and Rabbit met with the umpire at home plate for the coin flip. "Call heads, heads, heads," Darlene said.

"Does it matter?" the old man asked.

"Yes! We want to be the home team."

"I mean, don't we have the same chance whether we call heads or we call tails?"

"No. Larry usually always wins when he calls heads. If it ain't broke, don't fix it."

The old man smiled. Never mind the laws of probability, never mind the difference between correlation and causation, he loved the girl. So intense. So fierce. So free of doubt. So unlike him. That was to say, the old him. The new him was not fierce by any means but was loosely intense, eagerly relaxed, bemused by paradox.

Larry didn't fix it. He called heads and won the toss. "We're in the field, guys!" he yelled to the dugout as he and Rabbit shook hands.

"Yes!" Darlene said, and grabbed her glove, hugged Pat, and raced to right-center. The old man walked out to second in her wake. He turned and looked at the crowd. He was at ease. Not fierce, but not scared either. He wasn't worried about how he would perform for his team, how he would look to Liz Ann and the other spectators. He was serenely alert, fully absorbed, as he read the ground-hugging, skidding, spinning slice hit to him off the end of the bat by lead-off hitter Dick Dodge, shuffle-stepped to his left, welcomed it into his glove, and threw his man out smartly.

"All right, Wayne," Darlene yelled. "Great start."

The next batter, Buddy Budnick, lined one over the old man's head that Darlene charged but had to one-hop. "Shit!" she said, "Should have had it." Buddy had rounded first hard, as if to go to second, and Darlene ran in toward him, the ball cocked in her left hand, yelling "Go ahead, Buddy, try it!"

"Not on you, Dar," Buddy said, retreating to first with a grin.

Chuck Metcalf then grounded sharply to Pat at third and the old man hurried over to take the throw at second, just ahead of rapid Buddy, for the force-out, Classics wives kazooing their appreciation.

"Okay, guys, two down. Infielders play deep. I'll cover second," Larry said.

But he didn't get the opportunity, because Rabbit Watson ripped a single to center and Guy Fletcher lofted a deep fly over Billy's head for an inside-the-park home run, Hot Shot supporters cheering gleefully, before Doc Holiday flew out to Darlene to end the inning.

"Only down three, we're fine," Larry said. "Let's get 'em back. Here we go, Dar."

The team, the crowd, quieted excitedly to see what the explosive Darlene, a reticulation of quick-twitch fibers from her toes to her tongue, would do. She imploded, grounding directly to Dale at the first base bag, rendering her great speed meaningless. She jogged back to the dugout with her bat still in her hand.

"Jesus fucking Christ!" she said. "Fuck me! That won't happen again."

Johnny and Billie both flew out to end the unproductive inning.

The Hot Shots continued to attack in the second, Tim Clark and Frank Baxter hitting hard ground balls through the infield for singles and Jim Montgomery moving them over with a groundout to Dale at first. When pitcher RJ McCoy came to the plate, the old man, playing catcher, said, "I hope you throw me a lot of knuckle balls today, RJ."

"What're you trying to do, Brer Rabbit me?" RJ said.

The old man laughed, cocooned in equanimity. "Not at all. I'm ready for anything."

"Good for you," RJ said, then lined a double to left between Johnny and Billy, scoring both runners, giving the Hot Shots a 5-0 lead, before Dick popped up and Buddy flew out.

"Let's go, Classics!" boomed a young man's voice from the crowd as the teams changed sides.

This time they did. Gordy doubled to right-center and Pat scored him with a single to right. Vern moved Pat along with a single, and Dale walked to load the bases, bringing up the old man. The bleachers rang metallically as the Classsics fans stomped their feet.

"Wayne, I think RJ purposely walked Dale to get to you," catcher Tim Clark said. "No respect for his elders."

"Probably did. Not to worry."

"What are you—Alfred E. Neuman?"

"In a manner of speaking."

He loaded his body and emptied his mind. His receptors were attuned. Nothing existed except the ball. Perhaps wary of Brer Rabbit, RJ did not throw the knuckler. He arced a smooth pitch with topspin toward the middle of the plate, a pitch eminently affordable, and the old man was all over it, his Freak trampolining the ball with a resounding crack, the left-center fielder, who had drawn in a couple of steps, also in disrespect of age, desperately turning and running back as the ball climbed over his head and landed two hops from the fence, the old man scooting around the bases for a triple as three runs scored. The dugout was roaring. The bleachers rang again with prolonged stomping. Bernice, Margie, and Gloria kazooed cacaphonously.

"Yes, Wayne, yes!" Darlene screamed, and Gordy, coaching at third base, slapped hands with him.

The old man steepled his hands briefly and inclined his head slightly. Did he actually whisper "Namaste"? He did. Was his pulse rapidly slowing as he drew a couple of deep breaths? It was. Were the surge of adrenalin and the flood of dopamine already petering out? They were. Was he giddy? No. Was he, after the merest flash flush of success, back in the moment? Yes. Did he need to look at Liz Ann for validation? No.

Two pitches later, he scored the fifth run of the inning on Zee's hard ground single to right.

"All right, guys, way to answer," Larry said.

The Hot Shots sassed back, scoring two, and the top of the order for the Classics again failed to produce, making the score 7-5 after three. But they shut out the Hot Shots in the fourth, Pat smothering RJ's smash down the third base line and throwing him out and Darlene robbing Buddy with an all-out sprint to her left, extending her right arm as far as she could, snagging the ball, somersaulting when she lost her balance, and from a sitting position waving her glove for all to see that the ball was in it. Vern and Zee ran toward her to help her up, but she sprang to her feet and jogged in. The crowd whistled and clapped and cheered.

"Okay, guys, we've got the momentum now. Let's ride it!" Larry said.

Was that the spark the Classics needed? Was Darlene's play an inspirational turning point? Did it mark a change in momentum? Was momentum an actual thing? Could one good play be the catalyst for another and then another and then another? Could it be an attuning fork, turning attention toward clear signal and away from crackling noise? His teammates certainly believed so. Or was momentum just a subjective impression created by a statistically abnormal clumping of events, like a coin turning up heads six flips in a row or batters stringing together six hits in a row? Truly random if seen in a context of a million consecutive flips or at-bats, but seemingly other-directed if viewed myopically within the limitations of six flips or a single inning? The old man had always thought so. But now, in the moment as he was, he could almost sense himself vibrating with his teammates on the same iron string.

In any case, the Classics proceeded to string consecutive hits, starting with doubles by Gordy and Pat and singles by Vern and Dale, Gordy and Pat scoring and Vern getting to third. As he came to the plate the old man embraced the beauty of the day, the extraordinary ordinariness of the day, the towering dark green hemlocks and firs bordering the field beyond the fence, the glow of the emerald and henna carpet, the brilliance of the red and white uniforms of the Hot Shots, the look and heft of his smudged white Freak with the lyrical lime green horizontal stripe at the bottom of its barrel. What more could he ask for? He took his stance.

"You're getting the knuckler this time, Wayne," Tim said. "No more Mr. Nice Guy for RJ."

"Whatever."

RJ grinned at Wayne and threw him an ordinary top-spinner, too deep to be affordable. It clunked on the back of the plate for a strike.

"Knuckler for sure now, Wayne," Tim said.

It was. RJ adjusted his grip and tossed the ball with no follow through. Deprived of spin, the ball floated and quarked in the currents of the air. As it made its final jump toward the outside half of the plate, the old man, staying with it, paying divine attention, swung, contacting it at maximum bat speed precisely at its equator, and it gapped the right-side outfielders, who were surprised that the ball could be upon them so suddenly, and rolled to the fence.

Another triple, two runs scoring. Darlene, coaching third, said "Beautiful, Wayne," and bear-hugged him. The old man was brief in his "Namaste," quick to catch his breath while the crowd roared. RJ looked toward him and lifted his cap in salute. The old man nodded. Zee lined a single to right, and the old man scored. They had their five runs and led, 10-7. The Classics engaged in an orgy of high-fives and daps, the Hot Shots trudged off the field. Had the momentum shifted?

It certainly seemed so, the Hot Shots going down in order in the fourth. But then the Classics did the same thing in their half. Where *was* mo'? "Let's not lose momentum, guys," Larry said, as if it were simply a matter of keeping track of their car keys.

In the fifth, momentum strayed, or the Classics let it get away, or the Hot Shots stole it, or statistically normal regression to the mean occurred as the Hot Shots scored three runs on a single, a walk, and Rabbit's mad dash around the bases, hat in hand, grimace on face, arms pumping, knees churning, on his long drive to straightaway center. The Hot Shots all ran out to greet Rabbit at home plate. Their fans were stomping: momentum was theirs! Guy then doubled, and Doc hit a low line drive to the old man's left. Attuned and welcoming, he read the angle of the drive as best he could within the limits of his mac d, made a crisp crossover step and ran hard, gloving it at full extension on a hop as it passed through his retinal blur and into clearer sight, jump-stopping as in days past on the basketball court, reverse pivoting, and throwing the runner out by a step. "Great play, Wayne. That's a momentum breaker," Larry said. "Let's get those runs back."

They did. Finally, the top of the order produced. Darlene, grunting on her swing, laced one into the right field gap and sprinted all the way to third, up on her toes, head still, arms punching, legs driving. Johnny singled her home and then scored on Billy's double, and Gordy sliced an off-field triple down the left field line, to tie the score. But Pat and Vern, too eager to loft a sacrifice fly, each popped out to shallow left, too short for Gordy to gamble on, and Dale stranded Gordy with a grounder back to RJ.

Where was the momentum now? Were both teams getting

tight, or was that an unwarranted *post hoc ergo propter hoc* conclusion from the abnormal clumping of errors that followed? Zee let Doc's grounder roll right between his legs. Tim, out of sync and reaching desperately, landed a swinging bunt four feet in front of the plate that the old man pounced on, only to have Dale drop his throw. Bax grounded to Pat, who stepped on third for one out but got the ball stuck in his glove and was late on his throw to Zee at second. Trouble. But when Jim dropped a flare just back of Zee, Darlene charged, scooped the ball off the ground, and zinged a throw to Dale to nip Jim at first for the out, Tim and Bax advancing to third and second.

"Nice play, Dar," Larry said.

RJ was next. He waggled his black and orange Mikan DC41 and looked over the field before stepping into the box.

"Watch out for Larry's knuckler," the old man said.

"Larry doesn't have a knuckler. Larry doesn't have anything." And he lined Larry's first pitch up the middle, scoring Tim and Bax. *Quod erat demonstrandum.*

Dick forced RJ at second for the third out, but the Hot Shots had the lead, 12-10.

"Okay, right now, right now," Larry said as the Classics tossed their gloves on the dugout bench. "We don't want to wait till the seventh. We take the lead now, we put the pressure on them. Wayne, it's on you. Get us started."

Phenomenal, his stream of consciousness then, his awareness of body and self in time and space, of this fiction that he believed in, this invented microcosm bounded by clean lines and clear rules within which, by relinquishing control, by not getting in the way of his attention, he simply *was*, fearless and delighted, attuned, rapt, potentially potently kinetic. He rejoiced in the beauty of the day, the human-made richness of the situation. He neither sought it nor shunned it. He accepted it. He would eat his breakfast, he would wash his bowl.

"No triple this time, Wayne," Tim said as the old man came to the plate.

"Odds are you're right," the old man said. "Three triples in a row would indeed be a glaring statistical anomaly for anyone, let alone a guy my age."

He took his stance, loaded his back leg, emptied his mind. RJ shrugged, grinned, and threw his knuckler, a darter that landed in the middle of the plate for a strike, the old man, trusting his feeling, letting it go.

"Another one coming, Wayne?" Tim said.

"I wouldn't know, Tim." He would not distract himself by guessing. He would simply watch.

It was another knuckler, outside and deep, a ball.

The third pitch was a high spinner that reached the very top of the allowable 12-foot arc, and the old man waited and watched, and waited and wound his hips as it descended to chest level, and lashed it up the middle over RJ's head into center field for a single.

The Classics fans cheered. "All right, Wayne, good start," Larry yelled.

Zee followed with a ground ball up the middle past RJ. The old man, attuned to the speed and direction of the ball, got a good jump and ran toward second as hard as he could. Rabbit raced in, gloved the ball on the dead run, and without even planting his feet fired to Buddy at second for the force. But the old man, who hadn't slid in a game since he turned 70, fearing injury to his brittle bones and tight ligaments, surrendered to the moment and dropped into a perfect figure four to get the tip of his right shoe onto the base just before the ball arrived. "Safe!" the umpire, having hustled out to call the play, yelled.

The bleachers again rang metallically. "Great effort, Wayne," Pat called from the coaching box.

"Wayne, you're a mess. We need to get that cleaned up," the umpire said. He called time and the old man jogged to the dugout.

The friction from contact with the bristly fibers of the henna carpet had shredded the thin skin on the outside of his left leg from knee to mid-calf. The skin flapped in pieces and Eliquis-thinned blood ran into his sock as he jogged to the dugout.

Darlene grabbed the first-aid kit. "I got this!" She pulled on a pair of rubber gloves and used a gauze pad to sop up some of the blood. He embraced the pressure. She tore open a packaged alcohol wipe. "This is gonna hurt. Sorry, honey." She rubbed the pad all over the wounded area. He embraced the stinging. She extracted a four-by-six-inch bandage from a box in the kit, lubed it from a tube of Neosporin, pressed it on the wound, then wrapped it with adhesive spooled from a wide roll. "Okay, Wayne, go get 'em, baby!"

He returned to second. The wounded area was a little stiff but would not interfere with his running.

Larry was up. Zee clapped his hands. The old man was alert. Larry did his job, hitting a grounder to the right side that handcuffed Jim, his throw to second late because of his bobble. Bases loaded, and here came Darlene. The crowd hushed excitedly. She bent her knees, settled her weight into her compact, jutting butt, waggled her baby blue DeMarini Flipper. RJ, knowing Darlene was an impulsive, first-ball swinger, threw the ball a foot short of the plate. Darlene lifted her right foot and started a swinging motion but checked it. RJ threw short again, Darlene refrained again. RJ shook his head. His third pitch was a knuckler on the inside edge. Darlene was a little early, a little out in front, but had generated such bat speed that when she contacted the ball just above the sweet spot it flew down the right field line toward the corner. The old man jogged in to score, Zee loped in to score, and Larry, the heaviest, paunchiest, slowest runner on the team now that Tommy was gone, chugged past second and started toward third. Darlene, arms firing, stride lengthening, taking two steps to Larry's one, nipped the inside corner of the first base bag and closed on him, touching second when he was halfway to third, and continued to close, threatening to run right up his back, shouting "Go, Larry, Go! Score! Score!", and stopped at third clapping her hands as Larry lunged for home plate a step ahead of Jim's relay throw, inertia carrying him into the backstop screen, which he grasped while he gasped.

The Classics and their fans were laughing and cheering. "All right! All right," "That's living on the edge, Larry!" , "Way to push him, Darlene!"

After Larry made his way back to the dugout, past all of his teammates lined up for fist bumps and high fives, after the crowd had calmed down, Johnny skied to left, Darlene tagging and scoring easily, and then Billy and Gordy grounded out.

14-12, top of the seventh. "Hold 'em, guys," Larry said. "Heart of their order coming up. Everything you've got now. Let's end it here."

The old man, preternaturally alert, was back at second. Buddy led off with a triple that rolled between Johnny and Billy. Hot Shots fans cheered, Classics fans groaned. Chuck flew out to Vern in right, Buddy scoring. 14-13. Rabbit tripled to center, legs churning. Only strong relay throws from Billy to Gordy to Pat kept him from scoring. Who was faster? Rabbit or Darlene? Perhaps they would race sometime.

Two outs away from winning, one run away from a tie score, Guy at the plate. "Here we go, Larry, you got 'em," Darlene called. She was right. Guy hit a ground smash right back to Larry, who got his glove down to the ground just in time to snare it. He looked Rabbit back and threw to first.

Two down, Doc up. The old man knew that Doc usually came to the right side. He moved back a step, just in case Doc blooped one over his head. The colors of the shirts and caps of the crowd were an abstract of beauty. The crowd's murmuring was musical. He was at ease, he was poised. He rejoiced in being.

Larry tossed one short, which Doc disdained. Larry countered with a pitch high and deep, which Doc made the mistake of accepting. Reaching, flailing, unable to shift his weight or snap his wrists, he contacted the bottom of the ball with the handle of the bat and parachuted it toward the old man. "All right," Gordy exulted. "All you, Wayne." But the old man had to wait, rooted, looking into the sky, disoriented, until the ball passed through his retinal murk and entered readable space. It was deeper than he had guessed. Two seconds late, he pivoted and executed a wobbly turn-and-go, his balance deserting him, his glove and bare hand extended. He did not know where the ball was. He felt, rather than saw, it hit the tip of his glove and carom off his right shoulder. He felt it rolling down his back toward the ground, and his glove and bare hand swung around behind him and formed a cradle into which the ball settled. Astounded, he held the pose for a five-count to be sure of the catch as his teammates roared and raced to him, Rabbit standing fruitlessly at home plate and Doc at first shaking his head.

"Out!" the umpire called. "Ball game!"

After the hugging and back-pounding and high-fiving, after the rejoicing and the expressions of incredulity ("I've never seen anything like it, Wayne! How did you think of that?"), after the exchange of handshakes with the Hot Shots and the presentation of the championship trophy by Mary Bright, which Larry accepted in memory of Tommy, after they had all handed their phones to Bernice and Margie and Gloria and posed for team pictures, after Darlene had shouted "Pool party at the Dahl house in Emerald Hills at five o'clock, ribs and pulled pork and a keg, bring your spouses and your swimming suits!", the old man lingered for a few minutes near the concession stand with Liz Ann.

"Coach, you were on fire today!"

"No, Liz Ann, I was chillaxed today. I was open, I was receptive, I was ready to engage. I felt part of something larger than myself, immersed in a great web of being. I wasn't trying to have my way by wrenching or forcing. I was not an artist manipulating my material, I simply employed it as it presented itself. I was not a warrior battling an enemy, I was simply responding to the vicissitudes of a game. I was not anxious. I was not concerned about myself or the perception that others might have of me. I felt grateful, not entitled. I let the game come to me. Angst does not, as Sartre would have it, arise from the very nature of our consciousness. It arises from clinging to our consciousness, to our self. Letting go of the self is angst's antidote. Letting go of the self frees us to fully experience ludic life."

"Wow, Coach, this is such an unexpected transformation! You know I love and respect you, but I have to ask: aren't you mucking about for an undigested oat in a pile of horseshit? This language is so not you. Pronouns that disagree in number? Split infinitives? Paradoxes? Gaining control by not seeking to gain control? Given who you are, it just seems so devious. What brought all this about?"

"Two things. First, our beery discussion at 190 Sunset. As I was going all *sfumato,* immersed in the day and the scene and our conversation and our friendship, I began to sense the common sense in your remark about the paradoxical coexistence of fate and free will. As light can be both particle and wave, so life can be both determined and spontaneous. By opening our self"—

"There it is again!"

"—to mindfulness we can lift the veil of maya and enter the infinitely relaxed realm of the infinite no-mind, the realm of the ludic, truly, neither in control nor out of control, simply attuned to affordances. And second, my own abysmal failure. After months of working to rewire my brain, my game was falling apart."

"And you didn't think that age had anything to do with that? With the waning, if you will, of strength and speed and agility?"

"Indeed I will! Thank you. But the problem was deeper than that. The problem was my disconnect—-"

"Disconnect? Don't you mean disconnection? Or disconnecting? Who *are* you?"

"I am a person at ease, transcending the moment by being in the moment. Before, my disconnect from the whole, my desperate efforts to master my fate, to captain my soul, to be invincible, prevented me from realizing, in the sense of making real, actualizing, my self. I was trying to impose my will upon the game. It wasn't happening. I was making too many errors in the field, too many bad swings at the plate. The games began to fill me with fear. I did not want to hit, I did not want the ball hit to me. The more I tried to concentrate, the more I choked. The more I played, the worse I got. I could not get in sync. I was early, I was late, I was pulling off the ball. If I stayed on the ball it was stiffly so, no wind, no snap, no follow-through. Dread tired, I had about decided to just get the season over with and then quit the game. I had about decided not to go to St. George. And then you and I met for beer, and in the course of our discussion I began to get these vague glimmers."

"Something came over you? You who does not believe that there *is* a something that can come over one?"

"Let's just say that an awareness occurred. Not a flash of insight, not satori, but a gradual dawning, a hazy autumnal aurora, a pragmatic acceptance of the exquisite fictional truth of the union of atman with Brahman, there being nothing else for me."

"So now you believe in the soul? And an oversoul? And transcendence? And atonement?"

"I believe in the soul as a construct of the brain that dies with the brain. I believe in the oversoul not as something supernal or ethereal but as a pulsing of infinitely intricately interrelated quanta that one can, through mindfulness, be not at one with but attuned to, in transcendent harmony with. I no longer crave success nor fear failure. I look for and accept whatever is available to me. I still practice—but mindfully. As we talked about basketball that afternoon, I so admired your courage, your heart, the way you and Brenda played with abandon and willed the Mavericks to come back and win that championship game, like Liberty leading the people, brandishing musket and flag, and as I so admire Darlene's refusal to yield as well—"

"She *is* special, isn't she? Talk about drinking life to the lees."

—"but I understood that my gray spirit quailed at pressure. I could not meet it head on. I had to sidle up, lean gently into it, recognize it for what it was, a construct of interrelated quanta, a solvable puzzle if the mind was not burdened with hope and fear. And that's when I slowly began to rewire not my brain but my mind, began to re-teach myself all those old Hindu-Buddhist-Taoist fictional truths. Ever since, I have been playing better, with patience and poise and self-forgiveness."

"Well, if today is any indication, not just better but great."

"Today was an aberration. I was absolutely in my bag and in the zone. Even my clumsy play on that final pop fly exemplified a serendipitous finding of affordances. I misread the depth and trajectory, I stumbled when I pivoted, I had no idea where I was or where the ball was, but I put up my hands just in case, and the ball found me, hit my glove and then my shoulder, I felt it rolling, and instinctively, going with the flow, swung my hands behind my back and accepted it. In the future there will no doubt be occasions of regression to the mean, but I am happy to say that in the past few weeks the mean has been steadily rising."

"So what's next? St. George?"

"Yes, in early October. I'm going with a team of 80-year-olds drawn from Seattle and Bellevue. I'll keep working out and we'll have some practices down in Federal Way."

Liz Ann hugged him. "Well, good luck, Coach. I'm still a little taken aback by your mucking about in horseshit—I think active will has more to do with success than passive acceptance—but I'm so happy that you feel you've found an answer that works for you. Ride it as long as you can. Enjoy your celebration at the Dahl house today and text me from St. George. I'll be dying to know how you do."

[Hm-*hmm*. Sylvia]

[I shiver again, Wayne, this time at your acceptance of the exquisite fictional truth that the more we are at ease, the more we are engaged. As Jack Foster spoke of the sculler at ease, operating at peak relaxed performance in the midst of intense effort, so we can speak of you in your second coming as the batter at ease, all intunition (nice invention, that), your center holding midst the passion of your swing. Wish I'd been in town to see you play! Dave]

[Wayne, so pleased to learn of your success. I, too, wish I could have seen the game. To think of all the games I watched you play in high school without really paying attention, just kind of caught up in the sociability of it all—which girls were sitting with whom, who was wearing what. I kind of agree with Liz Ann, though. Who is this "serenity now" guy? Where's that angst-ridden existentialist I used to know? You're not going to start attending one of those evangelical mega-churches, are you? Solveig]

13

The Sleepers

The Windhover

To Christ our Lord

I caught this morning morning's minion, kingdom of daylight's
   dauphin, dapple-dawn-drawn Falcon, in his riding
   Of the rolling level underneath him steady air, and striding
High there, how he rung upon the rein of a wimpling wing
In his ecstasy! then off, off forth on swing,
   As a skate's heel sweeps smooth on a bow-bend: the hurl and gliding
   Rebuffed the big wind. My heart in hiding
Stirred for a bird--the achieve of, the mastery of the thing!

Brute beauty and valour and act, oh, air, pride, plume, here
   Buckle! AND the fire that breaks from thee then, a billion
Times told lovelier, more dangerous, O my chevalier!

   No wonder of it: sheer plod makes plough down silion
Shine, and blue-bleak embers, ah my dear,
   Fall, gall themselves, and gash gold-vermilion.

Gerard Manley Hopkins

The intercom buzzed at 10:00 a.m. as, shoulders hunched, he was trying to compose on his desktop in the southwest corner of the great room on a cool, partly sunny late September day. High above the town, glancing now and then at seagulls cruising rooftops, he had on a hunch typed out "The Windhover" and was waiting uneasily for words to emerge. Grateful for the excuse to pause but nettled by the obligation to respond, he went to the intercom phone hanging on the wall by the front door.

"Yes?"

"Hi, Wayne! It's Solveig."

His heart thumped once and then skittered. Apparently, his dosage of Sotalol was not sufficiently powerful to preclude all atrial fibrillation. His fingers shook. His lungs spasmed.

"SOLveig?"

"Yes!"

"Please come UP."

He buzzed her in and opened his unit door. How was his hair? Was his shirt—a black cotton tee—wrinkled? He heard slow, heavy steps climbing, sensed a pause at the first landing, heard slow, heavy steps again, heard panting, sensed a pause at the second landing. When thudding resumed, he edged out onto his own landing and beamed down upon Solveig seven steps below as she labored up, supporting herself with a hand on the railing, her compact black leather purse dangling from her left shoulder on a long, thin strap. She beamed back, puffing, probably sweating. How stout she was! Not obese, exactly, but certainly a couple of clicks north of *zaftig*, a BMI of 29, probably, in contrast to Diane's lifelong athletic 20. She wore a black diaphanous thigh-length wrap and a white, scoop-necked long-sleeved tee offering an inch of cleavage, untucked over ankle-length black slacks. Her feet were broadly visible in black, rhinestone-studded sandals with a strap at the ankle and another at the base of the toes, which were painted magenta, hyperlinking to her hair. Her hair! Still auburn, chestnut, henna! Surely, these grayer days, she was having her roots done? Still pulled back from her broad forehead, secured above the ears with combs, and extending to the middle of her back. And perched atop it, a black beret. Slowly she climbed, shrugging and rolling her ice-blue eyes behind hexagonal horn rim glasses, coppery red and rutilant beneath the stairway skylight.

"Sherpa!" she gasped. "Oxygen!"

Her ascension at last complete, she extended her arms wide, as he did his, and they embraced and squeezed. He could feel her heart pounding against his, felt some moisture seeping through the back of her shirt and wrap, scented the jasmine perfume radiating from her overheated body.

"SOLveig, what a shOCK! WHAT are you DOing here? I MEAN in EDmonds?"

"I wanted to see you, get more directly involved in your story."

"My STOry?"

"Yes. *A How Pretty Town.* I wanted to see this brave new Edmonds that you write of."

"How LONG has it been since you were HERE?"

"Forty years. Since my parents sold their business and retired in '78 and moved to the Virgin Islands. Before that I was here a few times after I graduated from Whitman and moved to Manhattan to look for some sort of editorial work in the book business. In '65 I came back to marry my boss at Pendant Publishing, Walter Lippmann, at the Everett Golf and Country Club in front of my parents' golfing friends and some of my sorority sisters and a few EHS friends like Sylvia and Dorothy and Carolyn and Dave. I was disappointed that you never responded to my invitation. Then I was here in the '70s on a few occasions to visit my parents and let them have some time with my children, Oscar and Samantha." She smiled. "I did not come back for my second marriage. Or my third."

"Well, my God, you look wonderful! Just a filigree of wrinkles around your eyes and your mouth. A few short vertical creases above and below your lips. Where are the DITCHES? Crevices? Sunbursts?"

"It's not Botox, if that's what you're hinting. It's just an abundance of my own subcutaneous fat. Although I would not disdain Botox if I thought I needed it. But look at you! I think you and I have reversed weights since our high school days. How skinny you are! About 40 pounds less than the doughy Wayne I used to know."

"So come on in. Sit down. Cool off." He led her to the camel-colored leather couch that faced the town-sea-mountainscape. "Can I get you a glass of something? Sparkling water, cranapple juice, an IPA, some chardonnay?"

She slipped off her wrap and sat. "Some water would be fine."

"BRB. Oh, no, I did *not* just say that!"

Solveig laughed. "AAMOF, I *love* text language!" she called to him as he entered the kitchen. "There's much to be said for condensation. Not that I don't love your prose style. DGMW!"

"YJMTU!" he called back, his head in the refrigerator.

"YGM!"

He returned with two tumblers of un-iced coppery gold liquid. "In honor of the occasion, how about some ginger beer?"

She smiled. "Are you referencing my hair?"

"Yes. An homage to the prettiest hair at EHS."

He clinked her glass and sat next to her, side-saddle, right leg crossed over left. They sipped and gazed at each other over the rims of the tumblers. He sensed the Sotalol beginning to brake his runaway heart. He noticed tiny random flecks of orange in her horn rims. Eventually Solveig glanced outward.

"Wayne, this view is just gorgeous! The little town could not be lovelier today. Wearing like a garment the beauty of the morning."

"The ships and shops and condos all bright and glittering, steeped for the moment in our peekabooing sun? For a long time now this room has been for me a fine prospect from which to recollect emotion in tranquility. A tranquility which I do not feel at the moment, BTW. But soft, I pray me, no more! I do feel lucky that Diane and I were able to afford this place on our middle-class incomes in 1985. Today it would cost five times what we paid for it."

They sipped. Solveig's jowls jiggled when she swallowed. "I like the ginger. The piquant woodiness."

"So when did you get in? How long are you staying? *Where* are you staying?"

"I arrived yesterday. Ubered out from SeaTac. I'm at the Harbor Square Best Western for a week. Sylvia has been my contact. Did Happy Hour with her at Salt and Iron. Vodka martinis and steak salad. Edmonds fooding has certainly changed since the heyday of Brownie's Cafe! She drove me up here this morning."

"And you're here to get more involved in my story?

"Yes. Is that it on the computer screen over there?"

"Yes. But what does getting involved even mean?"

"It means that I want to stimulate you and your thinking, your truing and skewing, and use you to do a little of that for myself. At this age I think we need each other. I kind of feel like Emily returning from the dead to Grover's Corners." She patted his free hand with hers.

He flinched with pleasure.

"There are so many things to share. I was hoping we could take some walks and have some talks. I'm a little jealous of Sylvia and Liz Ann."

"Well, sure, we can do that. I'd *love* to do that. You have the energy? You want to start now?"

"I have the energy for short walks. Not the full Gourmand Way or Ecclesiastical Way experience all at once, but perhaps a neighborhood at a time."

"Sure. Today's the Saturday Market. We could drive up past your old house on Walnut and park on 6th by the Christian Science church near Lumsden's old place and visit the Market, then see what you're up for after that. There are so many places I'd like to show or see anew with you."

"Good. Let me just use the bathroom first."

"Go down the hallway, through the bedroom, and use mine. You can see the ferry docking from the toilet."

"So I've read!" She handed him her empty glass and heaved herself up.

He rinsed the glasses in the kitchen sink and trailed her to his bedroom to get ready. His jeans were okay. He kicked off his slippers and laced up the two-tone black and silver Under Armour basketball high tops that he had bought online when he decided to enter the shooting contests at St. George. He heard the toilet flush. He pulled the tee shirt off, tossed it into the hamper, and lifted his clean blue-and-white checked short-sleeve shirt from its closet hanger. The bathroom door opened, and Solveig came out.

Shirtless, he tried with minimal success to roll his shoulders back, straighten his spine, suck in the half-inch ripple of flab that hung over the waistband of his 32-inch jeans.

"Well," she said, "quite an experience! Up too high to have Toms peeping at me, me peeping at them instead while I peed. I could see cars and pedestrians streaming northward on 5th. They're heading to the Market? I felt like I was hovering invisibly over the grandeur of the town, Holy Ghost-like brooding over the bent world—with warm breasts, if not bright wings!"

He laughed, dawdling a few seconds before putting on the shirt.

"You know, you're not exactly swole, but for a skinny guy, you've got some muscles. Tupac abs, training bra pecs, unleavened dinner roll bis. Your workouts are doing you good. Wayne Manley Adams! The windhoverer."

"Well, Hopkins *is* one of my favorite poets."

"Mine, too. And I'm thinking, in keeping with a theme of yours, that Hopkins' prosody, his sprung rhythm, is perhaps his unconscious intunition of quantum mechanics. His unpatterned variety of stressed and unstressed syllables is a kind of quantum entanglement that heightens the import of words put together in the quirky, quarky process of composition. 'In his riding of the rolling level underneath him steady air' is just so lovely, bits of language separately sprung and then strung together, staccato blending into lilting legato, syntactic rhythm turning diction photo-electric.

And ee cummings, too, now that I think about it! Quirky syntactic structures—'pretty how town,' 'up so floating many bells down,' 'down they forgot as up they grew'—casting words in a new light. Producing a kind of Higgs field through which words pass and gain mass and meaning."

"Ah, so this is why you came back—to enrich my thinking."

"Yes. But I also want to see, and help you to see, this town. So why don't you button up your shirt and we'll go?" She pinched some fabric and leaned forward to look at it. "That's the shirt you were wearing when you had a beer with Liz Ann, isn't it?"

"Yes."

He buttoned up and grabbed a navy blue UW baseball cap. He filled pockets with wallet, phone, and keys. "All set. I've got a catheter in the glove box of my car if I need it."

"Where you used to keep the condoms!"

They returned to the great room, where he saved his work and logged out.

"I have such a fear of forgetting to Save or of hitting a wrong button and erasing everything. Or of some invasive crooked worm gnawing at my computer's brains. Or of incurring a power surge that my suppressor fails to suppress."

"You don't make a hard copy as you go?"

"No."

"I would advise you to do that."

"Yeah, I'm sure you're right."

From the coat closet the old man selected a powder blue vest, "Tennis Championship Monte Vista 2009" embroidered in gold on its left breast, memento of the final time he and Diane had won together, she flying around the court to return difficult shots and give him a chance to score points on volleys at the net. Solveig slipped her wrap on and they stepped out to the landing. "Going down is sure to be easier on my heart and lungs, but I still need to be careful because of my arthritic knees, so I'm going to cling to the handrail."

They descended slowly, side by side. His balance was as

precarious as hers, but he was ready to grab her if need be. Coming out of the parking garage, he stopped the Santa Fe at the sidewalk for pedestrians passing, then nosed his way into traffic. "Morning Edition" had just concluded on KNKX, the NPR station, and Marian McPartland's "Somewhere (There's A Place For Us)" was playing on the mid-day jazz segment.

"That was one of Diane's favorites," the old man said.

"I know."

He drove to Walnut and turned right. Halfway up the block, choked with condos that had replaced single-family ramblers on wide, grassy lots, he pointed and said, "I lived right about there when I was a freshman at EHS."

"I know. I used to think about you now and then."

"Really? I did not know that."

They passed a parked truck the color of honey mustard whose driver was carrying bags of frozen food toward a condo entry.

"Wayne, look! We're taking Schwan's Way!"

He smiled.

"And look at what's become of my family's old place," she said when they reached 6th. "Our blocky old Cape Cod with the base-ment that my dad ran his plumbing business out of has become a multi-level with picture windows facing the Sound—or the Sea, I guess it's called now—and a wide cedar deck that runs the length of the house. Actually, I have to admit, it looks better. I don't miss the way it was, but in a sense I miss the way it is now. I mean, it might be good to live there."

"Why don't you come back?"

"I'm married, Wayne."

"Oh, right. Well, let's just crawl through this area, running from 6th to 7th and Walnut to Maple. It was called Cedar Valley back when my grandfather was a young man."

"What's it called today?"

"Nothing that I know of."

"I think in your story you should call it the Lower East Side, and then the area from 7th to 9th and from Pine to Bell, with all those big houses cantilevering their way up the hill, would be the Upper East Side."

"So that would make the area between 3rd and Sunset, from Main to Caspar, the Upper West Side? And between the beach and Highway 104, from the Dog Park to Main, would be the Lower West Side?"

"Exactly."

"Actually, I do often conceive of the Bowl as Manhattan, with scattered outer boroughs like Firdale and Five Corners and Perrinville and the International District comprising the rest of the city."

"I know you do. But what's special about the Bowl, as opposed to Manhattan, is that it remains scaled for humans. You can see the sky and, except near some of the newer condo developments, you don't feel cramped. How quiet it is right here! The Lower East Side is really a step back in time. It's almost the way it was when my family lived here in the late '40s and early '50s. Local traffic only, spacious yards. Houses still unpretentious, upgraded but modestly so, cedar-sided bungalows with composition shingles on the roof. A sprinkling of two-story places with dormers but, because of very sensible zoning restrictions, no McMansions. And look at this on the right—two really dumpy tiny ramblers with rotting roofs and siding! They must date back to the '30s. Amazing that they haven't been bought up and torn down and redeveloped. Sure, there's no view, but still this *is* the Bowl, and it would be a nice neighborhood for kids to grow up in. It was for me!"

They turned left at 7th. "Look, the alley's still here between Walnut and Alder! Gravel with a deep grassy median because it's so little used. Still perfect for playing hide-and-seek or kick-the-can."

They turned on Alder and drove back to 6th. "When I was four," the old man said, "I used to live right there on the west side of 6th, between a patch of woods on the south and Claudia Ward on the north."

"I know, although I wasn't here yet. We left Ballard and moved to Edmonds in 1946, when you were living on Maple Street. Claudia and I were friends in grade school. We never played—or urinated!—in the woods, but we could busy ourselves with dolls and dollhouses for hours. And look! I can't believe that her simple little old place with the hip roof and the white, horizontal cedar siding is still there. And that white picket fence! And the vegetable garden! This isn't exactly my 'How young Mama looks' moment, but it is agreeably touching. I'm so glad I came back."

"Me too."

He turned right, crossed Maple, and parked opposite the church.

"The old Lumsden place hasn't changed either," she said. "Same ramshackle rambler, same white cedar-plank fence."

"Remember Lenny? The butcher at Safeway?"

"Of course. He and my dad used to march for the American Legion, Frank Freese Post 66, in the 4th of July parades, before we moved out to Talbot."

They extricated themselves from the car, the old man zipped up his vest, and they walked across Dayton. The old man turned, hesitated, then pointed his key fob at the Santa Fe and locked it remotely.

"The Lower East Side a pretty rough neighborhood?" Solveig said. "Don't want anyone to steal your catheter?"

"My bat bag, containing my precious old Mikan Freak, my brand new DeMarini Nihilist, my Wilson A700 glove, and my Under Armour high-top softball shoes, is in the cargo area. We get very few car prowls in the Bowl, but I don't want to take a chance. Rather than entice any freebooting kids passing by, I'll risk a charge of xenophobia."

"There's actually a bat called the Nihilist? Who's the CEO of that company? Art Schopenhauer?"

"Yes, there is. It sells for $345 at so-called Cheapbats.com, but naturally I had to have it when I heard about it. Not sure who the CEO is. Fred Nietzsche, possibly."

They passed the Legion Hall. "Hasn't changed," Solveig said. "Same simple barnlike building it was when your dad was playing for New Year's Eve dances and my parents were out on the floor jitterbugging and fox-trotting."

They stopped at Main. Foot traffic had increased. Pedestrians passed on both sides of them.

"Remember here on the corner there was a fast-food drive-in called Day's? Later changed hands and became Dee's?"

"No, I think that happened in the '60s, after I left."

"Yeah, you're right. Diane and I used to go there for ice cream cones."

They waited for a pair of bike riders in helmets and blue and yellow spandex to zip by, then crossed to the west side of 6th.

"Remember the old Shopping Cart grocery store with the huge parking lot on this corner? Built by Ernie Vollan and Claude Savage? Later became Thriftway? It's now going to become—"

"Main Street Commons! The original building plus an Old World Plaza in a new Warehouse Style building. Touted in *My Edmonds News* as a refuge from urban distractions (*sic!*). Going to have an Artists' Alley, an outdoor stage, a family-friendly arcade and roller bowl, and restaurant space for healthy food—vegan spots, sushi spots, juice bars. Sure, why not? I know that you like to call the center of the commercial area Midtown, with the hub at the 5th and Main roundabout being Times Square, but this whole section from 6th down to 3rd and from Walnut to Main, I'm thinking, with its condos and galleries and art supply stores and restaurants and specialty shops, you could call, hinting at a brave new world, SoMa, and the section between 6th and 3rd and Bell and Daley, less commercial and more residential, NoMa. And the Arts Corridor that the Mayor talks about establishing, on 4th from Main to the Edmonds Center for the Arts at Daley, could be Greenwich Village."

He pulled out his phone and tapped. "Noted," he said.

They crossed Main and entered NoMa. On the corner stood a two-story house with a broad veranda and a prominent gable-roofed dormer and matching mini-gable protecting the front door, built years before the old man and Solveig were born.

"Doc Kretzler's old place!" Solveig said. "My family used to go to him. He kept his office in his home. Newly painted creamy yellow. Somebody has made it shine! New white picket fence, arched trellis at the gate, flower beds along the perimeter lush with blooming yellow and copper gladiolas. When I visualize '50s Edmonds, this image is one of the first to pop into my mind. There's something special about those Craftsman elements. Stalwart, substantial. Upright. A symbol of virtue, success, prosperity."

At Bell they encountered a vehicular barricade demarking the Market. To the right, a half-block north on 6th, lay the vacant Civic Field, barren of its old grandstand.

"Ah, the old, rude high school athletic fields and the Field House where we had second grade with Mrs. Hill, soon to be Olmsteded and become the Bowl's Central Park. Which of course would make 7th Park Avenue."

They turned west on Bell.

"Behold the Market," the old man said, gesturing to a canoply, extending the length of the block and then angling from 5th to Main, of open-sided tents erected on slender metal poles by nomadic artisan-merchants—farmers and gardeners and fishers and woodturners and silversmiths and jewelers and ceramicists and quilters and weavers and soapmakers—to mark their temporary turf and protect tables laden with boxes and trays of flowers and fruits and vegetables and meat and eggs and baked goods and confections and snacks and portable racks and trees of hanging artifacts. "Our little *agora*."

"It's charming," Solveig said.

"Uh-oh. Do I detect condescension?"

"Not necessarily. I urge you to refrain from prebuttal. Let's not either of us rush to judgment. Let's just wander and observe. Then find a place to sit down and reflect, because in another 15 minutes I am definitely going to need a rest."

They snailed their way through or around clusters of attentive shoppers, who were reading signs, pointing, touching, asking questions, deliberating, making choices, handing over cash or credit cards, smiling, munching something, or tucking purchases into their own reusable straw baskets or cloth shopping bags. As they neared Main, they came upon a jazz quartet of white teenage males in black fedoras launching the moody opening chorus of "Blue Monk."

"Break time," the old man said. "Let's stop right now and go sit on the Library steps that I skipped up and down so many times in my youth. I have got to hear this song."

"A good choice," Solveig said. "I love that warm old Carnegie building. We could almost think of it as the Edmonds truncated version of a brownstone. And too bad Monk Monken isn't here for some classic Monk bebop."

"He wouldn't be interested. He liked a little Glenn Miller and Benny Goodman, but 'modern' jazz bored him. Zee and I couldn't even get him to listen to Duke Ellington."

The thin kid on alto sax began soloing, bass and drums providing rhythmic ballast, trumpeter standing by, the absence of a piano visible and audible, Monk without Monk, no idiosyncratically jagged, angular, resounding, flatted, deliciously sour comping chords and tart punctuating single notes, but the foray a pleasure nonetheless, noodling runs, a soaring ascent to the top of a roller coaster and a precipitous drop into low register followed by a bit of plangent whimpering, then the drummer, à la Art Blakey, with a rolling flourish wiped the screen like a transition in a '30s Hollywood movie, and the old man irised in on the trumpeter who took the air with a crystalline restatement of the melody followed by a long run of wailing notes that ended in an epistrophe of sharp seagull cries before the other three rejoined him in a flatted reprise of the main chorus.

The old man's vigorous applause induced a few bystanders, and Solveig, to clap politely. He stood, extracted his wallet, fished a five from it, strode over to the saxophonist's open instrument case and tossed in the bill, the four nodding to him in appreciation as they began to play "Round Midnight."

"That was quite nice," Solveig said as he returned to sit beside her. "Tasty in the brackish, dry, mordant, almost fecal way that blue cheese and gorgonzola are."

"'Blue Monk,' blue cheese, the blues—yes! My kind of music. The minor key is the key of entropy. It's the poignant key of life. I'm pleased to see these young guys caring about classic bop. Like you and me, I doubt that it has much of a future, but it was lovely while it lasted."

"Don't be too sure of its demise. Esperanza Spalding and lots of other young musicians are playing Manhattan clubs all the time and evolving the form with fusions and infusions, according to what I hear. Bop-rooted jazz lives on. And so do you and I, for the moment. But what are we to make of this crowded Market? Who are the people coming here? They're not all Bowlers, are they?"

"Assuredly not. Many are from the outer boroughs of Edmonds or from Lynnwood, Shoreline, Woodway Park, Brier, Mountlake Terrace. Some even ride the ferry over from Kingston. But they are Bowl lovers. They delight in coming here."

"As we look around, certainly we can say that they are mostly white, although back on Bell we did see a handful of Asians and right over there, lining up for some crab rangoon won tons, is an African American couple. There are a few teenagers, a sparser few like you and me from the Silent Generation, a fair number of Millennials pushing strollers or holding the hands of toddlers, lots of Gen Xers, and a scattering of Boomers, more women than men but still many couples exploring together, to all appearances settled, comfortable, prosperous, self-assured folks, polite, considerate to each other and the merchants, no jostling or edging in, calmly enjoying the scene, never making a scene, not needing to *be* seen, not wanting to stand out, call attention to themselves, just wanting to be a part of, blend in, unhip, unchic in their bucket hats, floppy sunhats, tennis visors, ball caps, tucked in tees and blouses, crewneck sweaters, pullover sweatshirts sometimes pulled off and tied around their waists, Gore-Tex vests, poplin windbreakers, blue jeans, mom jeans, khakis, polyester slacks, cargo shorts, white tennis shoes, Rockports. Wardrobe by REI, Eddie Bauer, LL Bean, Nordstrom, Kohls. No pizzazz at all, except for that black couple, she in turned-up-cuff jeans with a multi-colored rope belt and a sewn-in matching thin rope running from thigh to knee on one leg, he in tight plus-four-length black jeans with long side zippers, long black socks, and silvery high tops very much like those Under Armours you're wearing."

"So the vibe is vapidity? Insipidity?"

"No, not exactly. You sense that the people are quietly excited to be here, turned on in their sedate way. There's a sense of community but not camaraderie or competition. They are here to enjoy the display, not to display themselves. Like Manhattan, the Bowl is a center, a hub, but it lacks Manhattan's edge, its swarming mix of races and ages and income levels, where the ethos is do unto others before they do unto you and the sartorial key to fitting in is not fitting in."

"It's also a far cry from the evening *passeggiatas* that Diane and I enjoyed observing in Milan, a range of ages parading, strolling, perhaps trolling, dressed to impress, greeting friends, gossiping."

"Yes. This is more like a secular religious celebration taking place in an open-air meme-plex. It produces a kind of *hygge,* a coziness of shared values. The Market is a safe space for the affluent and the liberal. The Sierra Club has a presence here, with its 'Save The Edmonds Marsh' banner. Another sign down by the intersection admonishes 'This is a Zero Waste Event/Please Use Our Recycle and Food Waste Bins.' People are not on the streets this morning to meet with or compete with their neighbors, nor are they here just to replenish their food supply or get a ceramic plate to hang on a wall. They're demonstrating their virtue, their piety, their belief in purposeful eating, in the nourishing and detectable, delectable, gustatory quality of pure, simple, wholesome, sustainable natural food produced on mini-farms in outlying valleys— the

Flying Tomato Farm, the Sky Valley Family Farm. Immaculate, pesticide-free, fresh-picked, vine-ripened fruits and vegetables grown in organically fertilized soils that are weeded by hand, home-made compotes and syrups, meat and dairy products untainted by antibiotics, fresh goat milk, eggs from free-range chickens and ducks, cuts from free-range chickens and humanely-raised pigs and lambs. They're here for Wilson Fish Market's local troll-caught fish and for gluten-free baked goods. For half an hour or so they are locavores, off the grid (although ready to jump back on at the ting of a text), paying nostalgic homage to an agrarian tradition, to '60s counterculture, to the artisanal, to capitalism writ small, to producers who labor with love and are not alienated from their products, to the environmental movement, to the greening of America. And they're seeking the ritualized sensory pleasure that the Market offers, bowing their heads to sniff astringent lilies and mums, lifting their heads to inhale the sweetish smoke from grills barbequing pork or to get a whiff of the metallic emanation from the hot oil in which caramel corn is sizzling and popping, delighting in the lurid colors crammed into a dizzying array of floral bouquets, fingering the fuzzy, doughnut-shaped peaches, the plump heirloom tomatoes, the glistening grainy blackberries, the red and golden beet goblets with their snaky umbilical-cord stems."

"So you're saying that we're spoiled? Smug? We're entitled, we're elitist, we're classist, we can afford to be environment-conscious and health-conscious and quality-conscious? Our quest for authenticity is inauthentic? We are contentedly playing our privilege card? Flaunting our taste for the fresh, the organic, the unusual, the wholesome? Didn't you say just a few minutes ago that the quiet Lower East Side is a great place to raise kids? Now you're saying that we have too much beauty, safety, comfort? We lack a salutary *frisson* of danger, surprise, shock? We need some panhandlers and muggers, we need some drunks pissing in the alleys or passing out in their own puke? We need con artists, guys running shell games, guys selling knock-off watches? In Lynnwood there are homeless people living in their cars on side streets or pushing shopping carts containing their entire estate down 196th while in the Bowl we deliberate over which kohlrabi might be the crispest? We need a grittier racial and ethnic mix of people, black rappers instead of white kids culture-appropriating black jazz or that bland flautist we had last week or that bluegrass banjo picker we'll have next week?"

"No, not exactly. The secular reverence is genuine. This new Edmonds truly is brave in its staunch support of progressive values. It puts on a splendid show that could not even have been imagined by our parents in the '50s. They had no concept of purposeful eating, of making political or moral or esthetic statements in their choice of aliment. It's just that...."

"It's a veneer?"

"Maybe so. Possibly there's a starker underlying reality. Possibly the Bowl is a place where superego tamps down restless id. There's a core of local patrons, sure, but I'm guessing that the Market is supported largely by wised-up outsiders. Probably most of the locals don't attend and possibly many either secretly resent or are indifferent to its principles. But enough about the Market. Shall we move along? Maybe find a place to get a bite?"

They walked a few steps south to Main and paused at Pelindaba Lavender. "The old brick Fourtner Building," the old man said. "It housed the post office and the Safeway and then Peggy Harris Gifts for so many years, and now it's a place for all things lavender, soothing, handcrafted items for personal care therapy and home decor, made from organically certified lavender produced on a San Juan Island farm, what the owners call a 'holistic and self-contained ecological adventure,' and for a women's clothing boutique called Sound Styles."

They strolled to the intersection and paused, looking up Main to the east.

"Oh, there's the new mural I've read about," Solveig said. "Let's take a look." They walked a few steps east past some pin oaks whose leaves were yellowing their way toward mocha, and gazed at, on the south side of the Fourtner, "A Mother's Love," 30 feet long and 12 feet high, a huge black and white mother Orca attended by a flight, a heavenly choir, of seagulls, tailing its cute young offspring on the surface of abstract blue and white waves. "It's so sweet, so charming! It's Disney, it's adorable! A romantic anthropomorphizing of nature. No *sturm*, no *drang*. I'm getting that *hygge* feeling again. I can hear Louis Armstrong singing 'What a Wonderful World.'"

"So you're saying that Edmonds and the Salish Sea are idealized here as safe spaces? That we're not edgy enough? That the town is full of art but most of it is bland? That we are *en garde* against the *avant garde*? That authentic, not ersatz, graffiti pulses with energy, rebelliousness, criticism, Kilroyan ululations? That the poetry readings at Cafe Louvre are not challenging or aggressive enough? That poems published in *My Edmonds News* by the Epic Poetry Group run heavily to nostalgia and 'observations'? You're wondering where are the experimental painters and writers? Where are the poetry slams? Where's our 'Howl' on the one hand, our 'Wasteland' on the other, our 'Idea of Order at Key West' on the third? You're thinking that everything here is sanitized? You're hard-hearted Hannah calling out the evil of banality? You're wondering where a guy can get a good lap dance in this town? Or where a girl can score some bud? Or where a TG can do a little vaping? You're thinking that this mural might as well be titled 'Helicoptering Nemo'? That the solicitous mother and innocent babe are at odds with the stark reality that is embodied in Hobbes's Leviathan or Melville's Moby Dick? That the mural is pretty much just a feel-good ad for the whale watch cruises that are available for a fee down at the harbor? That this is *so* Edmonds? No anarchic splashes of graffiti from anti-social taggers to be found anywhere—instead, authorized, subsidized, sublimated, domesticated street art expressing the town's idealized conception of its ethos?"

"Well, yes. But that doesn't mean that I don't love it. I'm in tune with its self-conception of its ethos, with the top-down direction from the super-ego that seems to rule here. But I still think the id needs to be heard from. Rather, will insist on being heard from."

He smiled. "Sing it, sister!"

She smiled back, tightly, and narrowed her eyes. "Wait a minute, have you been reverse Malcolming me, feigning ingenuousness, getting me to do all this unpacking, just to test my *bona fides*? You're *playing* me?"

"Ah, so, Macduff, but if so, Macduff, it's because I simply can't get enough of your talk of the town, your take on the town. When I hear you speak, I know I'm not dreaming. You corroborate me."

She widened her smile and relaxed her eyes. "Well, that's why I'm here."

He looked east and pointed. "Remember further up Main was Evans' Music Center, where my dad and I used to buy jazz records? "

"I do. That's where my parents bought the baby grand for our new house on Talbot."

"And then on the south side, where Epulo Bistro is now, was the old post office, after it migrated from the Fourtner Building? The Driftwood Theater moved into that site after a new post office was built at 2nd and Main. I appeared—'acted' would not be *le mot juste*— in a couple of plays there in '64 and '65—*The Waltz of the Toreadors* and *Nude with Violin*."

They edged their way across Main, wary of colliding with focused shoppers striding toward the Market.

"Ah, Starbucks. Might LaTasha be in there?"

"I doubt it. She only works the early shift. Gets off at 10:00."

"Might we bump into Liz Ann walking over from 4th on her way to work at the Museum?"

"I doubt it. Her shift doesn't start until 1:00."

They wandered south on 5th, pausing to look at the table of bargains displayed outside the doorway of the Edmonds Bookshop.

"I've always liked this little shop," the old man said. "Warm, tight, the air close. The old flooring creaks beneath the carpet when you walk. They have an impressive inventory for such a small space. Shelves and tables are really crammed together. You have to be careful not to bump butts with your fellow browsers when you move."

"Will *A How Pretty Town* lie in state on this table one day?"

"My remains on the remainder table?"

"Yes. Is that a consummation devoutly to be wished?"

He chagrinned. "Yes. It shouldn't matter to me now, because it won't matter to me then, but yes. I like to imagine the title catching the eye of a vacationing Adam Gopnik, *The New Yorker's* resident aphorist and elucidator of liberalism's thousand small sanities, who riffles through it, then turns to his daughter Olivia and observes that its sanities appear to be outnumbered by its inanities."

She smiled and helped herself to his arm, slipping her right inside his left, bicep to tricep, nudging him to the chivalric side of the walk. Her breast abutted his elbow. He began to tingle.

They crossed the alleyway, passed Engels' Tavern, and stopped in front of the Red Twig. Chattering patrons were brunching or lunching in the street-side courtyard.

"The last time I saw this place, it was still McKeever's Shell."

"We could eat here if you want."

"Fulfilling, as you used to with Diane, a Brousseauian social contract?"

"Uh-huh. But if you don't mind, I'd rather hit The Cheesemonger for a Beef and Blue sandwich. Your take on 'Blue Monk' has memed its way into my brain."

"Lead the way."

Drivers lined up three deep in all directions at Dayton's four-way stop waited patiently, all smiles, for the octogenarians to traverse the intersection's herringboned crosswalk of maroon brick pavers just a shade darker than Solveig's hair.

"I think they love us," Solveig said. "We *are* cute, aren't we? Fading *flâneurs*."

"Sadly, we are. I mean, yes, we are, and that is sad. I still cannot allow myself to use 'sadly' or 'hopefully' as a sentence modifier. In any case, I don't like being condescended to by younger generations as I devolve."

"You'd rather they honk irritably to tell us that we're too old and slow to be in the street anymore?"

"Well, no."

They reached the sidewalk. The cars began to move.

"So," Solveig said, "the old home of Yost's Suburban Transportation System Bus Garage and the Edmonds Motor Company."

"Yes. Zee and I used to stop in to buy Coke stubbies for a nickel from the vending machine in the passengers' waiting room. And then Ward Phillips, EHS class of '58—remember him?"—

"I do."

—"bought the complex in the '70s and turned it into a little two-story mall that he called Old Milltown, giving the storefronts an early 20th century look. Our destination is just ahead, in one of the old service bays."

They wound among sizeable planters filled with flowers in Hazel Miller Plaza, an oasis that fronted the shops, entered The Cheesemonger, studied the hand-written menu on the whiteboard above the counter, the old man leaning as far forward as he could to lessen the blurriness of the letters, ordered, the Beef and Blue for him, the Speck-tacular for her, paid separately, poured themselves glasses of water from an urn, and took a corner table.

"So, where were we?" the old man said.

"Examining the virtues, the progressive pieties, of the Bowl. It is in so many ways a shining city at the base of a hill. Shall we count those ways?"

"Okay. I'll start by saying that Edmonds was the first to participate in the statewide Sustainable Cities Partnership, the City Council has adopted a Climate Change Goals project to reduce the local output of greenhouse gases, the town holds frequent Styrofoam Recycling Events, as of 2020 it will no longer allow single-use Styrofoam or plastic cutlery and straws in eateries or at community sponsored events, and it's the first in the state to achieve 100% renewable energy for city buildings."

"Being an inveterate reader of *The Beacon* and *My Edmonds News* online, I can add (broad, Ada-like, 'a' there, vain Wayne—this *is* fun!) that The Arbor Day Foundation has named Edmonds a Tree City USA in recognition of its commitment to effective urban forest management."

"There exists an Edmonds Diversity Commission promoting 'diversity, equity, and inclusion'; it sponsored a Diversity Film Series at the Edmonds Theater in 2017-18, and in 2018 paraded a 4th of July banner reading 'Accept Respect Celebrate Diversity in Edmonds.'"

"We'll circle back to that," Solveig said. "On a related note, in 2017 the Council approved changing Columbus Day to Indigenous Peoples' Day to recognize that, while the European colonization of North America did lead to the development of a unique, diverse, and complex civilization, it also led to the suppression, forced assimilation, and genocide of indigenous peoples and their cultures."

"The Pride of Edmonds celebrates Pride Month with an LGBQT picnic at Hickman Park, and the Cascade Art Museum has scheduled an exhibit of work by gay and lesbian artists to show how their work has influenced the cultural identity of the Northwest."

"The Council has invested over a million dollars to clean up the salty Edmonds marsh, daylight Willow Creek, and restore salmon habitat." She gulped some water. "Needed that!"

He sipped from his glass in empathy. "It also passed a bill requiring gun owners to store firearms securely; however, when the bill was challenged by some residents, the State Supreme Court ruled that the Council had exceeded its authority."

"Circling back now, the Council has designated Edmonds a Safe City, and 600 gathered at Westgate in 2018 to protest Trump's zero tolerance policy for immigration law enforcement, chanting 'No hate, no fear, immigrants are welcome here.' Also in 2018 an Edmonds Bakery Valentine cookie with the message 'Build the Wall,' said by the owner to have been facetiously intended, was criticized by some locals as divisive, and the owners of the very Cheesemonger whose sandwiches our waitperson is now bringing us responded by creating some 'Build Love' cookies."

"Here you go," said the smiling middle-aged woman, setting down two baskets and two bags of popped corn. "Enjoy!"

With alacrity the old man two-handed half of his concoction—layers of thinly sliced roast beef and crumbles of blue cheese strewn with caramelized onions and bound with garlic mayo and dalmatia fig jam on grilled whole wheat—and Solveig did the same with her smoked prosciutto, laura chenel, fresh chevre, arugula, and dalmatia fig jam on grilled ciabatta.

"Mmm, so good," she moaned at first bite. "I walked up quite an appetite this morning."

"Love the fig jam," the old man said. "The dark sweetness atop the tangy cheese—an overtone but not an override. By the way, the name of your sandwich takes me back to the '40s and a silly song my uncle Ned used to sing: 'Oh once there was a Dutchman whose name was Johnny Burbeck, he used to deal in sausages and sauerkraut and speck.' How *is* the speck?"

"Tender, smoky, salty, spicy, fatty, rich. Love it."

"And may I say I also love having a companion?"

"In the literal sense of one you are sharing bread with?"

"Exactly. But back to our task. A Housing Strategy Task Force was appointed by the Mayor in 2017 to develop strategies to reduce homelessness and develop housing tailored to the specific needs of the community. Too few people live in too-big spaces, it was said."

"The State Arts Commission named Edmonds the state's first Creative District in recognition of the role arts and culture play in the town's economy, attracting and retaining a variety of creative-sector businesses—art museums and galleries and studios, theaters and music and dance venues."

"And the town is developing a 4th Avenue Cultural Corridor, which you have already given the sobriquet Greenwich Village, organizes monthly Art Walks and Wine Walks, and helps fund the many murals intended to capture (though they may also reveal inadvertently) the soul of Edmonds."

"The Council is proactively working to establish facilities to accommodate new wireless 5G technology."

"Edmonds is rated Snohomish County's Most Fiscally Healthy City, based on credit scores, and ranks 22nd in the state."

"And there's an abundance of parks, some of which have seamless, latex-free rubber surfaces accessible to all people, including those with disabilities."

The old man flashed 13 fingers at her.

"What's that— our gang sign?"

"No, that's 13 ways of looking at our backburb!" He tipped the bill of his cap to her. She lifted her chapeau to him. "Our little town fairly shines with virtue. It is so very much in tune with the Green New Deal. AOC might feel at home here. What could possibly be wrong with the town's official pieties?"

"What could be wrong, Mloclam, is that they are not truly representative. I absolutely love the pieties, but it's quite likely that many residents strongly oppose, or are at best lukewarm toward, progressive points of view. I have read the campaign platforms of Charlotte, Gary, and Monk in their race for Position 8, and I am guessing, based on events since the 2016 presidential campaign, that for every vote for Charlotte's AOC or Gary's Biden, there'll be one for Monk's Trump. I suspect that many sense and fear the presence of a Deep Town. I suspect that many feel that the city is moving too aggressively—and expensively— toward virtue."

"Are you virtue-shaming us?"

"No, but I am implying that virtue is in the eye of the beholder and that every view deserves to be expressed."

"*Tu quoque*, Solveig? Are you afflicted with the modern Trumpian defenses of bothsidesism and whataboutism and *argumentums ad populum* and *ad hominem*? Have you abandoned Aristotle and the Law of the Excluded Middle? Surely both sides can't be right."

"I'm just saying that probably a fair number of people want everything to just slow down."

"And by 'just slow down' they really mean 'stop!' They don't want the Bowl to change because change means imposing on their privilege. 'I've got mine, Jack, and I want to preserve it and the old Edmonds in amber.' "

"Perhaps they doubt whether, in forcing density upon the Bowl by the artificial means of regulations and subsidies, it will be possible to maintain the town's Hallmark movie *milieu* , its quaint charm."

"What they want to maintain is their sense of entitlement, that discriminating charm of the bourgeoisie. They fear an invasion of poorer, less-well-educated people (and I think you can add, though few will say it, non-white people) who won't love the quiet, clean, safe town the way they do."

"But it's also not a crime to look out for one's own self-interest or to fear change. Should there not be more debate? Not only would that be fairer, but taking seriously the concerns of the reactionary side might allay animosity."

"Or is calling for more debate just another way of stalling? Such comments tend to come from Boomers and Karens who grew up absurd, at least according to Paul Goodman, and are growing old absurd, spiritually empty, ideal-less, the products of the ethos of unfettered capitalism."

"Maybe so, my good man, and we may find it appalling, but surely there is a significant number of them. If 600 showed up to demonstrate against exclusionary immigration policies, thousands more locals did not. Of those who showed up, probably many were not Bowlers or even Edmonds residents. Perhaps a fair number of Bowlers actually want Trump to build his wall. Probably many see the historic displacement of indigenous peoples as a necessary evil. Probably many believe in assimilation, do not value diversity for its own sake, oppose the gun storage law as an invasion of privacy and an unlawful restriction of a constitutional right, oppose or at least don't wish to promote gay marriage, and don't care a feather or a dab of fig jam for the arts. Because they aren't walking around with 'MEGA' caps on their heads or 'Brackxit' buttons on their lapels, there's a tendency to think that people with an antipathy toward bigger, more powerful governments don't exist in this town."

"You're certainly right about their being a dearth of public conservative speech. In my walks around town I have seen only virtue-signaling signs in windows. In separate condos on 4th: 'LOVE' and 'Stop Hate Together.' In the C'est La Vie store on 5th: 'We Welcome All Races, Religions, Countries of Origin, Sexual Orientations, Genders. We Stand With You. You're Safe Here.' In a house on Main across from our old grade school: 'Take Action To Elect A Democratic Congress.'"

"But that's probably because the antis don't dare to broadcast a contrary opinion. They've been cowed by this new guilted age we're living in. Although we might not like their opinions, I think it's wrong to stifle them. Draw them out. Hear them out. Let id go. Repression is oppression."

The old man smiled widely, opened his arms widely. "Yes, yes, Macduff, whilom lover, star of my lucid dreams, corroborator, accreditor, I beg to agree. O, Edmonds, Edmonds! Your leaders suffer from motivation attribution asymmetry. They assume that their ideology is based on love and goodness, whereas that of their critics is based on hate and selfishness. Let a hundred flowers bloom— and after they do, don't foment a Cultural Revolution if you happen not to like the color or scent of the blossoms."

They smiled at each other. They looked into each other's eyes. They picked up their napkins, dabbed at their mouths, scrubbed grease from their fingers. Each took a fistful from their popcorn bags and crunched meaty kernels. The old man fetched a water pitcher and refilled their glasses. Each chugged, breathed, chugged again. Solveig's phone pinged in her purse. She looked in its direction and shrugged. He nodded.

"It's from Sylvia! She wants to know how it's going. What should I say?"

"Swimmingly?"

"'Swimmingly' it is," she said, tapping her reply. "All right, then! We've spent a good hour here. The sandwiches were delicious, and we got so much done. What's next? What I've been dreading? Time to put our *pieds* à *terre*?"

"Yes, let's just slowly work our way back to the car and then guiltily add to earth's superfluity of greenhouse gases by taking the Adams automotive tour of the Bowl, featuring arboreal and architectural highlights."

She doffed her beret, patted her hair, donned it again, and they got up and retraced their steps to Dayton and turned right. Solveig eyed the climb to 6th and said, "'Work' is right! If only I could cube my enthusiasm!" They plodded about forty yards and stopped in front of the Salish Sea Brewery, their attention drawn by the bright white Italian columns of the Masonic Temple across the street.

"Here's one highlight, no doubt," Solveig said. " And a real lodestone for me in my high school days. Repainted a gray-blue with white trim on the A-shaped roofline and the buttresses supporting the eave, freshened up, but otherwise the same as in the '50s."

"Yes, an erratic in the geological sense of not being native to the area in which it rests, those iconic columns inviting us to enter the fantasyland of the teen Canteen. Rock 'n' roll and ballads. 'Dream.' The moon never beams without bringing me dreams of the beautiful Solveig, *belle-lit*. I was a child and you were a child in this kingdom by the sea. You were my Kim Novak, dancing with Dickie. Somehow there I got the idea that you could be mine."

"And so I became."

"But only for a year."

She took his hand—how touchingly teen-age that felt. He assayed a single squeeze, she reciprocated, and they trudged up the hill, she on the chivalric side this time, past a succession of condos that had superseded '30s Craftsman houses and the O.C. Kelly Fuel wood and coal yard. By the time they reached the car, Solveig was panting and sweating again.

"Now you can relax," the old man said. "We'll drive around the Bowl the way we did in my '49 Ford when we were killing time, waiting for dark so we could park, only now we are more interested in Bowl exotica than in our own erotica. Let's start with the Upper Eastside."

He drove up Dayton, past the Anderson Center, to 8th, turned left, went to the intersection with Main. "Behold the elm."

The tree, in the yard of a two-story house on the northwest corner, was at least 60 feet tall, its dark-leaved branches dominating the yard and sprawling in high arcs from its forked trunk over the sidewalk and half of the street.

"Goodwin's old place! I never really noticed that tree when I was a kid. It must be nearly a hundred years old now. What an elegiac beauty! Creating a shady bower, a shrine to the Edmonds of our youth."

"It's one of *my* lodestones. Now on to the next one."

He coasted down Main to 4th, turned left, crossed Dayton, stopped at the power substation, and pointed at the gangly tree shrouding its gate. "The deodar cedar."

"Very pretty. Makes a good screen with all those lateral branches drooping and spreading. Love the long needles, the silvery-green color, the gray scaly bark, the pale green cones like Christmas lights. Not sure I ever noticed it when I lived here and went to visit Sylvia."

"Deodars are naturally pyramid-shaped and can grow to 50 feet, but the city keeps this one topped so as not to interfere with residential views. We have here another symbol of longevity, even eternity, and peace and holiness for some. So, ready for one more?"

"Wayne, this is so Woody Allen! I feel like Mariel Hemingway or Diane Keaton. *Ou comme Odette, avec Monsieur Swann.* If only we could get a carriage ride."

"No carriages available in the Bowl—but we could rent a Segway."

"No, thanks. I don't trust my balance for that."

"Me either."

He turned on Walnut, went to 3rd, headed north, crossed Main, and parked next to Claire's Restaurant.

"Oh, yes, of course, the horse-chestnut, *le marron*!" Solveig said, pointing to the tree across the street towering at least 100 feet, stout, pendulous, broad-leaved branches culminating in a domed crown. "Now this one I do remember. I used to see it all the time when I went to Patty's house. We would gather the nuts when they dropped in the fall. They were inedible but we polished them and our mothers used them in arrangements of fall leaves and flowers."

"For me it's a nondigital calendar that I watch year-round from my condo. Gold-green, then seaweed green, then maize, like now, then bare ruined choirs. Solveig, could I prevail upon you to go stand next to the tree's trunk for a Facebook picture?'

"Facebook? I unfriended myself from FB years ago. Instagram too, even though they helped me keep tabs on Oscar and Samantha and my grandchildren. But, if you really want to document my re-appearance in town...."

They got out of the car. The old man stood on the sidewalk and prepped his phone. Solveig waited for a wide break in the traffic, then slowly, brazenly, jaywalked across. She posed, mouth closed, staring the camera down, and he took two vertical shots, getting in all but the crown of the tree.

"Thank you," he called, waving, then selected a shot, tapped "Under the spreading chestnut tree the rufous Solveig stands," and posted.

After waiting a minute at the curb for the traffic to clear, she jaywalked back and they re-entered the Santa Fe.

"All right, we've done my favorite carbon-sequestering trees. Now let's pay our respects to the buildings that stand out to me. One, unfortunately, no longer exists: the original Hughes Memorial Methodist Church."

"I can still visualize it, though, its height and breadth commanding attention, its unapologetic mission-style design—terra cotta roof tiles, Roman arches, ecru stucco walls, belfries, stained glass— like something transplanted from the Old World to lend stature to our little town in the '40s and'50s."

"Then there's its first cousin, the two-story Beeson Building, built in the early 1900s, also with its ecru stucco, Roman arches, terra cotta tiles on the roof and the awning over the first floor shops, and deep red eyebrow awnings over the west windows on the second floor. Let's go look."

He pulled out of the parking space, turned right at Bell, turned right at 4th, and found a spot next to the Churchkey Pub. The western side of the Beeson gleamed in the sun, which was well past the meridian, while the northern side was shadowed.

"Since I was a kid living on 4th heading over to Swanson's for a *Sport* magazine," the old man said, "this afternoon image has stabbed me again and again, its offer of glory in the sun, a singularity inflating—O let there be light!— juxtaposed with deepening dark, a black hole contracting, yin and yang, an evocative phenomenon, so beautiful to me."

"Dare I, like most of your characters, use the word 'awesome?'"

"You may."

"You, of course, may not?"

"May— can't."

"Now what? '

"Can you tolerate a little more boulevardiering? We'll have to exit the car and walk a bit to get a good view of the next few."

"I'm okay with that as long as we just tootle."

They tootled to the corner and the old man pointed southwest to the Shumacher Building, a two-story wooden structure in the Western False Front style with a detailed façade and a parapet higher than the roofline. "This is about as old as we get here in the Bowl. Originally the site of a general store when built *circa* 1900," he said. "Several other businesses since then, Chanterelle now for many years."

"I never really thought about it when I lived here, but it's like something in *Shane* or *High Noon*," Solveig said. "A touching attempt to look brave and grand, imposing civilization—admittedly, a white version of civilization—upon the frontier, reaching for the stars, Edmonds style, as aspirational in its resource-challenged way as the Chrysler Building or the new Hudson Yards."

"And then there's what I call its city-cousin once-removed, the Leyda Building, originally built by Fred Fourtner."

They went east single-file against the foot-traffic in Times Square, shoppers with their bags full drifting away from the closing Market, passed the new 407 Coffee Shop, passed the theater, and settled on a sidewalk bench near the intersection. Built in the '20s, the Leyda was a sturdy, rectangular, two-story mixed-use (his aunt Mable and Uncle Ned had once lived in an apartment above Llubb's, an art gallery, in the '60s) building with a weathered dark brick façade busily ornamented with miniscule bas-relief arches below the roofline, interspersions of light-colored blocks above the broad street-level windows and the many narrow rectangular second-floor windows, and, in the last decade, flat wooden "Starbucks Coffee" awnings attached by cables to the building's masonry.

"It feels solid and sturdy, bourgeois, more sophisticated than the Schumacher but kind of heavy and earth-bound, advanced at the time of its building, no doubt, still interesting to look at. Sitting here under September's ochering oak leaves, listening to the water gushing from the fountain, we can almost imagine ourselves immersed in our own little tone poem of the Pins and Fountain of home."

"That's a stretch!"

"But that's what meta's for!

"Agreed! So let's take a shot at a few more metaphors before we bring our tour to a close." He ushered her across Main in a stream of pedestrians who outpaced them, then clasped her shoulder and led her into an about-face. "The Fourtner building from this perspective—what does it remind you of if you subtract about 21 stories?"

"A very flat Flatiron building!" she laughed. "Yes! From here it's a triangle."

"It always amuses me to imagine it so," he said. "Now let's look at the theater."

They tootled west and stopped in front of the bakery.

"Mmm, in my mind's nose I can still smell the maple bars of my youth," the old man said.

"Oddly enough, I seem to be still smelling the beer from the Edmonds Tavern that stood next to it!" Solveig said.

They gazed across the street. Also built in the '20s, the remodeled two-story Edmonds theater, *née* the Princess, was an Art Deco erratic, with a stucco façade painted desert-sand brown and ornamented with lighter tan stucco trim on the corners and a symmetrical roofline that was formed by five horizontal overlapping pieces, two on either side rising to the fifth at the apex, a tall vertical marquee, readable from east and west, affixed between two Roman-arched window frames, one glassed-in, functioning, the other stuccoed over in a frozen wink, and a cable-suspended awning over the windowed main entry and an adjacent doorway.

"I never really paused to look at it before, back when I was going to double-features in the '50s," Solveig said. "It looks like a piece from a jigsaw puzzle. It's appropriately playful. It suggests fun, escape, mystery, intrigue, problem-solving."

"Yes. I'm not going to call it beautiful, but it's definitely something out of the ordinary. Now what? Ready to drive over to the old high school?"

"Wayne, I actually think I could walk it if we slowly stroll and pause now and then. It's only three blocks and quite flat."

"Capital! We can time-travel through Greenwich Village."

They moseyed to 4th and crossed Main, exchanging waves with the driver of a Lincoln Navigator who had seen them waiting on the curb and stopped for them, and continued north, on the east side of 4th, for about 20 paces, to a cement walk beneath an awning on the side of which appeared "Motto Mortgage" in white letters.

"Now here's a little gem," the old man said, pointing to a set-back square single-story building, its façade a chalky-mortared interspersion of vermilion- and rust-toned bricks, with a centered triangular peak rising from the front edge of its flat roof. There were large windows, eyebrowed by a row of dun-colored bricks placed vertically, on either side of its front door, and the corners of the building, from bottom to top, were defined by dun bricks of alternating lengths placed horizontally.

"I do remember walking by here now and then. Used to be the offices of Dr. Kenney and Dr. Magnuson."

"Yes. Magnuson was our family dentist."

"I gave the building absolutely no thought as a girl, but now that I look it over, I like it! It's kind of jaunty, kind of saucy, the gratuitous peak and the corner piping announcing the offices as a place to do spirited battle against disease and decay."

"Agreed. But are you sure that the peak is gratuitous? Let's go up the walk and look a little closer. Do you see what's inside that diamond shape of dun bricks in the middle of the triangle? "

"Oh, yes! It's a caduceus etched in a gray diamond-shaped stone with the letter M on one side and the letter D on the other. How appropriate for the building's original purpose! Truly, I never noticed it as a kid."

"Me either. I never came here except when I was in pain. All I could think about when approaching the building was the abscessed tooth that Doc Magnuson was going to be pulling without giving me Novocain. But now I really dote on it every time I pass by."

"And there's kind of a visual echo of the Carnegie Library on 5th, too, which also has its corners defined by a lighter shade of brick."

"Quite!"

They walked on, the only pedestrians on the block, now that the Market had been closed for half an hour, paused at Rick Steves' two-story complex, whose Roman-arched portico and somber brown brick façade adorned with gargoyles and figures in high relief nodded to Old Europe, turned and noted, on the west side of the street, a couple of Victorian- style two-story houses with gables and a veranda roof supported by white-painted columns ("Kind of a *Belle* Époque feel," Solveig said) until they reached the North Sound Church at the corner.

"Ah, the old Edmonds Baptist Church—Dave's dad's place!" Solveig said. "I actually attended a vacation Bible camp here one summer along with Dave and Sylvia and Patty and Claudia. Had a great time!"

"Did you indeed? Shall we cross to the other side of 4th to get a better view?"

"Topping!"

They traipsed over the crosswalk's faded, chipped stripes of white paint. The old man noted empathetically the cracks in the street's asphalt and the shiny rivulets of tar that had been applied to seal the largest of them.

They faced about.

"Do you mind if I take this one?" Solveig asked.

"Not a tall."

"Now, this old church is definitely not an erratic," Solveig said. "Like the Schumacher building back on Main, it really looks like it belongs here, on the northwest frontier. It's just the right size for Edmonds. It basically fills up its wide lot, and it's two stories high, but it doesn't overwhelm. There's a modesty, a self-sufficiency, a this-will-do about it. The cladding is native cedar shakes painted stark white. The design is simple, yet visually interesting. Its roofline meets in a short triangular peak in the center, like the little brick offices that we just looked at, but the left side begins higher and runs horizontally until sharply angling toward the peak, the right begins lower and runs diagonally all the way to the peak. There's a complimentarity throughout. At the double-door entry, two columns support a small protective gable peak that salutes its superior at the roofline, and on the roof there's an unusual belfry telescoping out of a box-like base and surmounted by a half-dome supported by six short slender columns on top of which stands a cross. The fascia boards of each structure—gable, roof, and belfry—are painted dark brown, and the color correspondence, abetted by the upward slants from the gable and roofline peaks to the cross at the top of the belfry, creates a feeling of ascension. The vertical sets of rows of little window panes in the center of the building, the upper set's middle row longer and capped by additional panes that form a Roman arch, provide variety, reinforce the feeling of ascension, and also suggest the Trinity, as does the three-piece belfry. And enclosing the whole, leaving an opening only for a wide welcoming walkway, is a low white picket fence. The image is redolent of rectitude, cleanliness, virtue, purity, order. It's very traditional, very touching, very comforting. One of the town's nicest features. Thank you for bringing me back to it—and it back to me."

"My pleasure." He patted her shoulder. "Just one more now. Can you make it to our last stop?"

She mock-fluttered her silvery lashes over her ice-blue eyes. "I'll try!"

They crossed Bell and lumbered north, passed the house in which the old man had lived in 1950, he telling Sovleig how small the yard now seemed to him, wondering how was it even possible that eight or 10 of his friends used to gather there to play football games, then crossed Edmonds and Daley, Solveig doggedly matching his restrained pace, and stood in front of their old high school.

Once a Neo-Classical two-story rectilinear brick building, rigid, upright, stern, it had been jazzily transformed in the '30s by a new stucco Art Moderne façade, its flat westside front becoming a long, swelling, sweeping curve lightened by vertical windows on the first floor, its northern and southern corners now gracefully rounded off, softened, and lent an airy elegance by three supporting stucco columns separated by tall, slender second-floor windows.

"Did you just praise with a faint 'Damn'?" Solveig said.

"I did. I really like the other buildings that we've looked at today, but I love this one. It has a creamy warm glow, a voluptuous fecundity, yet it's also aerodynamic. It's lithe and supple. It flows. To me the transformation of the building from Neo-Classical to Art Moderne is like moving from the hieratic to the demotic."

"Or from Bach to Gershwin."

"Yes. 'Swonderfully accessible."

"And there's almost a nautical element to it as well. One can sort of visualize this entrance as the bow of a ship breasting the waves, transporting students out of ignorance."

"Or of full-breasted Liberty leading the pupils."

"In any case, we seem to be agreed that there is something warmly mammarian about it."

"Yes, we are. Alma mater indeed. And this completes our lodestone tour. Nothing magical or mystical about them, just beautiful parts of my reality for the past 80 years." He turned toward her. "It's 4:02 by my watch. So now what?"

"A visit to your bench on Sunset?"

"Why don't we go park?"

"What? Where?"

"At the beach. You haven't been to the beach yet. Let's come full circle. We'll go to the dog park, just south of where we used to sit in my '49 Ford. My Santa Fe's bucket seats will keep us chaste."

"Uh-huh. Actually, what I'd most like to do now is find a bathroom—and then get a cup of coffee to perk myself up. I'm exhausted."

"Should I jog back to the car and come pick you up?"

"Show off! Would you mind?"

"I could use the conditioning. I'll be back in an Edmonds minute."

He pivoted, closed his fists, and eased into a comfortable trot, running through intersections, making an evasive shuffle and feigning a stiff-arm as he passed his old front yard, kitty-cornering at Bell, and gliding to a stop beside the Santa Fe. Panting comfortably, he jumped in, pushed the starter button while belting up, made a right at Main, a right at 3rd, a right at Daley, and picked up Solveig at the corner of 4th.

He squeezed her hand briefly. "I have a suggestion. Why don't we go back to my place and we'll both use the bathroom and I'll make you a pour-over."

"Another climb up those stairs? That pour-over better be pretty damn good."

"I think you'll like it. I've got an unopened Starbucks bag of Sidamo beans from Ethiopia boasting of notes of ripe blackberry and creamy chocolate."

At the foot of the stairs she girded and he took her left elbow, abetting her, lifting her slightly while conveniently using her to maintain his own balance, as she jacked herself upward by gripping the railing with her right and pushing off.

"We'll just take our time," he said.

"Considering how little we have left, is this how I want to spend mine? Climbing up to your aerie?"

"I'm hoping yes?"

"Yes."

He squeezed her elbow in gratitude. "So, do you often think of dying?"

They reached the first landing. Solveig paused and panted. Her pinkening skin glistened. "Of course."

"Me too."

"But not quite as often as I think about living."

"Me either. But like what do you think about when you think about death?"

"For one thing, I think about how I would want to go. I would like it to be as free of pain as possible. I see no virtue in dying in agony."

"Me either. But, if agony does occur, bearing it stoically? Setting a good example? Biting down on a stick held between your teeth, the way you did in giving birth to your children?"

"Hah! Exercising my right to choose, I had elective C-sections for both Oscar and Samantha. The procedure was brief, pain-free, perfectly safe for both baby and me, and recovery was a breeze, although I do bear stitching scars, an uninked maternal tattoo, my paunchy belly resembling a football with laces the width of cooked fettuccini. I feel under no obligation to seek pain—I would never even run a city block, let alone a marathon—and when pain perversely seeks and finds me I am under no obligation to bear it nobly. I am free to wail and rail against it. Fain would I exemplify a manic defiance of the cult of imperturbability. I will not be wus-shamed!"

"She said, bearing her opprobrium nobly."

"She said, refusing to acknowledge opprobrium."

They baby-stepped over to the second flight.

"So, clearly you don't want to be stoned to death by some lottery-losing villagers, or chopped into pieces by an axe-wielding Mafia hitman who mistook you for an informer, or burned at the stake for practicing bitchcraft."

They resumed their climb.

"But what about a sudden violent but virtually painless death, instant lights out— massive cerebral hemorrhage, bullet fired into your brain by a mass murderer in a shopping mall, neck broken in a clumsy backward fall off a ladder, body blown to pieces when your plane crashes into the side of a fog-obscured mountain at 600 miles an hour, that sort of thing. No introspection, final review, taking stock, coming to terms with oneself and the universe, no saying goodbye to one's husband and children and grandchildren and friends, no goodbye to clocks ticking—no, wait a minute, that's only relevant if you happen to be enjoying the anachronistic tick-tick-tick of an auditory transition on '60 Minutes'—rather, goodbye to digits silently, inexorably, blinking up or blinking down, and to red wheelbarrows and leftover plums liberated from the refrigerator and tumultuous orgasms, just zip, rip off the bandaid, and it's over?"

They reached the second landing. Solveig leaned against the wall and fanned her flushed face. "It's not the climb, it's the memory of those tumultuous orgasms," she said. Her ice-blue eyes twinkled, her coppery glasses gleamed in the wavy particles flowing through the skylight.

"Yes, my point exactly, wouldn't you like to hang on to that, wouldn't you prefer an easing into death, a long fatal illness, multiple myeloma perhaps, negotiated under the hauspices of palliative care, a gradual decline like that which I imagine for myself—at first, propped up by bed pillows, maintaining muscle tone by practicing the dynamic-tension exercises of Charles Atlas, the way Zee and I did when we were kids, then, iPad on lap, fictionalizing, revising, Noting, anagramming, palindroming, gazing across the town and across the Sound to Skagit Head gleaming Doverishly, welcoming visitors, rubbing minds—Zee, Monk, Sylvia, Charlotte, Carolyn, Liz Ann, Dave, perhaps, if he happened to be in town, you, perhaps, making one last special trip to see me, everyone bringing books (Chomsky, Beckett, Rovelli, Kolbert, Pinker, Gopnik, Harris, Jim Holt, Richard Dawkins, Daniel Dennett, Yuval Harari, Joseph Henrich, Michael Gazzaniga) for me to fondle and flip through as I haphazardly true and skew, a nurse, serving as my death doula, climbing the stairs daily to microwave rice bowls for me (cashew chicken, shrimp with pineapple and green peppers), assist me with taking my pills, help me access my toilet and shower, within a few weeks connecting me to an IV and a Foley catheter, emptying my bedpan, wiping me, giving me a sponge bath, introducing morphine to the IV, then titrating it daily until time for the ultimate supercharge that painlessly eliminates me?"

"Of those painless alternatives, which would I prefer? It's a tough call, what with the orgasms and all, but I'm leaning toward instant death. My familial bonds are strong. I don't need to exchange last-minute terms of endearment with my husband, children, grandchildren, or even you, or even to say an official goodbye. In fact, that might be painfully maudlin for me. I might prefer to just disappear."

"Not me. I'm such a clinger. I cringe at my own craven sentimentality, but I want that slow winding down, that hanging on to phenomena, even if it's only Netflix reruns of *Seinfeld* on my iPad, until finally exhaustion and morphine-induced metabolic torpor render me apathetic and I lose my grip. I don't want to die unexpectedly, the way Diane did. I want to die the way my parents did, in bed, drugged, only not angry or sullen, not spitefully welcoming death as a refuge from life, just clinging to my unnecessary and meaningless life, a life that has always been unnecessary and meaningless but so absurdly absorbing and compelling, until I can no longer. I don't want it to end suddenly, arbitrarily. I want to lose heat gradually. I could never commit suicide."

Solveig inhaled deeply, her chest rising, and they began their final ascent. "But surely you would want someone to pull the plug if through accident or illness you became unconscious and entered a vegetative state?"

"True. If it's likely that I will never again be able to experience the rush of life, take me off the respirator and kill me softly with kindness."

"You have an Advance Health Care Directive?"

"I do. It's on file at the office of Dr. Robert Hope, Jr. And you?"

"I do. I'm covered legally. But my inner living will is that my dying will release me from earthly bonds, my atomic fetters, and I will graduate from this earthly high school."

"So it isn't over when it's over?"

They reached his unit door. Solveig gasped and leaned against him in relief. He inserted his key.

"I don't think so. I was raised as a Lutheran but, like Sylvia, I gave up organized religion long ago. However, the fictive stage manager within me feels that everybody knows, even you, Wayne, though you will not deign to admit it, that there is something, some essence, some quiddity, that is eternal about each person. I have to believe that consciousness does not die and that, apart from the dreadful physical pain that might occur in the process, death has no sting."

He pushed the door open wide, put his arm around Solveig's waist, and they entered together. "You have to believe because you *need* to believe?"

"I have to believe because I have no choice. I cannot close my mind's eye. Seeing is believing. I'm being empirical, not mystical. As I lie dead, I'm still awake. I find the end of consciousness literally unimaginable. You don't?"

"No, I do. In my mind's eye, I never die. But my physical eyes, severely macularly degenerated though one of them is, tell me that I will. My mind's eye offers only an ersatz empiricism, the physical ones offer the real epistemological maccoy. Through them I induce, from what is observable, measurable, testable, and repeatable, the theory that entropy rules the universe, systems fall apart, the electro-chemical system that is me being no exception."

He closed the door.

"And the electro-chemical system that is me says I gotta go. Same bathroom?"

"By all means. Enjoy!"

As Solveig passed the guest bathroom and quick-stepped down the long hallway, the old man began coffee preparations. The metal electric water heater and the thermally insulated quart carafe, both spouted and handled like a coffee pot, and the electric coffee grinder were at their home bases next to the stove. He extracted an eight-ounce glass measuring cup from a lower cupboard, filled it thrice with cold tap water, each time raising the cup to eye level, dribbling a few drops in or a few drops out as needed to get an exact eight ounces, then pouring it into the heater. He flipped the switch and took from an upper cupboard a plastic funnel, a number 4 brown Melitta filter, and an unopened bag of Starbucks beans. He inserted the funnel into the carafe, fitted the filter into it, noted the *Spokane* just coming in, and turned to find Solveig doing the same.

"Almost as much fun as the first time," Solveig said. "And I didn't bother to touch up my lip gloss, since we're going to be cupping."

"Excellent. Here's the bag we'll be drinking from." The bag was two-toned, powder blue on the upper two-thirds, black on the bottom, the tones separated by a thin magenta stripe. "Howard Schultz had me at powder blue," the old man said.

"It *is* a buoyant, cheerful color."

"Offering the dream of a blue yonder to a SAD denizen of the often calaginous, Stygian Edmonds Bowl where we both descry and decry 50 shades of gray, where we have 50 words for rain. Now let me just wrestle it open. They seal these things so tight that my arthritic digits are almost not a match for them." He unfolded the top and gripped the sealed edges with thumbs and index fingers and yanked. Nothing. He clenched his jaw and tried again. A nanometer of movement. He pressed his knees against the cupboard, held his breath, flexed his abs, and pulled again, grunting. A micrometer of movement. Once more he strained, thumbs throbbing, and finally created a millimeter of separation, gained a bit of momentum, and pressed his inertial advantage hard as the bag gradually opened wide.

"Well, quite an operation," Solveig said. "I could never put that much effort into making coffee."

"What do you usually do?"

"Sometimes I step out to a coffee shop on my block and have an Americano. Sometimes I make a K cup."

"A K cup?" He stroked the back of his neck.

"Disappointed in me, Wayne?"

"Of course not. Not seriously."

"Yes, you are. It's as plain as the no's on your face."

He smiled, lifted the bag to his nose, snorted. "Want a whiff?"

He extended the bag to her. She leaned forward to sniff, once, twice.

"What do you get?"

"Honestly? The interior of an old garage like McKeever's Shell with its blended smell of dirty drained oil and stacked rubber tires. But that's not a bad thing—I like it!"

"Me too! So let me just get this brew going." He took a scoop from a drawer and dropped six heaping tablespoonfuls of beans into the grinder. "Brace yourself," he said, and switched on the grinder, which growled its way into a whir, its pitch rising like the wail of an air raid siren as it hit full speed and raced for a good 20 seconds, Solveig muffling her ears with her hands.

"Yet another reason why I don't grind my own," she said.

The old man removed the plastic receptacle and poured its finely-ground contents into the filter levelly. The whooshing heater clicked off automatically when the water hit the boiling point, and he lifted it, aimed the spout, and slow-poured a steaming stream over the concupiscently spread grounds, wetting the outer edges evenly, washing them toward the center in slow, counterclockwise swirls, then drizzling the middle until all were soaked, reddish brown muff becoming a puddle of black, pausing a half-minute to let it steep and drip and dry, coming again with the swirls, urging the grounds to release all that they had, pausing again, then finishing with a final trickle to the center from the exhausted pot.

They stared into the filtered funnel until the oozing was done.

"Those were the days," the old man said.

"Yes, they were," Solveig said. "I have to admit, I like a man with a slow hand. But the proof of the puddling is in the drinking, *n'est-ce pas*? Let's find out how it tastes."

The old man lifted the filter from the funnel and dropped it into the garbage beneath the sink. He rinsed the funnel, set it in the sink, and screwed the cap into the carafe. He drew from a cupboard two slender porcelain mugs, white, and poured a couple of ounces into each.

"No, fill mine up," Solveig said. "I don't need to aerate and sniff. I get *bubkis* from that."

"Ohh-*kay*."

They carried their full mugs carefully to the couch and set them on the glass coffee table.

"While the coffee's becoming sippable, I'll just take a minute to run back and use a catheter. Please sit back and enjoy the view."

"Sure. And at the same time I'll check my phone with my evolving third eye."

"Excellent!" How nice it was to have an attentive reader.

He hurried to the bathroom, told himself to relax, relax, she would be there when he got back (early on in the self-cathing portion of his life he had impatiently rammed a catheter through the bladder wall and into his prostate, his hand the voluminous bowl incarnadining, turning the yellow sea red, and had driven himself to the emergency room at Swedish, where the doctor on duty, Horst Kloppelberg, fitted him with a Foley, which he had to wear for two weeks while the wound healed, causing him to miss four games with the Classics), set paper towel, catheter, and nitrile glove on top of the tank, unbuttoned, lowered jeans and underpants, slipped on the glove, opened the package, and carefully, mindfully, actually, inched the catheter into his bladder.

When he returned to the living room, Solveig, occupying the middle of the couch, her purse and wrap beside her right hip, had her phone to her ear. "Yes, dinner with Sylvia. Okay, sweetie, gotta go now. Love you. Bye."

She tucked the phone back into the purse.

"All right," the old man said, slipping off his vest, tossing it onto the Morris chair, then seating himself to her left, "let's drink some coffee."

They sipped from their mugs, reflected, swallowed.

"I definitely get the blackberry," Solveig said, "although I might not have come up with that word on my own. There's a winey ripeness, a deep flavor, that lingers on the palate and in the nose. It really is reminiscent of those wild berries we used to pick in the '40s and '50s, going out with our parents to areas like Picnic Point and Martha Lake that had been logged off but not developed, the thorny vines growing in tangles over left-behind stumps and branches, scratching our hands and arms when we reached deep under broad green leaves to get the biggest, juiciest berries, the ones that turned our fingers purple and stained our clothes when we wiped them off. A tart, anise-like flavor, aromatic, with a hint of tar, like the black licorice we used to buy at Bienz's."

"Agreed. And, accompanying the blackberry on the palate," the old man said, " I detect a bit of creamy chocolate along the edges of the tongue, a tri-toned berry-mocha-latte effect."

"Agreed. Maybe your labor-intensive coffee-making protocol is worth following after all. Or maybe what we just said is pretentious horseshit."

They smiled at each other. Solveig drank deeply, uncrossed her legs, and set her mug on the table.

"But the caffeine is definitely perking me up."

The old man took another tri-toned sip. The sun, glimpsed through gauzy herringbones of red and charcoal cirrus, was dropping toward the Olympics.

"So, where were we?" he said. "Where are we?"

"We *were* in love." She touched the hair at her left temple. She reached again for her mug, leaned back, recrossed her legs, swigged. "We *are* in Edmonds, quaint sylvan city of hunched shoulders where progressive superego and reactionary id vie for soul control."

"And also in limbo?"

"Maybe." She uncrossed her legs, set down her mug, scooted toward him, leaned into him.

He reached forward, deposited his mug, and sank back, reestablishing contiguity.

"Are we doing the movie thing?"

"The movie thing?"

"Yeah, you know. Except for a few specialized *oeuvres* like *My Dinner With Andre* or *Babette's Feast*, characters seldom finish even a cup of coffee, let alone a meal, in a movie or TV show, that would be way too boring, they just do a little stage business and then shade into something else—lovemaking, for instance."

He raised his right arm and extended it atop the back of the couch behind her. She fingered the earring dangling from her left lobe. She stroked her neck.

"Are we doing the *Quora* thing?"

"The *Quora* thing?"

"Yeah, you know. For each question like 'What did Einstein mean when he said that God does not play dice with the universe?' the daily *Quora* posting offers a half-dozen trite masturbation fantasies 'reported' in response to sham questions like 'Have you ever stopped and had a conversation with a hitch-hiker who offered you a special massage for a ride to their destination?' or 'What pleasantly surprised you when a neighbor took off their clothes?' or 'What is the most inappropriate experience you have had with your paternal aunt, your best friend's spouse, your uncle with the wooden leg, or your married ex-girlfriend?'"

"Alas, the few hitch-hikers I have picked up over the years have never offered me anything more than a grateful 'Thanks a lot, man,' none of my neighbors have ever taken off their clothes in front of me, I never had an inappropriate experience with my aunt Mabel or with Zee's spouse Janice or with my Uncle Ned who, although he didn't have a wooden leg, did have a cedar chest, he told me to my immense amusement when I was in third grade, or with my married ex-girlfriend."

He placed his left hand on hers, which lay fanned on her left quad, and smiled. She smiled back. He inched his right hand onto her right shoulder.

"And what *did* Einstein mean when he said that God does not play dice with the universe?"

"I *think* that he was plumping for a lawful, deterministic universe untainted by the randomness and uncertainties of quantum mechanics, a universe accessible to human reason but created by an impersonal, intangible force unconcerned with the fate and doings of humans."

He stroked her left hand once. She looked at him with wide-open eyes. Was she breathing faster?

"I think so, too."

"But I also think that he was wrong."

"God *does* play dice with the universe?"

"That I really don't know, but my sense is that the wacky quantum theorists are on to something with the charming uncertainty of their quarks. Einstein's God is too hidebound, too steeped in rationality, too antipathetic to quantum mysticism to suit me. His cool God does not exude the dearest freshness of deep down things. He lacks spirit, passion, compassion, playfulness. My exquisite fictional God is hella more than rational, is relational, is beautiful, sexy, transformative, is one who breathes fire into his equations, gives them what Steven Hawking called their ontic clout, is one with whom atonement brings an epiphany to the umpteenth power, a mind-blowing trip of awful intensity, like that experienced by a rodent in the embrace of a hawk or a salmon snared by a bear."

Stirred, he wanted to pull her into him with his right arm in a hawkish embrace, snare a breast with his left hand. Might she want that too?

"A rodent, a salmon? Leda mastered by the brute blood of the air, shiveringly, orgasmically, assimilating Zeus's knowledge with his power? Heart battered by a three-personed God, broken, blown, burned, made new?"

"Yes. The ultimate transmogrifying big deal. Delta S forever greater than 0, a fiction that you know from your feelings to be something else."

He risked raising his spread hand to her breast, felt the supporting wire of her D cup, risked saying "But what about #MeToo? Are you countenancing rape?"

"Only as a metaphor for the longed-for assault of atonement." She slid her right hand to his crotch. "Try to sudden-blow *me* and I'll crush your balls!"

They laughed. She did not remove her hand. A penile vein pulsed. His hackles horripilated. It had been 10 years. He swallowed. He cautiously pulled her closer with his right arm. He tentatively touched a clothed nipple. Outside his jeans, she fingered his glans. They looked at each other, leaned in, kissed by the book. He inhaled her tri-tone coffee breath. It was going to happen.

They drew their heads back, looked at each other, smiled. She removed her glasses and hat, set them on the table beside her mug. He followed suit. She closed her eyes and sighed.

"You're not thinking of England, are you?"

"No, only of you. Just trying to be in the moment. Eyes wide shut."

She found his glans again and his lips again. Yes, because she always did a thing like that, zeroed in, found signal in noise, like that first touch in the '49 Ford, Diane too, coming to sit by him, betting him across the board, he was her guy save for that one *contretemps*, whereas he equivocated, ambiguated, hesitated, factored in, contextualized, maintained his perimeter, eyes wide open, taking in her fine lashes, her high forehead, the brown redness of her hair, but also the green gem, town and Sound and mountains out there where the evening was about to meet the sky, mouth wide open too, his teeth clumsily clacking hers, Solveig chuckling for old time's sake, keeping eyes wide shut, fondling him, yes, teasing him to life on the couch where Diane used to affirm him, his hand slipping under her tee shirt, roaming, his cold shriveled root stirring, firming, lucky, yes, *think*, yes, given the truth as uttered forth in the fictions of Chomsky and Beckett and Rovelli and Kolbert and Pinker and Gopnik and Harris and Holt and Dawkins and Dennett and Harari and Henrich and Gazzaniga, for reasons unknown that time won't tell, *y-a-t-il quelque chose plutot que rien parce que l' univers est venu par hasard d'une fluctuation quantique du vide*, no matter, matter a mere matter of events, it is established beyond all doubt beyond that which clings to any fictions of humans *quaquaqua* scientific and philosophical and religious and social constructs, that everything changes, nothing endures, the Olympics disintegrate, the Pacific plate subducts, the earth rumbles and spouts, rumbles and spouts, its climate warms, the universe cools, the Bowl shapeshifts, a dime store dies, a lavender shop is born, ramblers fall, condos rise, Indians become indigenous peoples, in short, in brief, empires melt like ice cream, become anathema, the better angels of our nature emerge from their chrysalis, the facts are there, reams of data, on the whole, in general, prove material life less violent, safer, easier now, it matters not, people continue to waste and pine, waste and pine for salvation, for metempsychosis, the meta that matters most to most, his hand surfing the fulsome folds of her belly flesh with its fettuccini laces, his nose hunting pheromonal emanations, were those a real thing, was it time, yes, they drew back, they smiled, they stood, high above the town he helped her shrug out of her tee, her combs loosening, her tresses further confessing, unhooked her lacy black bra, slid the straps down her arms, tossed it to the end of the couch, her heavy breasts sprawling, overflowing his kneading hands, broad mauve areolas, rosier nipples erect, seeking contact, while she unbuttoned his shirt, skated her hands over his hairy pecs, unbuttoned his jeans, tugged them down till they sagged at his ankles, his black Jockeys too, stroking the veiny throbbing vee at the base of the circumcised glans, his selfish gene, in spite of the fact, as proved by neurologists, that he lacked a self, any one no one, no one any one, growing manic, lusting to be copied, to end run entropy, but whence the emergence of a rage to replicate in an RNA molecule four billion years ago and the evolution of selfish selflessness, love and law, billions of years later, summer winter autumn spring, wondering, hoping, could he be within an inch of the old, once so reliable, five-and-a-quarter, he glanced down, yes, if measured generously that is, he chuckled gratefully, she smiled approvingly, he unbuttoned her pants, unzipped her, let the pants slide to the floor, nearly swooning at the pink silk bikini panties stretched so tight across her broad cheeks and thighs, she wouldn't be waxed, would she, no, wanton strands of roseate pubic hair peeked out from their pouch, he sucked an extending nipple, squeezed her ass with both hands, tugged down her panties, cupped her slough as she widened her stance, her gene raging too, loving to live, why, so many fruitless years after menopause, stroked her clit, lipped his fingers, fingered her lips, companions sharing scallions, chives, they smiled, they kissed off book, muscularly, they drew back, they smiled, each kicked off their shoes, pants, underpants, he sat, opened his arms wide, she, soaked, knelt over him, woman-spreading, with her right hand held him straight, cathed him up, he arched his pelvis, abs and rectum tight, held the pose, a reverse plank, an asana, palindrome, beseeching her to grind him, she read his sine, tightened her vaginal grip, would not let him go except he blessed her, tugged and pushed, tugged and pushed, her knees on the couch, her eyes half-shut, middle-distancing, intuning, seeking the rhythm she needed to get them off, her breasts flopping as she went up and down, up and down, her hair falling over her ears, he felt firmer, longer, almost engorged, was he four and a half now, four and three-quarters—impossible!—yet it felt like it, yes, he was up to this, they were soaring, windhovering above the town, he was engaging, he was probing, he was ramming, ramming, ram-ming, his loving selfish gene demanding, Solveig, eyes wide open now, was jouncing, jouncing, jouncing, riding the roiling under-neath her choppy air, clinging, brute and beauty, pride and plume, buckling, grasping the wind as with gasps each burst and flamed, the achieve of, the mastery of the thing, wrung upon the wimpling of their lusting interlocked loins, galling, galling themselves, until at last, chafed, their whimpering embers gashed gold-vermilion.

He felt something cold and wet. He opened his eyes, reconnoi-tered. The sun had routed night and drenched his bedroom in wavy particles of bright light. 5:05. Was it possible? After 10 dry years? He extended his arms under the covers, unstuck his cotton sleep-ing shorts from his mons, touched the slimy pooled proof, touched the retreated tender glans, and guffawed. Guffawed! Chortled! Hilarious, that little death. A tenuous transcendence. Yes, yes, yes. Humpty Dumpty. Only senselessness made sense. He was in the bed where, on a day like any day, Sea, trees, clouds, rain, a hos-pice worker would supercharge his IV and cause his fictional self, that brief, conscious event known as Wayne Adams, to unhappen, some of its elements to be cut and pasted into other short stories by Science Care, the rest to be atomized and rebound by nature and read as leaves, as grass. But not today, not today. Today he would shower away the remnant of the night and take his pills and ask Alexa for the question of the day and walk and drink coffee and immerse himself in cyberspace and visit his bench and work out and shoot baskets and go to the batting cages and read and write and drink wine and watch the setting of the sun, which would be gold-vermilion in its dying.

Epiblog

A nd those, as far as I can tell, having thoroughly explored his home desktop computer, his iPad, his phone, and his metal filing cabinet containing three college-ruled notebooks of jottings from his reading and one that served as a bank for his verbal coinings, two fat manila folders of jumbled clippings from newspapers and magazines dating back to the '60s, and a boxed hard copy of *A How Pretty Town* in reverse order, each chapter dated and paper-clipped, "The Sleepers (1/20)" on top, were the last words Wayne Adams wrote for what he intended to be his *magnum opus*. Wayne's death in the ICU at Swedish Hospital from respiratory failure caused by COVID-19, on April 1, 2020, his birthday, caught those who knew him by surprise, given that prior to the state-issued shelter-in-place order in March he had seemed to be the picture of octogenarian health, plowing through each day energetically, walking around town, lifting weights, shooting baskets, frequenting batting cages with old pal and recently elected Councilman Gary Zylstra, and cramming the hours with reading, writing, and re-creational (he maintained that those looping sitcom reruns refilled his creative aquifers) TV watching. A phone call on April 2 from his lawyer and also lifelong friend Michael Monken, informing me that in January Wayne had revised his will and named me executor, surprised me as well. In keeping with his I daresay singular notion that the most we can ask of life is that it be a perpetual high school, he was leaving the majority of his modest financial estate to Edmonds School District 15, to be used at the District's discretion to enhance its high school academic and athletic programs, with a smaller amount going to the Edmonds Historical Museum to preserve the history of his beloved Bowl, and was ceding control of all his written material to me. But, dressed in a charcoal Levi's thick poly-cotton blend collared shirt, untucked, a thigh-length black leather coat, black skinny jeans, and his silver-black Under Armour high tops, he had told me on a mizzling afternoon in November as we drank beer seated in front of the fireplace at Brigid's Bottle Shop in Salish Crossing, that his immune system, growing increasingly confused and cantankerous with age, had become subversive. "I'm my own worst enemy," he said. "I sabotage myself. Fifteen years ago I had an auto-immune disease called polymyalgia rheumatica, severe inflammation of the hip and shoulder joints. I had never even heard of it, had no idea it was a thing. I had come home from a softball tournament in Las Vegas feeling sore and tired, which was to be expected after playing 10 games in three days and running hard. But day by day it got worse, not better. It hurt to have sex with Diane, what with the robust involvement of the hips, you know." He smiled briefly. "In fact, any attempt to use either the shoulders or the hips was painful. I couldn't lift my arm above my head. Diane had to shampoo and comb my hair, help me on with my shirts and jackets. To sit required an uncontrolled freefall of two feet. Bad enough when collapsing into my cushioned Morris chair but imagine my hesitancy to drop trou and plummet through hip-flexor spasms toward an unforgiving slippery toilet seat to go number two. Finally it hurt just to lie in bed for sleep. In less than 30 minutes pain would vice my shoulders and I would have to edge myself out and mince my way to the living room to take a little pressure off by sitting upright in the Morris, where I would watch TCM and Netflix, dozing off occasionally, until false dawn. Fortunately, when I went to see him a week later, Dr. Hope Jr. suspected what it was. He ordered some blood tests and put me on a steroid, Prednisone, 50 milligrams a day for two weeks before gradually dialing the dosage down. I was a junkie standing before the cupboard at 5:00 every a.m., shaking for my Preds. It took six months for me to get back to feeling normal. In addition, for the past 10 years I've had rheumatoid arthritis, another auto-immune disease, and it seems to be getting worse. At first it was just fingers, then it became knees and ankles, and now it's in the hips. It hurts to walk, let alone run or jump. At my upcoming quarterly appointment with my rheumatologist, Dr. Rahul Mehan, I'm going to demand an increase in my Methotrexate. I take six tablets per week now. I'm going to ask for 10 and won't settle for less than nine. What do I care about side effects? I might not even live long enough for the drug to exact its debilitating toll on my kidneys and liver. Then a year and a half ago my dry macular degeneration migrated to wet, my immune system, alarmed by my deteriorating vision, compounding the problem by creating rogue blood vessels intended to bring helpful oxygen to the area but only exacerbating the distortion because of the resultant increased swelling. And just last week my hematologist, Dr. Marshall Music, called to tell me that my recent bone marrow biopsy revealed an uptick in self-destructive cancer-causing white blood cells from seven to nine percent. I still have some strength—I bench-pressed 120 this morning—but I think it's quite likely that my quixotic immune system, in tilting at so many windmills over the years, has weakened and left me vulnerable to any new bacterial or viral strain that wafts along. I do get a flu shot every fall and a pneumonia booster every three years, but I doubt that's sufficient to deflect all incoming."

The firelight reflected off his face. I looked at him a little more carefully. I had to admit that he looked older than when I had seen him at the championship game in August. Although his hair, which he had worn combed straight back since I had known him, remained a mousy brown with just the odd strand of gray, the hairline had retreated perhaps an additional half inch. The skin between his sparse eyebrows was scored like a pastry chef's crimpings on the edge of a pie crust. The hollows beneath his eyes had a dusky tinge, his cheeks caved beneath their bones, his deep dimples, once resiliently round, now sagged into long convex grooves that obversely parenthesized his mouth, and the areas above and below his thin lips were fields of furrows. The grizzle of his three-day stubble (desperately trying to mask the wrinkles or too indifferent to shave?) did not work to his advantage, either.

"Are you really blaming yourself?" I countered. "I thought you were a rationalist. Haven't you put the ghost of Sigmund Freud, whom old Bokanov called 'the Viennese quack,' to rest? Psychosomatic illness? Come on! Bacteria, not stress, causes ulcers. The psychopathology of everyday life? There are no accidents? You forget your keys because of synaptic traffic problems, not for any meta reason like self-loathing or an imbalance in your id-ego-superego dynamics. The bogus interpretation of nocturnal dreams? Your brain is just tidying up its workshop, refreshing its screen, during REM sleep, not posing cryptic puzzles the solving of which will be therapeutic for you. Although it may bemuse us to see the immune system as a comic Quixote or as a tragic Othello who kills the very thing it loves, it has no subversive intent—no 'intent' of any kind. It's just doing the job it evolved to do, acting on its interpretation of limited data, lacking any ability to see the big picture. It's not the immune system's fault that it's myopic or experiences bouts of dyslexia, nor is it your fault that you have one that makes mistakes. Read Susan Sontag on the wrongness of seeing illness as metaphor."

And then he laughed. Those big guffaws that came from his belly. And grinned—showing those big, crooked, yellowish-white coffee-stained teeth—just enough to give me hope that he was still jonesing for a rush of some kind.

"Liz Ann, thanks," he said. "I needed that bracing splash of cold water in the face. I *have* read Sontag. I'd forgotten that—because of synaptic traffic problems, not repression of something painful, I agree! Freud's fiction is fascinating, full of stimulating fancies and conceits, concepts and tropes—the unconscious, wit and its relation to the unconscious, id-ego-superego, the Oedipus complex—that can occasionally, if not taken literally, be useful in the examination of some aspects of human existence, but overall it is not fiction that I believe willingly."

He lifted his half-full schooner of Brittany and Justin's Winter's Balm IPA, squinted at it, quaffed. "Passion fruit! What I need right now, enervated as I am. I haven't been able to write or tweet anything since my account of the August championship game, which I finished just before heading to St. George. I welcome your company and this bright infusion of sweet-tart-full-bodied- orange-mangoosity whose alluring perfume continues to linger on my palate after I swallow. So-named by Spanish missionaries in Brazil who fancied that the purple blossoms resembled Christ's five wounds."

"So you're taking communion, Coach? Drinking Christ's blood?"

"Hmm. That does present me with a dilemma."

"Many others—Diane, Dave, Zee, Monk, Charlotte, possibly Sylvia, possibly even Solveig—would say that the acknowledgement and internalization of that passion is exactly what you need."

"And what would you say?"

"Hmm. That does present me with a dilemma."

"What? You mean you're in the numinous and transcendence camp?"

"It's not a matter of which camp I'm in. Not a matter of camps at all." Trying to give it a *faux Suddenly Last Summer* or *Three Faces of Eve* ominous eeriness, I said, "Tell me about St. George, Coach. You texted me in October 'No gold. I was terrible.' and that was all I heard until you texted yesterday and invited me for a beer. What happened?"

I sipped some of Brittany and Justin's Umber Ale, a meaty brown brew with hints of walnut, maple, molasses, and, oddly, egg white.

He grinned. "In that championship game at Meadowdale in August, you saw me at the pinochle of my senior softball career."

I grinned back. "I like it! A deliberate malapropism in the midst of depression may be a sign of resilience. Of course it may also be a sign of quiet desperation, a whistling past the graveyard. Go on."

"Okay, I'm just gonna say it, at Meadowdale I was great. Could not have played better. Attuned, in the moment, mindfully mindless, not clinging to consciousness, immersed in the realm of the ludic, in a relationship with something beyond myself, my being and doing a yin-yang unity, chillaxed, angst-free, serenely joyful, open to affordances and serendipities."

"And then?"

"And then came that regression to the mean that I blithely predicted in our conversation after the game and privately airily dismissed as a mere bump in the road on my way to a gold medal and just possibly election to the United States Softball Association Hall of Fame."

"You just suddenly lost it? Fell out of tune? Went all Berg and Schoenberg on their asses?"

He chuckled. "Not quite. In September we had some practices at Celebration Park in Federal Way. In national tournaments, in divisions 65 and older, you play 11 guys in the field, so they put me at rover, the middle infielder. Teams usually put their best infielder at shortstop and their second best at rover. The position demands versatility—speed, good hands, good arm, good footwork around the bag—and even with my vision and balance problems, among the 80-year-olds I could provide that. Or so we all thought. But in our infield drills, although I was not a disaster, I wasn't sharp, a bit slow to react and get in front of balls, bobbling some, looping a few throws, pivoting a little clumsily at second base on double plays. In BP, which I approached with serene joy, confidently assuming I would be autonomically resuming my intuitive swing, I was at first surprised, then puzzled, though not disheartened, by my frequent failure to make clean contact with the ball. For every fairly solid line drive or reasonably deep back-spinning flyball there were two dribbled grounders or weak pop-ups. I was early, I was late, I was hitting off the handle or off the end of the bat. The old me would have stewed and groused, but the new me maintained equanimity, believing that my championship swing would return with the next pitch. 'Hey, it's been a while,' various teammates said. 'Your timing's a little off. It'll come back.'"

He drank some Winter's Balm. He seemed to be picking up

steam. "So we went to St. George. The basketball shooting contests were on Saturday and Monday, the softball competition Monday through Thursday. I flew into Vegas ahead of the other guys on Friday, rented a Kia Soul, skirted the Strip, which has little appeal to me—in the past 20 years, participating in softball tournaments, I've probably languished a total of 40 days and 40 nights in various garish, jangling casinos there—and drove the 100 miles north through the austere desert and the gorgeous sedimentary rock road cuts in the Virgin River canyon on 1-15 to the Ramada for a drama—as Kinbote found a cat-mouse game in muscat, so I hope you'll allow me my little botkin"(I was smiling. It cheered me to hear him eeigling and schmeeweigling again)—in St. George, a town that is 70% Mormon, laid out in that prototypical rectilinear Mormon grid with the gleaming white Temple near the center standing tall and proud, a conservative town that probably is not experiencing a battle for soul control between progressives and reactionaries, but is like the Bowl in some ways: clean, safe, orderly, busy, set amidst beauty (iron-rich red mesas and buttes, white sandstone cliffs, black-studded basaltic lava fields), and dependent on tourism (lush golf courses, proximity to Zion National Park, and home of the renowned Huntsman Games, which attract over 10,000 participants each year).

"Saturday morning I drove out to Snow Canyon Middle School on the west side of town for the Hot Shot competition. There were eight participants in my age group. Four of us shot at a time, each at a corner basket. I was ready. I had been practicing my jumpers for months. I was in shape. I knew I could get off 12 shots in one minute. At Harbor Square I had timed myself in that drill scores of times. The old rhythm and feeling were back. I was squaring up, I was getting off the floor six inches, quantum leaps for me, I was nothing but one smooth motion from my gather to my follow-through, with a song in my heart I was lasered on that space just over the front of the rim, ready to chord my movement to the rhythm of 'Hallelujah.' The red lights of the scoreboard timer blinked on: 1:00. The horn blared. I started with the required layup, then grabbed my ball out of the net ('Now you've heard there was a secret chord'), dribbled to the left baseline marker, pivoted, squared, shot, swish ('that you can play and please the Lord'), raced to retrieve the ball and dribble to the right baseline marker, pivoted, squared, shot, swish ('and you don't have no worries, do ya'), raced to retrieve the ball and dribble to the left 45-degree mark, pivoted, squared, shot, swish ('Well it goes like this, the fourth, the fifth'), raced to retrieve the ball and dribble with the left hand to the right 45-degree mark, squared, shot, a rim-rattler but good, ('the minor fall and the major lift, hallelujah'), raced to retrieve the ball, breathing a little harder now, dribbled behind my back and went to the top of the key, pivoted, squared, shot a hybrid push-jumper, lacking the strength for the pure J from that distance, swish, ('hallelujah, hallelujah,'), raced to retrieve the ball, headed for the left corner again, pivoted, squared, shot, a swirler but good, ('your faith was strong, needed no proof'), raced to retrieve the ball, headed for the right corner again, pivoted, squared, shot, hit the far side of the rim, and the ball caromed forward and rolled rapidly away from me, clear to the corner of the gym. That was it, Liz Ann, a perfect score to that point, and then disaster. My song and faith gone, I sprinted after the ball, pacemaker pounding, finally captured it, frantically dribbled back to the court and, exhausted now, cast off a desperate airball as the horn blared indifferently. I finished fifth."

He looked at me and shook his head. "I had that gold, man."

I tugged twice at the sleeve of his leather jacket. "That was just bad luck, not bad faith or bad karma. You were in tune, flowing, then you got a bad break. It wasn't your fault. There was nothing you could do about it."

"Yes, it was my fault. I could have lived with a miss or two that I could rebound, I could have still posted the highest score, but I shot the one shot that could kill me, not quite enough backspin, a little too flat, a little too long, a little too hard."

"But it was one error! Surely the other guys were making errors, too?"

"Yes, but they were erring on the side of caution, they weren't shooting themselves out of the competition."

"Then look at it this way, Coach. You have often lamented your tepidity and timidity, your tendency to be a quakebuttock"—

"E'en so, e'en so," he nodded.

—"but here you dared to be bold, to grab for the gold, you were Phoebe on the carousel."

"And then I missed and fell off."

"But you went for it. That's growth! And you were perfect—until you weren't. Your practice made myelin, and myelin almost made perfect. So much to be proud of there!"

He took a sip of his passion fruit, sucked some air over it, seemed to reflect. He shrugged. "It gets worse."

"Oh?"

"Yes. After agonizing all weekend over my failure to be a Hot Shot—overconfidence, a smug sense of privilege after making seven in a row leading to a lapse in attention—on Monday morning I'm back at Snow Canyon for free throws and 3-pointers. Free throws are my *métier*, my *forte*, my make-my-day. I set a team record in high school. I used to shoot with you girls in practice. I have rehearsed the form 10,000 times. I settle in at the line, a fellow contestant near the basket rebounding for me. Without a song in my heart this time, and without, it turned out, enough leg or wrist or follow-through, trying to think without thinking, I lofted my first shot, which, short and flat, hit the front of the rim and bounced back to me. Shocked, I tachycardiaed. My mind exploded. How is this possible! I'm too good for this! A single miss is my entire margin for error if I want to get the gold. I have to make all the rest. I slammed the ball off the floor, shook my head, took a deep breath—and missed again, clanking the right side of the rim. When my partner returned the ball I slammed it twice, dribbled it several more times, shifted my feet, seething, all right, goddamn it, now I'm pissed, it's the old me, you know how I get, fuck you world, angry adrenaline rises up in me, focuses me, out of spite I make the third shot, and the fourth and the fifth, I'm rolling, you can't stop me, they're all swishers, and I start to tighten as I get to 20, and tighten more at 24, I'm quaking, I might actually have a chance if I do well on my 3-pointers, I just need this last one, and in my craven need I jerk it slightly, pull it a little left, it lips out, and I have 22 points, goodbye gold. I beat myself again."

"But you still had a chance for silver or bronze."

"Yes. And I got the brass. I went on to make four of my six 3-pointers for a total of 34 points. The winner, from California, had 36, and the runner-up, from Pennsylvania, had 35."

"Bronze is good! And you came back! You climbed out of a hole to win it. You should have proudly posted a selfie on Facebook with your medal around your neck."

"Only with gold could I have done that. I wanted to be the best 80-year-old shooter in the nation—okay, small sample size, I'll grant you that! But brass was failure."

"So embrace the failure! Chew and stew and rue as you eat your bitter heart out. Grit over it! Aren't you the guy who celebrates the fact that he is not an animal, who revels in consciousness, who exults that he *can* daydream, make fictions, who sees suffering and joy as the double helix of life?"

"I was."

"Are."

"Maybe that was horseshit."

"Bullshit!"

He flinched. His eyes widened. Then he forced a smile and accepted the blow. "You could be right."

I smiled back and patted his sleeve, rather enjoying the pliancy of the leather. "What about the softball?"

"Yeah, the softball. We were scheduled to play a doubleheader at one o'clock. With my head buzzing, I drive my Soul back to the Ramada, change into my TUKWILA TITANS softball uniform (gaudy orange jerseys and caps, black shorts), pick up a protein box lunch and a tall cold brew at the Red Cliffs Mall Starbucks drive-through and down them on the way to the Snow Canyon Softball Complex, seven beautifully manicured fields of tightly clipped green grass, smoothly dragged henna infields, crisp white boundary lines. So lovely there in that little bowl with the white cliffs looming to the north and the buxom red hills enclosing us to the east."

"Lovely enough to return next year for another try?"

He drank some beer and looked into the fire.

"Anyway, our first game is against a local team, the St. George Dragons. When I arrive, the guys all say 'Hey, Wayne, how'd you do?' and I say 'Brass' and they say 'Great' and I say 'Yeah, thanks. Not really.' " I'm trying to put myself back together, find a comfortably confident persona somewhere between quakebuttock and coxcomb. My teammates all believe in me. It's my first year as an 80-year-old, I'm the young guy, lithe and lively, they brought me in to be a star. The Dragons are a weak team. We mercy them 15-2 in five innings, no thanks to me. I feel that I am ready, but I make a throwing error and go 0 for 3, two lazy flies and a chopped grounder, with a walk. Our second game is against the Minnesota Maulers. They beat us 8-5. Twice I muff grounders with two outs and a chance to end the inning with a force at second, and they go on to score after each error. At the plate I fail to hit a single ball on the sweet spot and go 0 for 3. Tuesday we have a single game against Scrapiron from Colorado. They beat us 10-9. I have one good play on defense. The shortstop and I both go for a grounder hit between us, I grab it backhanded and, not having time to turn and make the throw to second, without even thinking or looking zip it backward underhanded straight to the second baseman's glove for the out, bringing roars of approval from my teammates and an inner exaltation from me. An affordance! A serendipity! The next inning I drop a pop fly. On offense, again out of sync, I bloop a single to left on my first at-bat, then go out three times in a row on poorly timed swings. Later I go to Applebee's with the guys for beer and dinner, but my head is buzzing. I know they're all wondering when I'm going to start producing. In my room that night, watching an American League playoff game and reruns of *The Office*, in desperation I decide to forget serenity and fluidity and revert to a mechanical approach. At bat I will not swing until I get a called strike, hoping that will keep me from jumping on the first bad pitch. When the pitch is released I will utter my old mantra 'Wait, wait.' When I swing I will say 'Hammer it!' to keep my eyes focused on the ball and then force myself to keep my chin on my right shoulder so I don't move my head. In the field, I will say 'Down, down' on groundballs, and then 'Look it in.' I will be really intense, throw myself once more into the breach.

"It doesn't make any difference. Wednesday we begin double elimination medal play, seeded fifth, based on the results of our first three games, behind Top Gun from San Diego, Scrapiron, the Maulers, the Silvertips from Mesa, and ahead of St. George. We lose to the Silvertips, 14-5. I say 'Wait, wait,' but I don't wait. I'm out in front. I say 'Hammer it,' but I don't hammer it. I pull my head. Apparently my officious protective proprioceptors, a kind of adjunct to my immune system, commandeer my mind and will, privileging balance over performance. I rip one line drive down the left field line for an RBI triple, the only time when pulling my head and falling away don't mess me up because the pitch is way inside, and that's it. I simply cannot hit the ball on the screws. On defense I make one intuitive play. There's a pop up between me and the second baseman. I close on it, but it's his ball. At his side I defer to him but he bobbles it, it slips from his grasp and falls toward the ground, and mindfully mindlessly I reach out and snare it near my ankles—again to roars of approval. For the rest, I make a few routine plays but also a couple of errors each game. I'm looking up, I can't stay down, down. My frustration and depression increase with each game. My teammates go from encouraging me to pitying me to giving up on me. The second game, loser out, is a rematch with St. George, whom we mercied in our first meeting, and they rally to beat us, 10-8. In short, in sum, in fine, I stink and we go home in ignominy."

"Aw, sad," I said, and could not resist plucking at his sleeve once more. "But you had 11 players on your team. Those other guys must have been having defensive lapses and making bad swings, too."

"True. We all 'contributed' to the losses. But I expected more of myself. Had I hit .700 with power and made maybe only one error, I could have accepted not winning the gold. But to do what I did and then get knocked out is unacceptable."

"And yet you have to accept it, don't you?"

"Why can't I always be at my best?"

"Coach, surely you recognize that you've just committed the logical fallacy of the complex question? The stark truth is that you are. At any given instant, you are. In the next instant you might be better, or worse, but at that instant you are the best you can be. As you said in a different context, Coach, you see, you saw, you gee, you haw, you pitch, you yaw. That's you. Unalgorithmicable. Forever angst-ridden. Now shooting or swinging intuitively, now analytically, now mindfully mindless, now maniacally mechanical, now relaxed, now intense. Both work for you until, absurdly, they don't. Both so grow out of who you are, that perennial sophomore. You'll never find serenity. The graph of your life, of your teaching and coaching and playing and blog-writing careers, is a cascaded range of peaks and crevasses that will ultimately end in a steep entropic declivity. You reap less than you sow, you come then you go. All is vanity. As you have before, lean into that Sisyphean absurdity. Revel in your doing, your truing, your skewing. For you, only sense-lessness makes sense. That's your fiction."

He turned from me and stared at the forking flames of the fire for several seconds before turning back.

"And do you share my fiction?"

I shook my head. "Coach, no, I can't go there. Mechanico-morphism does not feel right to me. I get the rational arguments against the belief that the universe has purpose—deductive conclusions drawn from premises based on findings from physics and biology—but they don't quite stand up against my own intuitions. I look at the order and intricacy and beauty of nature—the solar system, our bodies, a glorious orange Oriental poppy—and I feel awe, reverence. Where you think emergence, I think design. I look at Jennifer and feel that she is in my life for some divine reason. And I can't imagine myself, or anyone else I used to know, truly dead dead. My parents, my grandparents, my deceased friends are all still here. I often sense their unbidden presence, a hovering, a looking in on, a shepherding. Though it's totally unempirical, un-demonstrable, it feels true. I *am* other than my electro-chemical system. I don't have a religion, but I am religious. Or maybe I'm a closeted Unitarian!"

We laughed and clinked glasses and took our last swallows of beer. I left a five on the little table beside me and we strolled through drizzle to our cars. We hugged.

"Thanks for offering the comfort today," he said. "Love you, Mann!"

"The cold comfort," I corrected him. "Love you, too, Coach."

Elizabeth Ann Mann
October 2020

Special thanks to Dick Curry, Judy Evans, Matt Evans, Gary Lee, Traci Lockhart-Hobbs, Jeff Lowman, Melinda Lucum, Kristin Thiel, and Don Vail, who read all or part of the original manuscript and offered helpful suggestions or positive reinforcement or both.

Printed in the USA
CPSIA information can be obtained
at www.ICGtesting.com
LVHW060544170823
755442LV00001B/27